BY LINWOOD BARCLAY

Bad Move

Bad Guys

Lone Wolf

Stone Rain

No Time for Goodbye

Too Close to Home

Fear the Worst

Never Look Away

The Accident

The Accident

The Accident

A NOVEL

LINWOOD BARCLAY

BANTAM BOOKS
NEW YORK

The Accident is a work of fiction. Names, characters, places, and incidents either are the product of the author's imagination or are used fictitiously. Any resemblance to actual persons, living or dead, events, or locales is entirely coincidental.

Published in the United States by Bantam Books, an imprint of The Random House Publishing Group, a division of Random House, Inc., New York.

BANTAM BOOKS and the rooster colophon are registered trademarks of Random House, Inc.

Library of Congress Cataloging-in-Publication Data
Barclay, Linwood.
The accident : a novel / Linwood Barclay.
p. cm.
ISBN 978-0-553-80718-9
eBook ISBN 978-0-553-90806-0
1. Wives—Death—Fiction. 2. Serial murders—Fiction. 3. Single fathers—Fiction. 4. Fathers and daughters—Fiction. I. Title.
PR9199.3.B37135A65 2011
813'.54—dc22 2010053042

Printed in the United States of America on acid-free paper

www.bantamdell.com

9 8 7 6 5 4 3 2 1

First Edition

Book design by Caroline Cunningham

For Neetha

The Accident

PROLOGUE

Their names were Edna Bauder and Pam Steigerwald, and they were grade school teachers from Butler, Pennsylvania, and they had never been to New York before in their entire lives. New York was hardly the other side of the planet, but when you lived in Butler, almost everything seemed that way. As Pam's fortieth birthday approached, her friend Edna said you're going to have a birthday weekend you are never, ever going to forget, and on that count she turned out to be absolutely right.

Their husbands were delighted when they heard this was a "girls only" weekend. When they learned it was going to be two full days of shopping, a Broadway show, and going on the *Sex and the City* tour, they said they would rather stay home and blow their brains out. So they put their wives on the bus and said have fun and try not to get too drunk because there's a lot of muggers in New York, everybody knows that, and you have to keep your wits about you.

They found a hotel near Fiftieth and Third that was, at least by New York standards, reasonable, although it still seemed like a lot considering all they were going to do was sleep there. They'd vowed to save money by not taking cabs, but the maps of the subway system looked like a schematic for the space shuttle, so they decided, what the hell. They went to Bloomingdale's and Macy's and a huge shoe outlet in Union Square that would have held every store in Butler and still had room left over for the post office.

"I want my ashes scattered through this place when I die," Edna said, trying on a pair of sandals.

They tried to get to the top of the Empire State Building, but the line to get in was huge, and when you had only forty-eight hours in the Big Apple you didn't want to spend three of them waiting in line, so they bailed.

Pam wanted to eat lunch at that deli, the one from that movie where Meg Ryan had the fake orgasm. Their table was right next to the one they used in the movie—there was even a sign hanging over it to mark the spot—but when they got back to Butler they'd tell everyone they got the actual table. Edna ordered a pastrami sandwich with a knish, even though she had no idea what a knish was. Pam said, "I'll have what she's having!" and the two of them went into fits of hysterics when the waitress rolled her eyes.

While having coffee afterward, Edna said, almost out of nowhere, "I think Phil's been seeing that waitress at Denny's." And then she burst into tears, and Pam asked why she suspected such a thing, that she thought Edna's husband, Phil, was a good guy who'd never cheat, and Edna said she didn't think he was actually sleeping with her or anything, but he went there for coffee every single day, so that had to mean something. And the thing was, he hardly ever touched her anymore.

"Come on," Pam said. "We're all busy, we got kids, Phil's working two jobs, who's got the energy?"

"Maybe you're right," Edna said.

Pam said, "You need to get your mind off that nonsense. You brought me here to have fun." She opened her New York Fodor's tourist guidebook to the spot where she'd put a sticky note and said, "You need more retail therapy. We're going to Canal Street."

Edna had no idea what that was. Pam said you could buy purses—designer purses, or at least purses that looked just like designer purses—for next to nothing down there. You have to ask around for the best deals, she said. She'd read in a magazine somewhere that sometimes the best stuff, it's not even out where the people can see it. You have to go into a back room or something.

"You're talkin' my language, honey," Edna said.

So they grabbed yet another cab and asked to be taken to the corner of Canal and Broadway, but at Lafayette and Grand the taxi came to a dead stop.

"What's happened?" Edna asked the driver.

"Accident," he said in an accent Pam thought could be anything from Salvadoran to Swiss. "I can't turn around. Is just few blocks that way."

Pam paid the driver and they started walking in the direction of Canal. A block up, a crowd had gathered. Edna said, "Oh my God."

She looked away, but Pam was transfixed. A man's legs were splayed across the hood of a yellow cab that had crashed into a streetlight. His upper body had gone through the windshield and was draped over the dashboard. A mangled bicycle was trapped under the car's front wheels. There was no one behind the wheel. Maybe the driver had already been taken to the hospital. People with FDNY and NYPD on their backs were inspecting the car, telling the crowd to move back.

Someone said, "Fucking bike messengers. Amazing it doesn't happen more often."

Edna took Pam by the elbow. "I can't look at this."

By the time they found their way to Canal and Broadway, they hadn't exactly put that horrible image out of their heads, but they'd been repeating a "These things happen" mantra that would allow them to still make the most they could out of this weekend.

Pam used her camera phone to get a shot of Edna standing under the Broadway street sign, and then Edna got a shot of Pam doing the same. A man walking past offered to take pictures of the two of them together, but Edna said no thank you, telling Pam later it was probably just a ploy to steal their phones. "I wasn't born yesterday," Edna said.

As they moved east on Canal the two of them felt as though they'd wandered into a foreign country. Weren't these what the markets in Hong Kong or Morocco or Thailand looked like? Stores jammed together, merchandise spilling out onto the street?

"Not exactly Sears," Pam said.

"So many Chinese people," Edna said.

"I think that's 'cause it's Chinatown," Pam said.

A homeless man wearing a Toronto Maple Leafs jersey asked for change. Another tried to hand them a flyer but Pam held up her hand defensively. Throngs of teenage girls giggled and gawked, some able to carry on conversations while music chattered from the buds stuffed into their ears.

The store windows were jammed with necklaces, watches, sunglasses. A WE BUY GOLD sign was positioned out front of one. A long, vertical sign hanging off a fire escape read "Tattoo—Body Piercing—Henna Temporary Supplies—Wholesale Body Jewelry—Books Magazines Art Objects 2nd Floor." There were signs pushing "Leather" and "Pashmina" and countless banners in Chinese characters. And even a Burger King.

The two women went into what they thought was one store, but it turned out to be dozens. Like a mini-mall, or a flea market, with each business ensconced in its own glass-walled cubicle. They all offered a specialty. Stalls for jewelry, DVDs, watches, purses.

"Look at this," Edna said. "A Rolex."

"It's not real," Pam said. "But it looks fabulous. Think anyone in Butler knows the difference?"

"Think anyone in Butler even knows what a Rolex is?" Edna laughed. "Oh, check out the bags!"

Fendi, Coach, Kate Spade, Louis Vuitton, Prada. "I can't believe these prices," Pam said. "What would you normally pay for a bag like this?"

"Way, way more," Edna said.

The Chinese man running the stall asked if they wanted help. Pam, trying to act as though she knew the territory, which was not easy when you had a New York guidebook sticking halfway out of your purse, asked, "Where do you have the *real* deals?"

"What?" he said.

"These are nice," she said. "But where do you keep the prime stuff?"

Edna shook her head nervously. "No, these are fine. We can pick from these."

But Pam persisted. "A friend told me, I'm not sure if it was your place specifically, but there might be some other bags, but not on display here."

The man shook his head. "Try her," he said, pointing deeper into the rabbit warren of shops.

Pam went to the next kiosk and, after giving the bags a cursory look, asked the elderly Chinese woman, dressed in a brilliant red silk jacket, where they were hiding the good stuff.

"Huh?" the woman said.

"The best bags," Pam said. "The best knockoffs."

The woman gave Pam and Edna a long look, thinking that if these two were undercover cops, they were the best she'd ever seen. Finally, she said, "You go out the back door, go left, look for door with number eight on it. Go down there. Andy'll help you."

Pam glanced excitedly at Edna. "Thank you!" she said, and grabbed hold of Edna's arm, tugging her to a door at the end of the narrow mall.

"I don't like this," Edna said.

"Don't worry, it's okay."

But even Pam was caught up short when they went through the door and found themselves in an alley. Dumpsters, trash strewn everywhere, abandoned appliances. The door closed behind them and when Edna grabbed it she found it locked.

"Great," she said. "Like that accident didn't freak me out enough."

"She said go left, so let's go left," Pam said.

They didn't have to walk far before they found the metal door with an "8" painted on it. "Do we knock or just go in?" Pam asked.

"This is your brilliant idea, not mine," Edna said.

Pam rapped lightly, and when no one came after ten seconds, she pulled on the handle. The door was unlocked. They were met with a short set of steps leading down a dark stairwell. But there was a glimmer of light at the bottom.

"Hello? Andy?" Pam called out.

There was no answer.

"Let's go," Edna said. "I saw some purses at the other place that were perfect."

"We're already here," Pam said. "Might as well check it out." She went down the stairs, feeling the temperature drop with each step. She peered into a room at the bottom, then turned and looked back up at Edna with a huge grin on her face. "This is *so* the place."

Edna followed her into a dense, cluttered, low-ceilinged room that was jammed with handbags. They were on tabletops, hanging from hooks on the walls, hanging from hooks in the ceiling. Maybe because it was cold, it reminded Edna of a meat locker, but instead of sides of beef dangling from above, it was leather goods.

"I must be dead," Pam said. "We're in Purse Heaven."

Tubular fluorescent lights flickered and buzzed above their heads as they began picking through bags on the display tables.

"If this is a fake Fendi, I'll eat Phil's hat," Edna said, inspecting one bag. "The leather feels so real. I mean, it is real *leather*, right? It's just the *labels* that are fake? I'd love to know how much this one is."

Pam noticed a curtained door at one end of the room. "Maybe that Andy guy is in there." She started walking toward it.

Edna said, "Wait. We should get out of here. Look at us. We're in some basement, off an alley, in New York City, and no one has any idea whatsoever where we are."

Pam rolled her eyes. "God, you're so *Pennsylvania*." She reached the doorway and called out, "Mr. Andy? The Chinese lady said you could help us?" As soon as she'd said "Chinese lady," she felt like an idiot. That really narrowed it down.

Edna had gone back to examining the lining of the fake Fendi.

Pam reached out and pulled aside the curtain.

Edna heard a funny sound, a kind of *pfft*, and by the time she'd looked over, her friend was on the floor. Not moving.

"Pam?" She dropped the purse. "Pam, are you okay?"

As she approached she noticed that Pam, who was on her back, had a red dot on the middle of her forehead and something was running out of it. Like Pam had sprung a leak.

"Oh my God, *Pam*?"

The curtain opened and a tall, thin man, with dark hair and a scar over his eye, stepped out. He had a gun, and it was pointed straight at her head.

In her last remaining second, Edna spotted, just inside the room beyond the curtain, an elderly Chinese man, seated at a desk, his forehead resting on it, a rivulet of blood draining from his temple.

The last thing Edna heard was a woman—not Pam, because Pam was done talking—saying, "We have to get out of here."

The last thing Edna thought was, *Home. I want to go home.*

TWO MONTHS LATER

ONE

If I'd known this was our last morning, I'd have rolled over in bed and held her. But of course, if it had been possible to know something like that—if I could have somehow seen into the future—I wouldn't have let go. And then things would have been different.

I'd been staring at the ceiling for a while when I finally threw back the covers and planted my feet on the hardwood floor.

"How'd you sleep?" Sheila asked as I rubbed my eyes. She reached out and touched my back.

"Not so good. You?"

"Off and on."

"I sensed you were awake, but I didn't want to bug you, on the off chance you were sleeping," I said, glancing over my shoulder. The sun's first rays of the day filtered through the drapes and played across my wife's face as she lay in bed, looking at me. This wasn't a time of day when people looked their best, but there was something about Sheila. She was always beautiful. Even when she looked worried, which was how she looked now.

I turned back around, looked down at my bare feet. "I couldn't get to sleep for the longest time, then I think I finally nodded off around two, but then I looked at the clock and it was five. Been awake since then."

"Glen, it's going to be okay," Sheila said. She moved her hand across my back, soothing me.

"Yeah, well, I'm glad you think so."

"Things'll pick up. Everything goes in cycles. Recessions don't last forever."

I sighed. "This one sure seems to. After these jobs I'm doing now, we got nothin' lined up. Some nibbles, did a couple of estimates last week—one for a kitchen, one to finish off a basement—but they haven't called back."

I stood up, turned and said, "What's your excuse for staring at the ceiling all night?"

"Worried about you. And . . . I've got things on my mind, too."

"What?"

"Nothing," she said quickly. "I mean, just the usual. This course I'm taking, Kelly, your work."

"What's wrong with Kelly?"

"Nothing's wrong with her. I'm a mother. She's eight. I worry. It's what I do. When I've done the course, I can help you more. That'll make a difference."

"When you made the decision to take it, we had the business to justify it. Now, I don't know if I'll even have any work for you to do," I said. "I just hope I have enough to keep Sally busy."

Sheila'd started her business accounting course mid-August, and two months in was enjoying it more than she'd expected. The plan was for Sheila to do the day-to-day accounts for Garber Contracting, the company that was once my father's, and which I now ran. She could even do it from home, which would allow Sally Diehl, our "office girl," to focus more on general office management, returning phone calls, hounding suppliers, fielding customer inquiries. There usually wasn't time for Sally to do the accounting, which meant I was bringing it home at night, sitting at my desk until midnight. But with work drying up, I didn't know how this was all going to shake down.

"And now, with the fire—"

"Enough," Sheila said.

"Sheila, one of my goddamn houses burned down. Please don't tell me everything's going to be fine."

She sat up in bed and crossed her arms across her breasts. "I'm not going to let you get all negative on me. This is what you do."

"I'm just telling you how it is."

"And I'm going to tell you how it will *be,*" she said. "We will *be* okay. Because this is what *we* do. You and I. We get through things. We find a way." She looked away for a moment, like there was something she wanted to say but wasn't sure how to say it. Finally, she said, "I have ideas."

"What ideas?"

"Ideas to help us. To get us through the rough patches."

I stood there, my arms open, waiting.

"You're so busy, so wrapped up in your own problems—and I'm not saying that they aren't big problems—that you haven't even noticed."

"Noticed what?" I asked.

She shook her head and smiled. "I got Kelly new outfits for school."

"Okay."

"Nice ones."

I narrowed my eyes. "What are you getting at?"

"I've made some money."

I thought I already knew that. Sheila had her part-time job at Hardware Depot—about twenty hours a week—working the checkout. They'd recently installed these new self-checkout stations people couldn't figure out, so there was still work there for Sheila until they did. And since the early summer, Sheila had been helping our next-door neighbor—Joan Mueller—with her own books for a business she was running from her home. Joan's husband, Ely, had been killed on that oil rig off the coast of Newfoundland when it blew up about a year back. She'd been getting jerked around by the oil company on her settlement, and in the meantime had started running a daycare operation. Every morning four or five preschoolers got dropped off at her door. And on school days when Sheila was working, Kelly went to Joan's until one of us got home. Sheila had helped Joan organize a bookkeeping system to keep track of what everyone owed and had paid. Joan loved kids, but could barely finger count.

"I know you've been making some money," I said. "Joan, and the store. Everything helps."

"Those two jobs together don't keep us in Hamburger Helper. I'm talking about better money than that."

My eyebrows went up. Then I got worried. "Tell me you're not taking money from Fiona." Her mother. "You know how I feel about that."

She looked insulted. "Jesus, Glen, you know I would never—"

"I'm just saying. I'd rather you were a drug dealer than taking money from your mother."

She blinked, threw back the covers abruptly, got out of bed, and stalked into the bathroom. The door closed firmly behind her.

"Aw, come on," I said.

By the time we reached the kitchen, I didn't think she was angry with me anymore. I'd apologized twice, and tried to coax from Sheila details of what her idea was to bring more money into the house.

"We can talk about it tonight," she said.

We hadn't washed the dishes from the night before. There were a couple of coffee cups, my scotch glass, and Sheila's wine goblet, with a dark red residue at the bottom, sitting in the sink. I lifted the goblet onto the counter, worried the stem might break if other things got tossed into the sink alongside it.

The wineglass made me think of Sheila's friends.

"You seeing Ann for lunch or anything?" I asked.

"No."

"I thought you had something set up."

"Maybe later this week. Belinda and Ann and me might get together, although every time we do that I have to get a cab home and my head hurts for a week. Anyway, I think Ann's got some physical or something today, an insurance thing."

"She okay?"

"She's fine." A pause. "More or less."

"What's that mean?"

"I don't know. I think there's some kind of tension there, between her and Darren. And between Belinda and George, for that matter."

"What's going on?"

"Who knows," she said.

"So then, what are you doing today? You don't have a shift today, right? If I can slip away, you want to get lunch? I was thinking something fancy, like that guy who sells hot dogs by the park."

"I've got my course tonight," she said. "Some errands to run, and I might visit Mom." She shot me a look. "*Not* to ask her for money."

"Okay." I decided to ask nothing further. She'd tell me when she was ready.

Kelly walked into the room at the tail end of the conversation. "What's for breakfast?"

"You want cereal, cereal, or cereal?" Sheila asked.

Kelly appeared to ponder her choices. "I'll take cereal," she said, and sat at the table.

At our house, breakfast wasn't a sit-down family meal like dinner. Actually, dinner often wasn't, either, especially when I got held up at a construction site, or Sheila was at work, or heading off to her class. But we at least tried to make that a family event. Breakfast was a lost cause, however. I had my toast and coffee standing, usually flattening the morning *Register* on the countertop and scanning the headlines as I turned the pages. Sheila was spooning in fruit and yogurt at the same time as Kelly shoveled in her Cheerios, trying to get them into herself before any of them had a chance to get soggy.

Between spoonfuls she asked, "Why would anyone go to school at night when they're grown up and don't have to go?"

"When I finish this course," Sheila told her, "I'll be able to help your father more, and that helps the family, and that helps you."

"How does that help me?" she wanted to know.

I stepped in. "Because if my company is run well, it makes more money, and *that* helps you."

"So you can buy me more stuff?"

"Not necessarily."

Kelly took a gulp of orange juice. "I'd never go to school at night. Or summer. You'd have to kill me to get me to go to summer school."

"If you get really good marks, that won't happen," I said, a hint of warning in my voice. We'd already had a call from her teacher that she wasn't completing all her homework.

Kelly had nothing to say to that and concentrated on her cereal. On the way out the door, she gave her mother a hug, but all I got was a wave. Sheila caught me noticing the perceived slight and said, "It's because you're a meanie."

I called the house from work mid-morning.

"Hey," Sheila said.

"You're home. I didn't know whether I'd catch you or not."

"Still here. What's up?"

"Sally's dad."

"What?"

"She was calling home from the office and when he didn't answer she took off. I just called to see how he was and he's gone."

"He's dead?"

"Yeah."

"Oh jeez. How old was he?"

"Seventy-nine, I think. He was in his late fifties when he had Sally." Sheila knew the history. The man had married a woman twenty years younger than he was, and still managed to outlive her. She'd died of an aneurysm a decade ago.

"What happened to him?"

"Don't know. I mean, he had diabetes, he'd been having heart trouble. Could have been a heart attack."

"We need to do something for her."

"I offered to drop by but she said she's got a lot to deal with right now. Funeral'll probably be in a couple of days. We can talk about it when you get back from Bridgeport." Where Sheila took her class.

"We'll do something. We've always been there for her." I could almost picture Sheila shaking her head. "Look," she said, "I'm heading out. I'll leave you and Kelly lasagna, okay? Joan's expecting her after school today and—"

"I got it. Thanks."

"For what?"

"Not giving up. Not letting things get you down."

"Just doing the best I can," she said.

"I love you. I know I can be a pain in the ass, but I love you."

"Ditto."

It was after ten. Sheila should have been home by now.

I tried her cell for the second time in ten minutes. After six rings it went to voicemail. *"Hi, you've reached Sheila Garber. Sorry I missed you. Leave a message and I'll get back to you."* Then the beep.

"Hey, me again," I said. "You're freaking me out. Call me."

I put the cordless receiver back onto its stand and leaned up against the kitchen counter, folded my arms. As she'd promised, Sheila had left two servings of lasagna in the fridge, for Kelly and me, each hermetically sealed under plastic wrap. I'd heated Kelly's in the microwave when we got home, and she'd come back looking for seconds, but I couldn't find a baking dish with any more in it. I might as well have offered her mine, which a few hours later still sat on the counter. I wasn't hungry.

I was rattled. Running out of work. The fire. Sally's dad.

And even if I'd managed to recover my appetite late in the evening, the fact that Sheila still wasn't home had put me on edge.

Her class, which was held at the Bridgeport Business College, had ended more than an hour and a half ago, and it was only a thirty-minute drive home. Which made her an hour late. Not that long, really. There were any number of explanations.

She could have stayed after class to have a coffee with someone. That had happened a couple of times. Maybe the traffic was bad on the turnpike. All you needed was someone with a flat tire on the shoulder to slow everything down. An accident would stop everything dead.

That didn't explain her not answering her cell, though. She'd been known to forget to turn it back on after class was over, but when that happened it went to voicemail right away. But the phone was ringing. Maybe it was tucked so far down in her purse she couldn't hear it.

I wondered whether she'd decided to go to Darien to see her mother and not made it back out to Bridgeport in time for her class. Reluctantly, I made the call.

"Hello?"

"Fiona, it's Glen."

In the background, I heard someone whisper, "Who is it, love?" Fiona's husband, Marcus. Technically speaking, Sheila's stepfather, but Fiona had remarried long after Sheila had left home and settled into a life with me.

"Yes?" she said.

I told her Sheila was late getting back from Bridgeport, and I wondered if maybe her daughter had gotten held up at her place.

"Sheila didn't come see me today," Fiona said. "I certainly wasn't expecting her. She never said anything about coming over."

That struck me as odd. When Sheila mentioned maybe going to see Fiona, I'd figured she'd already bounced the idea off her.

"Is there a problem, Glen?" Fiona asked icily. There wasn't worry in her voice so much as suspicion. As if Sheila's staying out late had more to do with me than it did with her.

"No, everything's fine," I said. "Go back to bed."

I heard soft steps coming down from the second floor. Kelly, not yet in her pajamas, wandered into the kitchen. She looked at the still-wrapped lasagna on the counter and asked, "Aren't you going to eat that?"

"Hands off," I said, thinking maybe I'd get my appetite back once Sheila was home. I glanced at the wall clock. Quarter past ten. "Why aren't you in bed?"

"Because you haven't told me to go yet," she said.

"What have you been doing?"

"Computer."

"Go to bed," I said.

"It was homework," she said.

"Look at me."

"In the *beginning* it was," she said defensively. "And when I got it done, I was talking to my friends." She stuck out her lower lip and blew away some blonde curls that were falling over her eyes. "Why isn't Mom home?"

"Her thing must have run late," I said. "I'll send her up to give you a kiss when she gets home."

"If I'm asleep, how will I know if I get it?"

"She'll tell you in the morning."

Kelly eyed me with suspicion. "So I might never get a kiss, but you guys would say I did."

"You figured it out," I said. "It's a scam we've been running."

"Whatever." She turned, shuffled out of the kitchen, and padded back upstairs.

I picked up the receiver and tried Sheila's cell again. When her greeting cut in, I muttered "Shit" before it started recording and hit the off button.

I went down the stairs to my basement office. The walls were wood-paneled, giving the place a dark, oppressive feel. And the mountains of paper on the desk only added to the gloominess. For years I'd been intending to either redo this room—get rid of the paneling and go for drywall painted off-white so it wouldn't feel so small, for starters—or put an addition onto the back of the house with lots of windows and a skylight. But as is often the case with people whose work is building and renovating houses, it's your own place that never gets done.

I dropped myself into the chair behind the desk and shuffled some papers around. Bills from various suppliers, plans for the new kitchen we were doing in a house up in Derby, some notes about a freestanding double garage we were building for a guy in Devon who wanted a place to park his two vintage Corvettes.

There was also a very preliminary report from the Milford Fire Department about what may have caused the house we'd been building for Arnett and Leanne Wilson on Shelter Cove Road to burn down a week ago. I scanned down to the end and read, for possibly the hundredth time, *Indications are fire originated in area of electrical panel.*

It was a two-story, three-bedroom, built on the site of a postwar bungalow that a strong easterly wind could have knocked down if we hadn't taken a wrecking ball to it first. The fire had started just before one p.m. The house had been framed and sided, the roof was up, electrical was done, and the plumbing was getting roughed in. Doug Pinder, my assistant manager, and I were using the recently installed outlets to run a couple of table saws. Ken Wang, our Chinese guy with the Southern accent—his parents emigrated from Beijing to Kentucky when he was an infant, and we still cracked up whenever he said "y'all"—and Stewart Minden, our newbie from Ottawa who was living with relatives in Stratford for a few months, were upstairs sorting out where fixtures were going to go in the main bathroom.

Doug smelled the smoke first. Then we saw it, drifting up from the basement.

I shouted upstairs to Ken and Stewart to get the hell out. They came bounding down the carpetless stairs and flew out the front door with Doug.

Then I did something very, very stupid.

I ran out to my truck, grabbed a fire extinguisher from behind the driver's seat, and ran back into the house. Halfway down the steps to the basement, the smoke became so thick I couldn't see. I got to the bottom step, running my hand along the makeshift two-by-four banister to guide me there, and thought if I started spraying blindly from the extinguisher, I'd hit the source of the fire and save the place.

Really dumb.

I immediately started to cough and my eyes began to sting. When I turned to retreat back up the stairs, I couldn't find them. I stuck out my free hand and swept it from side to side, looking for the railing.

I hit something softer than wood. An arm.

"Come on, you stupid son of a bitch," Doug growled, grabbing hold of me. He was on the bottom step, and pulled me toward it.

We came out the front door together, coughing and hacking, as the first fire truck was coming around the corner. Minutes after that, the place was fully engulfed.

"Don't tell Sheila I went in," I said to Doug, still wheezing. "She'd kill me."

"And so she should, Glenny," Doug said.

Other than the foundation, there wasn't much left of the place once the fire was out. Everything was with the insurance company now, and if they didn't come through, the thousands it would cost to rebuild would be coming out of my pocket. Little wonder I'd been staring at the ceiling for hours in the dead of night.

I'd never been hit with anything like this before. It hadn't just scared me, losing a project to fire. It had shaken my confidence. If I was about anything, it was getting things right, doing a quality job.

"Shit happens," Doug had said. "We pick ourselves up and move on."

I wasn't feeling that philosophical. And it wasn't Doug's name on the side of the truck.

I thought maybe I should eat something, so I slid my plate of lasagna into the microwave. I sat down at the kitchen table and picked away at it. The inside was still cold, but I couldn't be bothered to put it back in. Lasagna was one of Sheila's specialties, and if it weren't for the fact that I had so much on my mind, I would have been devouring it, even cold. Whenever she made it in her browny-orange baking pan—Sheila would say it was "persimmon"—there was always enough for two or three meals, so we'd be having lasagna again in a couple of nights, maybe even for Saturday lunch. That was okay with me.

I ate less than half, rewrapped it, and put the plate in the fridge. Kelly was under her covers, her bedside light on, when I peeked into her room. She'd been reading a Wimpy Kid book.

"Lights out, sweetheart."

"Is Mom home?" she asked.

"No."

"I need to talk to her."

"About what?"

"Nothing."

I nodded. When Kelly had something on her mind, it was usually her mother she talked to. Even though she was only eight, she had questions about boys, and love, and the changes she knew were coming in a few years. These were, I had to admit, not my areas of expertise.

"Don't be mad," she said.

"I'm not mad."

"Some things are just easier to talk to Mom about. But I love you guys the same."

"Good to know."

"I can't get to sleep until she gets home."

That made two of us.

"Put your head down on the pillow. You might nod off anyway."

"I won't."

"Turn off the light and give it a shot."

Kelly reached over and turned off her lamp. I kissed her forehead and gently closed the door as I slipped out of her room.

Another hour went by. I tried Sheila's cell six more times. I was back and forth between my office basement and the kitchen. The trip took me past the front door, so I could keep glancing out to the driveway.

Just after eleven, standing in the kitchen, I tried her friend Ann Slocum. Someone picked up long enough to stop the ringing, then replaced the receiver. Ann's husband, Darren, I was guessing. That would be his style. But then again, I was calling late.

Next I called Sheila's other friend, Belinda. They'd worked together years ago, for the library, but stayed close even after their career paths went in different directions. Belinda was a real estate agent now. Not the greatest time to be in that line of work. A lot more people wanted to sell these days than buy. Despite Belinda's unpredictable schedule, she and Sheila managed to get together for lunch every couple of weeks, sometimes with Ann, sometimes not.

Her husband, George, answered sleepily, "Hello?"

"George, Glen Garber. Sorry to call so late."

"Glen, jeez, what time is it?"

"It's late, I know. Can I talk to Belinda?"

I heard some muffled chatter, some shifting about, then Belinda came on the line. "Glen, is everything okay?"

"Sheila's really late getting back from her night class thing, and she's not answering her cell. You haven't heard from her, have you?"

"What? What are you talking about? Say that again?" Belinda sounded instantly panicked.

"Has Sheila been in touch? She's usually back from her course by now."

"No. When did you last talk to her?"

"This morning," I said. "You know Sally, at the office?"

"Yeah."

"Her dad passed away and I called Sheila to let her know."

"So you haven't talked to her pretty much all day?" There was an edge in Belinda's voice. Not accusing, exactly, but something.

"Listen, I didn't call to get you all upset. I just wondered if you'd heard from her is all."

"No, no, I haven't," Belinda said. "Glen, please have Sheila call me the minute she gets in, okay? I mean, now that you've got me worrying about her, too, I need to know she got in okay."

"I'll tell her. Tell George I'm sorry about waking you guys up."

"For *sure* you'll have her call me."

"Promise," I said.

I hung up, went upstairs to Kelly's door and opened it a crack. "You asleep?" I asked, poking my head in.

From the darkness, a chirpy "Nope."

"Throw on some clothes. I'm going to look for Mom. And I can't leave you alone in the house."

She flicked on her bedside lamp. I thought she'd argue, tell me she was old enough to stay in the house, but instead she asked, "What's happened?"

"I don't know. Probably nothing. My guess is your mom's having a coffee and can't hear her phone. But maybe she got a flat tire or something. I want to drive the route she usually takes."

"Okay," she said instantly, throwing her feet onto the floor. She wasn't worried. This was an adventure. She pulled some jeans on over her pajamas. "I need two secs."

I went back downstairs and got my coat, made sure I had my cell. If Sheila did call the house once we were gone, my cell would be next. Kelly hopped into the truck, did up her belt, and said, "Is Mom going to be in trouble?"

I glanced over at her as I turned the ignition. "Yeah. She's going to be grounded."

Kelly giggled. "As if," she said.

Once we were out of the driveway and going down the street, I asked Kelly, "Did your mom say anything about what she was going to do today? Was she going to see her parents and then changed her mind? Did she mention anything at all?"

Kelly frowned. "I don't think so. She might have gone to the drugstore."

That was only a trip around the corner. "Why do you think she was going there?"

"I heard her talking to someone on the phone the other day about paying for some."

"Some what?"

"Drugstore stuff."

That made no sense to me and I dismissed it.

We weren't on the road five minutes before Kelly was out cold, her head resting on her shoulder. If my head was in that position for more than a minute, it would leave me with a crick in my neck for a month.

I drove up Schoolhouse Road and got on the ramp to 95 West. It was the quickest route between Milford and Bridgeport, especially at this time of the night, and the most likely one for Sheila to have taken. I kept glancing over at the eastbound highway, looking for a Subaru wagon pulled off to the side of the road.

This was a long shot, at best. But doing something, anything, seemed preferable to sitting at home and worrying.

I continued to scan the other side of the highway, but not only didn't I see Sheila's car, I didn't see any cars pulled over to the shoulder at all.

I was almost through Stratford, about to enter the Bridgeport city limits, when I saw some lights flashing on the other side. Not on the road, but maybe down an off-ramp. I leaned on the gas, wanting to hurry to the next exit so I could turn around and head back on the eastbound lanes.

Kelly continued to sleep.

I exited 95, crossed the highway and got back on. As I approached the exit where I thought I'd seen lights, I spotted a police car, lights flashing, blocking the way. I slowed, but the cop waved me on. I wasn't able to see far enough down the ramp to see what the problem was, and with Kelly in the truck, pulling over to the side of a busy highway did not seem wise.

So I got off at the next exit, figuring I could work my way back on local streets, get to the ramp from the bottom end. It took me about ten minutes. The cops hadn't set up a barricade at the bottom of the ramp, since no one would turn up there anyway. I pulled the car over to the shoulder at the base of the ramp and got my first real look at what had happened.

It was an accident. A bad one. Two cars. So badly mangled it was difficult to tell what they were or what might have happened. Closer to me was a car that appeared to be a station wagon, and the other one, a sedan of some kind, was off to the side. It looked as though the wagon had been broadsided by the sedan.

Sheila drove a wagon.

Kelly was still sound asleep, and I didn't want to wake her. I got out of the truck, closed the door without slamming it, and approached the ramp. There were three police cars at the scene, a couple of tow trucks and a fire engine.

As I got closer, I was able to get a better look at the cars involved in the accident. I began to feel shaky. I glanced back at my truck, made sure I could see Kelly in the passenger window.

Before I could take another step, however, a police officer stood in my way.

"I'm sorry, sir," he said. "You have to stay back."

"What kind of car is that?" I asked.

"Sir, please—"

"What kind of car? The wagon, the closest car."

"A Subaru," he said.

"Plate," I said.

"I'm sorry, sir?"

"I need to see the plate."

"Do you think you know whose car this is?" thc cop asked.

"Let me see the plate."

He allowed me to approach, took me to a vantage point that allowed me to see the back of the wagon. The license plate was clearly visible.

I recognized the combination of numbers and letters.

"Oh Jesus," I said, feeling weak.

"Sir?"

"This is my wife's car."

"What's your name, sir?"

"Glen Garber. This car, it's my wife's car. That's her plate. Oh my God."

The cop took a step closer to me.

"Is she okay?" I asked, my entire body feeling as though I were holding on to a low-voltage live wire. "Which hospital have they taken her to? Do you know? Can you find out? I have to go there. I have to get there right now."

"Mr. Garber—" the cop said.

"Milford Hospital?" I said. "No, wait, Bridgeport Hospital is closer." I turned to run back to the truck.

"Mr. Garber, your wife hasn't been taken to the hospital."

I stopped. "What?"

"She's still in the car. I'm afraid that—"

"What are you saying?"

I looked at the mangled remains of the Subaru. The cop had to be wrong. There were no paramedics there; none of the nearby firefighters were using the Jaws of Life to get to the driver.

I pushed past him, ran to the car, got right up to the caved-in driver's side, looked through what was left of the door.

"Sheila," I said. "Sheila, honey."

The window glass had shattered into a million pieces the size of raisins. I began to brush them from her shoulder, pick them from her blood-matted hair. I kept saying her name over and over again.

"Sheila? Oh God, please, Sheila . . ."

"Mr. Garber." The officer was standing right behind me. I felt a hand on my shoulder. "Please, sir, come with me."

"You have to get her out," I said. The smell of gasoline was wafting up my nostrils and I could hear something dripping.

"We're going to do that, I promise you. Please, come with me."

"She's not dead. You have to—"

"Please, sir, I'm afraid she is. There were no vital signs."

"No, you're wrong." I reached in and put my arm around her head. It nodded over to one side.

That was when I knew.

The cop put his hand firmly on my arm and said, "You have to move away from the car, sir. It's not safe to stand here." He pulled me forcibly away and I didn't fight him. Half a dozen car lengths away, I had to stop, bend over, and put my hands on my knees.

"Are you okay, sir?"

Looking down at the pavement, I said, "My daughter's in my truck. Can you see her? Is she asleep?"

"I can just see the top of her head, yes. Looks like she is."

I took several shaky breaths, straightened back up. Said "Oh my God" probably ten times. The cop stood there, patiently, waiting for me to pull it together enough for him to ask me some questions.

"Your wife's name is Sheila, sir? Sheila Garber?"

"That's right."

"Do you know what she was doing tonight? Where she was going?"

"She has a course tonight. Bridgeport Business College. She's learning accounting and other things to help me in my business. What happened? What happened here? How did this happen? Who the hell was driving that other car? What did he do?"

The cop lowered his head. "Mr. Garber, this appears to have been an alcohol-related accident."

"What? Drunk driving?"

"It would appear so, yes."

Anger began to mix in with the shock and grief. "Who was driving that car? What stupid son of a bitch—"

"There were three people in the other car. One survived. A young boy in the back seat. His father and brother were the two fatalities."

"My God, what kind of man gets behind the wheel drunk with his boys in the car and—"

"That's not exactly how it looks, sir," the cop said.

I stared at him, trying to figure out what he was getting at. Then it hit me. It wasn't the father driving. It was one of the sons.

"One of his boys was driving drunk?"

"Mr. Garber, please. I need you to calm down for me. I need you to listen. It appears it was your wife who caused the accident."

"What?"

"She'd driven up the ramp the wrong way, then just stopped her vehicle about halfway, parking it across the road, no lights visible. We think she may have fallen asleep."

"What the hell are you talking about?"

"And then," he said, "when the other car came off the highway, probably doing about sixty, he'd have been almost on your wife's car before he saw it and could put on the brakes."

"But the other driver, he was drunk, right?"

"You're not getting me here, Mr. Garber. If you don't mind my asking, sir, did your wife have a habit of drinking and driving? Usually, by the time someone actually gets into an accident, they've been taking chances for quite some—"

Sheila's car burst into flames.

TWO

I'd lost track of just how long, exactly, I'd been standing there, staring into Sheila's closet. Two minutes? Five? Ten?

I hadn't poked my head in here much in the last two weeks. I'd been avoiding it. Right after her death, of course, I'd had to do some rooting around. The funeral home needed an outfit, even though the casket was going to be closed. They'd done the best they could with Sheila. The broken glass had torn into her like buckshot. And the subsequent explosion, even though it did not fully engulf the car's interior before the firefighters doused the vehicle, had only made the undertaker's job more challenging. They'd sculpted and molded Sheila into something that bore a remote resemblance to how she'd looked in life.

But I kept thinking about what it would do to Kelly, to see her mother that way at the service, looking only superficially like the woman she loved. And how everyone would be prompted to say how good she looked, what an amazing job the funeral home had done, which would only serve to remind us of what they'd had to work with.

We'll go with a closed casket, I'd said.

The director said that was what they would do, then, but they still wanted me to provide an outfit.

And so I selected a dark blue suit jacket and matching skirt, underwear, shoes. Sheila had more than a few pairs, and I picked a medium-height pair of pumps. I'd had a pair with higher heels in my hands at one point, then put them back because Sheila had always found that pair uncomfortable.

When I was building her this walk-in closet by shaving a few feet off the end of our large bedroom, she'd said to me, "And just so we're clear, this closet will be completely mine. Yours, that tiny, pitiful, phone-booth-sized thing over there, is all you're ever going to need, and there'll be no encroachment into my territory whatsoever."

"What I'm worried about," I'd said, "is if I built you an airplane hangar you could fill it, too. Your stuff expands to the space allotted for it. Honest to God, Sheila, how many purses does one person need?"

"How many power tools does one man need that do the same job?"

"Just tell me, right now, there'll be no spillover. That you'll never, ever, put anything of yours in *my* closet, even if it is no bigger than a minibar."

Instead of answering directly, she'd slipped her arms around me, pushed me up against the wall, and said, "You know what I think this closet is big enough for?"

"I'm not sure. If you tell me, I could get out my measuring tape and check."

"Oh, there's definitely *something* I want to measure."

Another time.

I stood, now, looking into the closet, wondering what to do with all these things. Maybe it was too soon to think about this. These blouses and sweaters and dresses and skirts and shoes and purses and shoeboxes stuffed with letters and mementos, and all of them carrying her scent, the essence of her that she had left behind.

It made me mournful. And it made me sick.

"Goddamn you," I said under my breath.

I could remember studying, back in my college days, something about the stages of grief. Bargaining, denial, acceptance, anger, depression, and not necessarily in that order. What I couldn't recall now was whether these were the stages you supposedly went through upon learning you were going to die yourself, or when someone close to you had passed away. It all seemed like horseshit to me back then, and pretty much did now. But I couldn't deny there was one overwhelming feeling I'd been having these last few days since we'd put Sheila in the ground.

Anger.

I was devastated, of course. I couldn't believe Sheila was gone, and I was shattered without her. She'd been the love of my life, and now I'd lost her. Sure, I was in grief. When I could find a moment to myself, certain that Kelly would not walk in on me, I gave myself the luxury of falling apart. I was in shock, I felt empty, I was depressed.

But what I really was, was *furious*. Seething. I'd never felt this kind of anger before. Pure, undiluted rage. And there was no place for it to go.

I needed to talk to Sheila. I had a few questions I wanted to bounce off her.

What in the goddamn hell were you thinking? How could you do this to me? How could you do this to Kelly*? What on earth possessed you to do something so monumentally fucking stupid? Who the hell are you, anyway? Where the hell did the smart, head-screwed-on-right girl I married go? Because she sure as hell didn't get in that car.*

The questions kept running through my head. And not just occasionally. They were there every single waking moment.

What made my wife get behind the wheel drunk out of her mind? Why would she have done something so completely out of character? What was going on in her head? What kind of demons had she been keeping from me? When she got into her car that night, totally under the influence, did she have enough sense to know what she was doing? Did she know she could get herself killed, that she could end up killing others?

Were her actions in some way deliberate? Had she wanted to die? Had she secretly been harboring some kind of death wish?

I needed to know. I *ached* to know. And there was no way to make that ache go away.

Maybe I should have felt sorry for Sheila. Pitied her because, for reasons I couldn't begin to comprehend, she'd done this astonishingly stupid thing and paid the ultimate price for her bad judgment.

But I didn't have it in me. All I felt was frustration and rage over what she'd done to those she'd left behind.

"It's unforgivable," I whispered to her things. "Absolutely un—"

"Dad?"

I spun around.

Kelly was standing by the bed in a pair of jeans and sneakers and a pink jacket, a backpack slung over one shoulder. She had pulled her hair back into a ponytail, secured with a red scrunchie thing.

"I'm ready," she said.

"Okay," I said.

"Didn't you hear me? I called you, like, a hundred times."

"Sorry."

She looked past me into her mother's closet and frowned accusingly. "What are you doing?"

"Nothing. Just standing here."

"You're not thinking about throwing out Mom's things, are you?"

"I wasn't really thinking anything. But, yeah, I'll have to decide what to do with her clothes at some point. I mean, by the time you could wear them they'll be out of fashion."

"I don't want to wear them. I want to *keep* them."

"Okay, then," I said gently.

That seemed to satisfy her. She stood there a moment and then said, "Can you take me now?"

"You're sure you want to go?" I asked. "You're ready for this?"

Kelly nodded. "I don't want to sit around the house with you all the time." She bit her lower lip, and added, "No offense."

"I'll get my coat."

I went downstairs and grabbed my jacket from the hall closet. She followed me. "You got everything?"

"Yup," Kelly said.

"Pajamas?"

"Yes."

"Toothbrush?"

"Yes."

"Slippers?"

"Yes."

"Hoppy?" The furry stuffed bunny she still took to bed with her.

"*Daaad*. I have everything I need. When you and Mom went away, she was always reminding *you* what to bring. And it's not the first time I've ever gone on a sleepover."

That was true. It was just the first time she'd been away overnight since her mother had gotten herself killed in a stupid DUI accident.

It would be a good thing for her to get out, be with her friends. Hanging around me, that couldn't be good for anyone.

I forced a smile. "Your mom would say to me, have you got this, have you got that, and I'd say, yeah, of course, you think I'm an idiot? And half the things she said, I'd forgotten, and I'd sneak back into the bedroom and get them. One time, we went away and I forgot to pack any extra underwear. How dumb, huh?"

I thought she might return the smile, but no dice. The corners of her mouth hadn't gone up much in the last sixteen days. Sometimes, when we were snuggled up on the couch watching TV, something funny would happen, she'd start to laugh. But then she'd catch herself, as though she didn't have the right to laugh anymore, that nothing could ever be funny again. It was as though when something made her start to feel happy, she felt ashamed.

"Got your phone?" I asked once we were in the truck. I'd bought her a cell phone since her mother's death so she could call me anytime. It also meant I could keep tabs on her, too. I'd thought, when I got it, what an extravagance a phone was for a kid her age, but soon realized she was far from unique. This was Connecticut, after all, where by age eight some kids already had their own shrink, let alone a phone. And a cell phone wasn't just a phone these days. Kelly had loaded it with songs, taken photos with it, even shot short stretches of video. My phone probably did some of these things, too, but mostly I used it for talking, and taking pictures at job sites.

"I have it," she said, not looking at me.

"Just checking," I said. "If you're uncomfortable, if you want to come home, it doesn't matter what time it is, you can call me. Even if it's three in the morning, if you're not happy with how things are going I'll come over and—"

"I want to go to a different school," Kelly said, looking at me hopefully.

"What?"

"I hate my school. I want to go someplace else."

"Why?"

"Everyone there sucks."

"I need more than that, honey."

"Everybody's mean."

"What do you mean, everybody? Emily Slocum likes you. She's having you for a sleepover."

"Everybody else hates me."

"Tell me, exactly, what's happened."

She swallowed, looked down. "They call me . . ."

"What, sweetheart? What do they call you?"

"Boozer. Boozer the Loser. You know, because of Mom, and the accident."

"Your mother was not a—she was not a drunk, or a boozer."

"Yes, she was," Kelly said. "That's why she's dead. That's how come she killed the other people. Everyone says so."

I felt my jaw tighten. And why wouldn't everyone be saying that? They'd seen the headlines, the six o'clock news. *Three Dead in Milford Mother DUI.*

"Who's calling you this name?"

"It doesn't matter. If I tell you, *you'll* go see the principal and *they'll* get called down and *everyone* will have to have a talk and *I'd* rather just go someplace else. A school where there's nobody that Mom killed."

The two people who'd died in the car that hit Sheila's were Connor Wilkinson, thirty-nine, and his ten-year-old son Brandon.

As if fate hadn't been cruel enough, Brandon had been a student at Kelly's school.

Another Wilkinson boy, Brandon's sixteen-year-old brother Corey, had survived. He'd been sitting in the back seat, belted in. He was looking forward through the front windshield and saw Sheila's Subaru parked across the off-ramp just as his father screamed "Jesus!" and hit the brakes, but not in time. Corey claimed to have seen Sheila, just before the impact, asleep behind the wheel.

Connor had not bothered with his seatbelt, and half of him was on the car hood when the police got there. His body had been taken away by the time I'd arrived, as had Brandon's. The boy had been wearing his seatbelt, but had not survived his injuries.

He'd been in sixth grade, three years ahead of Kelly.

I'd had a feeling things would be rough for her when she got back to school. I'd even gone in to talk to the principal. Brandon Wilkinson had been a popular kid, an A-plus student, a great soccer player. I was worried some students might want to take it out on Kelly, that her mother was being blamed for getting one of the school's most-liked kids killed.

I got a call Kelly's first day back at school. Not because of something someone had said to her, but because of something Kelly had done. One of her classmates had asked her if she got to see her mother's body in the car before they pulled it out, whether she'd been decapitated or anything cool like that, and Kelly'd stomped on the kid's foot. Hurt so bad the girl had to be sent home.

"Maybe Kelly's not ready to resume school," the principal had told me. I'd had a word with Kelly, even made her demonstrate for me what she'd done. She'd stepped around the front of this other girl, raised her knee, then driven her heel into the top of her classmate's foot. "She had it coming," Kelly'd said.

She promised not to do anything like that again, and returned to school the following day. When I didn't hear of any further incidents, I'd hoped things were okay. At least as well as could be expected.

"I'm not putting up with this," I told her now. "I'm going into that office on Monday and those little bastards who are saying these things to you are—"

"Can't I just go to another school?"

My hands tightened on the steering wheel as we drove down Broad Street, through the center of town, past the Milford Green. "We'll see. I'll look into it on Monday, okay? After the weekend?"

"It's always 'we'll see.' You say you will but you won't."

"If I say I'm going to do it, I'll do it. But it means you'll be with kids who don't live in your neighborhood."

She gave me a look. The "duh" was unspoken.

"Okay, that's the point, I get it. And that might seem like a good plan now, but what about in six months, or a year? You end up cutting yourself off from your own community."

"I hate her," Kelly said under her breath.

"Who? Is it a girl who's been calling you names?"

"Mom," she said. "I hate Mom."

I swallowed hard. I'd tried hard to keep my feelings of anger to myself, but why was I surprised Kelly felt betrayed as well? "Don't say that. You don't mean that."

"I do. She left us, and she got in that dumb accident so everybody hates me."

I squeezed the steering wheel. If it had been wood, it would have snapped. "Your mother loved you very much."

"Then why'd she do something so stupid and ruin my life?" Kelly asked.

"Kelly, your mother wasn't stupid."

"Wasn't getting drunk and parking in the middle of the road stupid?"

I lost it.

"Enough!" I made a fist and bounced it off the steering wheel. "Goddamn it, Kelly, you think I have the answers to everything? You don't think I'm going nuts trying to figure out why the hell your mother would do such a dumb thing? You think this is easy for me? You think I like that your mother left me to raise you on my own?"

"You just said she wasn't stupid," Kelly said. Her lip was quivering.

"Well, okay, what she *did,* that was stupid. Beyond stupid. It was as stupid a thing as anyone could do, okay? And it doesn't make a damn bit of sense, because your mother would never, *ever,* drink and drive." I banged the steering wheel again.

I could imagine Sheila's reaction, if she'd heard me say that. She'd have said I knew that wasn't exactly true.

It was years ago. We weren't even engaged. There'd been a party. All the guys from work, their wives, girlfriends. I'd had so much to drink I could barely stand. There was no way I could drive. Sheila probably would have failed a breath test, but she was in way better shape to drive than I was.

But it wasn't fair to count that. We were younger then. Stupider. Sheila'd never have done anything like that now.

Except she had.

I looked over at Kelly, saw her eyes welling up with tears.

"If Mom would never do that, why did it happen?" she asked.

I pulled the truck over to the side of the road. "Come here," I said.

"My seatbelt's on."

"Take the damn thing off and scoot over here."

"I'm fine here," she said, hugging the door. The best I could do was reach over and touch her arm.

"I'm sorry," I told my daughter. "The thing is, I just don't *know*. Your mother and I spent a lot of years together. I knew her better than anyone else in the world, and I loved her more than anyone else in the world, at least until you came along, and then I loved you just as much. What I'm saying is, this doesn't make any more sense to me than it does to you." I stroked her cheek. "But please, please don't say you hate her." It made me feel guilty when she said it, because I believed my feelings were rubbing off on her.

I was furious with Sheila, but I didn't want to turn her daughter against her.

"I'm just so mad at Mom," Kelly said, looking out her window. "And it makes me feel all sick inside, to be mad, when I'm supposed to be sad."

THREE

I put the truck back into drive. A short distance later I hit the blinker and turned down Harborside Drive. "Which house is Emily's again?"

I should have been able to spot it. Emily's mother, Ann Slocum, and Sheila had met six or seven years ago when they'd both signed up the girls for an infants' swim class. They traded tales of being new mothers as they struggled to get their girls in and out of their bathing suits, and had kept in touch since. Because we lived not too far from each other, the girls ended up in the same class at school.

Chauffeuring Kelly back and forth to Emily's house had usually been a duty that fell to Sheila, so I didn't instantly know which place was the Slocums'.

"That one," Kelly said, pointing.

Okay, I knew this house. I'd dropped Kelly here before. A one-story, built mid-sixties, would be my guess. It could have been a nice place if it got some attention. Some of the eaves were sagging, the shingles looked to be nearing the end of their lifespan, and a few of the bricks near the top of the chimney were crumbling from moisture getting into them. The Slocums weren't alone in putting off household repairs. These days, with money tight, people were letting things go until they couldn't be ignored any longer, and sometimes even then they weren't dealing with them. A leaky roof could be fixed with a pail a lot cheaper than new shingles.

Ann Slocum's husband, Darren, was living on a cop's salary, which wasn't huge, and probably even less than it used to be since the town started clamping down on overtime. Ann had lost her job in the circulation department at the New Haven paper sixteen months ago. Even though she'd found some other ways to make a living, I could imagine money was tight.

For about a year, she'd been running these so-called "purse parties" where women could buy imitation designer bags for a fraction of the price of the real ones. Sheila had turned our place over to Ann one night not long ago to run one. It was quite an event, like one of those Tupperware things—or at least what I imagine one of those Tupperware things are like.

Twenty women invaded the house. Sally, from work, came, as well as Doug Pinder's wife, Betsy. I was particularly surprised when Sheila's mother, Fiona, showed up, with her husband Marcus in tow. Fiona could afford a genuine Louis Vuitton if she wanted one, and I couldn't see her carrying around a bag that wasn't the real deal. But Sheila, worried that Ann would get a poor turnout, had begged her mother to come. It was Marcus who finally persuaded Fiona to make the effort.

"Be sociable," he'd apparently told her. "You don't have to actually *buy* one. Show up and support your daughter."

I hated to be cynical, but I couldn't help wondering whether his motives had little to do with making his stepdaughter happy. An event like this, you had to figure there'd be a lot of women there, and Marcus liked to check out the ladies.

Marcus and Fiona got to our place first, and when the women started arriving, he made a point of greeting them as they came through the door, introducing himself, offering to get each a glass of wine, making sure they all had a place to sit as they began to drool over leather and fake labels. His antics appeared to embarrass Fiona. "Stop making a fool of yourself," she'd snapped, taking him aside at one point.

Once Ann's sales pitch got under way and Marcus and I had retreated to the back deck with a couple of beers, he said, somewhat defensively, "Don't worry, I'm still madly in love with your mother-in-law. I just like women." He smiled. "And I think they like me."

"Yeah," I replied. "You're a stud muffin."

Ann did pretty well that night. Made a couple of thousand dollars—even knockoff purses could run several hundred bucks—and for hosting the event, Sheila got to pick any bag she wanted.

Even if the Slocums couldn't afford repairs to their house, purses and policing were paying well enough for Ann to drive a three-year-old Beemer sedan, and Darren had a Dodge Ram pickup that gleamed red. Only the pickup was in the driveway as we approached the house.

"Is Emily having any other friends sleep over?" I asked Kelly.

"Nope. Just me."

We stopped at the curb.

"You okay?" I asked her.

"I'm okay."

"I'll walk you to the door."

"Dad, you don't have—"

"Come on."

Kelly dragged her backpack, adopting a condemned-prisoner gait as we approached the house.

"Don't worry," I said. There was a For Sale sign with a phone number stuck to the inside back window of Darren Slocum's pickup. "It'll be fun, once you've ditched your dad."

I was about to ring the bell when I heard a car pull in to the driveway. It was Ann in her Beemer. When she got out of the car, she grabbed a Walgreens bag.

"Hey!" she called, more to Kelly than me. "I just got some snacks for your sleepover." Then she laid her eyes on me. "Hi, Glen." Only two words, but they were laced with sympathy.

"Ann."

The front door opened. It was Emily, her blonde hair pulled back into a ponytail just like Kelly's. She must have spotted us through the window. She squealed at the sight of Kelly, who barely had time to mumble a farewell to me as she and her friend ran off.

"So much for the tearful goodbye," I said to Ann.

She smiled, walking past me and taking me by the arm into the front hall.

"Thanks for taking Kelly tonight," I said. "She's very excited."

"It's no trouble."

Ann Slocum was in her mid-thirties, petite, with short black hair. Stylish jeans, a blue satiny T and matching bracelets. An outfit that looked simple enough but probably set her back more than what a new Makita rotary hammer, with variable speed and all the accessories, would have cost me. She had nice muscle tone in the arms, a flat stomach beneath her small breasts. She looked like someone who worked out, but I recalled Sheila saying once that Ann had dropped her gym membership. I supposed one could do that sort of thing from home. Ann gave off something, in the way she carried herself, the way she tilted her head when she looked at you, the way you knew she knew you were looking at her when she walked away, that was like a scent. She was the kind of woman who, if you didn't keep your head about you, you might find yourself wanting to do something stupid with.

I wasn't stupid.

Darren Slocum entered from the dining room. Trim, about a head taller than Ann and about the same age, but with prematurely gray hair. His high cheekbones and deep-set eyes gave him an intimidating look, which probably came in handy when he pulled people over for exceeding the Milford speed limits. He thrust out a hand. His shake was strong, just this side of painful, establishing dominance. But building houses gave you a pretty good grip, too, and I was ready for him, putting my palm firmly into his and giving as good as I got, the son of a bitch.

"Hey," he said. "How's it going."

"Jesus, Darren, dumb question," Ann said, wincing and looking apologetically at me.

Her husband shot her a look. "Excuse me. It's just something you say."

I gave my head a "Don't worry about it" shake. But Ann wasn't ready to let it go. "You should think before you talk," she said.

Oh what fun. I'd arrived in the middle of a spat. Trying to smooth things over, I said, "This is really good for Kelly. She's had no one to hang out with but me for two weeks, and I haven't exactly been a barrel of laughs."

Ann said, "Emily's been at us and at us to have a sleepover and she finally wore us down. Maybe it'll be good for everyone."

The girls could be heard in the kitchen, giggling and fussing about. I heard Kelly shout, "Pizza, *yes*!" Darren, distracted, looked off in the direction of the noise.

"We'll take good care of her," Ann said, then, to her husband, "won't we, Darren?"

He snapped his head around. "Hmm?"

"I said we'll take good care of her."

"Yeah, of course," he said. "Sure."

I said, "I see you're selling your truck."

Darren brightened. "You interested?"

"I'm not really in the market right—"

"I can give you a hell of a deal on it. It's got the three-ten horsepower engine and the eight-foot bed, perfect for a guy like you. Make me an offer."

I shook my head. I didn't need a new truck. I wasn't even going to get anything for Sheila's totaled Subaru. Because the accident was her fault, the insurance company wasn't going to cover it. "Sorry," I said. "What time should I pick Kelly up?"

Ann and Darren exchanged glances. Ann, her hand on the door, said, "Why don't we have her call you? You know how silly they can get. If they don't get to sleep in good time, they won't exactly be up at the crack of dawn, will they?"

When I pulled the truck in to my driveway, Joan Mueller was looking out her front window from next door. A moment later, she came outside, stood on the front step. A boy about four years old peered out from behind her leg. Not hers. Joan and Ely had had no children. This little guy would be one of her charges.

"Hey, Glen," she called as I stepped out of the cab.

"Joan," I said, planning to head straight into the house.

"How are things?" she asked.

"Managing," I said. It would have been polite to ask how things were with her, but I didn't want to get into a conversation.

"Do you have a second?" she asked.

You can't always get what you want. I walked across the lawn, glanced down at the boy and smiled.

"You know Mr. Garber, don't you, Carlson? He's a *nice* man." The boy hid another moment behind her leg, then ran back into the house. "He's my last pickup," Joan explained to me. "Expecting his dad along any minute. Everyone else has been by. Just Carlson's dad and that's it, then I'll have my life back for the weekend!" A nervous laugh. "Most people, they seem to pick up their kids early on a Friday, they get off ahead of schedule, but not Mr. Bain—Carlson's dad—he works right to the end of the day, Friday or not, you know?"

Joan had a way of rambling on nervously. All the more reason why I had hoped to avoid a chat.

"You're looking well," I said, and it was half true. Joan Mueller was a good-looking woman. Early thirties, brown hair pulled back into a ponytail. Her jeans and T-shirt fit her like a second skin, and she filled them well. If anything, she was a little too skinny. Since her husband's death, and starting an off-the-books child-care operation in her home, she'd lost probably twenty pounds. Nervous energy, anxiety, not to mention chasing after four or five children.

She blushed, tucked a stray lock of hair behind her ear. "Well, you know, I'm on the move all the time, right? You think you've got them all settled down in front of the tube or doing some crafts and then one wanders off and you get that one and then another one's on the go—I swear it's like kittens in a basket, you know?"

I was only a couple of feet away from her and was pretty sure I could smell liquor on her breath.

"Was there something I can help you with?"

"I—well, um—I've got a tap in the kitchen that won't stop dripping. You know, maybe sometime, if you had a second, but I know you're busy and all—"

"Maybe on the weekend," I said. "When I have a minute." Over the years, especially during other periods when work was tight, I'd done small jobs, unrelated to the company, for our neighbors. I'd finished off the Muellers' basement on my own a few years back over a month, working every Saturday and Sunday.

"Oh sure, I understand, I don't want to cut in on your free time, Glen, I totally understand that."

"Okay, then," I said, smiled, and turned to leave.

"So how's Kelly getting along? I haven't had her here, after school, since, you know." I had the feeling Joan Mueller did not want me to go.

"I've been picking her up every day after school," I said. "And she's at a sleepover with a friend tonight."

"Oh," Joan said. "So you're on your own tonight, then."

I nodded but said nothing. I didn't know whether Joan was sending out a signal or not. It didn't seem possible. Her husband had been dead for some time, but I'd lost Sheila only sixteen days ago.

"Listen, I—"

"Oh, look," Joan interrupted with forced excitement as a faded red Ford Explorer whipped into her driveway. "That's Carlson's dad. You really should meet him. Carlson! Your dad's here!"

I had no interest in meeting the man, but didn't feel I could vanish now. The father, a lean, wiry man who may have been in a suit but whose hair was too long and straggly for him to have a bank job, came up the walk. He had a kind of slow swagger. Nothing over the top. The kind of thing I'd noticed in bikers—I'd had one or two work part-time for me over the years—and I wondered whether this guy was a weekend warrior. He looked me up and down, just enough to let me know he'd done it.

Carlson slipped out the door, didn't stop to greet his father and headed straight for the SUV.

"Carl, I wanted you to meet Glen Garber," Joan said. "Glen, this is Carl Bain."

Interesting, I thought. Instead of "Carl Jr." his kid was named Carlson. I offered a hand and he took it. His eyes darted from Joan to me. "Nice to meet you," he said.

"Glen's a contractor," Joan told him. "Has his own company. He lives right next door." She pointed to my house. "In that house right there."

Carl Bain nodded. "See you Monday," he said to Joan, and went back to his Explorer.

Joan waved a little too enthusiastically as he drove off. Then she turned to me and said, "Thank you for that."

"For what?"

"I just feel safer having you next door."

She gave me a friendly look that seemed to go beyond neighborly as she retreated into the house.

FOUR

"What's it like?" Emily asked.

"What's what like?" Kelly said.

"Not having a mom. What's it like?"

They were sitting on the floor in Emily's bedroom amidst piles of clothing. Kelly had been trying on Emily's outfits and Emily had been modeling the clothes Kelly'd come in, and the one extra outfit she'd packed. Kelly had been asking if they wanted to swap tops for a week when Emily blurted out the question.

"It's not very nice," Kelly said.

"If my mom or dad had to die, I think I'd pick my dad," Emily said. "I love him, but it'd be worse for your mom to die because dads don't know a lot of things about stuff. Do you wish it was your dad instead?"

"No. I wish it hadn't been anybody."

"Wanna play spy?"

"How?"

"Have you got your phone?"

Kelly had it in her pocket and dug it out. Emily said, "Okay, so we hide in the house and try to get pictures of each other without the other person knowing about it."

Kelly grinned. This sounded like fun. "Like, just pictures, or video?"

"You get more points for video."

"How many?"

"Okay, you get one point for a picture, but you get one point for every second of video."

"I think it should be five points," Kelly said. They debated this briefly, and came up with five points for each picture and ten points for each second of video.

"If we both hide at the same time, how do we find each other?" Kelly asked.

Emily hadn't considered that. "Okay, you hide first, and then I'll try to find you."

Kelly was on her feet. "You have to count to five hundred. And not five, ten, fifteen, twenty, but one, two, three—"

"That's too much. A hundred."

"But not fast," she stressed. "Not one-two-three-four but one, two, three—"

"Okay! Go! Go!"

Kelly, phone firmly grasped in her fist, tore out of the room. She ran down the hallway, wondering where to hide. She looked quickly into the bathroom, but there really wasn't anywhere good there. If she was home, she could stand in the tub and draw the curtain across, but the Slocums had a shower with a glass door. She opened a door that turned out to be a linen closet, and the shelves came out too far to squeeze in.

She opened another door and saw a bed the same size as the one her parents slept in, although now her dad had the whole thing to himself. The spread was off-white and there were tall wooden posts at all four corners. This had to be Mr. and Mrs. Slocum's room. It had its own bathroom, but again, the shower—the best place to hide—had a glass door, and the tub was wide open without a curtain.

Kelly ran across the room and opened the closet. It was jammed with hanging clothes, and the floor was littered with shoes and purses. Kelly stepped in, nestling herself into the shirts and dresses that enveloped her. She didn't shut the door all the way. She left a two-inch gap so that when Emily came in, she'd be able to film her poking about the room. And then, when she opened the door, Kelly would scream, "Surprise!"

She wondered if Emily would wet her pants.

She tapped her phone and the screen illuminated. She activated the camera function and pressed the video icon.

Her foot nudged against something. She thought it was a purse. Something inside it jangled. Kneeling, she reached her hand in, felt what she thought had made the sound, and took it out.

She heard some motion. Through the crack, she saw the bedroom door open.

She tucked the item down into her front pocket. She kept her phone in her hand.

It wasn't Emily coming into the room. It was her mother. It was Ann Slocum.

Kelly thought, *Uh-oh.*

She wondered whether she'd get in trouble for hiding in the woman's closet. So she kept very still as Emily's mother came around the bed and sat on the edge. She reached for the phone on the bedside table and punched in a number.

"Hey," she said, holding the receiver close to her mouth. "Can you talk? Yeah, I'm alone . . . okay, so I hope your wrists are okay . . . yeah, wear long sleeves until the marks go away . . . you were wondering about next time . . . can do Wednesday, maybe, if that works for you? But I have to tell you, I've got to get more for . . . expenses and—hang on, I've got another call, okay, later—Hello?"

Kelly wasn't getting even half the conversation, what with Mrs. Slocum whispering so much. She listened, holding her breath, petrified she'd be discovered.

"Why are you calling this . . . my cell's off . . . not a good time . . . kid's got someone sleeping . . . Yeah, he is . . . but look, you know the arrangement. You pay and . . . something in return . . . mark us . . . down for a new deal if you've got something else to offer."

Ann Slocum paused, glanced toward the closet.

Kelly suddenly felt very frightened. It was one thing, hiding in a friend's mother's closet. That might make Mrs. Slocum angry. But hearing her private conversations, that might really make her mad.

Kelly dropped her arms to her sides and held them rigid, soldierlike, as though this might magically make her thinner, less noticeable. The woman started talking again.

"Okay, where do you want to do this... yeah, got it. Just don't be stupid... end up with a bullet in your brain—what the—"

Ann Slocum was looking right into the crack now.

"Hang on a sec, there's someone—what the hell are you doing in there?"

FIVE

I was sitting, having a beer, looking at the framed picture on my desk of Sheila and Kelly winter before last, bundled up against the cold, snow on their boots, wearing matching pink mitts. They were standing in front of an assortment of Christmas trees, the one on the far left the one we eventually chose to bring home and set up in the living room.

"They're calling her Boozer," I said. "Just thought you should know." I held a hand up to the picture, warding off any imagined rebuttals. "I don't want to hear it. I don't want to hear a damn thing you have to say."

I drew on the bottle. This was only my first. It was going to take a few more to get where I wanted to be.

It was lonely in the house without Kelly. I wondered if I'd be able to sleep when it came time to hit the sack. I usually found myself getting up around two, coming down to the living room and turning on the TV. I dreaded going upstairs, sleeping in that big bed by myself.

The phone rang. I snatched the receiver off its cradle. "Hello."

"Hey, Glenny, how's it going?" Doug Pinder, my second in command at Garber Contracting.

"Hey," I said.

"What are you doin'?"

"Just having a beer," I said. "I dropped Kelly off a little while ago at a sleepover. First night here without her, since."

"Shit, you're on your own?" Doug said excitedly. "We should do something. It's Friday night. Get out, live a little." Doug was the kind of guy who'd have told Mrs. Custer, within a week of her husband's last stand, to get herself down to the saloon, hoist a few, let loose.

I glanced at the clock. Just after nine. "I don't think so. I'm pretty beat."

"Come on. Doesn't have to be a going-out thing. I'm just sitting around here doing nothing. Betsy's gone out, I got the place to myself, so get in your truck and mosey over. Maybe rent a movie or something on the way. And bring beer."

"Where's Betsy?"

"Who knows. I don't question when good things happen."

"I'm just not up to it, Doug, but thanks for the offer. I think I'm gonna finish this beer, have another, watch some television, and maybe go to bed."

The thing was, I put off going to bed most every night. It was the place that, more than any other, reminded me of how different my life now was.

"Can't mope around forever, my friend."

"It hasn't even been three weeks."

"Oh, well, yeah, I guess that's not very long. Look, no offense, Glenny. I know sometimes I come across as insensitive, but I don't mean it."

"It's okay. Look, nice talking to you, and I'll see you Monday morn—"

"Hang on just a sec. I should have brought this up at work today, but there wasn't really a moment, you know?"

"What is it?"

"Okay, here's the thing. I hate to ask, honest to God I do, but you remember, a month or so ago, I asked you for a bit of an advance?"

I sighed to myself. "I remember."

"And I really appreciated it. Helped me over the hump. You're a fucking lifesaver is what you are, Glenny."

I waited.

"So, thing is, if you could find it in your heart to do that again, I'd be in your debt, man. I'm just going through a little rough patch at the moment. It's not like I'm asking for a loan or a handout or something, just an advance."

"How much?"

"Like, a month? Next four weeks' pay now, and I swear, I won't ask again."

"What are you going to live on for a month after you pay off whatever it is you have to pay off?"

"Oh, don't worry, I've got that under control."

"You're putting me in an awkward position, Doug." I felt the hairs rising on the back of my neck. I loved this guy, but I wasn't in the mood for any of his bullshit right now.

"Come on, man. Who pulled you out of that burning basement?"

"I know, Doug." This was the card he most liked to play now.

"And really, this is the last time I'm gonna ask. After this, things'll be totally cool."

"That's what you said last time."

A self-deprecating chuckle. "Yeah, you're probably right about that. But really, I'm just trying to sort out a few things, waiting for my luck to change. And I think that's going to happen."

"Doug, it's not a matter of luck. You've got to face a few realities."

"Hey, like, it's not like I'm the only one, right? The whole country's in the financial dumper. I mean, if it can happen to Wall Street, it can happen to anybody, you know what I'm—"

"Hang on," I said, cutting him off. "It's the other line."

I hit the button. "Hello?"

"I want to come home," Kelly said urgently, her voice nothing more than a whisper. "Come and get me now, Daddy. Please hurry."

SIX

Belinda Morton had told George she had a house to show tonight. "You know, that listing I just got, that couple moving to Vermont?"

George was watching *Judge Judy* at the time and didn't pay her any attention. All she needed was an excuse when she walked out the door, and when you were a real estate agent, you expected to have to head out at all hours. But just to be sure he wouldn't ask questions, she waited until her husband's favorite show was on. George loved *Judge Judy*. At first Belinda thought he was fascinated by all the various disputes—fights over unpaid rent, jilted lovers who keyed cars, girlfriends who wanted their men to pay back money they'd spent to bail them out—but she'd come to the conclusion it was the judge herself who kept George transfixed in front of the set. He had a thing for her. He was mesmerized by her stern nature, the way she dominated her court and everyone inside it.

Although, if George had been paying attention, he might have noticed that Belinda hadn't actually been going out that much lately. The real estate market was in the toilet. No one was buying. And people who needed to sell—like the ones who'd lost their jobs and spent months without success trying to find new ones—were getting downright desperate. The hospital was closing beds, laying off nurses. The Board of Education was talking about laying off dozens of teachers. Dealerships shutting down. Even the police department was letting a couple of officers go due to budget cuts. Belinda never would have guessed she'd see the day when people would just walk away. *Let the bank have it, we don't give a shit, we're out of here.* Just packing up their things and leaving their homes behind. Some houses, you could hardly give them away. Down in Florida, they had condo developments almost entirely empty, buyers from Canada coming down, picking up a $250,000 vacation spot for $30,000.

It was a world gone mad.

And how great it would be, Belinda thought, if a collapsing real estate market were all she had to worry about these days.

A few weeks ago, falling house prices, hardly any buyers, and no fat commissions going into the bank account had her tossing and turning all night. But at least back then, all she was worried about was her financial future. Keeping a roof over their heads, making the lease payments on the Acura.

She wasn't actually scared for her personal safety. She wasn't worried that someone might *hurt* her.

Not like now.

Belinda still needed to find a way to come up with $37,000. But even that was just in the short term. Ultimately, she'd have to get her hands on the whole $62,000. She'd maxed out her credit cards with cash advances totaling ten grand, put another five on her line of credit. And she was going to have to pay back her friends the eight thousand they'd kicked in. If they could get another fifteen or twenty for their truck, put that toward the debt, that'd be great, but Belinda would still have to reimburse them. She'd rather be in debt to them than their suppliers.

The suppliers wanted the money that was owed them. They'd made that very clear to her friends. And they didn't care whose fault it was.

But Belinda had been the one taking the blame. "This is your fault," they told her. "You don't fuck with these people. They want that money from us, and we want it from you."

Belinda had pleaded that it really wasn't her fault. "It was an *accident,*" she kept telling them. "It was just one of those things."

Hardly an accident, they told her. Two cars hitting each other for no reason, that's an accident. But when one of those drivers makes a decision to do something very, very stupid, well, that's a bit of a gray area, isn't it?

The car *burned up,* Belinda said. "What the hell do you want from me?"

No one was interested in excuses.

One way or another, she had to come up with the money. All the more reason to unload the stuff she still had. A few hundred here, a few hundred there—it all helped. If only these assholes would just take the product back. That would help wipe out a good chunk of the debt. But they weren't Sears. They had a "no return" policy. They just wanted their money.

She had a few deliveries she could make tonight. One guy in Derby who needed Avandia for his type 2 diabetes, and another customer only a couple of blocks over who was taking Propecia for baldness. Belinda wondered about pocketing a few of those herself, mashing them up and putting them in George's cream of wheat in the morning. The comb-over thing he'd been trying for several years wasn't fooling anybody. The other side of town there was a woman she delivered Viagra to, and Belinda wondered whether she was doing just that. Pulverizing the pill and hiding it in her husband's Heavenly Hash ice cream. Getting him ready for bedtime. And she thought she should place a call to that man in Orange, see if he was getting low on lisinopril for his heart.

She was going to set up a website, but she'd found word of mouth had been working pretty well for her. Everyone needed a prescription of one kind or another, and these days everyone was looking for a way to save on drugstore prices. Considering hardly anyone had a drug plan, and those who did were wondering how much longer they'd get to keep it, there was a demand for what Belinda had to offer. Her prescription drugs—which, by the way, were available without a prescription—were made God knows where, somewhere in China, maybe in the same factories that cranked out those fake Fendi bags Ann Slocum hawked. And just like those purses, they could be had for a fraction of the cost of the real deal.

Belinda told herself she was doing a public service. Helping people, and helping them save money.

Not that she felt good enough about this sideline to tell George about it. He could be a real tight-ass about the sanctity of trademarks and copyright protections. He'd just about had a fit one time when they were in Manhattan, about five years ago, and Belinda tried to buy a counterfeit Kate Spade bag from a guy selling them out of a blanket around the corner from Ground Zero.

So she didn't keep the drugs around the house.

Belinda kept them at the Torkin house.

Bernard and Barbara Torkin had put their house on the market thirteen months ago when they decided to move across the country to live with her parents in Arizona. He'd accepted a sales job at his father-in-law's Toyota dealership when GM killed its Saturn division and the dealership he'd worked at for sixteen years shut down.

The Torkins had a small two-story that backed onto a school playground. The house on one side was owned by a man who kept three dogs that never stopped barking. On the other, a guy who repaired motorcycles and listened to Black Sabbath 24/7.

Belinda could not unload the place. She'd advised the Torkins to drop their price, but they wouldn't budge. Damned if they were going to sell for forty percent less than they paid. They'd wait for the market to rebound, and then sell.

Don't hold your breath, Belinda thought.

The good news was the Torkin house made a great place for Belinda Morton to hide her product. And tonight, she would head over to her "pharmacy," as she liked to think of it, and fill some orders.

She was careful going down the cellar steps in her heels. It was cool down here, and she was losing the light as the door from the kitchen slowly started to swing shut. She reached, in time, the pull chain in the middle of the room that turned on the bare overhead bulb, but the corners of the room remained cast in shadow.

The basement wasn't much of a selling point for prospective buyers. Cinder-block walls, open stud ceiling. At least the floor was concrete and not dirt. A washer and dryer and a workbench were down here but not much else, except the furnace. It was behind there that Belinda headed.

She lowered her head to clear a heating duct, then squeezed into the three-foot space between the furnace and the wall. There was a gap at the top of the cinder blocks where the wooden beams rested. She stuck her hand up and reached in. She kept the jars just out of sight. There were fifteen of them in here, just the most popular stuff. Heart medications, drugs for acid reflux, diabetes, hard-ons. There was so little light back here she had to bring out the jars and set them on the worktable to sort out just what she needed.

She realized she was shaking. She knew that, even with a few sales tonight, she'd probably only make five hundred or so. She was going to have to come up with a better plan.

Maybe, she thought, she could talk the Torkins into some repairs.

Send them an email in Arizona, tell them she thought she could sell their house if they did a few minor upgrades. A bit of paint, replace the rotten boards on the front porch, get someone in to clear out the junk in the far corner of the property.

Tell them she could get it all done for a couple of thousand. Keep the money herself. What were they going to do? Hop a plane and come back to Milford to see if the work got done? Not likely.

She had two other out-of-town clients she might be able to talk into some repairs. Once she got out from under her debt, if she had to, she'd find a way to get the actual work done. If she got wind the owners were going to be back in the neighborhood, she'd have to move on it. Truth was, Belinda would rather explain to those people why the work wasn't done than have to explain to those other people why she didn't have their money.

She held the first jar up to the light so she could read the label. Those magical blue pills. George had tried them, once. Not these ones, not the knockoff variety. He'd gotten a prescription from his doctor, wanted to see what they'd do. What they did was give him one hell of a headache. The whole time he was on her he griped that he needed some Tylenols before his head exploded.

Belinda was unscrewing the lid when she heard the floor creak above her head.

She froze. There was nothing for a moment. She told herself she'd imagined it.

But then it happened again.

Someone was walking around in the kitchen.

She was sure she'd locked the front door when she'd come in. She didn't want anyone walking in on her while she conducted her dispensing duties. But maybe, somehow, she'd forgotten. Someone had seen the For Sale sign out front, her Acura parked at the curb, noticed the business card she kept on the dash, and decided this was an open house.

"Hello?" she called out tentatively. "Is there someone there?"

No one answered.

Belinda called out again. "Did you see the sign? Are you here about the house?"

If whoever it was upstairs was here for some other reason, like looking for a place to crash, or make out, or vandalize, they'd know now that someone was already here. And if they had half a brain in their head, they'd take off.

But Belinda hadn't heard anyone running for the front door.

Her mouth was dry and she tried to swallow. She needed to get out of here. But there was only one way out, and it was up those stairs, and the kitchen was at the top of those stairs.

She decided to call the police. She'd whisper into her cell phone, tell them to get here fast, that someone was in the house, someone was—

Her cell phone was in her purse. A fake Chanel bag she'd bought at one of Ann's purse parties. And it was sitting upstairs, on the kitchen counter.

The door at the top of the stairs opened.

Belinda considered hiding, but where would she go? Behind the furnace? How long would it take someone to find her there? Five seconds?

"You're trespassing!" she said. "Unless you're interested in buying this house, you've got no business being here."

A man's silhouette filled the doorway. He said, "You're Belinda."

She nodded. "That's—that's right. I'm the agent for this house. And you are?"

"I'm not here about the house."

With the kitchen lights illuminating him from behind, his face was difficult to see. But Belinda determined he was a good six feet tall, thin, with short dark hair, and wearing a dark tailored suit and white shirt, but no tie.

"What do you want?" she asked. "Is there something I can help you with?"

"You're running out of time." His voice was even, almost no inflection at all.

"The money," she said, her voice a whisper. "You're here about the money."

The man said nothing.

"I'm working on it," she said, struggling to make herself sound enthusiastic. "I really, really am. But just so you understand the situation. About the accident. There was a fire. So if the envelope was in the car—"

"That's not my problem." He descended a step.

"I'm just saying, that's why this is taking some time. I mean, if you folks took checks," and here she tried a nervous laugh, "I could write you one on my line of credit. Maybe not for all of it, not today, but—"

"Two days," he said. "Talk to your friends. They know how to reach me."

He turned, went back up the one step to the kitchen, and disappeared.

Belinda's heart fluttered. She wondered whether she was going to faint. She felt herself starting to shake again.

Just before she dissolved into tears, she realized that she'd just said something that had never occurred to her before.

So if the envelope was in the car—

If.

She'd always assumed it was. Everyone had. This was the first time she'd even considered it might not have been. Was there a chance in a million it still existed? And even if it had been in the car, was there the same chance it didn't go up in smoke? The car had burned, but from what Belinda knew, the fire had been extinguished before it was completely destroyed. Belinda'd heard the casket was closed more out of concern for the little girl than because the body had been consumed by flames.

There were questions she'd have to ask.

Hard questions.

SEVEN

I was back at the Slocum house in five minutes.

I thought Kelly would be waiting at the front door, watching for me, but I had to ring the bell. When no one showed up after ten seconds, I leaned on it again.

Darren Slocum, opening the door, looked surprised to see me. "Hey, Glen," he said, his eyebrows slanted down quizzically.

"Hi," I said.

"What's up?"

I'd assumed he'd know why I was there. "I'm picking up Kelly."

"You are?"

"Yeah. She called me. Can you get her?"

Hesitant. "Yeah, sure thing, Glen. Wait here a second and I'll go see what's going on."

I stepped into the foyer without being asked as he headed off through the dining room to the left. I stood there, looking around. To the right, a living room with a big-screen TV, a couple of leather couches. Half a dozen remotes lined up on the coffee table like prone soldiers.

I heard someone coming, but it was Ann, not Kelly.

"Hello?" she said. She looked as surprised to see me as Glen had. I didn't know whether I was reading her right, but she seemed troubled, too. She had a black cordless phone in her hand. "Is everything okay?"

"Darren's gone to find Kelly," I said.

Was it alarm that flashed across her face? Just for second?

"Is something wrong?"

"She called me," I said. "She asked me to come pick her up."

"I didn't know that," Ann said. "What's wrong? Did she say what was wrong?"

"She just said to come and pick her up." I could think of any number of reasons why Kelly might have decided to bail on her sleepover. Maybe she wasn't ready to be away from home this soon after her mother's death. She and Emily could have had a fight. Maybe she'd had too much pizza and felt sick to her stomach.

"She never asked to use the phone," Ann said.

"She has her own." Ann was starting to irritate me. I just wanted to get Kelly and go.

"Yes, well," Ann said, and seemed momentarily distracted. "Eight-year-old girls with their own phones! It wasn't like that when we were kids, was it?"

"No," I agreed.

"I hope the girls didn't have an argument or anything. You know how they can be. Best of friends one minute, mortal enemies the—"

"Kelly!" I shouted into the house. "Daddy's here!"

Ann raised her hands as if to shush me. "I'm sure she's coming. I think they were watching a movie in Emily's room, on the computer, for a while. We told her she couldn't have a TV in there, but when you have a computer, who needs a TV, you know? You can watch all the TV shows online now anyway. And I think they were writing a story, making up some sort of adventure or something like—"

"Where's Emily's room?" I asked, starting for the dining room, figuring I could find my way through the house faster than the Slocums could get Kelly to the door.

But then, suddenly, she appeared, coming from the living room, with Darren trailing after her. Kelly seemed to be making an effort to stay ahead of him.

"Found her," he said.

"Hey, Dad," she said sullenly.

She had her jacket on, backpack in hand, and stopped at my side, pressing into me. The backpack hadn't been fully zipped, and one of Hoppy's ears was sticking out.

"You okay, sweetheart?" I asked.

She nodded.

"You sick?"

She hesitated a second, then nodded. "I want to go home," she insisted.

"I don't know what her problem is," Darren said to me, like Kelly wasn't even there. "I asked her and she wouldn't say a thing."

Kelly wouldn't look at him. I mumbled a thank-you and guided her out to the front step. Ann and Darren muttered something in return before closing the door behind us. I stopped Kelly and leaned over to zip up her jacket. Inside the house, I could hear voices being raised.

Once I had Kelly buckled in and was pulling away from the Slocum house, I asked, "So what happened?"

"I don't feel good."

"What is it? Stomach?"

"I feel weird."

"Pizza? Too much soda?"

Kelly shrugged.

"Did something happen? Did something happen with Emily?"

"No."

"No, nothing happened? Or no, nothing happened with Emily?"

"I just want to go home."

"Did Emily or somebody say something? About your mother?"

"No."

"You looked like you didn't even want to talk to Mr. Slocum. Did something happen with him?"

"I don't know."

"What do you mean, you don't know?" The hairs were standing up on the back of my neck again. I was getting a bad vibe off him there. I didn't know what it was. But there was something I didn't like. "Did he . . . did he make you feel uncomfortable?"

"Everything's *fine,*" Kelly said, but she wouldn't look at me.

My mind was taking me places I didn't want to go. There were questions I felt I needed to ask, but it wasn't going to be easy to ask them.

"Look, honey, if something happened, you need to tell me about it."

"I can't."

I glanced over at her, but she was still looking straight ahead. "You can't?"

Kelly didn't say anything.

"Something happened, but you can't talk about it, is that what you're saying?"

Kelly's lips tightened. I felt a spike of anxiety.

"Did someone make you promise not to say anything?"

After a moment, she said, "I don't want to get in trouble."

I kept my voice as even as possible. "You're not going to get in trouble. Sometimes, grown-ups, they'll make kids promise not to tell something, but that's wrong. Any time a grown-up does that, it's to cover up something that they've done. It's not because of anything bad you've done. And even if they say you're going to get in trouble if you tell, you won't."

Kelly's head went up and down a fraction of an inch.

"This thing... that happened," I said, tentatively. "Was Emily there? Did she see it?"

"No."

"Where was Emily?"

"I don't know. She hadn't found me yet."

"Found you?"

"I was hiding, and then she was going to hide."

"From her father?"

"No," she said impatiently. "We were hiding from each other. In different parts of the house, but then we were trying to sneak up on each other."

"Okay," I said, starting to clue in. "Did she come in later? Did she find you?"

A shake of the head.

We were by the hospital, the point where we'd normally turn down Seaside Avenue to our place, which was neither by the sea nor within view of it. But I felt, now that Kelly was talking, pulling in to the driveway might shut her down. So I went past our street and wandered down Bridgeport Avenue. If Kelly noticed we were missing the turn to our place, she didn't mention it.

Okay, no more stalling. This was my life—*our* life—now. Dad and daughter had to talk about things that Dad would have been very happy to hand over to Mom.

"Sweetheart, this is really difficult for me to ask, but I have to, okay?"

She looked me in the eye, then turned away.

"Did Mr. Slocum do something to you? Did he touch you? Did he do something that you didn't want him to do? Because if he did, that's wrong, and we need to talk about it." It seemed unthinkable. The guy was a *cop,* for crying out loud. But I didn't care if he was the goddamn head of the FBI. If he touched my kid, I was going to beat the living shit out of him.

"He didn't touch me," she said.

"Okay." I started to imagine different scenarios. "Did he *say* something to you? *Show* something to you?"

"No, he didn't do any of those things."

I let out a long breath. "Then what, honey? What did he do?"

"He didn't do *anything,* okay?" Kelly turned and looked at me directly, as though getting ready to accuse me of something. "It wasn't him. It was *her.*"

"Her? Who?"

"It was Emily's mom."

EIGHT

"Emily's *mom* touched you?" I asked, bewildered. That seemed even more unthinkable.

"No, she didn't *touch* me," Kelly said. "She got *mad* at me."

"Mad at you? Why would she get mad at you?"

"I was in their room." Now she wouldn't look at me.

"Their room? You mean, their bedroom?"

Kelly nodded. "We were just playing."

"Playing in Emily's parents' bedroom?"

"I was only *hiding*. In the closet. I wasn't doing anything bad. But she got all mad because she didn't know I was there and she was on the phone."

I was upset, but part of me was relieved, as well. The worst-case scenario appeared to be off the table. Kelly being where she wasn't supposed to be, hiding in Ann and Darren Slocum's bedroom—well, if I'd found Emily hanging out in my bedroom closet, I'd probably be pissed about it myself.

"Okay, so let me get this straight," I said carefully. "You were hiding in Mr. and Mrs. Slocum's bedroom and then Mrs. Slocum came in to use the phone?"

Kelly nodded. "She came in and sat on the bed right near the closet and phoned somebody and I was really scared she was going to see me because the door was open a little bit but I thought if I tried to close it, she'd see that, so I didn't do anything."

"Okay," I said.

"So she was talking to one person and then she started talking to another person and—"

"She hung up and called someone else?"

"No, it was like another call came in while she was talking to the first person. And when she was talking to the second person, that's when I guess she heard me breathing in the closet and she stopped talking and she opened the door and she got really mad and told me to come out."

"You shouldn't have gone into their room," I said. "Especially their closet. It's private in there."

"So you're mad, too."

"No, I'm just saying. What did she say to you?"

"She asked me if I'd been listening."

Before I knew it, we were all the way to Devon, so I hung a left on Naugatuck and started working our way back on Milford Point Road. "Mrs. Slocum probably wouldn't have said what she was saying on the phone if she knew someone was in the room with her."

"Yeah, that's for sure," Kelly muttered.

"What?" I asked. "What was she saying?"

She gave me a look. "You mean you want me to tell you? Even though I wasn't supposed to hear? Doesn't that mean you're sort of listening in, too?"

I shook my head. "Okay, it's none of my business what she said, just like it was none of yours. But I mean, generally, what was it about? Why was she so upset you heard her?"

"The first person or the second?"

"Both, I guess."

"Because she wasn't mad at the first person. She was mad at the second person."

"The second caller? She was mad at that person?"

A nod.

"Do you know who it was?"

A head shake.

"So what was she saying?"

"I can't talk about it," Kelly said. "Mrs. Slocum said I wasn't supposed to."

I weighed that. Kelly had eavesdropped on a conversation she wasn't supposed to hear. What Ann Slocum had to say on the phone wasn't my business, either. But at the same time, I needed to get to the bottom of this. I needed to know whether Ann's response was within reason, or if she'd crossed a line.

"Okay, let's not worry about what exactly she said on the phone, but what did she say to you after?"

"She asked me how long I'd been hiding there, and then she asked me if I heard what she was saying on the phone and I said no, not really, which wasn't exactly true, and then she said I shouldn't have done that and she said I wasn't supposed to tell anyone what she was talking about."

"Like me," I said.

"Not, like, *anybody*. She said I wasn't supposed to tell Emily and I wasn't supposed to tell Mr. Slocum, either."

That was interesting. It was one thing, Kelly overhearing something that was Slocum family business, that shouldn't be discussed outside their home. But now it seemed what my daughter had heard was a little more specific than that. "Did she say why?"

Kelly fingered her backpack. "Nope. She just said not to tell. She said if I ever told anyone, she wouldn't let me and Emily be friends anymore." Her voice wobbled. "I don't have very many friends and I don't want Emily not to be my friend."

"Of course you don't," I said, trying very hard to hide my anger at Ann Slocum's insensitivity. Kelly had just lost her mother, for crying out loud. "What happened then?"

"She left."

"The bedroom? She left the bedroom?" A nod. "Didn't you both leave?" A shake. "Wait a minute. She got mad because you were hiding in her bedroom, and then you stayed there? Why would you do such a thing?"

"She *made* me. She told me to stay right there, because she had to think about what to do with me. She said it was like a time-out. And she took the talking part of the phone with her."

I was feeling prickly all over. What the hell was the woman thinking?

"That's when I called you," Kelly said. "I'd put my phone back into my pocket just before she opened the door and she didn't know I had it."

"Why did you have your phone out?"

"When Emily opened the door to look for me I was going to shout 'Surprise!' and wanted to see her scream on video."

I gave my head a small shake. "Okay, so when she left the room and told you to stay there, that's when you called me." She nodded. "That was smart. When she left the room, did she lock the door?"

"I don't know. I don't even know if it has a lock on it. But Mrs. Slocum told me not to move and I didn't want to get in trouble so I stayed there. But she didn't tell me I couldn't phone you, so I did. But I thought she might get mad, so that's why I was whispering. When you got there, Mr. Slocum started yelling for me and that's when I came out."

"Honey, what she did, that was wrong. You shouldn't have been there, in her closet, but she shouldn't have done that. I'm gonna have a word with her tomorrow."

"Then she'll know I told you, and Emily won't be my friend anymore."

"I'll make sure she doesn't do that."

Kelly shook her head forcefully. "She might get mad."

"Honey, Emily's mom's not going to hurt you or anything."

"Maybe she'll hurt *you*."

"What? What's she going to do to me?"

"She might put a bullet in your brain," Kelly said. "That's what she said she was going to do to the person she was talking to."

NINE

Once Glen Garber had left with his daughter, Darren Slocum said to Ann, "What the hell was that all about?"

"I don't know. She felt sick, she went home. She's a kid. She probably ate too much junk. Or maybe she misses her mom, I don't know." When she turned to walk away from him, he grabbed hold of her elbow.

"Let go of me," Ann said.

"What was she doing in our bedroom? That's where I found her, you know. When I asked her what she was doing there, she said you told her to stay there. I don't want some kid nosing around our bedroom."

"The girls were playing hide-and-seek," Ann explained. "I told her it was okay for her to hide in there."

"The kids should not be playing in our room. That's off limits as far as—"

"Okay, fine! Jesus, do we have to make a federal case out of this? You don't think I've got enough to worry about?"

"*You?* You think you're the only one with things to worry about? You think they think you're in this on your own? Let me tell you something. If they take you down, they're taking me with them."

"I know, okay, you're right. All I'm saying is, there's enough shit going on around here that I don't have time to have some stupid fight about where the girls are playing in the house."

"Letting Emily even have a sleepover was a stupid idea," Darren said accusingly.

Ann gave him a look of exasperation. "What are we supposed to do? Just stop having *lives* while we try to sort this out? What do you want me to do? Ship Emily off to live with my sister or something until everything is back to normal?"

"And how the hell much did you spend on pizza?" he asked. Waving his arms in the air, he said, "You think we've got money to just throw around?"

"Right, Darren. That twenty bucks I spent on pizza, that'd make all the difference right now. We tell them, hey, look, here's twenty bucks, cut us some slack."

He turned away angrily, then just as quickly turned back.

"Were you on the phone a while ago?"

"What?"

"The light on the extension in the kitchen. It came on. Was that you?"

Ann rolled her eyes. "What's going on with you?"

"I'm asking, were you on the phone?"

"The kid called her dad, remember? He just left?"

That shut him up for a moment. The whole time he'd been talking, Ann had been thinking, *I have to get out of here*. But she needed a reason. Something believable.

The phone rang.

There was a cordless extension in the living room. Ann was closer. She snatched up the receiver. "Hello?"

A voice shrieked, "He came to see me!"

"Jesus, Belinda?"

"He said I was running out of time! I was in the basement, I was getting some prescriptions ready and—"

"Just calm down for a second and stop screaming in my ear. Who came to see you?"

Darren said, "What's going on?" Ann held up a palm.

"The guy," Belinda said. "The one you deal with. Honest to God, Ann, I thought, just for a second there . . . I didn't know what he was going to do. I have to talk to you. We have to come up with this money. If we can just come up with thirty-seven thousand for him, and whatever you put in, I swear on my mother's grave, I'll pay you back."

Ann closed her eyes, thought about the money they needed. Maybe her earlier caller, the one she was going out to meet, could do more to bail them out. Say something like, *This is it, this is the absolute last time, after this, I'll never ask you for anything again.*

Something to think about.

"Okay," Ann said. "We'll figure something out."

"I need to see you. We need to talk about this."

Perfect. "Okay," Ann said. "I'll head out now. I'll call you on my cell in a minute and we'll figure out where to meet."

"Okay," Belinda said, sniffing. "I never should have got into this. Never. If I'd had any idea that—"

"Belinda," Ann said sharply. "I'll see you soon." She hung up and said to Darren, "He's leaning on her."

"That's just great," he said.

"I'm going out."

"Why?"

"Belinda needs to talk about this."

Darren ran his fingers into his hair and pulled. He looked like he wanted to hit something. "You know we're totally fucked, right? You never should have brought Belinda into this. She's an idiot. That was *your* call. Not mine."

"I have to go." Ann brushed past him, grabbed her jacket, car keys, and a purse that was on a bench near the front door, and left.

Darren turned around and saw Emily standing, tentatively, at the far end of the living room.

"Why's everyone always fighting?" she asked.

"Go to bed," her father said, his voice like low, rumbling thunder. "Go to bed right this second."

Emily turned and ran.

Darren pulled back the curtain on the front door window, watched as his wife backed her Beemer out of the drive, took note of which direction she headed.

Ann was grateful to Belinda for calling when she did. It made her exit from the house a lot simpler. But it didn't mean Ann had to meet up with her right away. She had to get this other meeting out of the way first. Let Belinda sweat it out for a while. After all, she had only herself to blame.

It was dark down by the harbor, and the stars were out. It was cold, in the mid-fifties. Every few seconds there was a wind gust, sending dead leaves fluttering down from the trees.

Ann Slocum parked up close to the edge of the pier and, because of the cold, decided to wait in the car, with the motor running, until she saw headlights approaching. There were still boats moored down here, but the harbor was deserted. Not a bad place to meet if you didn't want to be seen.

Five minutes later, headlights flared in her rearview mirror. The car came straight up from behind, the lights so bright Ann had to adjust her mirror to keep them out of her eyes.

She opened her door and walked around to the back of her car, her shoes crunching on the gravel underfoot. The driver of the other car opened his door and jumped out hurriedly.

"Hey," Ann said. "What are you—"

"Who was it?" the man asked, charging toward her.

"Who was who?"

"When you were on the phone, *who was it?*"

"It's nothing, it's nobody, it's nothing for you to worry—Get your hands off me!"

He'd grabbed her by the shoulders and was shaking her. "I need to know who it was!"

She planted both her palms on his chest and shoved, forcing him back enough that he released her. She turned and started walking back to get into her car.

"Don't you walk away from me," he snarled, grabbing her left elbow and spinning her around. She stumbled, braced herself against the back of the car. He closed in on her, grabbing her wrists and pinning them to the trunk lid. He pressed himself up against her, put his mouth to her ear.

"I'm not taking any more of this shit," he said, softly. "All of this, it's over."

She brought up a knee and connected.

"Shit!" he screamed, and again relaxed his grip on her.

Ann twisted under his weight, skittered along the trunk lid, turned up the passenger side of the car. There was little more than a couple of feet between it and the edge of the pier.

"Goddamn it, Ann." The man reached for her again, grabbing her jacket. But he didn't have much of a hold on it, and she jerked herself away. She pulled so hard, however, that she stumbled toward the pier's edge.

Ann attempted to regain her balance, but she'd have needed another couple of feet to do it. She went over, her head striking the edge on the way.

A second later, there was a splash, and then nothing more.

The man peered over the side. The water was black as the night, and it took a moment for him to spot her. She lay facedown in the water, arms extended. Then, with a quiet grace, her arms pulled into her body and she rolled slowly onto her back. She stared up lifelessly for several seconds as an invisible force dragged her legs downward. A moment later, the rest of her followed, her face a pale jellyfish slipping beneath the surface.

TEN

Once I'd tucked Kelly into bed and done my best to assure her I was not angry, at least not with her, and that she had nothing to worry about regarding her encounter with Ann Slocum, I went down to the kitchen, poured myself a scotch. I took it with me to my basement office.

I sat there and thought about what to do.

The Slocums' number was probably already in the speed dial of the upstairs phones, the ones Sheila used, but it wasn't programmed into my office phone. I didn't feel like trudging back upstairs now that I had my drink and a place to sit, so I hauled the phone book over and looked up their number. I picked up the phone, prepared to start punching in digits. But my index finger failed to move.

I replaced the receiver.

I had tried, before putting her to bed, to get Kelly to recall as much as she could of what Ann had said on the phone, after first persuading her that I'd do everything I could to make sure Emily remained her friend.

Kelly had sat curled up against a nest of pillows, hugging Hoppy, and using the same technique she employed when spelling words, or reciting memorized verses of poetry. She closed her eyes.

"Okay," she had said, eyes squeezed shut. "Mrs. Slocum phoned this person to ask if their wrists were okay."

"Are you sure?"

"She said, 'I hope your wrists are all better and you should wear long sleeves in case there are marks.'"

"She was talking to someone who broke their wrists?"

"I guess so."

"What did she say to them?"

"I don't know. Something about seeing them next Wednesday."

"Like another appointment? Like someone's wrists were in a cast and the cast comes off next week?"

She nodded. "I think so. But that was when the other call happened. It might have been one of those calls you hate so much."

"What do you mean?"

"Like, when they call at dinner and ask you to give them money or buy the newspaper?"

"A telemarketer?"

"Yeah."

"Why do you think it was a telemarketer?"

"Well, the first thing Mrs. Slocum said was, 'Why are you calling?' And something about her cell phone being off."

This wasn't making any sense. Why would Ann Slocum care if Kelly overheard her on the phone with a telemarketer?

"What else did she say?"

"She said something about paying for something, and getting something back, or something like that. She was trying to get a good deal."

"I'm not getting this," I said. "She was trying to make a deal with a telemarketer?"

"And then she said don't be stupid because you'll get bullets in your brain."

I massaged my forehead, baffled, although I could imagine myself telling a telemarketer I'd like to shoot him in the head.

"Did she say anything about Mr. Slocum?" I asked. After all, Ann had made Kelly promise not to mention the call to her husband. Maybe that meant something. Although none of this made sense. Kelly shook her head no.

"Anything else?"

"Not really. Am I in trouble?"

I stooped and kissed her. "No. Absolutely not."

"Mrs. Slocum isn't going to come here and get mad at me again, is she?"

"Not a chance. I'll leave your door open, so if you have a bad dream or something, I'll hear you, or you can come and see me. But I'm going downstairs right now. Okay?"

She said okay, tucked Hoppy in, and turned off her light.

Slumped wearily at my desk, I tried to reason it out.

The first part of the conversation, which sounded like Ann checking up on someone who'd been injured, seemed innocuous enough. But the second call was more puzzling. If it was just a nuisance call, maybe Ann was pissed that she'd had to cut off the first caller to deal with it. I could understand that. Maybe that was why she made some kind of threat about shooting the person.

People threatened things all the time they didn't really mean. How often had I done it? In my line of work, pretty much every day. I wanted to kill our suppliers who didn't deliver on time. I wanted to kill the guys at the lumberyard who sent us warped boards. The other day I'd told Ken Wang he was a dead man after he'd driven a nail through a water line that was just behind the drywall.

Just because Ann Slocum said she wanted to put a bullet in someone's brain didn't mean she had any intention of doing it. But she might not have been happy to find out a small child was listening to her lose her cool. And she wouldn't want her daughter to know she'd spoken to someone that way on the phone.

But had she really said anything that she'd care if her husband found out about?

All that aside, my one concern was Kelly. She didn't deserve to have been frightened that way. I could accept that Ann would be upset finding Kelly hiding in her closet, but getting that angry with her, threatening her with the loss of Emily as a friend, then ordering her to stay in the room and taking the cordless phone with her so Kelly couldn't make a call—what the fuck was that?

I picked up the phone again, started to dial.

Hung up.

And what the hell was all that at the door when I came to get Kelly? Clearly, Ann didn't know my daughter had a phone on her. Suppose Kelly hadn't called me to come get her? What, exactly, would Ann have done next?

I thought about what I would say to Ann when I got her on the phone.

Don't you ever pull that kind of shit with my daughter again.

Something like that.

If I called.

Even though my opinion of Sheila's judgment had taken a nosedive in recent weeks, I couldn't help but wonder how she'd handle this situation. After all, she and Ann were friends. Sheila always seemed to know, far better than I, how to handle a prickly situation, how to defuse a social time bomb. She was best at it with me. Once, after a guy in an Escalade cut me off on the Merritt Parkway, I'd sped after him, hoping to catch up and pull alongside so I could flip him the bird.

"Look in your rearview mirror," Sheila said softly as I leaned on the accelerator.

"He's in front of me, not behind me," I said.

"Look in your rearview mirror," she said again.

I thought, *Shit, a cop's tailing me.* But when I looked in the mirror, what I saw was Kelly in her booster seat.

"If giving this guy the finger trumps your daughter's safety, then by all means," Sheila said.

My foot came off the gas.

Quite a wise approach from a woman who drove up the wrong ramp and killed herself and two others. The memories of that night did not square with those I had of Sheila as a calm, reasonable person. I thought I knew what her prevailing view of my current predicament would be.

Suppose I did get Ann Slocum on the phone and gave her a piece of my mind? I might get some satisfaction out of it. But what would the fallout be for Kelly? Would Emily's mom turn her daughter against Kelly? Would it send Emily into the enemy camp at school, with the kids who called Kelly "Boozer the Loser"?

I emptied my glass and debated whether to go back upstairs for a refill. As I sat there, feeling the warmth spread through my body, the phone rang.

I grabbed the receiver. "Hello?"

"Glen? It's Belinda."

"Oh, hey, Belinda." I glanced at the clock. Nearly ten.

"I know it's late," she said.

"That's okay."

"I was thinking I should give you a call. I don't think I've even seen you since the funeral. I was feeling bad I hadn't been in touch, but I wanted to give you your space, you know?"

"Sure."

"How's Kelly doing? Is she back at school?"

"She could be better. But she'll get through this. We'll get through this."

"I know, I know, she's such a terrific girl. I just . . . I just keep thinking about Sheila. I mean, I know she was only my friend, that your loss is so much greater, but it hurts, it just hurts so much."

She sounded as though she might start to cry. I didn't need this right now.

"I wish I could have seen her one last time," she continued. What did she mean by that? That she wished she could have spent time with Sheila one more time before she died? "I guess, what with the car catching on fire . . ."

Oh. Belinda was referring to the closed casket. "They got the fire out before it took over the inside of the car. She wasn't . . . touched." I pushed away memories of the shattered glass sparkling in her hair, the blood . . .

"Right," Belinda said. "I think I'd heard that, although I'd wondered, whether Sheila . . . you just don't like to let your mind go there, thinking about how badly . . . I really don't know how to say this."

Why did she have to know whether Sheila was burned beyond recognition? Why on earth would she think I'd want to talk about this? This was how you comfort a man who's just lost his wife? Ask whether there was anything left of her?

"I felt a closed casket was best. For Kelly."

"Of course, of course, I can understand that."

"It's kind of late, Belinda, and—"

"This is very difficult, Glen, but Sheila's purse . . . was it recovered?"

"Her purse? Yes, it was. I got it from the police." They'd searched the bag, looking for evidence, receipts. Wondering where she'd bought the bottle of vodka they'd found, empty, in the car. They didn't find anything.

"The thing is—this is *so* awkward, Glen—but the thing is, I'd given Sheila an envelope, and I was wondering—this is horrible, I shouldn't even be asking you this . . ."

"Belinda."

"I wondered if maybe it had been in her purse, that's all."

"I went through her belongings, Belinda. I didn't notice any envelope."

"A brown business envelope. Oversized, you know."

"I didn't see anything like that. What was in it?"

She hesitated. "I'm sorry?"

"I said, what was in it?"

"Um, there was a bit of cash in it. Sheila was going to pick up something for me next time she was in the city."

"In the city? New York?"

"That's right."

"Sheila didn't go into New York all that often."

"I think she'd been planning a girls' day out, a shopping trip, and there was something I was going to have her get for me."

"I can't see you missing out on a trip like that."

Belinda laughed nervously. "Well, that week was pretty hectic for me and I didn't think I was going to be able to make it."

"How much was in the envelope?"

Another pause. "Not that much, just a little."

"I didn't see anything like that," I said. "It might have burned up in the car, but if it was in her purse, it would have survived. Did Sheila tell you she was going into the city that day?"

"That was . . . that was the sense I had, Glen."

"She told me she had some errands to run, but she didn't mention anything about going into Manhattan."

"Listen, Glen, I never should have even brought this up. I should let you go. I'm so sorry for calling."

She didn't even wait for me to say goodbye. She just hung up.

I still had the receiver in my hand, debating with myself again whether to call Ann Slocum and give her hell for the way she'd treated Kelly, when I heard the doorbell ring upstairs.

It was Joan Mueller. Her hair, freed from its ponytail, was falling on her shoulders, and she had on a snug, scooped T that revealed a hint of a purple lace bra.

"I saw you pull in a little while ago and saw the lights were on," she said once I had the door open.

"I had to pick up Kelly at a friend's," I told her.

"She's gone to bed?"

"Yeah," I said. "Did you want to step in?" I regretted it as soon as I suggested it.

"Well, okay," she said brightly, brushing me as she went past. She stood at the entrance to the living room, wondering, maybe, whether I was going to invite her to sit down. "Thanks. I love Friday nights. No kids getting dropped off in the morning. That's the good part. Not knowing what to do with myself, that's the tough part."

"What can I do for you, Joan? I haven't forgotten your kitchen tap."

She smiled. "I just wanted to thank you for earlier." She stuck her hands into the front pockets of her jeans, her thumbs tucked into the belt loops.

"I'm not sure I understand."

"I kind of used you," she said, and grinned. "Like a bodyguard." She had to be talking about when Carl Bain showed up. "I needed a big strong man beside me, if you know what I mean."

"I don't think I do."

"The two parts of my day I hate the most are when Carl drops off his kid and when he picks him up at the end of the day. He creeps me out, that guy. I get this bad vibe off him, you know? Like he's just waiting to blow up?"

"Has he said something to you? Threatened you?"

She slipped her hands out of her pockets and waved them about as she answered. "Okay, the thing is, I think he's worried about what his kid might be saying when he comes over. Carlson, he's just a little guy, and they say whatever comes into their head, you know?"

"Sure."

"And the odd time, he'll say something about his mother. Alicia? That's the mother's name. Although he calls her his mommy, he doesn't call her Alicia." She rolled her eyes. "Of *course*. Like I need to tell you that. Anyway, sometimes, you know, you ask a kid, Hey, what's your mother doing today? And this one time, he says his mother had to go to the hospital because she broke her arm. And I'm like, Oh no, how did she do that, and Carlson says because his dad pushed her down the stairs."

"Jeez."

"Yeah, no shit? But the next day, he says to me, he was wrong. She didn't get pushed down the stairs. His dad told him that his mommy tripped. So I figure, he must have gone home, right? And said to his dad, Oh, I was telling the babysitter about Mommy going to the hospital after she got shoved down the stairs, and he must have freaked, tells his kid that he's got it all wrong, she tripped." She stuck out her lower lip and blew out hard enough that a few strands of hair momentarily floated.

"So every day he comes by, you think he's wondering what you're thinking," I said.

"Kinda, yeah."

"When did the boy say this?"

"First time he mentioned it was around three, four weeks ago. He—the dad, Carl, I mean—seemed okay, but lately, he's been kind of on edge, asking me, did I make any phone calls or anything?"

"Phone calls about what?"

"He didn't say. But I wonder if someone might have called the police about him or something."

"Did you?"

She shook her head very slowly. "No way. I mean, I thought about it, Glen. But the thing is, I can't afford to lose a customer, you know what I'm saying? I need every one of those kids, at least till the money from the oil company comes through. I just don't want Carl taking it out on me, if someone did put in a call to the police. And I thought, if he knew I had a strong man living next door to me, maybe he'd think twice before he did anything like that."

I thought she put a little emphasis on "strong man."

"Well, I'm glad I could help," I said.

She tilted her head to one side and looked me in the eye. "It's going to come in, you know. I mean, eventually. And it's going to be a good settlement. I'll be pretty well fixed."

"That's good," I said. "It's about time."

She let that hang out there a moment. "Anyway, what I wondered was, you don't think Sheila might have reported him, do you?"

"Sheila?"

"I was talking to her, I guess a few days before the accident and all, wondering what I should do about what Carlson said had happened to his mother, thinking it was kind of a bad thing, knowing some woman got her arm broke and not doing anything about it. I was saying, you think I should make an anonymous call kind of thing, and if they arrested him, did she think I'd still get to babysit Carlson?"

"You talked about this with Sheila?"

Joan nodded. "Just the once. Did she mention anything to you about this? That she was thinking of calling the police or anything?"

"No," I said. "She never did."

Joan nodded again. "She mentioned you were under a lot of stress, with that house you were building that burned down. Maybe she didn't want to burden you with it."

She sighed and slapped her hands on her thighs. "Anyway, look, I should go. What a joy, right? Your neighbor bringing her problems over late at night." She slipped into a mocking voice. "Hey, neighbor, got a cup of sugar and by the way could you be my bodyguard?" She laughed, then stopped abruptly. "So, I'll see you," she said.

I watched her walk back to her house.

I decided not to call Ann Slocum that night. I would sleep on it. In the morning, I'd decide what to do.

When I went upstairs, Kelly was out cold in my room, curled up on her mother's side of the bed.

Saturday morning, I let Kelly sleep in. I'd carried her back into her room the night before, and peeked in on her as I headed down to the kitchen to make coffee. She had her arm wrapped around Hoppy, her face buried into his (her?) furry ears.

I brought in the paper, scanned the headlines while I sat at the dining room table, sipping coffee and ignoring the shredded wheat I'd poured.

I wasn't able to focus. I'd settle on a story and be four paragraphs in before I realized I wasn't retaining anything, although one article interested me enough to read it to the end. When the country was going through a shortage of drywall—particularly in the post-Katrina building boom—hundreds of millions of square feet of the stuff that was brought in from China had turned out to be toxic. Drywall's made from gypsum, which contains sulfur, which is filtered out in the manufacturing process. But this Chinese drywall was loaded with sulfur, and not only did it reek, it corroded copper pipes and did all sorts of other damage.

"Jesus," I muttered. Something to be on the lookout for from now on.

I tossed the paper aside, cleaned up my dishes, went down to the study, came back upstairs, looked for something in the truck I didn't need, came back indoors.

Stewing.

Around ten, I checked on Kelly again. Still asleep. Hoppy had fallen to the floor. Back in my office, sitting in my chair, I picked up the phone.

"Fuck it," I said, under my breath.

No one locks my daughter in a bedroom and gets away with it. I dialed. It rang three times before someone picked up and said hello. A woman.

"Hello," I said. "Ann?"

"No, this isn't Ann."

She could have fooled me. Sounded just like her.

"Could I speak to her please?"

"She's not . . . who's calling?"

"It's Glen Garber, Kelly's dad."

"This isn't a good time," the woman said.

"Who's this?" I asked.

"It's Janice. Ann's sister. I'm sorry, you'll have to call back later."

"Do you know when she'll be in?"

"I'm sorry—we're making arrangements. There's a lot to do."

"Arrangements? What do you mean, arrangements?"

"For the funeral," she said. "Ann . . . passed away last night."

She hung up before I could ask her anything else.

ELEVEN

Sheila's mother, Fiona Kingston, was never a fan of mine. Sheila's death only served to reinforce that opinion.

Right from the outset, she'd believed her daughter could have done better. Way better. Fiona never came right out and said it, at least not to me. But I was always aware she thought her daughter should have ended up with someone like her own husband—her first husband—the late Ronald Albert Gallant. Noted and successful lawyer. Respected member of the community. Sheila's father.

Ron died when Sheila was only eleven, but his influence persisted. He was the gold standard by which all prospective suitors for Fiona's daughter were measured. Even before she'd reached her twenties, when the boys she went out with were unlikely to become lifelong companions, Sheila was subjected to intense interrogations about them from Fiona. What did their parents do? What clubs did these boys belong to? How well were they doing in school? What were their SAT scores? What were their ambitions?

Sheila had only had her father for eleven years, but she knew what she remembered about him most. She remembered that there wasn't much to remember. He was rarely home. He devoted his life to his work, not his family. When he was home, he was remote and distant.

Sheila wasn't sure that was the kind of man she wanted. She loved her father, and was devastated to lose him at such a young age. But there wasn't the void in her life she might have expected.

Once Fiona's husband was dead—a heart attack at forty—whatever tenderness she might have had as a mother, and there was never that much to begin with, was displaced by the burden of running a household solo. Ronald Albert Gallant had left his wife and daughter well fixed, but Fiona had never managed the household finances and it took her a while, with the help of various lawyers and accountants and banking officials, to figure everything out. But once she had it all down, she became consumed with overseeing her business affairs, investing wisely, studying her quarterly financial statements.

She still had time, however, to run her daughter's life.

Fiona didn't take it well when her little girl, whom she'd sent to Yale to become a lawyer or a titan of industry, who with any luck should fall in love with some high-powered attorney-in-training, met the man of her dreams not in law class arguing the finer points of torts, but in the ivy-draped building's hallways working for his father's company, installing new windows. Maybe, had Sheila not met me, she would have completed her schooling, but I'm not so sure. Sheila liked to be out in the world, doing things, not sitting in a classroom listening to someone pontificate on matters she didn't give a rat's ass about.

The irony was, of the two of us, I was the one with the degree. My parents had sent me north to Bates, in Lewiston, Maine, where I'd majored in English for reasons that now elude me. It wasn't exactly the sort of degree that had prospective employers begging you to submit a résumé. When I graduated, I couldn't think of a thing I wanted to do with my piece of paper. I didn't want to teach. And while I liked to write, I didn't have the Great American Novel in me. I wasn't even sure I wanted to read another one, at least for a while. I'd had Faulkner and Hemingway and Melville up to here.

That fucking whale. I never did finish that book.

But despite that piece of paper, I belonged to that class of people who were invisible to Fiona. I was an ant, a worker bee, one of the faceless millions who kept the world running smoothly and whom, thankfully, you didn't have to spend a lot of face time with. Fiona probably appreciated, on some level, that there were people to build and renovate houses, just as she was pleased there were others who picked up the trash every week. She lumped me in with the folks who cleared out her gutters and cut her lawn—when she still had her big house—and tuned her Caddy and fixed her toilet when it wouldn't stop running, even if you jiggled the handle. It didn't seem to matter to her that I had my own company—granted, it had been handed down to me by my father—or that I employed several people, had a reputation as a reliable contractor, did okay for myself, that I was not only able to put a roof over my, my wife's, and my daughter's heads, but that I was able to build the damn roof myself. The only person who worked with his hands who might impress Fiona would be the latest darling of the gallery crowd, some twenty-first-century answer to Jackson Pollock whose paint-stained trousers were evidence of talent and eccentricity, not just of trying to make a living.

I'd had clients like Fiona over the years. They were the ones who wouldn't shake your hand, afraid their soft palms might get scratched by your calluses.

Since I'd first met Fiona, I'd had a hard time getting my head around the fact that Sheila was really her daughter. While there was a physical resemblance, in every other way the two women were different. Fiona cared deeply about maintaining the status quo. That translated into protecting tax breaks for the wealthy, praying that same-sex marriage never became legalized, and double life sentences for petty thefts.

Fiona's horror at Sheila marrying me was matched only by her disdain for her daughter's occasional volunteer work at a legal aid clinic and the time she spent volunteering on Democratic senator Chris Dodd's campaigns.

"Do you do it because you really care? Or because you know it drives your mother nuts?" I asked her once.

"Because I care," Sheila answered. "Driving Mother nuts is just a bonus."

The first year we were married, Sheila told me, "Mother's a bully. I've learned over the years the only thing you can do is to stand up to her. You'll never know the things she said to me when I told her I was marrying you. But you have to know the most hurtful things she said were not about you, Glen. They were about me. For the choices I've made. Well, I'm proud of those choices. And of the ones you've made, too."

I had chosen to build things. Decks, garages, additions, entire houses. After graduation, I sought employment at my father's contracting company, where I'd worked every summer since I was sixteen.

"I'm gonna need references," he'd said when I walked into his office right after college, when I was twenty-two.

I loved what I did. I pitied friends who spent their days sitting in cubicle prisons, who went home after eight hours unable to point to a single thing they'd accomplished. But I made buildings. Things you could point to as you drove down the street. And I was building them with my father, I was learning from him every day. A couple of years after I started working with him, I met Sheila on that window job, and before long we'd moved in together, something that didn't sit well with my parents any more than it did with Fiona. But two years later we stopped living in sin, as my own mother liked to call it, in part because Mom was dying of cancer, and knowing we were legally married would give her some peace of mind.

Four years later, there was a child on the way.

Dad lived long enough to hold Kelly in his arms. After his passing, I became the boss. I felt orphaned and overwhelmed. The shoes were too big to fill, but I did my best. It was never the same without him, but I still loved what I did. I had a reason to get up in the morning. I had a purpose. I felt no need to justify the life I'd chosen to Sheila's mother.

Sheila and I were both surprised when Fiona started seeing someone.

His name was Marcus Kingston, and while his first wife was still somewhere out in California, his second had died eight years earlier when some yahoo in a souped-up Civic ran a red light and broadsided her Lincoln. Marcus had been an importer of clothing and other goods, but had recently wound up his business when Fiona met him at a gallery opening in Darien. He'd spent a career mixing with the well-off and well connected, just the kind of people Fiona liked to be associated with.

When they decided, four years ago, to get married, Marcus sold his Norwalk house and Fiona put her place in Darien on the market. They went in together on a luxury town house that overlooked Long Island Sound.

Sheila's theory was that Fiona woke up one morning and thought, *Do I want to live the rest of my life alone?* I had to admit that it had never occurred to me that Fiona might have any emotional needs. The woman put up such a chilly and independent front that one could be forgiven for thinking that she didn't need people. But beneath that icy exterior was someone who was very lonely.

Marcus came along at the right time for her.

Sheila and I had wondered, on more than one occasion, whether Marcus's motivations were slightly more complicated. He, too, had been on his own, and it made sense that he might want to wake up in the morning with someone next to him. But we also knew that Marcus had not sold his business for what he'd hoped to get, and that a sizable portion of his income still went to his first wife in Sacramento. Fiona, who'd been so careful—I might be inclined to say "tight"—with her money for so many years, appeared to have no problem spending it on Marcus. She'd even bought him a sailboat, which he moored in the Darien harbor.

Marcus still did some consulting here and there for importers who valued his expertise and connections. He dined out a night or two a week with these people, and liked to brag about how the business world just wouldn't let him rest. Sheila and I had, privately, observed that he could be a bit of a blowhard, an asshole, frankly. But Fiona appeared to love him, and seemed happier with him in her life than she had been before he showed up.

They visited a lot so Fiona could see her grandchild. I could find plenty of reasons to dislike Fiona, but there was no question that she did adore Kelly. She took her shopping, to the movies, to Manhattan to visit museums and attend Broadway shows. Fiona even endured the occasional trip to the Toys "R" Us in Times Square.

"Where was this woman when I was a kid?" Sheila had asked me more than once.

Fiona and I maintained a kind of truce through these years. She didn't like me, and I didn't care much for her, but we remained civil. There was no out-in-the-open warfare.

That pretty much ended with Sheila's accident.

After that, there was no holding back. Fiona blamed me. If I knew Sheila had a drinking problem, why hadn't I done something about it? Why hadn't I spoken to Fiona about it? Why hadn't I forced Sheila into a program? What was I thinking, letting her drive around half the state of Connecticut, when she might very well have been under the influence?

And how often had she been drunk like that with Kelly—their granddaughter, for Christ's sake—in the car?

"How could you not have known?" Fiona asked me at the funeral. "How the hell could you not have seen the signs?"

"There were no signs," I told her, dazed and unhappy. "Not really."

"Yeah, that's what I'd say if I were you, too," she shot back at me. "That's what you have to believe, isn't it? Gets you off the hook. But believe me, Glen, there had to have been signs. You just had your head too far up your ass to notice."

"Fiona," Marcus said, trying to pull her away.

But she wouldn't stop. "You think she just decided one night, Hey, I think I'll become an alcoholic and get plastered and fall asleep at the wheel in the middle of an off-ramp? You think someone just does that all of a sudden?"

"I suppose *you* saw something," I said, stung by her fury. "*You* never miss a trick."

She blinked. "How was *I* supposed to see anything? I didn't *live* with her. I wasn't there with her seven days a week, fifty-two weeks a year. But you were. You're the one who was in a position to see something, and in a position to do something about it when you did. You let us down. You let Kelly down. But most of all, you let Sheila down."

People were staring at us. If it had been Marcus saying these things, I would have decked him. But that wasn't an option with Fiona. But maybe the reason I so badly wanted to do it was because I knew she was right.

If Sheila'd had a drinking problem, surely I'd have seen *something*. How could I not have known? Had there been signs? Had there been warnings I'd chosen to ignore? Was it because I didn't want to face the fact that Sheila was going through some kind of difficulties? Sure, Sheila liked a drink, like everyone else did. On special occasions. Lunch with her friends. Family get-togethers. We'd been known to kill off a couple of bottles of wine at home when Kelly was staying over with Fiona and Marcus in Darien. I even caught her one time when her foot slipped on the carpet as we headed upstairs on one such occasion.

But those couldn't have been signs of something more serious. Or was I just kidding myself? Did I not want to see the truth?

Fiona was right: A woman didn't just decide one night to get blind drunk and set off in her Subaru.

Three nights after Sheila's death, I quietly tore the house apart after Kelly had gone to bed. If Sheila had been a closet drinker, she'd have been hiding liquor somewhere. If not in the house, then the garage, or the shed out back where we kept the lawnmower and rusted, old garden chairs.

I searched everywhere and came up with nothing.

So then I talked to her friends. Everyone who knew her. To Belinda, for starters.

"Okay, once, at lunch," Belinda recalled, "Sheila had one and a half Cosmos and she got a little tipsy. And another time—George just about had a fit when he found us, he's such a tight-ass—we smoked up. I had a couple of joints and we kind of mellowed out one evening when we were having a girls-only night. It was just a bit of fun. But she never really lost it, and any time she'd anything more than one drink she insisted on calling herself a cab. She had good sense. She was a smart girl. It doesn't make any sense to me, either, what happened, but I guess we never know what someone else is going through, do we?"

Sally Diehl, from the office, had a hard time making sense of it, too. "But I had this cousin once—well, I still do—and she had a coke habit like you wouldn't believe, Glen, but what was really unbelievable was how well she'd kept it hidden for so long, until one day, the cops came into her house and busted her. No one had any idea. Sometimes—and I'm not saying this was the case with Sheila—but sometimes, like, you just don't know anything about people that you see every day."

So it seemed there were two possibilities. Either Sheila had a drinking problem and was extremely good at hiding it, or Sheila had a drinking problem and I wasn't good at picking up the signals.

I supposed there was a third possibility. Sheila did not have a drinking problem, and did not get behind the wheel drunk. For that possibility to be true, all the toxicology reports had to be wrong.

There wasn't a shred of evidence to suggest they were.

In the days after Sheila's death, as I struggled to make sense of something that made no sense at all, I tracked down students from the course she'd been taking. Turned out she never even went to class that evening, although she had shown up for all the other sessions. Her teacher, Allan Butterfield, said Sheila was the top student in the all-adult class.

"She had a real reason to be there," he told me over a beer at a roadhouse down the street from the school. "She said to me, 'I'm doing this for my family, for my husband and my daughter, to make our business stronger.'"

"When did she say that to you?" I'd asked.

He thought a moment. "A month ago?" He tapped the table with his index finger. "Right here. Over a couple of beers."

"Sheila had a couple of beers here with you?" I asked.

"Well, I had a couple, maybe even three." Allan's face was flushed. "But Sheila, actually, I think she was having one. Just a glass."

"You did this often with Sheila? Have a beer after class?"

"No, just the once," he said. "She always wanted to get home in time to give her daughter a kiss good night."

The way the police figured it, Sheila had skipped her class that night to drink away her evening somewhere. They never found out where she'd gone to do it. A check of area bars didn't turn up any sightings of her, and no area liquor stores remembered selling her any booze that night. All of which meant, of course, nothing.

She could have sat in the car for hours drinking stuff she'd bought at another time, in another town.

I asked the police several times if there was any chance there'd been a mistake, and each time they told me toxicology reports didn't lie. They provided copies. Sheila had a blood-alcohol level of 0.22. For a woman of Sheila's size—about 140 pounds—that worked out to about eight drinks.

"I don't just blame you for not picking up the signals," Fiona fumed, at the funeral when Kelly was out of earshot. "I blame you for making her turn to drink. You swept her off her feet, no doubt about it, with your common touch, but over the years she was never able to stop thinking about the life she could have had. A better life, a richer life, the kind you'd never be able to give her. And it wore her down."

"She told you this?" I said.

"She didn't have to," she snapped. "I just knew."

"Fiona, honestly," Marcus said, in a rare moment that made me quite like the guy. "Dial it down."

"He needs to hear this, Marcus. And I may not have it in me to tell him later."

"I doubt that," I said.

"If you'd given her the kind of life she deserved, she'd never have had to drown her sorrows," she said.

"I'm taking Kelly home," I said. "Goodbye, Fiona."

But like I said, she loved her granddaughter.

And Kelly loved her in return. And Marcus, too, to a degree. They doted on her. For Kelly's sake, I tried to put aside my animosity toward Fiona. I was still reeling from the news that—evidently—Ann Slocum was dead, when I heard a car pull in to the driveway. I eased back the curtain and saw Marcus behind the wheel of his Cadillac. Fiona sat next to him.

"Shit," I said. Before Sheila died, Kelly would stay at their town house one weekend out of six. If I'd been informed that this was one of those weekends, I'd certainly forgotten. I was confused. Neither Kelly nor I had seen Fiona or Marcus since the funeral. I had spoken to Fiona a few times on the phone, but only until Kelly had picked up the extension. Each time, Fiona made it clear she could barely be civil to me. Her contempt for me was like a buzz over the phone line.

I bounded up the stairs and poked my head into Kelly's room. She was still asleep.

"Hey, kiddo," I said.

She rolled over in bed and opened one eye, then the other. "What is it?"

"Grandmother alert. Fiona and Marcus are here."

She sat bolt upright in bed. "They *are?*"

"Did you know they were coming today?"

"Uhhh . . ."

"Because I sure didn't know. You better get moving, kiddo."

"I kind of forgot all about it."

"Did you know?"

"I might, sort of."

I gave her a look.

"I might have been talking to Grandma on Skype," she confessed. "And I might have said it would be okay to come out and see me, but I didn't say an actual day. I don't think."

"Like I said, you better get moving."

Kelly slithered out from under the covers just as the doorbell rang. I left her to get herself dressed and went down to answer the door.

Fiona was up front, ramrod stiff and stone-faced. Marcus hovered just behind her, looking uncomfortable.

"Glen," she said. Her voice could cut ice.

"Hey, Glen," Marcus attempted. "How's it going?"

"This is a surprise," I said.

"We came to see Kelly," Fiona said. "To see how she's doing." Her tone implied she doubted my daughter was doing well.

"Was this one of those weekends?"

"Do I need it to be one of 'those weekends' to see my granddaughter?"

"We might not have been home. And I'd hate for you to come for nothing." This sounded reasonable to me, but Fiona flushed.

Marcus cleared his throat. "We thought we'd chance it."

I stepped back to give them room to come inside. "You've been talking to Kelly over the Internet?" I asked Fiona.

"We've had some chats," Fiona said. "I'm very worried about her. I can just imagine what she's going through. When Sheila lost her father, she was older than Kelly, but she still took it so very hard."

"The thruway was a son of a bitch," Marcus said, still trying to cut through the tension. "Seems like they're ripping up the roads all over the place."

"Yeah," I said. "They do that."

"Look," he said, "I told Fiona, you know, maybe this isn't such a great idea, just showing up without calling or—"

"Marcus, do not apologize for me. There's something I want to discuss with you, Glen," Fiona said, in a tone MacArthur might have used when he got the Japanese to surrender.

"What's that?"

"Kelly was telling me, during our Skype chat, that things aren't going very well for her at school."

"Kelly's doing fine. Her grades are even a little better than last year."

"I'm not talking about her grades. I'm talking about her social situation."

"What about it?"

"I understand the other children are being horrible to her."

"It hasn't been an easy time for her."

"Yes, well, I wouldn't think so, considering that the boy who died in that accident was a student at Kelly's school. She's being tormented. That's not a good environment for the child."

"She told you about the kids calling her Boozer."

"She did. So you *do* know."

"Of course I know."

"I guess I thought, if you knew, you would have done something about it."

I felt that familiar prickling at the back of my neck. I didn't want to get into this with her, but couldn't let her get away with it. "I'm doing something about it, Fiona. Rest easy."

"Are you moving her to another school?"

"Fiona, she only told me about this last night. I don't know what it was like where you went to school, but in Milford the schools aren't open on weekends. But I'll be getting in touch with the principal first thing Monday morning."

Fiona glared at me a moment, then looked away. When she met my eyes again, she seemed to have made an effort to soften her look. "I had an idea that might preclude you from having to do that, Glen."

"What might that be?"

"Marcus and I talked about the possibility of Kelly going to school in Darien."

He gave me another uncomfortable look. It seemed clear this idea had not originated with him.

"I don't think so," I said.

She nodded, as though she anticipated my reaction. "I can understand your reluctance. But let's look at the situation objectively. All the stress Kelly is being subjected to now can't be good for her academic performance. If she were in another school, where the other students don't know her situation, or that other boy, it would be a fresh start for her."

"It'll pass," I said.

"And," she continued, ignoring me, "there are several schools within a few miles of our place that come very highly recommended. Their test scores are far superior to the results being achieved in the public schools. Even if Kelly had not suffered such a tragedy, were not being subjected to this harassment at her school, it would be an alternative worth considering. These are good, solid institutions with impeccable credentials. Many of Fairfield County's more prominent families have enrolled their children in these schools."

"I'm sure they can afford them," I said.

Fiona shook her head. "Money's not a problem, Glen. I'll look after any tuition-related expenses."

I thought I glimpsed something in Marcus's face at that moment. I told Fiona, "I think it would be a bit much for Kelly to commute from here to Darien every day for school."

She smiled slyly at me. "Kelly would be with us through the week, of course, and back here with you on weekends. We've already been talking to a designer, someone Marcus knows, about making over the room Kelly stays in when she sleeps over now. She'd have a place for her computer, a desk where she could do her homework, and—"

"You're not taking her away from me," I said bluntly.

"Not at all," Fiona said, feigning offense. "I can't believe you'd think such a thing. I'm trying to help you, Glen. You and Kelly. Believe me, I know how hard it is to raise a child on your own. I've been there. I understand what it must be like for you, trying to juggle work and being a father. You're probably only just getting back into the swing of things, but you wait and see. You're on a job site, outside of town, you're waiting for a delivery or an inspection or a client—I don't know, I don't pretend to understand what you do—and suddenly realize you have to be at the school to pick Kelly up."

"I'll have to roll with it," I said.

Fiona reached out and touched one of my folded arms, quite a gesture for her. "Glen—I know you and I, we haven't always seen eye to eye. But what I'm proposing here, it's in Kelly's best interest. Surely even you can see that. I'm trying to give her every possible opportunity."

The thing was, it wasn't an entirely terrible idea, if I could swallow my pride about who'd be paying for it—there was no way I could afford to send Kelly to a private school here or anywhere else. And if I believed Fiona's motives were genuine, I might have been willing to entertain the proposal. But I couldn't help but feel this was an attempt on her part to drive a wedge between my own daughter and me. With Sheila gone, Fiona wanted control over her granddaughter.

"I told you," Marcus said to his wife. "I told you this would come across as too pushy."

"This really doesn't involve you, Marcus," she said. "Kelly is my granddaughter, not yours. There's no blood connection."

He looked my way, as if to say, *I know what you're going through, pal.*

"I am involved," Marcus insisted. "Kelly would be coming to live with *us*." He glanced at me again and clarified. "Through the week. And I'm okay with that, but don't say it doesn't involve me, goddamn it. Don't say that for one second."

"Kelly's staying with me," I said.

"Well," Fiona said, not accepting defeat, "clearly you need some time to think about it. And of course, we'll want to see what Kelly has to say. She might like the idea very much."

"It's my call," I reminded her.

"Of course it is." She patted my arm again. "Where is the little princess, anyway? I was thinking we could at least take her on a little excursion for the afternoon—maybe to the Stamford mall. Get her a new winter coat or something."

"I think Kelly should stay at home today," I said. "The thing is, something's happened, something I haven't even had a chance to tell Kelly about yet, and I don't know how she's going to react, but I think she's going to be very upset."

"What?" Marcus was frowning. Probably anticipating his wife lighting into me again, whatever the problem.

"You know Sheila's friend Ann? She has a daughter named Emily who's friends with Kelly?"

Fiona nodded. To Marcus, she said, "You remember her. She had the purse party here."

Marcus looked blank.

"I can't believe you don't remember. She was a real dish," Fiona said with more than a hint of disapproval. To me, "What about her?"

"We saw her only last night. Kelly had gone over for a sleepover. But Kelly called me to pick her up early, she wasn't having a good time, and sometime after that—"

"Daddy!"

The three of us turned our heads toward the stairs as Kelly screamed.

"Daddy, come here! *Quick!"*

I took the stairs two at a time and was in her bedroom a good ten seconds before either Fiona or Marcus could get there. Kelly was at her desk, still in her yellow pajamas, perched on the edge of her chair, one hand on the mouse, the other pointing at the screen. She was on one of the sites where she chats with her friends.

"Emily's mom," she said. "It's about Emily's mom—"

"I was going to tell you," I said, getting my arm around her and giving Marcus and Fiona a look that said *Get out of here*. They retreated. "I just found out myself, honey—"

"What happened?" There were tears in Kelly's eyes. "Did she just *die*?"

"I don't know. I mean, yeah, I guess she did. When I called their house this morning—"

Kelly squirmed in my arms. "I told you not to call!"

"It's okay, honey. It doesn't matter. I thought it was Emily's mom who answered, but it was her aunt, her mother's sister. She told me that Mrs. Slocum had died."

"But I *saw* her. Last night. She wasn't dead then!"

"I know, sweetheart. It's a shock."

Kelly thought a moment. "What should I do? Should I call Emily?"

"Maybe later, okay? Emily and her dad, they need some time alone."

"I feel all weird."

"Yeah."

We sat there for what seemed a very long time. I held on to her, cradling her in my arms as she cried.

"My mom, and now Emily's mom," she said softly. "Maybe I'm, like, a bad luck charm or something."

"Don't say that, sweetheart. Never say that. It isn't true."

When she stopped sobbing, I knew I needed to broach the subject of our visitors. "Your grandmother and Marcus want to take you out for the afternoon."

Kelly sniffed. "Oh."

"And I think your grandmother wants you to go to school in Darien. Any idea why she might want that?"

She nodded. She didn't look very surprised. "I guess I might have told her I hate my school."

"Online," I said.

"Yeah."

"Well, now your grandmother wants you to live with her through the week and go to school in Darien, come back here to me on weekends."

She slipped her arms tight around me. "I don't think I want to do that." A pause. "But at least, if I did, the kids there wouldn't know anything about me, they wouldn't know what Mom had done."

We held each other for another minute.

"If Emily's mom had a disease or something, like Evian flu, will I catch it? Because I was in her bedroom?"

"I don't think someone could come down with the flu and die from it in just a few hours," I said. "A heart attack, maybe. Something like that. But not something you could catch. And it's *avian* flu, by the way."

"You can't catch a heart attack?"

"No." I looked her in the eye.

"She doesn't look even a little bit sick in the video."

That stopped me. "What?"

"On my phone. She looks fine."

"What are you talking about?"

"When I was in the closet, I had my phone ready to take video of Emily when she opened the door. I *told* you that, Daddy."

"You didn't tell me you shot video of her mother. I thought when Mrs. Slocum came in you put your phone away."

"Like, pretty soon after."

"You still have it?" I asked.

Kelly nodded.

"Show me."

TWELVE

"Darren, I need to ask you some questions."

He was sitting in the front passenger seat of a car parked in his driveway. Behind the wheel was Rona Wedmore. She was a short, stocky black woman in her mid-forties. She had on a tan leather jacket and jeans, and there was a gun holstered to her belt. Her short hair was sensibly styled, although lately she had been streaking just a few strands, so there was this pencil-thin line of silver-gray that swept across the top of her head. The sort of thing that said she was her own person, without shouting it from the rooftops.

They were sitting in an unmarked police car. Darren Slocum had his hand on his forehead, shielding his eyes. "I just can't believe it," he groaned. "I just can't. I can't believe Ann's gone."

"I know this is a tough time. But I need to go over a few things with you again."

Rona Wedmore knew Darren. Not well, but they did have the same employer, after all. He was a Milford street cop and she was a police detective. They'd worked several crime scenes together, knew each other well enough to say hello, but they were not friends. Wedmore was aware of Slocum's reputation. At least two complaints of excessive force. Rumors, never proven, that he'd helped himself to some cash at a drug bust. And everyone knew about Ann's purse parties. Darren had once asked Wedmore if she'd consider hosting one, and she had declined.

"Go ahead," he said now.

"What time did Ann go out last night?"

"It would have been nine-thirty, quarter to ten, around then."

"And did she say why she was going out?"

"She got a phone call."

"Who called her?" Wedmore asked.

"Belinda Morton. They're friends."

Darren Slocum knew that wasn't the only call. He knew there had been one before that. Ann had spoken to someone else. He'd seen the light on the extension come on. And he knew, from talking to Emily later, that the Garber kid had her own cell phone. That she hadn't, as Ann had suggested, used their landline to call her father to pick her up.

"Why were they getting together, Belinda and Ann?"

Darren shook his head. "I don't know. They're friends. They talk to each other all the time, cry on each other's shoulders. I figured they were going to grab a drink somewhere."

"But Ann never met up with her?"

"Belinda called back here around eleven, asking for Ann. Said she'd tried to raise her on her cell but she wasn't picking up. Wondered what had happened to her. That was when I started to get worried."

"What did you do then?"

"I tried her cell, too. No luck. I thought about driving around, trying to find her, look for her car at places where she might have gone, but Emily was asleep, and I didn't want to leave her in the house alone."

"Okay," Wedmore said, taking down some notes. "So what time did you call it in?"

"I guess, around one?"

Wedmore already knew the answer. Slocum had called his department at 12:58 a.m.

"I didn't want to call 911. I mean, I work there, I know all the numbers, so I called in on the nonemergency line, got hold of Dispatch, asked, kind of unofficially, you know? Asked if everyone could kind of keep an eye out for Ann's car, that I was worried about her, that I was afraid maybe she'd had an accident or something."

"And you heard back when?"

Slocum ran his hands over his cheeks, smearing tears. "Uh, let me think. I think it was around two. Rigby called me."

Officer Ken Rigby. *Good man,* Wedmore thought. "Okay. I'm just trying to get a sense of the timeline, you understand."

"Did anyone see anything?" Darren Slocum asked. "Down by the harbor? Did anyone see what happened?"

"We're canvassing for witnesses now, but this time of year, there's hardly anyone down there.. There are some nearby houses, so maybe we'll get lucky. You never know."

"Yeah," Slocum said. "Let's hope someone saw something. But, what do you think happened?"

"It's early, Darren. But what Officer Rigby found was, the car was running, the driver's door was open, and the right rear tire was flat."

"Okay," Slocum said. Rona wasn't sure he was listening. The guy seemed dazed.

"The passenger side of the car was pulled up right next to the edge of the pier. We're just guessing so far, but it's possible that she went around to see what was wrong, and when she bent over to check the tire, she lost her footing."

"And that's when she fell into the water."

"Possibly. The water's not that deep there and there's not much current. When Rigby was shining his light around, he spotted her. It looks like an accident. There's nothing to suggest it was a robbery. Her purse was sitting on the passenger seat. Doesn't look like it was touched. Her wallet and credit cards were all still there."

Darren shook his head stubbornly. "Why didn't she just call me? Or a tow truck? Something? I mean, what was she thinking? That she was going to change a tire by herself down there in the middle of the night?"

"I'm sure we'll know more as the investigation continues," Wedmore told him. "Do you have any idea why Ann would be driving down around the harbor? Is that where she was going to meet Belinda?"

"Maybe. I mean, maybe instead of going for a drink, they were just going to take a walk."

"But if that's where they'd planned to meet, Belinda wouldn't have called you to ask where she was," Wedmore pointed out. "She'd have called to say she'd found her car, but that Ann wasn't anywhere around."

"Yeah, yeah, that makes sense," Darren agreed.

"So that brings me back to my question. What would Ann have been doing down at the harbor? Is it possible she was going to meet someone else before she was going to meet up with Belinda?"

"I... I can't think of anyone." Darren Slocum was crying again. "Rona, look, I don't think I can do any more... I've, I've got a lot to do..."

She looked out her windshield at Darren's pickup, noticed the For Sale sign in the window. Looking out, from between the living room drapes, was Emily.

"This must be a terrible thing for your daughter," Detective Wedmore said.

"Ann's sister, she lives in New Haven, came over around five in the morning," he said. "She's helping pull things together."

Wedmore reached out and patted Slocum on the arm. "You know we're going to do everything we can."

Slocum looked at her with bloodshot eyes. "I know. I know you are."

He watched Wedmore drive away and once she had turned the corner he got out his cell and punched in a number.

"Hello?"

"Belinda?"

"Oh my God, Darren, I still can't—"

"Just listen to me. You have —"

"I'm going out of my mind," she said breathlessly. "First, that man comes to see me, threatens me, and then you call at four in the morning and tell me Ann—"

"Would you just shut the fuck up for a second?" When there was silence at the other end, Darren continued. "Rona Wedmore is coming to see you."

"Rona who?"

"She's a Milford police detective. I know her. She's coming to see you because she knows you and Ann were talking, that you and she were going to meet up."

"But—"

"You tell her it was just girl talk. Maybe, I don't know, you had a fight with George or something and needed to talk. Nothing about the business, or that guy who visited you."

"But, Darren, what if he killed her? We can't just—"

"He didn't kill her," Darren said. "It was some kind of accident. She fell into the water and hit her head or something. But listen to me, you don't talk about the other things. Not one word. Are we clear?"

"Yes, yes, okay. I got it."

"And tell me again what Glen said when you talked to him last night."

"He said . . . he said the car didn't burn up. Sheila's purse, it wasn't lost in the fire. And he said there was no envelope in it."

"He actually said that?"

"That's right," Belinda said, her voice breaking.

Darren thought about that. "So there's a chance the money's still around somewhere." He paused. "Or maybe Glen's already found it."

THIRTEEN

Kelly's cell phone was sitting next to her mouse. She tapped a few commands into it, then handed it to me. "I paused it," she told me. The image on the small screen was narrow and vertical, like a mail slot flipped sideways. In the sliver of image, I could make out a bedroom, a bed in the foreground.

"Why does it look like this?" I asked.

"The closet door was only open, like, a crack," Kelly said.

"Right, okay. So how do I make it go?"

"Just press—here, let me do it."

She thumbed something, and the image began to move. Kelly's hand must have been shaking slightly as she filmed, for the sliver of light moved side to side, the bed shifted up and down.

Beyond the bed, a door opened.

"This is when Emily's mom came in," Kelly said. "Okay, now she's sitting on the bed."

The woman was probably no more than four feet from the closet door. She reached for something just out of camera range, and now she had a cordless phone in her hand. She entered a number and put the phone to her ear.

The sound quality was poor. *"Hey,"* Ann Slocum said. *"Can you talk? Yeah, I'm alone."*

"Can you make this any louder?" I asked Kelly.

She frowned. "Not really."

"*. . . your wrists are okay,*" Ann said. "*Yeah, wear long sleeves until the marks go away.*"

"See?" Kelly said. "She's not sick. She's not coughing or anything."

"*. . . about next time . . . can do Wednesday, maybe—*"

"This is when she got the other call," Kelly said.

"Shh."

"*. . . okay, later—Hello?*"

"Right here."

"Kelly, quiet."

"Right here, she kind of looks over and—"

"Shh!"

"*—us . . . down for a new deal if you've got something else to offer.*" At this point, Ann glanced in the direction of the closet.

And then the image disappeared.

"What happened?" I asked.

"That's when I put my phone down. When she looked over at me. I got scared."

"Was that when she stopped talking?"

"No, she hadn't actually seen me yet. She talked a little more. About the other stuff I told you. Where she got real mad and everything."

I handed the phone back to her. "Can you download that into your computer?" She nodded. "And then can you email it to me? As a file or something?" Another nod. "Do that."

"Am I in trouble?"

"No."

"Why do you want me to send you the video?"

"I just . . . I might want to look at it again later."

From downstairs, Fiona shouted, "Is everything okay?"

"Just a minute!" I shouted back.

Kelly bit her lip and asked, "So what should I do about Grandma and Marcus?"

"What do you want to do?"

She hesitated. "If I can't do anything about Emily, I guess I could go out with them for a while. But if I did, could you do me a favor?"

"Sure," I said. "What?"

"Could you find out what happened to Emily's mom?"

I wasn't so sure I wanted to get involved in that, but I promised, "I'll let you know what I find out."

"What's happened?" Fiona demanded when I returned downstairs.

I told the two of them what little I knew. That Kelly's friend's mother had died, but I didn't know under what circumstances.

"The poor kid," Marcus said, meaning Kelly, not Emily. "It's just one thing after another."

"I'm sure we'll find out soon enough what happened. It'll be on the news, or there'll be a death notice in the paper, a Facebook memorial, something. Kelly will probably get a text message before any of us learn a damn thing."

"Will she still spend the day with us?" Fiona wasn't going to let some tragedy derail a day with her granddaughter.

Fifteen minutes later Kelly bounded down the stairs, dressed and ready for an outing. Before they got into Marcus's Caddy and drove off, however, she gave me a private hug in the kitchen. I knelt down and wiped a tear from her cheek.

"I never knew anyone else whose mother died," she whispered. "I know Emily's got to be really sad."

"She will be. But she'll be strong, like you. She'll get through this."

Kelly nodded, but the corners of her mouth trembled.

"You don't have to go with them if you don't want to," I told her.

"No, it's okay, Daddy. But I don't want to live with them. I always want to come home and be with you."

Once I had the house to myself, I made a pot of coffee. This had always been Sheila's job, and I was still struggling to get it right—the number of spoonfuls, running the water from the tap until it was really cold. I filled a mug and went out onto the back deck. It was a cool day, but with a light jacket on it was nice out there, if somewhat bracing. I sat down, took a sip. Not nearly as good as Sheila's, but drinkable. That was all coffee really had to be for me.

Aside from a soft breeze that was liberating the last of the fall leaves from the three oak trees in our backyard, it was oddly still out there. The world seemed, briefly, calm. The last couple of weeks had been hell, but the preceding fifteen hours had been a maelstrom. The aborted sleepover,

Kelly's tale of the overheard phone call, Fiona's unexpected visit and unwanted school proposal. And, overshadowing everything, Ann Slocum's death.

Christ on a cracker.

"What do you make of that, Sheila?" I said aloud, shaking my head. "What in the hell do you make of that?"

Two little girls from the same class, both losing their mothers within a couple of weeks. And while I hadn't wanted to actively follow up on Kelly's request that I find out what happened to Ann, I was curious just the same. Could it have been a heart attack? An aneurysm? Some crazy thing that struck her dead in a second? Had there been some kind of accident? Did she fall down the stairs? Slip in the shower and break her neck? If she'd been ill, surely Sheila would have known about it and told me? Everyone told Sheila their troubles.

Would Darren Slocum have reason to feel about his dead wife the way I did about Sheila? Would anger displace grief? Maybe it would, regardless. If Sheila had died instantly of a stroke, I might be just as enraged, but my fury would be directed elsewhere. Instead of asking Sheila what the hell she was thinking, I'd save that question for the man upstairs.

"I still don't get it, Sheila," I said. "How'd you pull it off? How'd you hide a drinking problem?"

There was no answer.

"I've got stuff to do." I tossed the rest of my coffee onto the grass.

I decided to make good use of the day. With Kelly occupied, I could go into the office and do things that were impossible through the week. I could tidy up, replace a few saw blades, make sure no one had walked off with any of the tools. I could catch up with the voicemail, maybe even return a few calls rather than leave them all for Sally on Monday morning. Most likely all of them would be from customers wondering why their jobs weren't moving along more quickly. There weren't many projects that got done on time, despite our best intentions. Organizing the different trades—plumbers, tilers, electricians, just for starters—was akin to setting up dominoes. If you could get them in order and on time, everything fell into place. But it never happened that way. Supplies didn't show when promised. People got sick. You got called back to other jobs you thought were finished.

You did the best you could.

As I was getting out of my deck chair I heard a car door slam around the front. Coming around the side, I saw a white pickup truck I recognized parked across the end of the drive. *Theo's Electric* was stenciled onto the door, and Theo himself, a wiry guy in his mid-thirties who, at six feet, had about four inches on me in the height department, was sliding out from behind the wheel.

The passenger door opened a second later, and out got Sally. She was twenty-eight, with dirty-blonde hair and a body that was big-boned but not fat. She'd gone out for gymnastics and track and field back in high school, and while not quite the athlete she was then, she still ran three miles every morning and could pitch in and help unload a flatbed of two-by-fours when needed. She stood an inch taller than me, and liked to joke that if she didn't get a decent Christmas bonus, she could take me. I didn't like to admit she had a sporting chance.

She had a pretty face and a winning smile, and had been working for me for the better part of a decade. When she was in her early twenties, and looking for extra cash, she often babysat Kelly. But before long she'd concluded she was too old for that sort of thing, and picked up the occasional shift at Applebee's.

She and Theo had been going together for about a year, and even though it seemed soon to me, Sally had already been talking in the office about marriage. It wasn't my place to talk her out of it, but I'd done nothing to encourage the idea. My opinion of Theo Stamos had taken a nosedive in recent weeks, even before the fire. While he had his charms, he was famous for not showing up when he said he would, and his work was often sloppy. I hadn't used him on a job since the fire; I was sorry I hadn't cut him loose sooner. The so-called truck nuts—molded rubber testicles that had inexplicably become popular in the last few years—that were hanging from the pickup's rear bumper made me want to get out a pair of tin snips and perform a castration.

"Theo," I said. "Hi, Sally."

"I told him we shouldn't do this," she said, moving quickly so she could get between Theo and me.

"This is only going to take a sec," Theo said. He loped toward me, his arms swinging lazily at his sides. "How's it going there, Glen?"

"Okay," I said, noncommittally.

"Sorry to be bugging you on a Saturday, but we were in the area, and it seemed like as good a time as any."

"As good a time as any for what?"

"I notice you haven't been calling on me in a while."

I nodded. "Things are slowing down, Theo."

"I know that," he said. "But Sally here says you've still got some work lined up before things fall off." Sally winced, clearly not happy Theo was using her this way. "So it's not like things have dried up completely. You haven't used me since that house burned down, and that's not fair."

"You wired it," I said.

"With all due respect, Glen, do you have some kind of proof that says it was my fault?"

"I haven't found anything that says it wasn't."

He glanced down, kicked a pebble with the toe of his work boot, then looked at me. "I don't think that's right," he said evenly. "You've gone and convicted me without any evidence."

I hated to tell Theo the truth in front of his girlfriend, especially when Sally was a friend of mine, but he wasn't making it easy for me. "That's my prerogative," I told him. When Theo blinked, I realized he didn't know what I meant. While I didn't want to hire him anymore, it wasn't my intention to insult him, so I added, "It's my company. I get to choose who works for me and who doesn't."

"That's just not right," he insisted. "Give me one good reason why you won't hire me anymore."

Sally leaned up against the truck and closed her eyes. These were things she did not want to hear. But I think she knew what was coming.

"You're not dependable," I told Theo. "You say you're going to show up, and you don't. Even aside from this fire, your work isn't up to snuff. You cut corners."

"You know how it is," he said defensively. "Some jobs get backed up, you can't get to the next one right away. And I don't know what you're talking about, saying my work's not good. That's just horseshit."

I shook my head. "When I promise a client you're going to be there in the morning, and then you aren't, it reflects badly on me and the company."

"I told you not to do this, Theo," Sally said.

"What did the fire department say?" Theo's voice was starting to rise. "Did they say I wired it wrong?"

"I'm waiting on their final report, but they say the fire started in the area of the electrical panel."

"The *area*," he said. "So, somebody could have left some oily rags in that *area*, and that's what caused the place to go up in smoke."

"I do what my gut tells me," I said.

"Yeah, well, your gut sucks."

He was wasting my time. I'd made up my mind not to use him again and that was it. My eyes wandered down to the truck nuts hanging from his back bumper.

Theo saw me eyeing them. "Need a pair?" he asked.

"Another thing," I said. "Anybody shows up at one of my jobs with those hanging off the back of the truck gets sent home. I won't have my daughter walking past garbage like that."

"It's none of your business how I or anybody else dresses up his truck."

"That's right," I agreed. "But I decide whose trucks come to my job sites and whose don't."

Theo's hands fisted at his sides.

"Theo, knock it off," Sally said, stepping forward. "I *told* you not to do this but you wouldn't listen." To me she said, "Glen, I'm so sorry. I swear, I told him."

"Get in the truck," Theo told her. His face had gone beet red with fury. He got in and slammed the door but Sally didn't join him.

I felt a pang of guilt. "I don't mean to disrespect your boyfriend in front of you, Sally. But he asked, and I told him."

"He's not what he seems, Glen. He's got a lot of good points. He's got a good heart. The other day, at Walgreens, the lady gave him too much change and he gave it back."

What can you say to that?

Sally's head drooped when I didn't answer. Then she sighed and shook her head. "There's something else I need to talk to you about," she said.

I waited.

"I feel funny telling you about this. I don't want to get him into trouble."

"Theo?"

"No. Doug." She sighed again. "He asked me to double his paycheck for a week, then not write him one the next week. I said if he wanted an advance, he had to clear it through you. He said it could be our little secret."

Now it was my turn to sigh. "Thanks for telling me, Sally."

"I think he's having big-time money problems, him and Betsy."

"He called me about this last night."

"I know you'll have to tell him I told you, but when you do, please tell him I felt bad about it."

"Leave it with me." I reached out and touched her arm. "How you doin'?" I didn't have to ask her how long it had been now since her father had died. She'd lost him the same day I'd lost Sheila. "At the office, it's hard to get a moment."

"Okay," she said. "I miss him. I miss him so much. It's just so weird," she continued. "Me losing my dad, and a few hours later..."

"Yeah," I said, and forced a smile. Then, even though Theo was glaring at both of us through the windshield and would probably disapprove, I gave her a quick hug. The last time I'd done that had been at her father's funeral, which had been held a day before Sheila's. Given my own circumstances at the time, I might have been inclined to give the service a pass. But Sally had no family, no siblings, and was carrying a heavy load alone. My own sorrow was so raw I'd known how much it would mean to Sally if I spent two hours helping her deal with hers.

In the couple of weeks since, they'd figured out what had happened. Sally's dad was on meds that slowed down blood clot formations and thereby reduced his risk of another heart attack. Sally gave him his dose in the morning, but shortly after she'd left for work, he'd apparently become confused and given himself another shot. The overdose caused him to bleed to death internally.

"We pick ourselves up and keep on going," I told her as Theo glared at us. "There's not really much else we can do."

"I guess," she said. "How's Kelly doing? Is she home?" Sally remained Kelly's favorite babysitter, even though Sally hadn't sat her since she was four.

"She's with her grandmother. She'll be sorry she missed you." I hesitated. I wasn't big on self-revelation, but found myself saying,

"Nobody told me it would be so hard. Some father-daughter discussions are easier than others."

"Oh yeah," Sally said, and grinned. "I can just hear you giving her the talk about her monthly visitor."

"Yeah, I'm really looking forward to that." Maybe I could recruit Fiona when the time came. Or better yet, Sally.

"If you need me to talk to her about—"

"Thanks," I said. "I'll keep it in mind. Listen, you should go. Theo looks like he's going to blow a fuse."

She tipped her head toward the pickup's rear bumper. "Sorry about the truck nuts."

"I wouldn't let Kelly ride in a truck that had those on them," I said.

She flushed. My words had shamed her.

"See you Monday," she said, turning away, and got back into the truck. Theo squealed the tires as he pulled away from the curb.

I went back inside and poured another cup of coffee I knew I wouldn't drink. Sally and I had always had a kind of little sister–big brother thing going on, so my criticism must have felt like a harsh judgment. I was still brooding about that when the phone rang. "Hello?"

"You're home," said a male voice I thought I recognized.

"Who's this?"

"Darren Slocum. You and I need to talk right now."

FOURTEEN

I went out on the porch and waited for Darren Slocum to show.

My curiosity was piqued. Why would Slocum want to talk to me? I would have thought that other matters, like picking a casket, would be more of a priority.

I was only out there about five minutes when Slocum's red pickup came cruising down the street and came to a stop in front of the house.

"Darren," I said, descending the porch steps and extending a hand as he came up the walk. "I'm so sorry about Ann."

We shook, Slocum accepting my condolences with a nod. "Yeah," he said. "It's a bit of a shocker."

"Tell me about Emily."

"She's a disaster. Kid loses her mom, all of a sudden. I guess you know what that's about."

"What happened, Darren?"

He thrust out his jaw and looked up, as though trying to draw some strength first. "There was an accident."

The word sent an unexpected chill down my spine. "A car accident?" I asked.

"Sort of, but not exactly."

"What do you mean?"

"She'd gone down High Street, by the harbor, and it looks like she got a flat tire on the passenger's side, pulled over and got out to have a look—the door was open and the engine was still running—and anyway, she was parked up close to the edge there and it looks like she lost her footing, and went into the water. A guy I know, another Milford cop, spotted her just under the water there."

"Jesus," I said. "I'm very sorry. I really am."

"Yeah, well, thanks."

"I don't know what else to say."

"I thought you should know, what with our girls being friends and all."

"Sure," I said.

"Does your girl—Kelly—does she know?"

I nodded. "After I spoke to—I guess it was your sister-in-law—on the phone, I was going to tell her, but she found out on her own chatting online with her friends. Maybe even Emily."

"Okay," he said softly. "Must be a shock for her, too."

"Yeah," I said.

"What I was wondering," Slocum said, "was whether it would help if I had a couple of words with Kelly, let her know what happened."

"You want to talk to Kelly?"

"Yeah. Is she here?"

"No, she's not. But I've talked to her. It's okay." I couldn't think of a single good reason for Darren Slocum to tell Kelly how his wife died. I'd be the one to tell her, and comfort her.

He moved his jaw from side to side. "When's she going to be back? She off playing with another friend or something?"

A small muscle by his right eye was twitching. He was so tightly wound, he looked like he might snap. I wasn't eager for that to happen, so I kept my voice low and calm.

"Darren, even if she were here, I don't think you talking to her would help. She's just lost her mother, and now her best friend has lost hers. I think the best one to get her through this is me."

A look of frustration crossed his face. "Okay, Glen, let me just cut to it here."

Mentally, I went into a defensive stance.

"What the hell happened last night?" he asked.

I pushed the inside of my cheek with my tongue. "What are you talking about, Darren?"

"Your kid. Why'd she ask you to come get her?"

"She wasn't feeling well."

"No, no, don't give me that. Something happened."

"Whatever happened, it happened at *your* house. I might ask you the same thing."

"Yeah, well, whatever happened, I don't know what it was. But I think something happened between my wife and your kid."

"Darren, where are you going with this?"

"I need to know. I've got my reasons."

"Does this have something to do with your wife's accident?"

His jaw moved around some more but he didn't answer right away. Finally, he said gruffly, "I think my wife got a phone call. I think that phone call might have been the reason she went out to the harbor. I need to know who made that call."

I'd had enough. "Darren, go back home and be with your family. I'm sure they need you."

Darren kept pushing. "The girls were playing hide-and-seek. I think Kelly was hiding in our bedroom, and maybe she was there when Ann was on the phone. She might be able to tell me who Ann was talking to."

"I can't help you," I said.

"When you showed up, and I went looking for your girl, I found her standing right there in the middle of our bedroom. She said Ann had told her to wait there, like she was being punished."

I didn't say anything.

"If Kelly'd busted something, or gotten into something she wasn't supposed to, Ann would have mentioned it to me. But the fact that she didn't, that's curious. She kinda glossed over the incident before she went out. And she lied to me about being on the phone. She said Kelly must have used it to call you, but Emily told me she has her own cell phone. That right?"

"I got her a phone after her mother died," I said. "Look, Darren, I don't know what to tell you. How could Kelly know who Ann was talking to? And really, why does it matter? I mean, you just said what happened to Ann was an accident. It's not like, you know, someone *lured* her to the harbor. I mean, if that's what you thought, you'd be talking about it with the police, right?"

I continued, "And if, somehow, that *is* what you think, then maybe I should be talking to whoever's investigating your wife's accident, because I'm guessing it's not you. That wouldn't be the way they'd do things, right?"

"I've got every right to know the circumstances surrounding my wife's death," he said.

That struck a chord.

Wasn't that exactly how I felt about Sheila? Her death was an accident, but the circumstances made no sense to me. Hadn't I been doing the same thing Darren Slocum was doing now? When I sought out the other students and teacher from her night class, wasn't I searching for the truth? When I tore the house apart, trying to determine whether my wife had been hiding booze in places where I wouldn't find it, wasn't I looking for answers?

If there were things Ann didn't want him to know when she was alive, wasn't it conceivable that he was entitled to know them now that she was dead?

And yet, I didn't want to get dragged into this mess. I certainly knew I didn't want Kelly getting dragged into it.

"Look...," I started to say. But before I could decide what, exactly, I was going to tell him, he cut me off.

"Why'd you call my house this morning?"

"Excuse me?"

"You heard me. You called and got my sister-in-law. You said you wanted to talk to Ann. Why?"

"Just..." I wasn't ready to be straight with him yet. "I was going to ask her if she'd seen Kelly's stuffed bunny. Hoppy. But then she found it."

"Bullshit. You think you can be a cop as long as I have and not tell when people are lying to you? Why were you calling? Did Kelly tell you what happened? And you wanted to talk it over with Ann?"

I shook my head. "For Christ's sake, Darren, if that damn phone call is so important to you, why don't you just check your phone's history?"

He smiled sourly. "I thought of that. And guess what? Ann cleared the incoming and outgoing call list. What d'ya make of that? That's why I want to talk to Kelly."

"Look." I tried to adopt a conciliatory tone. "I don't know what kind of problems you and Ann were having, and I'm sorry, whatever they might have been, but I'm not getting dragged into them. My daughter's been through enough these last few weeks. She's lost her mother. The other kids—not your daughter, and thank you for that—have been hateful to her, because Sheila, what she did, it left one of the kids from that school dead. Now, Kelly's friend's mother dies. She's going to need a lot of time to get through this. I won't have you interrogating her. Not you, not *anybody*."

Slocum's body sagged. A moment ago, he looked ready to slug me. Now, not so much.

"Help me out here, man," he said.

A few seconds of silence passed between us. I knew what he was feeling, how desperate he was for answers. "Okay," I said. "Kelly and I talked, after I picked her up."

"Yeah?"

"Here's the deal. I'll tell you what she told me, and we're done. You don't talk to her." I paused, then added, "Ever."

Slocum only had to think a second. "Okay."

"Kelly was hiding in the closet, waiting to surprise Emily, when Ann came into the bedroom to use the phone."

He nodded. "I thought it was something like that."

"Kelly said the first person your wife talked to was—"

"Wait a minute. First person? There was more than one call?"

"Kelly had the idea there were two. The first person your wife talked to must have been a friend or something. Someone who'd hurt their wrist. Ann was calling to see if this person was okay. Then the line beeped and Ann took another call."

"So the first call, she placed that one herself," Slocum said, more to himself than me. Then, "So this first call, she was asking somebody how they were? They got hurt?"

"Something like that. But then the other call came in. Kelly said at first she thought it was a telemarketer or something, because Ann said there was some talk about a deal. And then she got a little angry."

"Angry how?"

"Ann said something like, don't be stupid or you'll end up shot in the head. Something like that."

Slocum tried to process it. "Shot in the head?"

"Yeah."

"What else?"

"That's really it."

"What about a name? Ann must have said someone's name?"

"No, there were no names."

He looked like he'd come to a fork in the road and didn't know which way to turn. This new information only seemed to frustrate him more. It was my turn for a question.

"What the hell's going on, Darren?"

"Nothing."

"Bullshit," I said. "You're in some kind of mess, and you're in over your head."

He shot me a sly grin. "I might not be the only one."

"Excuse me?"

"The way I figure it, you may have come into a little windfall lately. Like, within the last few weeks."

"I'm not following you, Darren."

His grin shifted into something menacing. "I'm just giving you a heads-up. That windfall, it's not yours. And hanging on to it, that's a real risky thing to do. You take a day or two to think it over and do the right thing, because after that, you'll be running out of options."

"I don't have a goddamn clue what you're getting at, and now it's my turn to tell you something: threatening me, that's a risky thing, too. I don't care what you do for a living."

"Couple of days," he repeated, as if I hadn't spoken. "After that, I won't be able to help you."

"Go home, Darren. Your family needs you."

He started walking back to his truck, then stopped. "I gotta say, it's a hell of a thing."

"What's that?"

"Your wife, my wife, both friends, both with little girls that play together—both dying in accidents within a couple of weeks. What are the odds of that?"

FIFTEEN

Kelly made the point, once she was in the car with Fiona and Marcus, that she hadn't had any breakfast, and since it was almost lunchtime, maybe they should get something lunchlike to eat. It was Fiona's plan to take Kelly, first, to the Stamford Town Center and buy her a new winter coat because she'd outgrown the one she'd worn last year and Fiona was not confident Glen would notice. Then, after that, they'd backtrack to Darien, where it was Fiona's plan to take a tour of two of the local private schools, give Kelly an idea where she could go once Fiona had managed to sell Glen on the idea.

"We'll eat at the Stamford Town Center," Fiona decided. Kelly said they had a pretty good food court, so she could wait. Fiona would have preferred a sit-down restaurant where someone took your order and brought it to you, but she was inclined to indulge the child, because there were some things she wanted to ask her about what had happened with her friend's mother, and she wanted the girl to be forthcoming.

Once the three of them sat down, Marcus and Fiona each with a latte from Starbucks and Kelly with a slice of pepperoni pizza, Fiona asked about the sleepover.

"I thought it was going to be fun but it was really not so good."

"Why's that?"

"I came home early. I called Dad to pick me up."

"Weren't you having a good time?"

"I was sort of at first, but then it wasn't fun anymore."

Fiona leaned in a little closer. "And why was that?"

"Well," Kelly said, "Emily's mom got really mad at me."

"She did?" Fiona asked. "Why did she get mad at you?"

Kelly said, "I'm really not supposed to talk about this."

"I don't see why you can't talk about it with me. I'm your grandmother. You can tell your grandmother anything."

"I know, but . . ." Kelly studied her slice, picked off a pepperoni slice and popped it into her mouth.

"But what?" Fiona said.

"I kinda promised not to tell anybody, except I told my dad because he's my dad."

"Who did you promise?"

"Emily's mom."

Fiona nodded. "Well, she's not with us anymore," she said matter-of-factly, "so you can't really break a promise to her now if you talk about it."

"It's okay to break promises to dead people?" Kelly asked.

"Absolutely."

Marcus was starting to shake his head. "Fiona, what are you doing?"

"Excuse me?" she snapped.

"Look at her. You're upsetting her. She's starting to cry."

It was true. Her eyes had filled with tears. One threatened to spill over and trickle down her cheek.

"I know this may be troubling, dear," Fiona told Kelly, "but sometimes, talking about a traumatic event can be therapeutic."

"Huh?" said Kelly.

"If you talk about what makes you feel bad, it can end up making you feel better."

"Oh. I don't think so."

"What sort of promise did Emily's mom ask you to keep?"

"She didn't want me to tell anyone about the phone call."

"Phone call," Fiona said. "A phone call. What phone call was that?"

"The one I heard her make."

Marcus was shaking his head disapprovingly, but Fiona ignored him. "You were listening in on someone else's phone call?"

"Not on purpose," Kelly said hastily. "I wouldn't do that. That would be eavestroughing."

"Eaves*dropping*, Kelly," Fiona said, not even cracking a smile. "So if it wasn't on purpose, how did you happen to be hearing this conversation?"

"I was just hiding," Kelly said. "From Emily. I didn't really hear that much of it anyway because she was whispering a lot." The tear finally spilled down her cheek. "Do I have to talk about this?"

"Kelly, it may not be pleasant to go over this, but I think—"

"Can I talk to you a minute?" Marcus said to his wife.

"What?"

"Sweetheart," Marcus said, taking out his wallet and handing a ten to Kelly, "take this and go get yourself something for dessert."

"But I haven't even finished my pizza yet."

"If you get it now, then when you've finished your pizza, you can start on it immediately."

She took the ten from him. "Okay." They watched her scamper over to the ice-cream stand.

"What the hell is wrong with you?" Marcus asked his wife.

"Absolutely nothing."

"That girl's mother is dead. Now her best friend's mother is dead. We're supposed to be taking her out for a nice day and you're conducting a fucking interrogation of her."

"Don't use that tone with me."

"Fiona, sometimes... sometimes you just don't know the effect you have on people. You can't... Is empathy beyond you?"

"How dare you," she seethed. "I'm only asking her these questions because I *care* about her welfare."

"No," he said, shaking his head. "There's something else going on with you. Is it because there's something about this Ann Slocum you've never liked?"

"What are you talking about?"

"I saw the way you acted with her at that purse party or whatever it was called. You had nothing but contempt for her. You were looking down your nose at her all night."

She stared at him. "That's nonsense. I don't know where you're getting this."

"I'm just saying, I'm shutting this down. You're not going to hound this child anymore. We'll take her shopping, we'll drive her around to those schools if you want to, although I swear, what makes you think Glen's going to give up his daughter Monday to Friday I have no idea, and then we're going to take her home."

"She's my granddaughter, not yours," Fiona said.

"Funny, then, that I'm the only one who's worried about her."

Fiona started to say something, but then realized that Kelly was standing two feet away, an ice-cream sundae in one hand and her cell in the other.

She held it out to Fiona. "My dad wants to talk to you."

SIXTEEN

I felt shaken as I went back into the house following Darren Slocum's visit. I dialed Kelly's cell the moment I was in the kitchen.

"Hi, Dad," she said.

"Hi, sweetheart. Where are you?"

"Getting some ice cream at the mall."

"Which mall?"

"Stamford."

"Could you put Grandma on?"

"Just a second. She's at the table."

I could hear mall background noises—people talking, bland music—and then Kelly saying, "My dad wants to talk to you."

"Yes, Glen?" Fiona's voice was as warm as the ice cream Kelly was eating.

"Fiona, you up to taking Kelly for overnight?" I knew Kelly already had pajamas and a toothbrush and several days' worth of clothes at Fiona's house.

A pause, then she whispered, "Isn't it a bit soon, Glen?" It occurred to me that she was trying to keep Kelly from hearing.

"Excuse me?"

"For you to have someone over? Is it that woman who lives next door? The Mueller woman? Sheila told me about her. I saw her hanging out the door, watching as we drove off. My daughter hasn't even been dead three weeks, you know."

I felt the anger welling up inside me. "Ann Slocum's husband came over here after you left, very distraught." I closed my eyes a moment, counted to three.

"What?"

"He was being, I don't know, pretty unreasonable. He wanted to talk to Kelly, and I can't see any good coming out of that. Just in case he decides to come back here later and try again, I think it'd be better if Kelly stayed with you."

"What do you mean, *unreasonable*?"

"It's a long story, Fiona. What would really help me, at this moment, would be if you could keep Kelly until tomorrow. Until I know this has all blown over."

"What's going on?" I heard Marcus ask.

"In a sec," Fiona told him. To me, she said, "Yes, of course, she'll stay with us. That's fine."

"Thank you," I said, and waited to see whether she might offer up even the slightest apology for what she'd first assumed my motives were.

Instead, she said, "Kelly wants to talk to you."

"Dad? What's going on?"

"You're going to spend the night at your grandmother's. Just the one night."

"Okay," she said, not excited, but not disappointed, either. "Is something wrong?"

"Everything's fine, sweetheart."

"Did you find out what happened to Emily's mom?"

"It was an accident, honey," I said. "She got hurt when she got out to check a flat tire."

Kelly paused a moment to take it in, then said, "So now Emily and me really have something in common."

While Darren Slocum had claimed to be satisfied that I'd told him the extent of what Kelly had heard his late wife say on the phone, some instinct told me he was lying. As I'd told Fiona, I was worried he might come back, and keeping Kelly at a distance for another day seemed like a good idea. And I had no idea what he was talking about when he'd suggested I'd come into a windfall recently. The grass wasn't even growing yet on

Sheila's grave, and he was intimating I'd had some kind of good fortune because of her fatal accident?

I didn't know what else to do but chalk it up to the distressed ramblings of a man who'd just lost a wife himself.

I did end up going to the offices of Garber Contracting after lunch. The business was off Cherry, just before you get to the Just Inn Time hotel and about half a mile down the road from the Connecticut Post Mall. While I was able to do some general tidying, I wasn't able to concentrate when I started checking the voicemails. I'd had every intention of calling these people back, but suddenly I couldn't face talking to any of them or going by their houses to listen to their complaints about why things weren't done. But I made notes of the messages so Sally could get back to everyone on Monday. While her choice in boyfriends was, to my mind, suspect, Sally was always on the ball at work. We called her our multitasker, who could keep the details of countless projects in her head at once. I'd seen her carry on a complicated phone conversation with a tile supplier about what we needed at one job while making notes about plumbing supplies we required at another. She liked to say she had several programs running in her head at once, adding that she'd earned the right to have a total system meltdown one day.

After the office was locked up, I went to the nearby ShopRite to pick up a few things. A steak for myself for dinner, some salami and tins of tuna and carrot sticks for lunches for Kelly and me through the week. I wasn't big on the carrot sticks, but Sheila would have wanted to see them not only in Kelly's lunch, but mine. It was odd. I was mightily pissed with my late wife, but still wanted to honor her wishes.

When Kelly was attending first grade, the first time she'd had to take a lunch with her every day, she begged Sheila and me to include a bag of potato chips. Her friend Kristen got potato chips every day, so why couldn't she have them? Well, if Kristen's mom wants to give her that kind of crap every day, that's her business, we said. But we're not doing it.

Kelly asked if Rice Krispie squares would be okay. Even if they had melted marshmallow in them, the cereal was healthy, right? So Sheila had helped her make up a batch. Melted the butter and marshmallow, mixed everything up in an enormous bowl, flattened them out in a pan.

The two of them had made a huge mess in the kitchen. Kelly happily took a square to school with her every day.

About a month later, when Kristen was over playing with Kelly, she happened to ask if we could put chocolate chips in the Rice Krispie squares. She really liked them that way. She'd been trading her potato chips for Kelly's squares every day.

As I was passing through the cereal aisle, the recollection made me smile. It seemed like a long time ago. It would be fun to make some one night with Kelly. Sometime around the start of third grade, she'd actually developed a liking for them herself.

I reached for a box just as someone else—a woman in her late thirties, early forties—decided to do the same. Shopping alongside her was a boy. Dark hair, jeans, and a jean jacket and running shoes with stripes and swirls all over them. I put his age at sixteen or seventeen.

"Excuse me," I said to the woman when we bumped elbows. "Go ahead."

Then I looked at her and did a double take. It didn't take more than half a second to realize who this woman, and the boy with her, were.

Bonnie Wilkinson. Mother of Brandon and husband of Connor.

The two people who died when they crashed into Sheila's car.

The teenage boy with her had to be her son Corey. His eyes looked dead, as though they'd cried out every tear he'd ever have.

Her blouse and slacks seemed to hang off her, and her face was drawn and gray. Her mouth opened and stayed that way when she realized who I was.

I backed up my cart to wheel it around them. I didn't need Rice Krispies. Not right now. "Let me get out of your way here," I said.

Finally, she could speak, although only just barely. "You just wait," she said.

I stopped. "Excuse me?"

"You're going to get yours," she said. "You're going to get it good." Her son's dead eyes bored into me.

I left my half-full cart and walked out of the store.

I picked up what I needed at the Super Stop & Shop. And instead of buying Rice Krispies, I bought all the ingredients I thought I'd need to make lasagna. I knew I couldn't make it as well as Sheila did, but I was going to give it a try.

I took the long way home so I could visit Doug Pinder.

My father had hired him to work at Garber Contracting about the same time I graduated from Bates. At twenty-three, Doug had been a year older. We worked side by side for years, but it was always understood I'd eventually be the guy in charge, even though no one expected it to happen quite so soon.

Dad, overseeing the construction of a ranch house in Bridgeport, had just unloaded two dozen four-by-eight sheets of plywood from a truck when he clutched his chest and dropped to the ground. The paramedics said he was dead before his head landed in the soft grass. I rode in the ambulance with him to the hospital, picking the blades out of his thinning gray hair.

Dad had been sixty-four. I was thirty. I made Doug Pinder my assistant manager.

Doug was a good right-hand man. His area of expertise was carpentry, but he knew enough about all the other aspects of construction to supervise the rest of the trades, and pitch in when needed. And where I was reserved, Doug was outgoing and jovial. When things got tense on a job, Doug knew just what to say and do to keep everyone's spirits up, better than I could. For years, I don't know what I would have done without him.

But things hadn't been right with Doug the last few months. He wasn't the life of the party anymore, or at least when he tried, it seemed forced. I knew he was under pressure at home, and it didn't take long to figure out it was financial. When Doug and his wife, Betsy, moved in to a new house four years ago, they'd gotten one of those too-good-to-be-true, subprime mortgages with almost nothing down, and when it had come up for renewal last year their monthly payments had more than doubled.

Betsy had been working in the accounting department of a local GM dealer that had closed its doors. She'd found a part-time job at a furniture store in Bridgeport, but had to be bringing in half of what she used to, if that.

The salary I paid Doug had remained constant through all this, but at best, he had to be treading water. More likely, he was drowning. While the construction and renovation business had slowed, I had, up to now, resisted cutting the pay of anyone who worked for me. At least those on staff, like Doug, Sally, Ken Wang, and our kid from north of the border, Stewart.

The Pinders had a wood-sided two-story off Roses Mill Road, near Indian Lake. Both their cars—Doug's decade-old Toyota pickup with a cargo cover and Betsy's leased Infiniti—were in the drive when I pulled up out front.

I could hear loud voices inside as I raised my hand to rap on the front door. I held it there a moment and listened, and while I could determine the mood inside that house—"ugly" was the word that came to mind—I couldn't make out any actual conversation.

I rapped hard, knowing I might not be heard over the commotion.

The shouting stopped almost immediately, like a switch had been flipped. A moment later, Doug opened the door. His face was red and there were beads of sweat on his forehead. He smiled and pushed open the aluminum screen.

"Hey! Whoa! Will you look who's here! Hey, Bets, it's Glenny!"

From upstairs somewhere, "Hi, Glen!" Cheerful, like they hadn't been tearing into each other five seconds earlier.

"Hi, Betsy," I called out.

"Can I get you a beer?" Doug asked, leading me into the kitchen.

"No, that's—"

"Come on, have a beer."

"Sure," I said. "Why not."

As I came into the kitchen my eye caught a pile of unopened envelopes sitting by the phone. They all looked like bills. There were bank and credit card logos in the upper left corners of several of them.

"What'll it be?" Doug asked, reaching into the fridge.

"Whatever you've got is fine."

He took out two cans of Coors, handed me one, and popped his. He extended it toward me so we could clink cans. "To the weekend," he said. "Whoever invented the weekend, there's a guy whose hand I'd like to shake."

"Yeah," I agreed.

"Good of you to drop by. This is terrific. You want to watch a game or something? There must be something on. I haven't even looked. Gotta be some golf, at least. Some people, they don't like watching golf, think it's too slow, but I like it, you know? So long as you got enough people playing, camera can go hole to hole, so you don't waste a whole lot of time watching people walk up the fairway."

"I can't stay long," I said. "I've got groceries in the car. Some stuff that has to go into the fridge."

"You could put it in ours for the time being," Doug offered enthusiastically. "Want me to go out and get them? It's no problem."

"No. Look, Doug, there's something I need to talk to you about."

"Shit, there a problem at one of the sites?"

"No, nothing like that."

Doug's face went dark. "Goddamn, Glen, you're not laying me off, are you?"

"Hell, no," I said.

A nervous smile crossed his lips. "Well, that's a relief. Christ, you gave me a start there."

Betsy popped into the kitchen, came over and kissed my cheek.

"How's my big strong man?" she said, but in her heels, she was nearly as tall as I was.

"Bets," I said.

Betsy was a tiny thing, barely an inch over five feet, but often wore killer heels to compensate. With them, she wore a super-short black skirt, tight white blouse, and jacket. She had a handbag hooked over her elbow, the word PRADA emblazoned on the side. I figured she got it the night Ann Slocum used our house to hawk her fake designer bags. If I were Doug, I wouldn't feel good, my wife heading out of the house looking like, if not quite a hooker, at least like someone who was on the prowl.

"How long you gonna be?" Doug asked her.

"I'll be back when I'm back," she said.

"Just don't..." Doug's voice trailed off. Then, "Just take it easy."

"Don't worry, I won't do anything crazy," she said. She flashed me a smile. "Doug thinks I'm a shopaholic." She shook her head. "An alcoholic, *maybe*." She laughed and then, just as quickly, adopted a look of horror. "Oh my God, Glen, I'm so sorry I said that!"

"It's okay."

"I just didn't think." She reached out and touched my arm.

"That's your whole problem," Doug said.

"Fuck you," she said to him, her tone no different than as if she'd blessed him after a sneeze. Her hand still on my arm, she asked, "How you holding up, anyway? How's poor Kelly?"

"We're managing."

She gave my arm a squeeze. "If we had a dollar for every time I put my foot in my mouth, we'd be living at the Hilton. Give that little girl of yours a hug from me. I gotta go."

"Glenny and me are gonna chill out a bit," Doug said, even though I thought I'd made it clear I didn't have a lot of time. I was relieved Betsy was leaving. I didn't want to say the things I had to say to Doug in front of his wife.

I didn't expect Betsy to give her husband a kiss goodbye, and I was right. She just turned on her killer heels and left. When the front door closed, Doug grinned nervously and said, "Storm front's moving out."

"Everything okay?"

"Oh yeah, sure! Everything's peachy."

"Betsy's looking good," I said.

"Oh, she's not one to let herself go, you can take that to the bank." He didn't say it proudly. "If there was anything *in* the bank." Now it was his turn to force a laugh. "I swear, sometimes, the way that woman shops, you'd think she had a printing press in the basement. She must have a secret stash someplace."

His eyes landed on the stack of unopened bills by the phone. He stood in front of them, opened a drawer and swept them into it. There were more envelopes already in there.

"Need to keep the place tidy," he said.

"Let's go sit outside," I said.

We took our beers out onto the deck. Beyond the trees, I could hear traffic rushing by on 95. Doug brought a pack of smokes with him, tapped one out, and stuck it between his lips. He was a heavy smoker when he joined the company, but quit a few years later. He'd picked up the habit again in the last six months. He lit up, drew in smoke, blew it out through his nostrils. "Gorgeous day," he said.

"Beautiful."

"Cool, but they're still out there golfing."

"Sally dropped by today," I said.

He shot me a look. "Yeah?"

"With Theo."

"Jesus, Theo. You think she's really going to marry him? It's not that I don't like the guy, but I think she could do better, you know what I mean?"

"Theo wanted to know why I haven't been using him."

"Whadja tell him?"

"The truth. That his work isn't up to par, and that electrical panel he wired in's probably why the Wilson house burned down."

"Ouch." A drink of beer, another puff. "So, that was it?"

"Sally ratted you out, Doug."

"Huh?"

"She's sorry she had to do it, but you didn't leave her any choice."

"I'm not sure I get where you're going, Glenny."

"Don't play dumb. We've known each other too long."

His eyes met mine, then he looked down. "I'm sorry."

"If you need an advance, you ask *me*."

"I did, and you said no. This last time."

"Then that should have been it. If I can do it, I will. If I can't, I won't. And we're going through some tough times now. The jobs are drying up, and if the Wilson place isn't covered by insurance we're really gonna be behind the eight ball. So don't ever, *ever,* do an end run around me and ask Sally to do it for you."

"I was in kind of a bind," he said.

"I don't like to tell people what to do, Doug. I figure how other people live their lives is none of my business. But in your case I'm going to make an exception. I see what's going on. The requests for pay advances. The unopened bills. Betsy off to the mall when you're up to your eyeballs in debt."

He wouldn't look at me. Suddenly his shoes were of tremendous interest.

"You need to get a handle on things, and you need to do it now. You'll probably have to lose the house, get rid of a car, sell off some things. You may have to start over. But you're going to have to do it. The one thing you can count on is your job with me. Just so long as you don't pull any fast ones."

He put down his beer, tossed the cigarette, and put his hands over his eyes. He didn't want me to see him crying.

"I'm so fucked," he said. "I am so totally, totally fucked. They sold us this bill of goods, you know."

"They?"

"Everyone. Said we could have it all. The house, the cars, the Blu-ray players, big flat-screen TVs, anything we wanted. Even while we were sinking, we'd get more credit cards in the mail. Betsy, she grabs them like they're lifesavers, but they're just more anchors dragging us down to the bottom."

He sniffed, rubbed his eyes, finally looked at me. "She won't listen. I keep telling her we have to change things, and she says not to worry, we'll be okay. She doesn't get it."

"Neither do you," I said. "Because you're letting it go on."

"You know what we're doing? We've got, like, twenty credit cards now. We use one to pay off the balance on another. I can't even keep track of it anymore. I can't bring myself to open the bills. I don't want to know."

"There are people," I said. "People who can help you get through these things."

"Sometimes I think it'd be easier to just blow my brains out."

"Doug, don't think that way. But you need to get hold of the problem. It's going to take you a long time to dig yourself out of this hole, but if you start now, you'll be coming out sooner. You can't count on me for money every time you're short, but you can talk to me. I'll help you where I can." I stood up. "Thanks for the beer."

He couldn't stand. He was back to looking at the ground.

"Yeah, thanks," he said, but his tone lacked sincerity. "I guess with some people, gratitude only lasts so long."

I weighed whether to respond or walk out. After a few seconds, I said, "I know I owe my life to you, Doug. I might never have found my way out of that smoke-filled basement. But you can't play that card every time. That's separate from this."

"Yeah, sure," he said, looking out over his yard. "And I guess, I guess you wouldn't want me making any calls."

That stopped me. "Calls about what?"

"I've known you a long time, Glenny. Long enough to know that not every job's on the books. Long enough to know you've got a secret or two yourself."

I stared at him.

"Tell me you don't have something tucked away for a rainy day." His voice was gaining confidence.

"Don't do this, Doug. It's beneath you."

"One anonymous phone call and you'd have the IRS so far up your ass they could count your cavities. But no—you can't help out a guy when he's having a few problems. Think about that, why don't ya, Glenny."

SEVENTEEN

Darren Slocum, standing out back of his house with cell phone in hand, made another call.

"Yes," said the man who answered.

"It's me. It's Slocum."

"I know who it is."

"Have you heard?"

"Have I heard what?"

"About my wife."

"Suppose you tell me."

"She's dead. She died last night. She went off the pier." Slocum waited for the man to say something. When he didn't, Slocum said, "You don't have anything to say? You're not curious about this? You don't have a single fucking question?"

"Where should I send flowers?"

"I know you saw Belinda last night. Put the fear of God into her. Did you call Ann? Did you ask her to meet you? Was it you? Did you fucking kill my wife, you fucking son of a bitch?"

"No." A pause. Then the man asked, "Did you?"

"What? No!"

The man said, "I drove past your place last night, must have been around ten or so. I didn't see your wife's car or your truck in the driveway. Maybe *you* threw her off the pier."

Slocum blinked. "I was out for just a couple of minutes. When Ann left I tried to follow her, but I didn't know which way she'd gone and I came home."

Neither of them spoke for a couple of seconds. Finally, the man said, "Is there anything else?"

"Anything else? *Anything else?*"

"Yes. Is there anything else. I'm not a grief counselor. I'm not interested in what happened to your wife. I'm a businessman. You owe me money. When you call me, I expect news on how you're coming along with that."

"You'll get your money."

"I told your friend she had two days. And that was a day ago. I'm willing to give you a similar deadline."

"Look, if you could give me some extra time, there's going to be some money. This wasn't how I was expecting to pay you back, but Ann . . . she had life insurance. We just got these policies, so when they pay up, there'll be more than enough—"

"You owe me money now."

"Look, it'll *come*. And right now, I'm planning a funeral, for Christ's sake."

The man at the other end said, "I'm sure your wife told you what she witnessed when she delivered a payment to me down on Canal Street."

The dead Chinese merchant. The two women in the wrong place at the wrong time.

"Yes," Slocum said.

"He owed money, too."

"Okay, okay," Slocum said. "The thing is, in the meantime, I think I may know where the money is."

"*The* money?"

"Garber told Belinda the car didn't totally burn up. They recovered her purse, and there was no money in it."

"Go on."

"I mean, I suppose it could have been somewhere else in the car, like the glove compartment, but I'm thinking, it makes the most sense that if she had the envelope with her, she'd have had it in her purse."

"Unless," the man said, "one of the first officers at the scene, one with your sterling ethical code, found it."

"I've worked a lot of accident scenes, and believe me, a cop, rifling through a dead woman's purse, I don't see it. I mean, the most you could expect is a few bucks or some credit cards. No one's expecting to find an envelope with more than sixty grand in it."

"Then, where is it?"

"Maybe she never intended to deliver it. Maybe she kept it for herself. Her husband's company's got financial problems."

The man was quiet.

"You there?"

"I'm thinking," the man said. "She called me, earlier that day, left a message. Said she'd run into a problem, was going to be delayed. Maybe the problem was her husband. He saw the money, took it from her."

"It's a possibility," Slocum said.

Several seconds of silence. Then: "I'm going to do you a favor. Consider it a bereavement leave. I'll see Garber."

"Okay, but listen, I know you'll do what you've got to do, but just don't do anything in front of—I mean, the guy's got a kid."

"A kid?"

"A daughter, same age as mine. They're friends."

"Perfect."

EIGHTEEN

My father was a good man.

He took pride in his work. He believed in giving 110 percent. He felt that if you treated others with respect, you'd get it in return. He didn't cut corners. If he bid twenty grand to remodel someone's kitchen, it was because he believed that's what the job was worth. For that money, he'd provide quality materials and excellent workmanship. If someone told him they could get someone to do it for fourteen, Dad would say, "If you want a fourteen-thousand-dollar job, then that's the guy you should go with, and God bless you." And when those people called him later, wanting him to fix everything the other contractor did wrong, Dad would find a nice way to tell them they'd made their choice, and now they had to live with it.

You couldn't do an under-the-table job with Dad. People were always taken aback by that. They thought, if they paid in cash, Dad could cut them some slack on the price because he wouldn't have to declare the income.

"I pay my taxes," Dad used to say. "I wouldn't go so far as to say I'm always thrilled about it, but it's the right thing to do, goddamn it. When I call the cops at one in the morning because someone's trying to break in to my house, I want them to show up. I don't want to hear I'm on my own because they've had to lay off cops because there's not enough money in the budget to pay 'em. People not paying their taxes, that hurts all of us. It's bad for the community."

It was not a commonly held opinion. Not back then, and not now. But I respected him for it. My father was a principled individual, sometimes to the point of driving my mother and me crazy. But he held to his beliefs. He was no hypocrite.

He would have had a dim view of some of the things I'd done.

I consider myself a pretty law-abiding individual. I don't rob banks. When I find a lost wallet, I don't empty it of cash and then pitch it into the garbage. I make sure it gets returned to its rightful owner. I try, within reason, to keep to the speed limit. I signal my turns.

I've never killed anyone, or even hurt anyone. A couple of bar fights in my youth, sure. I gave as good as I got, and afterward, we all had a few more drinks and forgot about it.

I've never gotten behind the wheel drunk.

And, every year, I've filed my return and paid my taxes. Just not all of them.

But, I admit, there have been times over the years when things were slow, when I have participated in the so-called "underground economy." A few hundred here, a couple of grand there. Usually jobs that did not go through the company. Jobs I did on weekends, on my own time—when I was still working for my father, and since I took over running the company. A deck for someone down the street. Finishing off a basement for the neighbors. A new roof for a buddy's garage. Jobs that might be too small for the company, but were perfect for me.

Or, if I needed a bit of help, I'd bring in my good friend Doug. And I'd pay him out of the cash I got.

While I'd had to tap into it during lean times, I'd managed to sock most of it away. I didn't want a record of the money, so I didn't bank it. I kept it at home, concealed behind a removable strip of wood paneling in my downstairs office. Sheila and I were the only ones who knew the cash—just under seventeen thousand dollars—was hidden there.

Although Doug didn't know how much I'd managed to save, or where I kept it, he knew I'd made money that was never reported. So had he, for that matter. But when he made his threat, he knew I had more at stake. I owned the company.

I hadn't ripped off the government for millions. I wasn't Enron or Wall Street. But I'd hung on to a few thousand the IRS would have been quite happy to pocket for themselves. If they found out, and could prove I owed them money, I'd find a way, over time, to pay them back.

But not before they'd turned my life inside out. They'd audit me, and when they were done doing that, they'd audit Garber Contracting. I knew those books were clean as a whistle, but it'd probably cost me several grand in accountants' fees to prove it.

I knew what my father would say, if he were alive today. He'd sing me a few of the old standards. "You reap what you sow," he'd have said. "If you'd kept your nose clean, you wouldn't be in this mess."

And he'd be right.

Later on Saturday, I grabbed my tools and rang Joan Mueller's doorbell. She looked delighted to see me. She was in a pair of jean shorts and a man's white dress shirt, the tails knotted at the front.

"I almost forgot," I said. "About the tap."

"Come in, come in. Don't worry about your shoes, keep them on, it's okay, God knows if I was worried about the carpets I wouldn't be taking in half a dozen kids every day, would I?" She laughed.

"No, I guess not," I said. I'd been in this house before and knew my way to the kitchen. There was half a bottle of Pinot Grigio on the kitchen table, and a nearly empty wineglass not far from it. Between the two, an issue of *Cosmopolitan*.

"Can I get you a beer?" Joan asked.

"I'm fine."

"Are you sure?" She opened the fridge. "I've got some Bud, a couple of Coors, and a Sam Adams. I seem to remember Sheila saying you liked Sam Adams."

"Thanks, but I'm okay."

She looked disappointed as she closed the fridge. "I didn't think there was a man alive who didn't like a cold beer."

"It's this one?" I asked, setting my toolbox on the counter next to the sink.

"Yup," she said.

The tap wasn't dripping. "It looks fine." I turned the cold on, then off, then did the same with the hot.

"It's kind of intermittent," Joan said. "It'll do it and then it won't. It won't do it all day, then I'll be in bed and I can hear it going *drip, drip, drip,* just driving me mad till I come down here and turn the taps off harder."

I'd been staring at the end of the faucet for nearly a minute and not a single drop had come out of it. "It looks okay, Joan. If it starts up again, give me a shout."

"Well, I'm really sorry to have put you to any trouble. I feel like a total idiot. Why don't you sit down for a second, anyway."

I took a seat across from her at the kitchen table.

"So, Joan, tell me again about this conversation you had with Sheila, about Mr. Bain."

She waved a hand dismissively at me. "It's no big deal."

"But you told her about him. About his son saying he beat up on his wife."

"Well, little Carlson didn't say that exactly, but it was certainly my take on the matter."

"And you talked to Sheila about whether you should call the police?"

Joan nodded. "I wasn't going to do it, and I wondered, maybe she did, but you know, she never mentioned anything." She smiled sympathetically at me. "I guess, in the bigger scheme of things, it doesn't really matter now, whether she did or not."

I thought about that. "I suppose. Except for the fact that this jerk may still be beating up on his wife. And wondering whether you might have called the cops about him. Maybe what you should do is, tell him you're cutting back, you've got too many kids, and give him two weeks' notice to find someplace else to put his kid."

"I don't know about that," she said. "I mean, he's going to know I'm singling him out. And what's to say, even if I don't look after his kid anymore, that he won't come back here to get even if he thinks I've ratted him out?" She filled her wineglass. "But I'm only going to have to do this for a little while longer anyway. Once the settlement comes in . . . did I tell you about that?"

"Yes, you did."

"Half a mil is what they tell me." She downed a third of the glass in one swig. "I'll be fixed pretty good. I guess I'd still work—five hundred grand won't last forever—but I'd stop babysitting. It's too hard, too stressful. House is always a mess." She paused. "I like to keep a neat house. And

I'd still look after Kelly, after she gets home from school. I'll always be happy to do that for you. She's a wonderful child. Have I told you that? She's just wonderful. It must be terrible for her, not having a mother."

She reached out and patted my hand appreciatively, letting it linger for just a second.

"Sheila was so lucky to have you," she said.

"I should be going," I said.

"You sure about that beer? It's no fun to drink alone, although if you have no choice . . ." She laughed.

"I'm positive." I stood, grabbed my toolbox, and found my way out.

I lay awake most of Saturday night, wondering whether Darren Slocum would show up the following day, insisting again that he talk to Kelly. I hoped I'd given him enough that he wouldn't feel the need. I kept wondering about the significance of Ann's phone call, the one Kelly'd overheard. I wondered whom she might have been talking to, and why she didn't want her husband to know. And why he was so determined to find out.

When I wasn't worrying about Darren, I was thinking about Doug, and whether I should throw a few hundred bucks his way. Not because I actually believed he'd bring the wrath of the IRS down on me. I was convinced it wasn't a serious threat on his part. Despite some of our differences, we'd been friends a long time. I was debating whether to give him some money because he needed it. But I also knew if I started giving him extra money, it would never end. I didn't have enough, not even taking into account what I had hidden behind the paneling, to solve Doug and Betsy's financial crisis.

I tossed and turned and thought about that house of mine that had burned down. I thought about whether the insurance company would cover my losses. I worried about whether the economy was going to pick up, whether there'd be any work for Garber Contracting five months from now.

I thought about the kids who called Kelly "Boozer the Loser."

I thought about the man Joan Mueller was worried about, and the unwelcome interest she seemed to be taking in me. Sheila had told me one time, jokingly, that I better watch out for her. This was even before Ely died on the oil rig. Sheila'd said, "I know that look she gives you. It's the same one I gave you. Of course," she'd smiled, "that was a long time ago."

I thought, briefly, about Belinda Morton, and her strange question about whether there'd been an envelope in Sheila's purse.

But mostly, I thought about Sheila.

"Why?" I said, staring up at the ceiling, unable to sleep. "Why did you do it?"

Still so angry with her.

And needing her so desperately.

When Kelly came through the door just after six on Sunday, I was expecting her to be followed in by Marcus and Fiona. But it turned out to be just Marcus.

"Where's your grandmother?" I asked Kelly.

"Marcus brought me by himself," she said. Kelly never referred to Fiona's second husband as "Grandpa" or "my grandfather." Fiona wouldn't allow it. "So we could have some 'just us' time."

Marcus smiled sheepishly. "Whenever it's the three of us, it's all girl stuff. So I asked Fiona to let me bring her back on my own."

"And she let you?" I asked.

He nodded, acknowledging that it was quite a triumph. "I think she was feeling a bit off, to tell you the truth."

Kelly asked, "What smells?"

"That's lasagna."

"You bought some lasagna?"

"I *made* some lasagna."

Kelly's look bordered on outright fear. "We had chicken fingers on the way back."

"It's true," Marcus said. "Glen, I wonder if you might have a moment . . ."

"Yeah, sure," I said. "Kelly, honey, why don't you head up to your room and unpack?"

"I didn't pack anything when I left, remember?"

"Then just scoot."

She gave me a hug and did, and Marcus came into the kitchen, pulled out a chair, and made himself comfortable at the table. Although, to be honest, he didn't look all that comfortable.

"So how are you doing?" he asked. "I mean, *really*?"

I shrugged. "Like my dad used to say, you play the hand you're dealt."

"Know what my dad used to say?" Marcus countered.

"I give up."

"'That lady over there's got a nice ass.'" He lightly slapped his palm on the table. "I thought that was funny."

"Sorry, Marcus. I'm not much for laughs these days."

"I know. Forgive me. You just made me think of my old man. He was a son of a bitch." He smiled wistfully. "And yet, my mom, she always took him back. I guess because deep down, no matter what he did that might make you think otherwise, he loved us." His smile seemed to wash away, and he looked a little lost.

When he didn't speak for a moment, I said, "I'm guessing something's on your mind."

"Yeah, I guess there is."

"Something you don't want to talk about with Fiona here." A nod. "Does that mean it's about Fiona?"

"I'm worried about her," he said. "She's taking all of this very hard. Losing a daughter and all."

"Luckily, she has me to blame. That must help."

Marcus shook his head. "She'd never show it in front of you, but I think she blames herself as much as she does you. Maybe more."

I got out the bottle of scotch and two tumblers. I poured us each two fingers and handed him his glass. He knocked it all back at once. I didn't take all that much longer.

"Go on," I told him.

"She goes into the bedroom and closes the door and I can hear her crying in there. One time I heard her saying, between sobs, that it was her fault. I asked her about it later and she denied even saying it. But I think she's been asking herself what she's been asking you—why didn't she see the signs? Why didn't she notice that there was something wrong with Sheila?"

"She's never indicated to me she'd like to shoulder any of this guilt I'm carrying around."

"Fiona can be a difficult woman," Marcus said. "I know that, Glen. But beneath that tough exterior, there is a heart."

"She probably ripped it out of someone else's chest and put it there," I said.

He grimaced. "Yeah, well." He shook his head. "There's something else."

"About Fiona?"

"About Fiona." He paused. "And Kelly."

"What?"

"A couple of things, actually. First, this idea of Fiona's to have Kelly come live with us and go to school in Darien, I'm okay with it but—"

"It's not going to happen," I said. "I don't want her gone from me five days out of every seven. That's just not on."

"Well, I kind of agree with you, but for a different reason."

"What reason?"

"Fiona's got money problems."

I poured myself another scotch. Marcus held out his tumbler and I obliged. "What's going on, Marcus?"

"I guess you've heard about this Karnofsky guy."

The Wall Street investment genius who turned out to be running a massive Ponzi scheme. Countless people had lost millions of dollars and were never going to get a cent of it back. "I watch the news," I said.

"Fiona had a lot of her money invested with his company."

"How much?"

"About eighty percent of it."

I felt my eyebrows soar. "How much is gone?"

"She doesn't share all her financial details with me, but from what I can tell, we're talking about two million, give or take."

"Holy shit," I said.

"Yeah."

"What's she going to do?"

"Even if she loses the two mil, she won't starve. But she's going to have to cut back quite a bit. She'll still have some of her nest egg, but she knows it still has to last a few years. And when she started talking about sending Kelly to school—Glen, you got any idea how much those schools cost?"

"More for a semester than I charge to build a house."

"About that. So if you're against the idea, I think you just have to put your foot down. In a way, it'll be a relief to her. She'll have made the offer, and felt good about doing it, but she'll have to defer to you."

"You said there were a couple of things."

"Yeah, well, Fiona started pushing Kelly pretty hard about this sleepover thing and what happened there."

"She did? Why?"

"I don't know. Kelly was getting really upset. I really had to get tough with Fiona, tell her to lay off. The kid's been through a lot, and Fiona wasn't making things any better, putting Kelly through a goddamn cross-examination."

"Why would she do that?" I asked.

Marcus threw back his second scotch, and said, "You know Fiona. She's always got some kind of hidden agenda."

Kelly came downstairs and didn't make much of the fact that Marcus had left without saying goodbye. "He seemed tired," she told me. "He said we'd do lots of talking but he hardly said a thing."

"Maybe he's got a lot on his mind," I said.

I'd taken the lasagna out of the oven and it was cooling atop the stove. Kelly inspected it, gave it a sniff.

"It's supposed to have sauce on the top," she said.

"Well, I put cheese there instead."

She took a fork from the cutlery drawer and dug into the middle of it. "Where's the ricotta? Is there ricotta?"

"Ricotta?" I said.

"And you used the wrong dish to make it in," she said. "It'll taste funny if you make it in a different dish."

"It was the only one I could find. Look, do you want to eat it or not?"

"I'm not hungry."

"I'm going to try it." I shoveled some onto a plate and grabbed a fork from the drawer. Kelly took a seat to watch me, like I was a science experiment or something.

"Something happened that'll make you mad," she said.

"What's that?"

"Grandma took me around to a couple of the schools I could go to. But I only got to see them from the outside because it was the weekend."

"I'm not mad."

"If I did go to school there, would you come and live with me at Grandma and Marcus's? My room there is really big. They could put another bed in there. But you wouldn't be allowed to snore."

"You won't be going to school in Darien," I said. "I'm going to see if there's another school here in town, if you still want to switch."

Kelly thought about that a moment. Then she said, "So, Emily's dad came over here yesterday?"

"That's right."

"Did he come by to give us an invitation to the funeral?"

"No. And that's not exactly how it works. People don't go around inviting—let's not worry about that now."

"So why did he come over?"

"He wanted to be sure you were okay, you being Emily's best friend and all."

She digested that, but she still looked worried. "There was nothing else?"

"Like what?" I asked.

"He didn't want anything back?"

I focused in on her. "Like what?"

Kelly was suddenly looking very anxious. "I don't know."

"Kelly, what would he want back?" I asked.

"I already got in trouble for being in their bedroom. I don't want to get into any more trouble."

"You're not in trouble."

"But I'm gonna be," she said, starting to tear up.

"Kelly, did you take something from the Slocums' bedroom?"

"I didn't mean to," she said.

"How could you not mean to take something?"

"When I was in the closet, there was a purse bumping up against my foot, so I reached down to move it, and there was something clinking inside it, so I took it out, but it was too dark to see what it was, so I put it in my pocket."

"Kelly, for God's sake."

"I just wanted to see what it was, and when Emily found me and I could see, I'd look at what it was. But then Emily didn't come in, her mom did, so I just left it in my pocket. It kind of made my pocket stick out, so I sort of held my hand over it when Mrs. Slocum made me stand in the middle of the room."

Wearily, I closed my eyes. "What was it? Jewelry? A watch?" She shook her head. "Do you still have it? Is it here?"

"I hid it in my shoe bag." Her eyes were large and moist.

"Go get it."

She ran to her bedroom and was back in under a minute, carrying by its drawstring a blue gingham bag with a sailboat on the side.

She handed it to me. Whatever was inside was heavier than I expected. I felt the item through the fabric before opening the bag, and my guess was that Kelly had left the Slocum house with a pair of bracelets.

I reached into the bag and took out the item. Heavy, bright and shiny, with a nickel finish.

"It's handcuffs," Kelly informed me.

"Yeah," I said. "So they are."

NINETEEN

"You think Mr. Slocum came over because he wanted these back?" Kelly asked. "You're sure he didn't ask for them?"

"He definitely did not." I was examining the cuffs, which had a tiny key stuck to them with a piece of clear tape. I returned Kelly's empty shoe bag to her. "If these were in his wife's purse, he might not even know about them."

"She's not a police lady."

"I know."

"But maybe sometimes she helped Mr. Slocum when he was being a policeman."

"I suppose that's possible."

"Are you going to give them back?" she asked. She sounded frightened.

I took a long breath. "No," I said. "I think we'll just forget about this."

"But I did the wrong thing," Kelly said. "I kind of stole them. But not really. I just didn't want Emily's mom to know I'd taken them from her purse."

"Why didn't you put them back when Mrs. Slocum left you in the room?"

"I was scared. She made me stand in the middle of the room, and if I was in the closet when she came back I thought I'd get in even more trouble."

I gave Kelly a hug. "It's okay."

"What if we put them in a box and mailed them to Mr. Slocum but you didn't write on the box who it was from?"

I shook my head. "Sometimes people just lose things. If he even knows about these, he probably won't be looking for them for a very long time."

"But what if a bad guy breaks in to their house at night and Mr. Slocum goes to get the handcuffs from the purse to keep him there until other police come?"

It was a relief I didn't have to explain what, exactly, I thought they might have been used for. "I'm sure that won't happen," I told my daughter. "And we're not going to talk about this again."

I shooed Kelly off and put the cuffs in the drawer of my bedside table. Maybe, when it was trash day, I'd drop these into a garbage bag and send them off on their way. My guess was, if these cuffs were in Ann Slocum's purse, not only did her husband not have a clue about them, they weren't being used in the Slocum house at all. No wonder she didn't want Kelly telling her husband about the call.

I wondered whose wrists had been of such concern to her.

I drove Kelly to school in the morning. "And I'll be picking you up, too," I said.

"Okay." That had been our routine for the last week, ever since Kelly had gone back to school since Sheila's death. "How long are you going to do this for?"

"For a while," I said.

"I think I can start riding my bike again soon."

"Probably. But we'll do this for a little longer, if that's okay with you."

"Okay," she said, with some dejection in her voice.

"And if Mr. Slocum shows up at the school, wanting to see you, you're not to talk to him. Go find a teacher if he does."

"Why would he do that? Because of the handcuffs?"

"Look, I'm not expecting him to do anything, but just in case. And we're not talking about the handcuffs anymore, and you're not to tell any of your friends about them."

"Not even Emily?"

"Especially not Emily. No one, you understand?"

"Okay. But I can talk to Emily about other things, right?"

"She won't be at school today. She'll go back in a few days, I'd guess."

"But I still talk to her online."

Of course. I was thinking like someone from another century.

Kelly asked, "Are we going to the visitation?" A word she didn't even know a month ago. "Emily said there's a visiting today and she wants me to come."

I wasn't so sure that was a good idea. First of all, I was worried it would be upsetting for Kelly. She'd just been to her mother's funeral, and wept through most of it. I was worried about how she'd handle another one so soon. Second, I didn't want her anywhere near Darren Slocum.

"I don't know, sweetheart."

"I have to go," she said. "To the visiting."

"No, you don't. People would understand if you didn't go."

"You mean, they'd think I didn't want to go? Because that's not true. I don't want people thinking I'm a chicken."

"You're not—that's not what they'd think."

"That's what I'd think. I'd think I was a huge pussy for not going."

"A what?"

She blushed. "A chicken. And besides, Emily and her parents came to Mom's funeral."

Kelly was right about that. The Slocums had been there. But a lot had changed in the interim. And the situation between us and the Slocums was different.

"If I don't go, then Emily will hate me forever," she said. "If that's what you want, then I guess I won't go."

I glanced over at her. "What time's the visitation?"

"It's at three."

"Okay, I'll pick you up at school at two. We go home and get changed, and we go to the visitation. But here's the deal: You stay with me. You don't wander out of my sight. Are we clear?"

Kelly nodded. "Got it. And you won't forget your promise, will you?"

We had reached her school. I pulled over to the curb. "I won't forget."

"You know which one I mean?"

"I know which one you mean. About looking into another school for you."

"Okay, I was just checking."

From there, I went into work, and told Sally I'd left her some phone message details.

"Done," she said.

"And there were some other voicemails—"

"And done," she said. "Okay, some of the places, they weren't in yet, but I left messages."

"Anyone looking for estimates?" I asked.

"Sorry, boss."

We did a quick review of what work we did have going on. Our three active job sites were a kitchen renovation in Derby, a double garage in Devon out back of someone's house, and finishing off the basement of a five-year-old house in East Milford. For the first time in a couple of years, we weren't building an actual house from the ground up.

"Stewart and KF are at the garage," she said. Stewart was our Canadian kid, and "KF" referred to Ken Wang, and was actually an abbreviated version of his nickname, which was Kentucky Fried Wang, or KFW, given that he hailed from the South. "Doug's headed off to Derby, and there's no one at the basement reno."

"Okay."

"Can we talk?" she asked, coming into my office. "I feel bad about Saturday," she said, sitting down across from me.

"Don't worry about it," I said. "You and Theo okay?"

"I kind of chewed him out a bit after. I understand it's your company and you get to make the call about who works for you and who doesn't."

"Yup," I said.

"Even though I think he's a good electrician, you know? He's doing some work now in my dad's—in my house." Sally had moved in to her father's place as his health had declined. He'd been a crusty old bastard, but that had also been his charm. He'd been a Civil War fanatic, had a considerable gun collection, old and new, that he'd been very proud of—an enthusiasm I had not shared. I knew how to handle guns, but had never owned one. I hadn't shared many of his political views, either. He'd liked to argue incessantly that Richard M. Nixon was the best president the United States ever had, so long as you looked past that stupid shit he did opening up relations with China.

Sally quickly learned her father had no savings that would have allowed him to move in to a decent care facility, so she did the best she could, slipping out of the office at noon to make sure he'd eaten the lunch she'd left him, and that he'd taken his meds. The cost of prescriptions had been a killer. She'd spent what savings her father'd had on various drugs: insulin for diabetes, plus lisinopril, warfarin, and the heparin injections for his heart ailments. His Social Security didn't come close to covering it, so Sally began dipping into her own savings. Pretty much all the money she saved on rent after moving in with her dad was going to drugs. If he'd lived much longer, Sally probably would have had to sell the house and find a small apartment for the two of them. But now the place had been left to her.

"Theo replaced a lot of my old outlets and put a ceiling fixture in the front hall, and when he's done the bathroom it's going to have one of those heated floors. I can't wait to feel a warm floor under my toes when I get up on a cold morning. The tiling, well, that's another thing. He's doing that this week, and tiling's not really his area, you know, but I can get someone else to fix that up later. Maybe Doug, if he'd do it."

"Great," I said, and thought about the words we'd had on Saturday.

"All I'm saying is, I respect your decision, and I'll do what I can to make him respect it, too."

I didn't much care whether he respected it or not, just so long as he stayed away from any of my projects, but kept the thought to myself. "I appreciate that, Sally."

She gnawed her lip, like she was working up to something. "Glen . . ."

"What's on your mind?"

"What do you think of him? I mean, as a guy. A guy for me."

"Sally, I've known you a long time, even before you started babysitting for Kelly. And I've got no problem telling you what to do around the office, but your private life is none of my business."

"Okay, let's say you knew Theo and I hadn't met him yet, is he the kind of guy you'd set me up with?"

"I don't set people up."

Sally rolled her eyes. "God, you're impossible. Let's say I'd never met him, but saw him on the site, and I said to you, 'Hey, that guy, he's cute, should I let him ask me out?' What would you say?"

"He's . . . a good-looking guy. Handsome. I can see that. And it looks like he cares about you. And he can be polite, until he's . . . pushed."

She studied me. "There's a 'but' coming. I can tell."

For a moment, I considered dodging, but Sally deserved the truth from me. "I would say maybe you can do better."

"Well," Sally said. "So."

"You asked."

"And you delivered." She forced a grin and slapped her thighs. "Was that so hard?"

"Kinda."

"I mean, I know what you're saying. But what if I *can't* do better?"

"Don't sell yourself short, Sal."

"Come on, look at me," she said. "I'm, like, seven feet tall. I'm a circus freak."

"Stop it. You're gorgeous."

"And you're a skilled liar." She got up and lingered a minute at the door. "Thanks, Glen."

I smiled, then I fired up the computer and googled "Milford schools." First, I looked to see what might be the next-closest public elementary school, jotted down a couple of possibilities, then looked at the private schools. There were several Catholic ones, but I didn't know what the chances were of getting into one of those, considering we were not Catholic. We weren't much of anything, when you got right down to it. Sheila and I were never churchgoers, and had never had Kelly baptized, much to Fiona's horror.

I wrote down a few more school names and phone numbers, figuring I could make calls throughout the day when I had a minute. Plus, I left a message for Kelly's principal. Not to rat out the kids who'd called her Boozer, but to sound him out about moving her to another school, given the awkwardness of her situation.

Then I drove to our closest job, the double garage in Devon. The client, a retired insurance agent in his mid-sixties, had two classic Corvettes—a 1959 and a 1963 Sting Ray with the split rear window—but no place to properly store them.

It was a simple job. No basement, no plumbing, other than a spigot for car washing. Just a solid structure with storage units and a workbench, good lighting and plenty of electrical outlets. The client had said no to powered doors. He didn't want to risk them going haywire someday and coming down on one of his treasures.

As I got out of the truck, Ken Wang approached.

"Hey there, Mr. G, y'all lookin' fine today."

You never got used to it.

"Thanks, KF. How goes it here?"

"Excellent. I tell you, I'd give my left tit for one of these here 'Vettes."

"Nice cars."

"Some guy was sniffin' around earlier lookin' for ya."

"He say what it was about?"

Ken shook his head. "No. Might be more work. So don't go wanderin' off or nuthin'." He grinned at me.

I went into the new garage to see how it was coming. The interior walls were drywalled—I found a stamp on a drywall sheet to allay any fears that it might be that toxic stuff from China—and Stewart was getting ready to sand the seams. "Pretty good, eh?" he said.

After giving the two of them some guidance about where to put the shelving units, I walked back out to the truck to pour myself some coffee from my thermos and make a couple of school calls. A small blue car pulled up and a short man in a blue suit got out with an envelope in his hand. Maybe this was the guy Ken had seen earlier. As he approached the truck, I powered down the window.

"Glen Garber?" he said.

"That's the name on the truck," I quipped.

"But you *are* Mr. Garber?"

I nodded.

He handed the envelope to me through the window and said, "You've been served." Then he turned and walked away.

I set my thermos cup on the dashboard and tore open the envelope, withdrew the papers from inside, and unfolded them. Some law firm letterhead. I scanned the paperwork. It was written in legalese I could barely understand, but I was able to get the gist of it.

The Wilkinson family was suing me for $15 million. Negligence. The crux of it was this: I had failed to identify my wife's condition and intercede, which ultimately resulted in the death of Connor and Brandon Wilkinson.

I tried to read it more thoroughly but things seemed to go blurry. My eyes were tearing up. I closed them, leaned my head back against the headrest.

"Nice going, Sheila," I said.

TWENTY

"It's interesting, that's for sure," said Edwin Campbell, sitting in his legal office. He took off his wire-rimmed reading glasses and set them next to the papers I'd been delivered a couple of hours earlier. He shook his head. "A bit of a stretch, I think, but very interesting."

"So you're saying, what, I don't have to worry about it?" I said, leaning forward in the leather padded chair. Edwin had been my father's lawyer for years, and I'd kept going to him not only out of family tradition and loyalty, but because he knew his stuff. I'd called him about the lawsuit right after the papers had been served, and he'd agreed to get me in to his office right away.

"Well, now, I wouldn't go so far as to say that," Campbell replied. "There's plenty of nuisance cases that have taken years to work their way through the system and needlessly cost people a considerable sum to defend themselves. So we're going to have to respond to this. They'll have to produce evidence you knew Sheila had a drinking problem and that it was very likely you knew she would get behind the wheel of a car in an inebriated condition."

"I've told you I never noticed any—"

Edwin waved a hand at me. "I know what you've said. And I believe you. But I think—and I'm sure you've done this already—but I think you need to go over everything about Sheila in your head one more time. Is there something you've overlooked, something maybe you've ignored be-cause you haven't wanted to acknowledge it? Something you don't want to admit to yourself? This is the time you need to be honest with yourself, painfully so, because if there's something out there, some small shred of evidence that suggests you could have reasonably assumed that Sheila was capable of doing what she did, we need to confront that and deal with it."

"I told you, there's nothing."

"You never saw your wife under the influence?"

"What, *never*?"

"That's what I asked you."

"Well, shit, of course, there were times when she'd had enough to feel it. Who hasn't?"

"Describe these circumstances."

"I don't know—Christmas, family gatherings, an anniversary maybe, if we'd been out to dinner. Parties."

"So Sheila had a habit of drinking too much at all those kinds of events?"

I blinked. "Jesus Christ, Edwin!"

"I'm just playing devil's advocate, Glen. But you see how these things can turn bad in a hurry. I know and you know there's a huge gulf between having a couple of drinks at Christmas and getting behind the wheel when you shouldn't. But all Bonnie Wilkinson needs is a handful of witnesses from those types of occasions, where you might have been present, to start building a case."

"Well, she's going to have a hard time doing that," I said.

"What about Belinda Morton?"

"Huh? Belinda was a friend of Sheila's. What about her?"

"I made a couple of calls before you came over, one to Barnicke and Trundle, the firm that's handling this for Mrs. Wilkinson, and they weren't afraid to tip their hand to me, suggesting that we might want to settle this thing before we even get to court."

"What are you talking about?"

"They already have a statement from Ms. Morton that when she and Sheila and another woman would go out for lunch, they'd get pretty looped."

"So maybe they had a few drinks. Sheila always took a cab home from those. She usually took a cab *to* those, since she knew she might be having a few."

"Really?" Edwin said. "So she'd go to lunch knowing full well she'd be having a lot to drink?"

"It's not like they got drunk. They just had a good time at lunch. You're making too much out of it."

"It won't be me who does it." He paused. "There's also this thing about marijuana."

"About what?"

"Belinda has apparently said she and Sheila smoked it."

"*Belinda* said that?" This woman, who was supposedly my wife's friend?

"So they say. They are, I understand, only alleging a single incident. A year ago, at the Morton home, in the backyard. Apparently the husband arrived and became quite perturbed."

I was shaking my head in disbelief. "What's she trying to do to us? To Kelly and me?"

"I don't know. To give her the benefit of the doubt, she may not have appreciated the implications of her comments when she was making them. My understanding is it was her husband, George, who felt she had an obligation to be forthcoming."

I slumped down in the chair. "That guy's got a pole up his ass. Even if they could prove Sheila liked to have a glass of wine or a Cosmo at lunch, how do they go from there to proving that it's my fault that she might have gotten behind the wheel drunk the night of the accident?"

"Like I said, it's a stretch. But anything can happen where a case like this is concerned, so we have to take this seriously. Leave it with me for now. I'll draft a response and run it by you."

I felt my world unraveling. Just when you thought things couldn't get any worse. "God, what a week."

Edwin looked up from the note he was making. "What?"

"I still don't know what's going to happen with the insurance on that house that burned down. I got a guy working for me who's going into financial ruin and keeps hitting me up for pay advances. Kids are calling my daughter Boozer at school because of Sheila's accident, plus her friend's mother died in an accident a couple of nights ago, and the woman's husband is bugging me because of some phone call Kelly heard when she was over there for a sleepover. On top of all that, the Wilkinsons want to sue my ass off."

"Whoa," said Edwin.

"Yeah, no shit."

"No, go back a bit."

"Which thing?"

"Your daughter's friend's mother died and what?"

I told him about Ann Slocum's death, and how Darren Slocum had come over demanding to know what Kelly had heard at the sleepover.

"Ann would have been that other woman at the lunches," I added glumly.

"Well, this is interesting," Edwin said.

"Yeah."

"Did you say Darren Slocum?"

"That's right."

"Milford cop?"

"Right again. You know him?"

"I know *of* him."

"That sounds ominous," I said.

"There've been at least two internal investigations concerning him, that I know of. Broke one guy's arm during an arrest following a bar fight. In the other incident, he was being looked into for some missing drug money, but I'm pretty sure that one was dismissed. There were half a dozen cops who had access to the evidence, so there was no way they could pin it on him."

"How do you know this?"

"You think I just sit here all day and work on my stamp collection?"

"So he's a bad cop."

Edwin paused a moment before answering, as if there might be others in the room and he didn't want to get sued for slander.

"Let's say he's got a cloud over him."

"Sheila was a friend of his wife's."

"I don't know that much about his wife. Other than that she wasn't his first."

"I never knew he was married before," I said.

"Yeah. When someone was telling me about his troubles, it came up that he was married years ago."

"Divorced?"

"She died."

"Of?"

"No idea."

I thought about that, then, "Maybe this all starts to fit. Him being a sketchy cop, his wife selling knockoff designer purses out of their house. I think they were bringing in good money with the purses." I didn't mention that it was probably all off the books. People in glass houses and all that.

Edwin's lips puckered. "The force might take a dim view of a cop and his wife selling knockoff merchandise. It's illegal. Not owning a knockoff bag, but making them and selling them."

"When Slocum came to see me, Saturday morning, he was pretty rattled. There seemed to be, in his mind, some connection between the phone call his wife took and the accident that killed her."

"Explain."

"I guess if she hadn't been going out to meet whoever called her, she might have had that flat tire some other time, in a safer place, and never would have fallen into the water and died."

Edwin's lips did some more puckering.

"What are you thinking?" I asked.

"Do you know whether the police are treating Ann Slocum's death as suspicious?"

"I have no idea."

Edwin moved his tongue across the front of his teeth. I'd seen him do this before when he was deep in thought.

"Glen," he said tentatively.

"I'm right here."

"Do you believe in coincidences?"

"Not so much," I said. I had a pretty good idea where he was going.

"Your wife loses her life in an accident that is, I think we would concur, difficult to reconcile. About two weeks later, her friend is killed in another accident, the circumstances of which are curious, if not equally so. I'm sure this has not escaped your attention."

"No," I said, and felt myself roiling inside. "It hasn't. But, Edwin, beyond that observation, I don't know what to make of it. Look, you know that trying to make sense of what Sheila did, how she died—it's all I've been thinking about. What did I miss? How could I not have known she had some kind of problem? Christ, Edwin, she didn't even like vodka, so far as I knew, and yet there was an empty bottle of it in her car."

Edwin strummed the fingers of his left hand on his desk. He cast an eye toward his bookshelf. "You know I've always been an Arthur Conan Doyle admirer. A fan, I suppose."

I followed his eye. I stood, took a step closer to the shelves, and tilted my head slightly to read the words on the spines. *A Study in Scarlet. The Adventures of Sherlock Holmes. The Sign of the Four.*

"They look really old," I said. "May I?"

Edwin nodded and I pulled out one of the books, opened it delicately. "Are these all first editions?"

"No. Although I do have some, sealed and safely put away. One that's actually signed by the author. Are you familiar with the works?"

"I can't say that I—maybe the one about the hound. The Baskervilles, isn't it? When I was a kid. And Sheila and I saw that movie, the one with the guy who also played Iron Man."

Edwin closed his eyes briefly. "An abomination," he said. "Not *Iron Man.* I liked that." He looked disappointed, possibly at the gaps in my literary education. There were many.

"Glen, let me ask you this, a straightforward question. Do you believe it is at all possible—even remotely so—that Sheila would willfully consume a bottle of vodka and bring about the accident that took her life and the lives of two others? Knowing what you do about her?"

I swallowed. "No. It's impossible. But yet—"

"In *The Sign of the Four,* Holmes says, and I think I have this right, 'When you have eliminated the impossible, whatever remains, however improbable, must be the truth.' You know the phrase?"

"I think I've heard it. So you're saying, if it's impossible that Sheila would do such a thing, then there must be some other explanation for what happened, even if it seems . . . really out there."

Edwin nodded. "In a nutshell."

"What other explanations could there be?"

He shrugged. "I don't know. But in light of these recent developments, I really think you need to be considering them."

TWENTY-ONE

I was driving away from Edwin's office when my cell rang. It was one of the private schools I'd called. The woman answered my questions about tuition fees (higher than I expected), whether Kelly would be allowed to switch in the middle of the school year (she would), and whether her academic record qualified her for admission (maybe).

"And of course you know we are a residential school," she told me. "Our students live here."

"But we already live in Milford," I explained. "Kelly would be able to live at home with me."

"That's not the way we do it," the woman stated. "We believe in a more immersive educational experience."

"Thanks anyway," I said. That was just dumb. If Kelly was going to be right in town with me, she was going to live with me. Maybe some parents were happy to farm their kids off to a school 24/7, but I wasn't one of them.

I phoned Sally to remind her that I was going to the visitation for Ann Slocum and likely wouldn't be at the office or at any of our job sites the rest of the day. When I got to Kelly's school I parked and went into the office to tell them I was taking her out of school for the afternoon. The woman in the office said a couple of other kids, as well as Kelly and Emily's teacher, planned to attend.

When Kelly came into the office to meet me, she had a small envelope in her hand. She didn't look me in the eye when she held it out to me. I tore it open and read the note as we headed out to the truck.

"What's this?" I asked. "This is from your teacher?"

Kelly mumbled something that sounded remotely like a yes.

"You stomped on another kid's foot? You did it *again*?"

She whipped her head around to look at me. Her eyes were red. "He called me Boozer. So I let him have it. Did you find me a new school yet?"

I put my hand on her back and guided her across the parking lot. "Let's go home. You need to get changed for the visitation."

I was in the bedroom, taking a third run at doing up my tie so the broad end wasn't shorter than the thin, when Kelly appeared. She was wearing a simple navy blue dress—something her mother had bought for her at the Gap—and matching tights.

"Does this look okay?" she asked.

She looked beautiful. "Perfect," I said.

"Are you sure?"

"Positive."

"Okay." She scampered off, and just in time. I didn't want her to see my face. It was the first time that she had ever asked her father for an opinion on an outfit.

The funeral home was just off the downtown green. The parking lot was full. A number of the cars were police cruisers. I took Kelly by the hand as we walked across the lot. Once we were inside, a man in a perfect black suit directed us to the reception room for the Slocum family.

"Remember, stick close," I whispered down to her.

"I know."

We'd barely stepped into the room, where about thirty people were milling about chatting in subdued tones, awkwardly holding coffee cups and saucers, when Emily came charging in our direction. She wore a black dress with a white collar. She threw her arms around Kelly and the two girls clung to each other as though they'd not seen each other in years.

They both burst into tears.

Slowly, the small talk descended into a murmur as everyone focused on the two small girls, propping each other up, bonding in a way that few of us could imagine for ones so young. They were joined by grief, and a sympathy and understanding for each other.

I, like most everyone, felt overwhelmed. But I couldn't bear to see the two of them dealing with this alone, and so publicly, so I knelt down, touched a hand lightly to each of their backs, and said, "Hey."

Another woman knelt on the other side of them. She looked, at a glance, like Ann Slocum. She flashed me an awkward smile. "I'm Janice," she said. "Ann's sister."

"Glen," I said, taking a hand off Kelly's back and offering it.

"Why don't I get the girls some refreshments?" she said. "Somewhere a little more private."

I hadn't wanted to let Kelly out of my sight, but at that moment, letting the girls be together seemed to make a lot of sense. "Sure," I said. Janice led Kelly and Emily, walking with their arms around each other, out of the room. In one respect, however, I was relieved. Across the room, the casket containing the body of Ann Slocum, unlike my wife's, was open. I didn't want Kelly to see Emily's mother in repose. I didn't want to have to explain why Ann's face could be made suitable for viewing and her mother's could not.

"That just broke my heart," a woman said behind me. I turned. It was Belinda Morton. Standing beside her was her husband. "Never in my life have I seen anything so sad."

George Morton, in a black suit, white shirt with French cuffs, and a red tie, extended a hand. I took it, somewhat reluctantly, since he was reputedly the one who'd pushed his wife to open up to the Wilkinson lawyers.

"This is all just, so, I just don't know where to begin," Belinda said. "First Sheila, and now Ann. Two of my best friends."

I didn't have it in me to offer any words of comfort. I was too angry with Belinda. But this wasn't the time to get into that.

"We have to believe there's a purpose in the way life unfolds," George said, affecting his usual wise manner. I could see the purpose in punching him in the nose. He had a way about him, that he was smarter than the rest of us, talking down to us. Quite a trick, since he was an inch shorter. I had a good view of his comb-over. What surprised me, looking at his eyes beyond the lenses of his heavy, black-framed glasses, was how troubled he appeared. His eyes weren't red the way his wife's were, but they looked sorrowful and tired.

"It's a terrible thing," he said. "Such a shock. Just horrible."

"Where's Darren?" I asked.

"I've seen him around," Belinda said. "Did you want me to find him for you?"

"No, that's okay." I didn't want to talk to him, I just wanted to keep track of him. "Will you be home later?" I asked.

"I would imagine," she said.

"I'll give you a call."

She started to speak, then stopped herself. George was looking off to one side, at the other people paying their respects, and she took advantage of the moment to lean in and ask, "Did you find it?"

"I'm sorry?"

"The envelope? You found it? Is that why you want to call?"

I hadn't thought about that in a while. "No. It's something else."

She looked even more upset than when she'd watched the girls consoling each other.

"What?" George said, returning his gaze to us.

"Nothing," Belinda told him. "I'm just . . . Glen, it was nice to see you." There was nothing in her voice that suggested she meant it.

She steered George off in another direction to mingle. I had a sense Belinda knew exactly what I wanted to talk to her about. I wanted to deliver a few choice words about her decision to help Bonnie Wilkinson wipe me out financially.

I was left standing there with no one I immediately recognized to talk to. There were several tall, broad-shouldered men with short haircuts clustered together. Fellow cops—it didn't take a genius to figure it out—but Darren wasn't among them. I went over to where the coffee was set up and bumped shoulders with a short black woman doing the same thing.

"Excuse me," I said.

"No problem," she said. "I don't think we've met."

"Glen Garber." I put down my cup and saucer so we could shake hands.

"Rona Wedmore," she said.

"Were you a friend of Ann's?"

She shook her head. "I'd never met her. I'm with the Milford PD." She tipped her head in the direction of the men I'd just noticed. "I don't work directly with Darren, but we're always running into each other. I'm a detective."

"Pleased to meet you," I said, then added, "It always seems dumb to say 'pleased' or 'nice' to meet you at things like this."

Rona Wedmore nodded understandingly. "Sure." She looked at me curiously. "What did you say your name was again?"

"Garber. Glen Garber."

"Your daughter, she was staying over with the Slocums that night."

I wondered how she knew this, and whether she was somehow involved in the investigation of the accident.

"Well, Kelly was going to stay over, but she came home early." When Rona Wedmore narrowed her eyes, I added lamely, "She wasn't feeling well."

"She's okay now?"

"Yes, well, she's upset, too. Emily's her friend."

"Was that your daughter, was that Kelly that was just . . ."

"Yes."

"Your girl, she seemed to be taking her friend's mother's death pretty hard," the detective said.

"She lost her own mother—my wife, Sheila—a few weeks ago."

"I'm very sorry for your loss. Your wife, she . . ." Wedmore seemed to be processing information, trying to retrieve data buried in her head.

"An accident."

"Yes. Yes, I know the one."

"It wasn't in Milford."

She nodded. "But I'm aware of it."

"First Sheila, then Ann," I said. "I think it's hardest on the girls. Speaking of which, I'm going to find mine now, if you'll excuse me."

Wedmore smiled as I moved away. Carrying my coffee, I worked my way through the crowd and over to the door. I thought maybe I'd find the two girls out in the hall, but they weren't there. The funeral home had several other reception rooms, and as far as I could tell the only one in use was the one for the Slocums.

I moved down the hall, poking my head into one room, then the next. I heard someone scurrying behind me, and saw Emily. She was alone.

"Emily!" I called softly.

She whirled around. "Hi, Mr. Garber."

"Where's Kelly? Isn't she with you?"

The girl shook her head and pointed to a closed door. "She's in there." And then she darted off.

The door was marked KITCHEN and instead of a knob had a brass plate. I pushed and the door gave way on its swing hinges. It was bigger than a standard kitchen, no doubt used to prepare foods for events that demanded more than just coffee.

"Kelly?" I called.

I stepped into the room and saw Kelly sitting on one of the counters, her legs dangling over the side. Standing before her was Darren Slocum. He would have had to pick Kelly up for her to be sitting there, almost eye to eye with him.

"Glen," he said.

"Daddy," Kelly said, her eyes wide.

"What the hell are you doing?" I asked, closing the distance between Slocum and me.

"We were just talking," he said. "I was just asking Kelly here a couple of questions about—"

My fist caught him squarely on the chin. Kelly screamed as Slocum stumbled back into a shelving unit loaded with oversized pots. Two of them went crashing to the floor. Orchestra cymbals would have made less noise.

It wasn't long before the screams and the pots brought us an audience. One of the funeral home directors, a woman I didn't know, and a couple of big guys I suspected were cops burst through the door. They saw Slocum rubbing his chin, feeling the trickle of blood that was coming down from the corner of his mouth. And then they saw me, my hand still shaped into a fist.

The cops started to move on me.

"No, no!" Slocum said, holding up his hand. "It's okay. It's okay."

I pointed a finger at him and said, "Don't you ever, ever talk to my daughter again. Go near her again and I'll take a fucking two-by-four to your goddamn head."

I scooped Kelly up in my arms and headed for the parking lot.

I could just imagine what Sheila would have said. *"Punching out a guy at his own wife's visitation. Smooth."*

TWENTY-TWO

"What was he asking you?" I asked Kelly as we drove home.

"Why did you hit Emily's dad?" she whimpered. "Why did you *do* that?"

"I asked you a question. What was he talking to you about?"

"He wanted to know about the phone call."

"What did you tell him?"

"I said I wasn't supposed to talk about it anymore."

"And then what did he say?"

"He said he wanted me to think really hard about everything I'd heard and then you came in and then you hit him and now everyone's going to hate me. I can't believe you did that!"

I was gripping the wheel so hard my knuckles were white. "You know you were supposed to stay with me."

Tears running down her face, Kelly said, "You let me go with Emily's aunt."

"I know, I know, but I *told* you I didn't want you to talk to Mr. Slocum. Didn't I tell you that?"

"But he came into the kitchen and he told Emily to go and I didn't know what I was supposed to *do*!"

I realized, at that moment, how astonishingly unreasonable I was being. She was eight years old, for God's sake. What did I expect her to do? Tell Darren Slocum to piss off and walk out? I had no business being furious with her. I could be furious with him, and I could certainly be furious with myself for letting her out of my sight. But I had no reason to take it out on Kelly.

"I'm sorry. I'm sorry. I'm not mad at you. I'm not—"

"I hate you. I just hate you."

"Kelly, please."

"Don't talk to me," she said, and turned her back to me.

We didn't say anything else to each other the whole way home. When we got there, she ran straight to her room and slammed the door.

I went into the kitchen and put a tumbler and the bottle of scotch on the table. I poured myself a drink. By the time I reached for the phone some twenty minutes later, I'd refilled my glass twice. I punched in a number.

The phone picked up after two rings. "Hello? Glen?"

Belinda had been looking at the caller ID. "Yes."

"My God, Glen, what happened? Everyone's talking about it. You *hit* Darren? Is that what you did? With his wife dead in the next room? Did you really do that? You couldn't possibly have done that."

"What the hell did you tell them, Belinda?"

"What?"

"The lawyers."

"Glen, I don't know what—"

"You make Sheila having a drink at lunch sound like she's an alcoholic, and then you tell them about the time the two of you smoked some marijuana?"

"Glen, please, I never meant—"

"Where's your head at?"

"What was I supposed to do, lie?" she asked. "I get called into a law office and I'm supposed to lie?"

"You didn't have to *lie,*" I said. "You just could have kept a few things to yourself. She wants fifteen million, Belinda. Bonnie Wilkinson is suing me for fifteen million dollars."

"I'm so sorry, Glen. I didn't know what to do. George said—you know what George is like, he's all by-the-book—he said if I didn't tell the truth they could charge me or hold me in contempt or something like that. I don't know, it was all so confusing. I certainly never meant to—"

"And they might just get it because of you. I just wanted to call and say thanks."

"Glen, *please.* I know I screwed up, but you don't have any idea of the kind of stress I've been under lately." Her voice was starting to break. "I've made some stupid decisions, everything's starting to unravel, I—"

"Anyone suing you for fifteen mil, Belinda?"

"What? No, no one—"

"Well then, consider yourself blessed." I hung up.

Not long after that, the doorbell rang. Kelly had still not emerged from her room.

I opened the door and found a man in a dark blue suit standing on the porch, holding some sort of identification in his hand. I put him in his late forties, about five-ten, with thinning silver hair.

"Mr. Garber?"

"That's right."

"Arthur Twain. I'm a detective."

Oh shit, I thought. Darren Slocum was filing charges.

Maybe I had police detectives stereotyped in my mind but Twain seemed well turned out for one. The suit—at least to my untrained eye—looked expensive, and his black leather shoes were polished to a high gleam. His silk tie probably cost more than everything I had on, and that included my shockproof watch. Despite his fashion sense, he had a small paunch and bags under his eyes. Well turned out, but weary.

"Yeah, okay," I said. "Come in."

"Sorry to drop in unannounced."

"No, that's okay. I mean, I suppose I should have been expecting you."

He blinked. "Oh?"

Kelly, evidently curious about who'd come to the door, had ended her self-imposed exile and come downstairs. She poked her head into the foyer.

"Honey, this is a detective, Arthur . . ." I'd already forgotten his last name.

"Twain," he said.

"Hi," Kelly said, pointedly not even looking at me.

"What's your name?"

"Kelly."

"Nice to meet you, Kelly."

I said, "Did you want to talk to Kelly first, or me, or both of us? I mean, she was there. Or should I be calling my lawyer?" That, I suddenly realized, would be the smartest course of action.

Arthur Twain said, cautiously, "I think I'll talk to you, Mr. Garber."

"Okay, honey," I said to Kelly, "we'll call you if we need you." Still managing not to look at me, she went back to her room.

I showed Twain into the living room. I wasn't sure whether I was to call him Mister, Officer, or Detective.

"Have a seat, uh . . . Is it Officer?"

"Arthur's fine," he said, sitting down. That struck me as pretty informal for a police detective.

"You want some coffee or something?" I was naïve enough to think that being a good host might get me out of an assault charge.

"No, thanks. First of all, I'd just like to say, I'm very sorry about Mrs. Garber."

"Oh," I said, taken aback. I wasn't expecting the detective to know, or ask, about Sheila. "Thank you."

"When did she pass away?"

"Nearly three weeks ago."

"A car accident." Not a question. I supposed that if Rona Wedmore could know about it, I shouldn't be surprised that Twain was up to speed.

"Yes. I guess the different forces all share information."

"No, I've just done some checking."

That seemed odd to me, but I let it go. "You're here about the incident this afternoon."

Arthur cocked his head slightly. "What incident would that be, Mr. Garber?"

I laughed. "I'm sorry, what? I mean, if you don't know about it, I'm hardly going to tell you."

"I'm afraid you have me at a disadvantage here, Mr. Garber."

"You did say you're a detective, right?"

"That's right."

"With the Milford police."

"No," Arthur said. "I'm with Stapleton Investigations. I'm not a police detective, I'm a *private* detective."

"What's Stapleton? A private investigation company?"

"That's right."

"Why's someone like that give a damn about my decking a Milford cop?"

"I don't know anything about that," Twain said. "I'm here about your wife."

"About Sheila? What do you want to know about Sheila?" Then I figured it out. "You're with that law firm, the one that's suing me, aren't you? Well, you can get the hell out of here, you son of a bitch."

"Mr. Garber, I'm not working for a law firm, and I'm not representing anyone who's launched any sort of action against you."

"Then, what are you here for?"

"I'm here to ask you about your wife's possible connection to criminal activity. I'm here to ask about her involvement in selling counterfeit purses."

TWENTY-THREE

"Get out," I said, moving toward the door.

"Mr. Garber, please," Arthur Twain said, rising reluctantly off the chair.

"I said get out. No one comes in here and says things like that about Sheila. I've listened to all the shit I want to about what my wife may or may not have done. I'm not listening to any more." I opened the door.

When Twain didn't move, I said, "I can pick you up and throw you out on your ass if that's how you'd rather do it."

Twain looked nervous, but he held his ground. "Mr. Garber, if you think you know everything there is to know about what your wife may have been involved in before she died, if you don't have a single question left unanswered, then fine, I'll go."

I got ready to throw him out on his ass.

"But if you have any doubts, any questions at all, about your wife's activities before she died, then maybe it would be worth your while to listen to what I have to say, maybe even answer a couple of my questions."

I still had my hand on the door. I was aware of my own breathing, the coursing of blood through my temples.

I pushed the door closed. "Five minutes."

We moved away from the door and went back to sitting in the living room.

"Let me start by telling you who, exactly, I work for," Twain said. "I'm a licensed private detective with Stapleton Investigations. We've been engaged by an alliance of major fashion conglomerates to track down operations trading in counterfeit goods. Fake purses chief among them. You're aware of the trade in knockoff merchandise, I assume."

"I've heard about it."

"Then let me get right to it." Arthur Twain pulled an envelope from inside his jacket and withdrew from it a folded sheet of paper. He opened it up and held it out for me. It was a printout of a photo. "Do you recognize this person?"

Reluctantly, I took the photo from him and glanced at it. A tall man with black hair, lean and fit looking, with a scar above his right eye. The picture appeared to have been taken on a New York City street, although it could have been any major city.

"No," I said, handing the photo back. "I've never seen him."

"You're sure?"

"Positive. Is there anything else?"

"Don't you want to know who he is?"

"Not really."

"You should."

"Why?"

"Your wife placed a call to him on the day of her accident."

"Sheila phoned him?"

"That's right."

My mouth was dry. "Who is he?"

"We don't know, exactly. He's gone by Michael Sayer, Matthew Smith, Mark Salazar, and Madden Sommer. We think his name is Sommer. The people he works for refer to him as their solver."

"Solver?"

"He solves problems."

"My wife never knew anyone by any of those names."

"She called Sommer's cell in the early afternoon." He reached into his jacket again. It was a small notebook, a Moleskine. He fingered through the pages until he found what he was looking for, then said, "That's right, here we are. Just after one p.m. Let me read you a number here."

He read off a series of digits that made my heart sink even if I hadn't dialed them in several weeks.

"Recognize it?" he asked.

"That's Sheila's cell."

"Your wife's cell called Sommer's at 1:02 the day she died."

"She must have dialed wrong. And how the hell do you even know this? Where did you get these phone records?"

"We work in cooperation with several law enforcement agencies. They have provided some of their surveillance information. This number your wife called, by the way, it's not a phone he has anymore. He goes through cell phones the way I go through cheesecake." He gave his paunch a light pat.

"Okay, so Sheila called Sommer. Who the hell is he? I mean, what's he do?"

"The FBI links him to organized crime."

"This is ridiculous."

"No, it's not," Arthur Twain said. "Sommer gets a lot of calls from women—and plenty of men, too—who are unaware he has those kinds of criminal connections. They may think he's a little shady, but figure what they don't know won't hurt them. They just think he's a businessman, a representative for a company that imports the items they're interested in selling."

"What items? When you walked in here you said purses. This guy moves *purses*?"

"Among other things."

"He looks more like someone you'd go to to get guns or drugs."

"He can get you those, too. Especially the latter. Of a certain kind."

"I don't believe any of this. I don't get a ladies' handbag vibe off this character."

"Sommer moves whatever can make him money, and purses is one of those things."

"So what are you saying? That my wife tried to buy a knockoff purse from this criminal?"

"It wouldn't have been just one, if it was purses at all. Sommer's people offer a full range of products. But knockoff bags are a distinct possibility. Have you ever heard of a purse party, Mr. Garber?"

I went to open my mouth, to say, "Are you kidding? We had one right here." But I stopped myself.

"I'm sure you have," he continued. "They're pretty popular. Women get together to buy fake designer bags for a fraction of what the real things cost. It's all a lot of fun, a girls' night out, they put out some cheese and crackers, open some wine. A woman goes home with some fancy Prada or Marc Jacobs or Fendi or Louis Vuitton or Valentino bag that looks pretty darn close to the real thing. Only one who doesn't know it's real is her. And all the women at the party, of course."

I studied him. "Don't you have *real* crimes to investigate?"

Arthur smiled knowingly. "That's what a lot of people say. But selling knockoff bags is a crime. A federal one."

"I can't believe police are wasting time on this when there's people getting murdered out there and drugs coming into the country and terrorists plotting God knows what. So a few women walk around with bags that aren't a real Marc Fendi—"

"Marc Jacobs, or Fendi," he said.

"Whatever. So they're walking around with a fake bag. If that's all they can afford, then they weren't going to buy the real one anyway. So who gets hurt?"

"Where would you like me to start?" Twain said. "With the legitimate companies that are having their copyrighted and trademarked work ripped off? The millions of dollars that are effectively stolen from them, and those who work for them, by this kind of crime?"

"I'm sure they're getting by," I said.

"Your daughter, Kelly, how old is she?"

"What's this have to do with Kelly?"

"I'm guessing she's what, seven years old?"

"Eight."

"Can you picture her, right now, working nine or ten or more hours a day in a factory, making knockoffs? That's what boys and girls her age do in China, working for a dollar a day. Working—"

"That's right, play the exploited-children card when all those companies really care about is losing profits—"

"Working their fingers to the bone in some sweatshop to make a bag, all so some woman from Milford or Westport or Darien can stroll about trying to fool people into thinking she's worth more than she really is. Do you know where the money goes, Mr. Garber? When a woman here in Milford drops thirty or fifty or a hundred bucks on some bag, do you know where the money ends up? The woman running the purse party will get her cut, of course, but she has to pay her supplier to get those bags. That money goes to produce other knockoffs, but not just other handbags. Counterfeit DVDs, video games, children's toys—covered with lead paint with parts that can snap off and choke a kid to death—substandard building parts with counterfeit approval stamps on them, even knockoff baby formula, if you can believe that. There are even imitation prescription drugs out there that look like the real thing, even have the same product identification stamps on them, but don't have the same ingredients, there's no regulation at all. I'm not talking about less expensive drugs from Canada. I'm talking pharmaceuticals from India, China. Some of these pills, Mr. Garber, they don't do *anything*. So you have someone on a limited pension, low income, he can't afford his heart medication or whatever, he finds what he thinks is the same drug on the Internet, or he buys it off a friend of a friend, starts taking it, next thing you know, he's dead."

I didn't say anything.

"You know who's making money from all that? Organized criminal organizations. Chinese gangs, Russian gangs, India, Pakistan. You name it. And plenty of good ol' Americans, too. The FBI says some of this money even gets funneled to terrorist operations."

"Really," I said. "Some lady down the street buys a Gucci bag and suddenly we've got planes flying into buildings."

Arthur smiled. "You make light, but I saw the expression on your face, a moment ago, when I mentioned building supplies. You're a contractor, am I right?"

The words had registered with me, and I may have blinked.

"Yes," I said.

"Imagine," he said, "if someone working for you were to install into one of your houses, I don't know, knockoff electrical components. Parts made in China that look, on the outside, exactly like name-brand ones manufactured and approved for use here, but on the inside they're just junk. Made with wire of insufficient gauge. They overheat, they short out. Breakers don't trip. It doesn't take a genius to figure out what might happen."

I rubbed my hand over my mouth and chin. For a moment, I was back in that smoke-filled basement. "So why are you here? If this is such a big deal, why aren't the police asking me about this instead of you?"

"We work with the police wherever we can, but they don't have the resources to deal with this problem. Counterfeit goods are a five-hundred billion dollar-a-year-business, and that's probably a conservative estimate. The fashion industry has turned to private security and investigation firms to track down counterfeiters. That's where I come in. Sometimes, it's pretty simple. We find a woman who's been holding purse parties, naïvely thinking there's nothing wrong with what she does, and we let her know she's committing a crime, a federal crime, and that may be enough. She stops, we don't charge her. Sometimes. When we find shops that are selling these goods, we notify the merchants, and the landlords, that what they're doing is illegal, and that we're prepared to bring in the police to prosecute to the fullest extent of the law. And we often do. But just the threat of it is often enough to get landlords to act. They get rid of those tenants and bring in ones that obey the law, that sell legitimate merchandise."

"What about just buying a purse? Owning a knockoff? Is that a crime?"

"No. But would your conscience be clear, if you were a woman and were carrying around a knockoff, and knew that this kind of thing could be happening?" He was looking in the envelope for a couple more pictures. He handed them to me.

"What are—oh Jesus."

They were crime scene photographs. If I was going to have to look at pictures like these, I would have preferred to see them in black-and-white. But these were in Technicolor. The bodies of two women, pools of blood beneath them. All around them, purses. On tables, hanging from the walls, from the ceiling.

"Dear God."

I looked at the next picture. A man, apparently shot in the head, his upper body sprawled across a desk. I thrust the pictures back at Twain. "What the hell is this?"

"The women's names are Pam Steigerwald and Edna Bauder. A couple of tourists from Butler, Pennsylvania. In New York for a girls' weekend. They were looking for bargain-priced purses on Canal Street and happened to be in the wrong place at the wrong time. The man is Andy Fong. A merchant, and an importer of knockoff purses manufactured in China."

"I don't know anything about these people."

"I show this to you because it's an example of what can happen when folks get mixed up in this whole counterfeit business."

I was angry. "This is disgusting, trying to make a point by showing me something like this, trying to scare the hell out of me. This has nothing to do with Sheila."

"The police believe our man with the many names, the one we'll call Madden Sommer, may have done this. The man your wife phoned the day she died."

TWENTY-FOUR

Madden Sommer sat in his car across the street, and three houses down, from the Garber house.

He had his hand on the door when another car pulled up. A black GM sedan. A well-dressed man got out. Soft looking. The rounded stomach hanging over his belt. The way he carried himself. When the front door opened, the man flashed some ID to Garber.

Interesting, Sommer thought, taking his hand off the door. He didn't get the sense the man was a cop, but anything was possible. He took note of the car's license plate, then placed a call on his cell.

"Hello?"

"It's me. I need you to run a plate for me."

"I'm not exactly at work right now," Slocum said. "I'm with family. My wife's sister is here."

"Write this down."

"I just said—"

"F, seven—"

"Hang on, hang on." Sommer could hear Slocum scrambling to find paper and a pencil.

"Christ's sake, go ahead."

Sommer read off the rest of the plate. "How soon?"

"I don't know. It depends who's on."

"I'll call you back in an hour or so. Have it for me by then."

"I told you, I don't know if I can get it right away. Where are you? Where's this car you—"

Sommer slipped the phone back into his jacket.

Garber had let the man inside his home. Sommer could see shadows in the living room. He'd also been watching the other windows of the house. There was a light on upstairs. Occasionally, a shadow crossed the curtains, and at one point, someone had peeked through them to take a look at the street.

A child. A young girl.

TWENTY-FIVE

I stood up, so angry I was shaking. The idea that Sheila had any dealings, even so much as a phone call, with a thug like Sommer was deeply disturbing to me. And I'd already had enough troubling revelations about Sheila.

"You're wrong. Sheila didn't call that guy."

"If she didn't, someone using her phone did. Did she lend her phone out to people?" Twain asked.

"No. But—it doesn't make sense."

"But your wife has purchased knockoff purses?"

I remembered when I was standing in the closet on Friday, wondering whether it was finally time to do something with Sheila's things. There were dozens of purses in there.

"There might be a couple," I said.

"Would you mind if I looked at them?"

"Why?"

"When you've been doing this as long as I have, you learn to spot certain characteristics. Just as someone could note the differences between a Coach and Gucci bag, I can sometimes notice differences between a bag made in one factory in China versus a bag made somewhere else. It gives me an idea which counterfeiters are making more of a dent in the market, for one thing."

I hesitated. Why help this man? What difference did it make now? If anything, Arthur Twain was going to tarnish Sheila's memory. Why help him do that?

As if reading my mind, he said, "I'm not here to hurt your wife's reputation. I'm sure Mrs. Garber never knowingly broke the law, or intended to. This is one of those things like, like stealing cable. Everyone does it, so no one thinks that there's anything—"

"Sheila *never* stole cable. Or anything else."

Arthur held up a defensive hand. "Sorry. It was just an example."

I said nothing, ran my tongue over my lip. "She hosted a party here," I said. "Once."

Arthur nodded. "When was that?"

"A few weeks—no, a couple of months before Sheila died."

"When you say hosted, did she sell the merchandise? Or did she turn that over to someone else?"

"Someone else." I hesitated, wondering whether it was fair to drag anyone else into it. Except the person I was going to name was as immune from prosecution as Sheila. "A woman named Ann Slocum. A friend of Sheila's."

Arthur Twain looked up something in his Moleskine. "Yeah, I have that name here. My information is that she was in regular contact with Mr. Sommer. I'll be wanting to talk to her, too."

"Good luck," I said.

"What do you mean?"

"She died the other night."

For the first time, Arthur looked taken aback. "When? What happened?"

"Late Friday night, or maybe early Saturday morning. She had an accident. Got out to check a flat tire, stumbled off the pier."

"Oh my. I didn't know." Twain was taking it all in.

So was I. The day that Sheila died, she'd put in a call to some kind of mobster. A man Twain was telling me was a suspect in a triple homicide. I thought about what Edwin had said, quoting Conan Doyle. How when something seemed impossible, the other possibilities, no matter how improbable, had to be considered.

Sheila had called a suspected killer. And before the day was out, she was dead.

She hadn't died the way the people in those photographs had. She hadn't been shot. No one had walked up to her and put a—

A bullet in her brain.

That wasn't what had happened to her. She'd died in an accident. An accident that had never made sense to me. Sure, all fatal accidents seemed senseless to those who were left behind to grieve. The deaths seemed so random, so cruelly arbitrary. But Sheila's accident was different.

Her accident went against character.

Sheila would never have gotten drunk enough to do what they claimed she did. Deep in my heart, I was certain of that.

Was it possible? Was it conceivable Sheila's death wasn't what it appeared to be? That while it seemed to be an accident, it was actually—

"Mr. Garber?"

"I'm sorry?"

Arthur Twain said, "You were going to let me have a look at some of those purses your wife had?"

I'd forgotten. "Wait here."

I went upstairs, passing by Kelly's room. She had left her door open and was sitting at her desk, on the computer. I stepped in. "Hey," I said.

"Hey," she replied, her eyes on the screen. "What does that man want?"

"He wants to see some of your mom's purses."

She looked at me, alarm flashing across her face. "Why does a *man* want to see Mom's purses? Does he want one for his wife? You're not giving them away, are you?"

"Of course not."

"Are you selling them?" Her tone was accusing.

"No. He just wants to see them. He tries to find out who makes fake designer purses and put them out of business."

"Why?"

"Because the people who make them are copying the originals."

"Is that bad?"

"Yeah," I said. Here I was, making Arthur's arguments when moments earlier I'd been trying to knock them down. "It's like, if you copy off another kid's work at school. It's not your work."

"So it's cheating," Kelly said.

"Yeah."

"So Mom was a cheater because she had some?"

"No, your mother was not a cheater. But the people who make those bags are."

Kelly was struggling with a decision. I was guessing it was whether to like me again. "I'm still mad at you."

"I understand."

"But can I help you?"

"With?"

"The purses?"

I motioned for her to follow me to Sheila's closet. There were about a dozen bags on the shelf above the hangers, and as I handed them down to Kelly she ran the straps up her arms. She looked pretty adorable, lugging them all down that way to the living room, struggling to keep her balance as she did so.

"Well, look at you," Arthur said as Kelly nearly stumbled into him. She dropped her arms and let the bags fall into two heaps on either side of her.

"Sorry," she said. "They're heavy."

"You're a pretty strong girl to carry those all the way downstairs."

"I have big arm muscles," Kelly said. She demonstrated, adopting a muscleman pose.

"Wow," he said.

"You can feel," she offered.

"That's okay," he said, keeping his hands to himself. "Your mother had a lot of purses."

"This isn't all of them," Kelly told him. "Just the ones she liked. Sometimes, if she had a purse she never used, she would donate it to the poor people."

Arthur looked up at me and flashed a brief smile. "These bags here, are they ones that your mom would have bought in the last couple of years?"

I was about to say I wasn't sure, but Kelly spoke up first. "Yes. This one," and she picked up a black one with an oversized black leather flower on it that was labeled *Valentino,* "she got when she went into the city with her friend Mrs. Morton."

Some friend.

"You can tell it's not real," Kelly said, opening the bag, "because there's no label inside telling you where it was made, and the lining isn't as nice, and if you try real hard you can peel the sticker off on the outside."

"You're good at this," Arthur said.

I said, "I'm raising Nancy Drew."

"And this one Mom got after the party Emily's mom had at the house," Kelly said.

Arthur made a close inspection. "A pretty good Marc Jacobs copy."

Kelly nodded in astonishment. "My dad would never be able to tell something like that." She glanced up at me.

"And this one," Twain said, "is an excellent Valentino knockoff."

"Oh my God," Kelly said. "You're like the only dad in the world who would know that! *Are* you a dad?"

"Yes, I am. I have two little boys. Well, not so little anymore."

She held up one of the purses. "Mom also really liked this one."

It was a tan fabric bag with leather trim, a slender strap, a mosaic of "F" symbols all over it.

"A Fendi," Arthur said, holding the bag to inspect it. "Nice."

"A good copy?" I asked.

"No," he said. "Not a copy at all. It's the real deal. Made in Italy."

"Are you sure?" I asked.

Arthur nodded. "Your wife might have found it on sale, but if you were to buy this on Fifth Avenue it would run you two thousand dollars."

"Grandma bought that one for Mom," Kelly said. "For her birthday. Remember?"

I didn't, but that explained it. Fiona wasn't the type to buy anything but the real deal. She'd be as likely to buy her daughter a knockoff bag as take her to lunch at Wendy's.

As Twain dropped the bag on the floor, it made a sound. Like something rattling around inside it.

Jesus, I thought. Not another pair of handcuffs. I wouldn't know what to make of that kind of discovery. But the rattle had not sounded metallic.

"There's something in here," he said, grabbing it by the strap.

I reached over and took it from him. "Whatever's in there was Sheila's," I told him. "The bags may be your business, but what's in them isn't."

I left Kelly and Arthur Twain in the living room. I went into the kitchen, undid the clasp on the top of the purse, and opened it wide.

Inside, there were four plastic containers, each one about the size of a jar of olives.

Each one carried a different label. Lisinopril. Vicodin. Viagra. Omeprazole.

Altogether, hundreds and hundreds of pills.

TWENTY-SIX

I returned the containers to the purse and shoved it into one of the overhead cupboards. When I returned to the living room, Twain was looking at me expectantly. But when I offered no details of what I'd found, he said, "Well, thank you for your time."

He left me his card, encouraged me to get in touch if I remembered anything that might be helpful, and left.

"He seemed nice," Kelly said. "What was in Mom's purse?"

"Nothing," I said.

"It had to be *something*. It was all noisy."

"It was nothing."

She knew I was lying, but she also knew I wasn't going to say anything more.

"Fine," she said. "I think I'll just go back to being mad at you." She stomped up the stairs and returned to her room, slamming the door behind her.

I took the drug-filled purse from the cupboard and went to my downstairs office. I emptied the bag onto my desk and watched the containers roll out.

"Son of a bitch," I said to the empty room. "What the hell is all this, Sheila? What in the hell is this?"

I picked up each of the small plastic jars, unscrewed the caps, peered inside. Hundreds of little yellow pills, white pills, the world-famous blue pills. "God, how many of these did you want me to take?"

I remembered what Twain had said, that there was a huge market not only in such things as knockoff purses and DVDs and construction supplies, but prescription drugs, too.

What had Sheila said to me that last morning we had together?

"I have ideas. Ideas to help us. To get us through the rough patches. I've made some money."

"Not like this," I said. "Not like this."

Now that I'd seen what was in this purse, I wondered what the hell might be in all her others. I checked the ones still in the living room, then went back upstairs—Kelly remained behind the closed door of her room—and looked through the remaining bags in Sheila's closet. I found old lipsticks, shopping lists, some change. No more drugs.

I returned to the basement. The purse Sheila had with her at the time of the accident had—as I'd told Belinda—survived, but not in good shape. It had been lightly scorched, then drenched after the fire department arrived. I'd thrown out the bag—I didn't want Kelly to see it—but saved everything that had been in it. I felt the need, now, to take a look at all those items.

Everything was stored in a shoebox that a pair of Rockports had come in. The shoes had already been worn out and tossed, but the box would probably last for years to come. I put it on my desk, gingerly, as if it were loaded with explosives. Then, with some hesitation, I removed the lid.

"Hey, babe," I said.

It struck me as a stupid thing to say. But looking at this collection of Sheila's effects, it seemed perfectly natural. In their own way, these mementos were close to Sheila in a way I never was. They were with her in her final moments.

A pair of stud earrings, with blood-red flecks on them. A necklace—an aluminum pendant on a leather string—that was even darker with Sheila's blood. I took it in my hand and brought it up to my face, touched it to my cheek. I laid it gently back into the box and examined the items from her purse that were not bloodied. Dental floss; a pair of reading glasses in a slender metal case; two metal hair clips, each with a strand of Sheila's hair still caught in them; one of those things from Tide that looked like a Magic Marker that's supposed to remove stains instantly. Sheila was always ready for any fast-food catastrophe. Tissue. A small package of Band-Aids. Half a pack of Dentyne Blast Cool Lime gum. When we would head out to see friends, or visit her parents, she'd tell me to lean close in the car and catch a whiff of me. "Chew one of these," she'd say. "Fast. You've got breath like a dead moose." There were three ATM receipts, other receipts from drug and grocery stores, a handful of business cards, one from a department store cosmetics counter, a couple from New York shopping excursions. There was a tiny container of hand sanitizer, some small hair elastics she kept in her purse for Kelly, a Bobbi Brown lipstick, eyedrops, a makeup mirror, four emery boards, a set of headphones she'd bought on the plane when we had gone to Toronto for a long weekend more than a year ago. A longtime hockey fan, she wanted to eat at Wayne Gretzky's restaurant. "Where the hell is he?" she asked. "In the kitchen," I told her. "Making your sandwich."

A memory attached to nearly every item. And not a single liquor store receipt to be found anywhere. And no pills, either.

I lingered over many of these things, but there was one thing in particular I wanted to have a look at.

Sheila's cell phone.

I took it out of the box, flipped it open, and hit the button to turn it on. Nothing happened. The phone was dead.

I opened my top desk drawer, where I kept the charger for my own phone—a duplicate of Sheila's—and inserted one end into the phone and shoved the plug into the wall outlet. The phone tinkled to life.

I had not yet gotten around to canceling it. It was part of a package deal with mine, and now Kelly's. When I'd gotten her phone, I could have canceled Sheila's, but found I didn't have it in me to do it.

Once the phone appeared to be working, and charging, the first thing that occurred to me was to call it from my desk phone.

I dialed the number I still knew by heart, heard it ring in my ear and watched as the phone rang and vibrated in front of me. I waited for the end of the seventh ring, at which point I knew it would go to voicemail, and I would get to hear my dead wife's voice.

"Hi. This is Sheila. I'm either on the phone, away from it, or too scared to answer because I'm in traffic, so please leave a message."

And then the beep.

I started to speak. "I . . . I just . . ."

I hung up, my hand trembling.

I needed a minute to pull myself together.

"I just wanted to say," I said, standing there in the room alone, "that I've said some things, since you've been gone, that now . . . I've been so angry with you. So goddamn angry. That you'd have done this, that you'd . . . do something so stupid. But in the last day or so, I don't know . . . Things made no sense before, and they're making even less sense now, but the less sense they make, the more I'm starting to wonder . . . to wonder whether there's more to this, that maybe . . . that maybe I haven't been fair, that maybe I'm not seeing . . ."

I sat in the chair and let the feelings wash over me, just let it happen. Allowed myself a minute or so to let it out. Like releasing pressure on a valve. You have to let it off, even just a little, so you don't get an explosion.

And when I finished sobbing, I grabbed a couple of tissues, wiped my eyes, blew my nose, took a few deep breaths.

And got back to it.

I went into Sheila's phone's call history. Arthur Twain said Sheila had called this guy Sommer the day of her accident, just after one.

I found a number in the history of outgoing calls. There it was, at 1:02 p.m. A New York area code.

I snatched up the receiver from my desk phone and dialed it. There was half a ring, and then a recording telling me the number was no longer in service. I hung up. Arthur Twain had said Sommer was no longer using that phone.

I got out a pen and a piece of paper and started writing down all the other numbers Sheila had called the day of, and the days leading up to, her accident. There were five calls to my cell, three to my office, three to the house. I recognized Belinda's number. There was the Darien number I knew to be Fiona's place, and another one I recognized as Fiona's cell.

Then, as an afterthought, I checked the list of incoming calls on Sheila's phone. There were the ones I would have expected. Nine from me—from the home phone, work phone, and cell. Calls from Fiona. Belinda.

And seventeen from a number I did not recognize. Not the number I believed belonged to Sommer. Not a New York number. All the calls from that number were listed as "missed." Which meant Sheila either didn't hear the ring, or chose not to answer.

I wrote down that number, too.

She'd been called by that number once on the day she died, twice the day before, and at least twice a day, every day, in the seven days leading up to her death.

I had to know.

Again, I dialed out from the house phone. It rang three times before going to voicemail.

"Hi, you've reached Allan Butterfield. Leave a message."

Allan who? Sheila didn't know anyone named—

Wait. Allan Butterfield. Sheila's accounting teacher. Why would he have been calling her so frequently? And why would she have been refusing to take his calls?

I tossed the phone onto the desk, wondering what else there was to do. So many questions, so few answers.

I kept looking at the pills. Where would Sheila have gotten prescription drugs? How would she have paid for them? What was she planning to do with—

The money.

The money I socked away.

The only people who knew about the cash I had hidden in the wall were Sheila and myself. Had she gone into that? Had she used that money to buy these drugs with the idea of reselling them?

I opened my desk drawer and grabbed a letter opener. Then I went around the desk to the opposite corner of the room. I worked the opener into a seam in the wood paneling, and in a couple of seconds had a rectangular opening seventeen inches wide and a foot tall and about three inches deep.

I could tell, very quickly, whether the money stored between the studs was all there. I kept it in $500 bundles. I quickly counted, and found thirty-four of them.

The money I'd saved from years of under-the-table jobs was all there.

And so was something else.

A brown business envelope. It was tucked in behind the cash. I pulled it out, felt how thickly it was stuffed.

In the upper left corner, some writing: *From Belinda Morton*. And then, scribbled under that, a phone number.

I recognized it right away. I'd only seen it a couple of minutes ago.

It was the number Sheila had dialed at 1:02 p.m. the day she died. The number Arthur Twain said belonged to Madden Sommer.

The envelope was sealed. I worked the letter opener under the flap and made a nice clean cut, then stepped over to my desk and dumped out the contents.

Cash. Lots and lots of cash.

Thousands of dollars in cash.

"Holy Mother of God," I said.

Then I heard the shot.

A shattering of glass.

Kelly screaming.

TWENTY-SEVEN

I was up the two flights of stairs in less than ten seconds.

"Kelly!" I shouted. "Kelly!"

Her door was still closed and I threw it open so fast I nearly pulled it off its hinges. I could hear Kelly screaming, but I didn't see her. What I did see was shattered glass scattered across the floor and Kelly's bed. The window that faced the street was a jagged nightmare.

"Kelly!"

I heard muffled crying and bolted for her closet door. I swung it wide and found her huddled in there atop a pile of shoes.

She leapt up and flung her arms around me.

"Are you okay? Honey? Are you okay? Talk to me!"

She pressed her head against my chest and sobbed, "Daddy! Daddy!" I was holding her so tightly I was afraid I'd break her.

"I've got you, I've got you, I've got you. Are you hurt? Did you get hit? By glass or anything?"

"I don't know," she whimpered. "It scared me!"

"I know, I know. Honey, I have to see if you're okay."

She sniffed and nodded and allowed me to hold her a foot away. I was looking for blood and didn't see any.

"You weren't hit by the glass?"

"I was sitting there," she said, pointing to the computer. Her desk was up against the same wall as the window, which meant that all the glass came in beside and behind her.

"Tell me what happened."

"I was just sitting there, and I heard a car going really fast and then there was a big bang and all the glass came in and so I ran into the closet."

"That was smart," I said. "Hiding like that. That was good." I pulled her into my arms again.

"What did it?" she asked. "Did somebody shoot at the house? Is that what happened?"

There were other people who'd help us get the answers to those questions.

"Well," said Rona Wedmore. "We meet again."

She arrived soon after several Milford police cars showed up. The street was closed off and there was yellow police tape cordoning off our property.

"Small world," I said.

Wedmore spent several minutes talking just to Kelly. Then she wanted to talk to me privately. When Kelly looked frightened at the thought of being separated from me, Wedmore called over one of the uniformed officers, a woman, and asked Kelly if she'd like to see what the inside of a police car was like. My daughter allowed the woman to lead her away only after I promised her it would be okay.

"She'll be fine," Wedmore assured me.

"Really?" I said. "Detective, someone just tried to kill my daughter."

"Mr. Garber, I know you're very upset right now, which, if you weren't, I'd think there was something wrong with you. But let's take this a step at a time, and sort out what we know and what we don't know. What we know is pretty straightforward. Someone took a shot at your house, blew out your daughter's bedroom window. But unless there's something you know you're not telling me, that's about all we know for sure right now.

"In fact, judging by where your daughter was sitting when the shot was fired, it doesn't seem likely anyone was aiming for her. She wouldn't even have been visible from the street. On top of that, the curtains were pulled shut almost all the way. Add to that the fact that Kelly's only eight, not very tall, and no one shooting up from the street through a window, at that angle, could expect to have hit anyone that small anyway."

I nodded.

"All that said, someone still shot out the window of your daughter's bedroom. You have any idea who might want to do that?"

"No," I said.

"No one's got a bone to pick with you? No one's upset with you?"

"I got more people pissed off at me than I can count, but none that would take a shot at my house. At least, I don't think so."

"I guess Officer Slocum would be on the list of those pissed off at you." I looked at her and said nothing. "I was at the visitation," she reminded me. "And I know what you did. I know you took a swing at Officer Slocum."

"Jesus, you think Slocum did this?"

"No," she said sharply. "I do not. But who else have you taken a swing at lately that you've forgotten about? Do I need to start making a list?"

"I haven't forgotten—look, I'm a bit rattled, okay?"

"Sure." She shook her head. "You're lucky, you know?"

"What? That someone took a shot at my house?"

"That you weren't charged with assaulting a police officer."

It had occurred to me.

"He isn't pressing charges. I spoke to him about it personally. But you're lucky. If some guy hit me, at my spouse's visitation, that guy would be charged. Big-time."

"Why isn't he?"

"I don't know. I don't get the idea you guys are good friends. My guess is, he'll find a way to settle it on his own. I don't think he'd shoot up your house, but I'd keep an eye on your speed. If he doesn't pull you over, one of his buddies will."

"Maybe one of those buddies did it."

Wedmore's face was awash with concern. "I suppose that's something we have to consider, isn't it? When we dig that bullet out of your wall, we'll be taking a look at it, seeing if it's a likely match with a police officer's weapon. But now that you've had a moment to think, is there anyone else whose toes you've stepped on lately?"

"It's been a kind of... kind of a strange few days," I admitted.

"Strange how?"

"I guess... I suppose it started with the sleepover."

"Wait, the one at the Slocums'?"

"That's right. There was kind of an incident there."

"What kind of incident?"

"Kelly and Emily, the Slocums' little girl, were playing hide-and-seek. Kelly was hiding in the Slocums' bedroom closet when Ann came into the room to make a call. When she spotted Kelly there, she got very angry. She upset Kelly so much that Kelly called me to come take her home."

"Okay," Wedmore said. "Was that it?"

"Not . . . really. Darren figured out Kelly had heard some of this phone conversation, which his wife had not told him about, and he wanted to know everything Kelly'd heard. He came by here Saturday, looking for her. Throwing his weight around. I told him what Kelly heard, which was next to nothing, and he promised not to bother her. But then I found him questioning her, without my knowledge, or permission, at the funeral home." I looked down. "That was when I hit him."

Wedmore put her palm on the back of her neck and rubbed. "Well. Okay. Why was Officer Slocum so concerned about that phone call?"

"Whoever it was, he thinks it was why his wife left the house that night. And then she had that accident down by the pier."

When Wedmore didn't say anything for a moment, I said, "It was an accident, right?"

A male uniformed officer came into the room and said, "Excuse me, Detective. The woman who lives next door, Joan . . ."

"Mueller," I offered.

"That's right. She happened to be looking out her window at the time and she says she saw a car drive past quickly at the time of the shot."

"Did she get a look at the car? Get a plate or anything?"

"No plate, but she said it was a small car, but squared off at the back, like a station wagon. Sounds to me like a Golf, or maybe a Mazda 3, something like that. And she said she thought it was silver."

"She get a look at the driver?" She didn't ask the question with any hope in her voice. It was night, after all.

"No," the cop said, "but she thought there were two people in the car. In the front. Oh yeah, and something on the end of the antenna. Something yellow, like a little ball."

"Okay, keep knocking on doors. Maybe somebody else saw something, too."

The cop left and Wedmore turned her attention back to me. "Mr. Garber, if you think of anything else, I want you to call me." She reached into her pocket and produced a card. "And if we find out anything, I'll be sure to let you know."

"You didn't answer my question."

"What was that?"

"Ann Slocum. Her death. That was an accident, right?"

Wedmore gave me an even look. "That investigation is ongoing, sir." She put the card into my hand. "If you think of anything."

TWENTY-EIGHT

Slocum answered his cell before the second ring.

"You tracked down that plate?" Sommer asked.

"Jesus Christ, what did you do?"

"Excuse me?"

"The Garber kid's window?" Darren was practically screaming into the phone. "The girl's bedroom! Is that how you lean on people? Kill their kids?"

"Did you get the plate?"

"Are you hearing me?"

"The plate."

"You're unbelievable, you know that? Unfuckingbelievable."

"I'm ready to write down the information."

Slocum tried to catch his breath. He'd been shouting so loud he was nearly hoarse. "The car's registered to an Arthur Twain. Out of Hartford."

"An address?"

Slocum gave it to him.

"What'd you find out about him?"

"He's a detective. Private. With something called Stapleton Investigations."

"I've heard of them."

Slocum took another breath and did his best to speak calmly. "Listen to me, and listen to me carefully. You can't go around shooting up kids' bedrooms. Not just because it's fucking wrong. It attracts way too much—"

Sommer ended the call.

TWENTY-NINE

There were still cops up in Kelly's bedroom when I went back down to the study. The money I'd found in the brown envelope was no longer on my desk. I'd dashed down here, bringing Kelly with me, between the time I'd called 911 and the arrival of the first squad car, stuffed the money back into the wall and replaced the panel. I'd had her stand outside the office door while I did it.

Just as well, because the police were all through the house. There were only so many questions I wanted to deal with.

I dialed Fiona.

"Hello? Glen? Good God, do you know what time it is?"

"I need a favor."

I could hear Marcus, on the other side of the bed. "Who is it? What's going on?"

"Shh! What kind of favor? What are you talking about?"

"I'd like you to look after Kelly for a while."

I could sense Fiona trying to figure out what I was up to. Maybe she'd return to her earlier suspicion, that I wanted Kelly out of the house so I could have a woman over.

"What's the problem?" she asked. "Have you decided you *do* want to send her to school here?"

"No," I said. "But I would like her to stay with you. For a few days, anyway."

"Why? I mean, I love having her here, but what's your thinking?"

"Kelly has to get out of Milford for a while. No school, nothing to worry about. She's been through a rough time and it might be just the thing for her."

"Won't she fall behind in her studies?" she asked. "At that school where they call her Boozer?"

"Fiona, I need to know whether you can do this for me."

"Let me talk to Marcus and get back to you in the morning."

"I need an answer now. Yes or no."

"Glen, what's this about, really?"

I paused. I wanted Kelly out of town, someplace where it would be more work for Darren or anyone else to find her. I knew Fiona's house had a full security system that was directly wired into the police, and that Fiona had it on all the time.

I said, "It's not safe here."

There was an even-longer pause at the other end of the line. Finally, Fiona said, "Fine."

I went upstairs and asked Kelly to come into my room, out of earshot of the police still in the house. I sat her on the bed next to me.

"I've made a decision and I hope you're going to be okay with it," I said.

"What?"

"I'm taking you to your grandparents in the morning."

"I'm going to school there?"

"No. It'll be like a vacation."

"A vacation? Where?"

"I don't know that they'll actually take you anywhere, but I suppose that would be okay," I said.

"I don't want to be away from you."

"I don't like that, either. But it's not safe here, and until I'm sure it is, it'd be better if you were someplace else. You'll be safe with Fiona and Marcus."

She thought about it. "I'd like to go to London. Or maybe Disney World?"

"I don't think you should get your hopes up about that."

She nodded, then thought a moment. "If it's not safe for me here, then it's not safe for you here. Are you going to go on a vacation, too? Can't we both go?"

"I'm going to stay here, but I'll be okay. I'll be very careful. I'm going to find out what's going on."

She slipped her arms around me. "My bed's got glass on it," she said. "You stay here with me tonight."

After the police had left, Kelly got into her pajamas and slipped under the covers of my bed. She nodded off fairly quickly, which surprised me, given the events of the evening. But I guessed her system was telling her to sleep, that she needed to recharge her batteries to cope with all the confusing things that were going on.

My system didn't work that way, not after someone had taken a shot at the house. I felt a need to do regular patrols. I turned off all the lights except for one in the kitchen and a night-light in the hall outside my bedroom. I'd check in on Kelly, head downstairs, take a look at the street, go back upstairs and check on Kelly again.

Sometime around three, I was starting to feel pretty beat. I went up to my room, lay down on the bed on top of the covers next to my daughter.

I listened to her breathing. In, and out, and in, and out. So peaceful. It was the only reassuring sound I'd heard in some time.

My intention was to stay up, to maintain my watch, but sleep finally overtook me. But my eyes opened with the suddenness of a fire station door. I looked at the clock and saw that it was just after five. I got up to do another perimeter patrol and decided there was no point in going back to bed.

I did a few things around the house, dealt with a couple of bills online that I'd forgotten to pay by the due date, made a note that we were nearly out of orange juice and cereal.

This was also the morning they picked up the trash. I gathered together all the household garbage, including the handcuffs Kelly had taken from the Slocum house that I'd tucked into the drawer of my bedside table. I stuffed them way down into one of the bags, put two cans out on the street, and by seven the truck had been by and taken everything away.

Shortly after that, I had the garage door open and was doing some tidying in there when I realized someone was standing by the front of the truck. It gave me a start.

"Morning," Joan Mueller said. "You're up awful early today. Most days, I don't see you heading out until nearly eight. I guess you're pretty shook up and all."

"Yes," I said.

"Did the police tell you I saw a car?"

"They did. Thank you for your help."

"Well, I don't know how much help I was. I didn't see much. No license plate or anything like that. How's Kelly?"

"Like you said, we were both pretty shook up."

"Who'd do such a thing? Shoot at a window? You know what I think it was? I bet it was just kids goofing around. Stupid, stupid kids, you know? Would you like a coffee? I just started a pot and I'd be happy to go get you some."

I shook my head. "I've got a few things to do, Joan. And you must have kids getting dropped off soon."

"What if, and this is a huge thing to ask, but what if I brought you over a coffee when Mr. Bain drops off Carlson? Would you have any problem with that? He still kind of has me worried, that man does, and the more he gets the idea that I've got someone next door looking after me—and I'm not saying that's what you're actually doing because I sure wouldn't want to impose or anything—the more I think he's not going to give me a hard time about anything I might have heard his son say about his mom falling down the stairs the other day, if you get my drift. Maybe if you're sort of standing out here at the front of your garage and when he comes you can wander over and say something like 'Hey, where's that coffee you promised me?'"

I sighed. Even without the events of the night before, I would have been exhausted.

"Sure," I said.

I saw the red Explorer pull in to the drive about fifteen minutes later. Carl Bain, dressed in what looked like the same suit I'd seen him in the other day, came around the truck and opened the back door to free his son from the straps of the safety seat. I started walking over, looking down at the lawn as though I hadn't even noticed him.

As we both neared the front door, I looked up and said, "Oh, hey. Morning."

"Morning," he said. His son said nothing.

"Just, uh...Joan told me to grab a coffee if I felt like it." I felt like a damn fool. How had I allowed myself to be talked into this?

The door swung open and Joan stood there smiling, a mug already in her hand. "Well, if it isn't the three strongest, handsomest men I know. Morning, Carlson! How are you today?"

The boy maintained his silence as he slipped into the house. Joan handed me my coffee. "There you go, neighbor. How are you today, Mr. Bain?"

He shrugged. "See you around six."

"Okay then, well, you boys have a super day." With that, Joan closed the door on both of us. Me standing there with a stupid cup of coffee as Bain started back for his Explorer.

No more, I thought. *I won't be dragged into this again. This has to be dealt with.*

"Hey," I said. "Wait up."

Bain stopped and turned. "Yeah?"

"This is...this is awkward. Joan—Ms. Mueller—she's been feeling kind of on edge lately."

He looked instantly concerned. "She okay? She's not gonna stop babysitting, is she? It took me a long time to find someone, and Carlson, he's real happy here and—"

"No, it's nothing like that. She...she has the idea you might be concerned about something with regard to your wife. I don't know anything about you, Mr. Bain, and I don't know what goes on in your home, but you need to know that Ms. Mueller never made any calls to anyone about—"

"What the hell are you getting at? What about my wife?"

I'd regretted agreeing to Joan's stunt about the coffee, and was quickly starting to regret wading into this conversation. "All I'm saying is, if there are problems between you and your wife, if someone's been to see you about rumors, I hope you're getting the help you need, but you have to know that Joan—"

"I don't know what the hell this is about, pal, but if you know something about my wife, and where I might find her, I'd love to hear it. Otherwise, mind your own goddamn business."

That stopped me short. "Where you might *find* her?"

"Christie took off shortly after Carlson was born," he said bitterly. "Ran off on both of us. I haven't seen that woman in nearly four years. Carlson hasn't seen her since he was four months old. He wouldn't know that woman if she got her own show on the Disney Channel."

THIRTY

I could have gone back and knocked on Joan Mueller's door and asked her what the hell was going on, why she was playing me this way, whether she'd simply lost her mind, but I had a better plan. Stay as far away from her as possible.

When Kelly was eating her frosted flakes, I said, "After you get back from staying with your grandmother, you won't be going to Ms. Mueller's house after school anymore."

"Why not?"

"She's got enough kids to look after." And I wasn't so sure she should be looking after them, but I had my own problems right now. "We'll check into an after-school program or something."

"If I'm even *at* that school anymore," Kelly reminded me.

I called Sally Diehl at the office.

"I don't know when I'm going to make it in today," I said. "I'm taking Kelly to her grandparents' place."

"Nice," Sally said. "She's getting a day off school."

"She's going to be off for a little while," I said. "Change of scenery. I want you to call Alfie over at the fire department." Alfred Scranton was a deputy chief, and the point man on investigations.

"Sure," Sally said. "What's up?"

"I was talking to someone last night about bogus electrical parts. Stuff from China or wherever, looks legit but inside it's nothing but shit."

"Daddy," Kelly scolded me.

"Is this about the fire?" Sally asked. A tender spot for her, considering her Theo wired the house that went up in flames. But there was no shielding her from this. She worked in the office and everything went through her desk sooner or later.

"Yes," I said. "I want to know if they had a close look at the parts that came out of that breaker panel. I want to know if they were the real deal."

"Come on, Glen, Theo wouldn't put stuff like that in one of your houses."

"Sally, just make the call, okay?"

"Got it," she said, but she didn't sound happy. "You haven't just got it in for him, have you?"

"How well do you know me, Sally?"

"Okay, I take it back. I'll make the call." Wanting to get off the subject, she said, "So what's with Kelly? She okay? You pulling her out of school?"

Kelly got up, rinsed her cereal bowl in the sink, and left the room.

"Truth is, we had a bit of an incident last night," I said.

"What?"

"Someone took a shot at the house."

"What? God, Glen, what happened?"

I told her.

"I just can't believe it. She okay?"

"Yeah, she's fine, considering everything. First her mother dies, then her friend's mother, and then this. She needs a break from Milford. So, tell Doug he's the main guy today. Any problems, you can always reach me on my cell."

Sally promised she'd be in touch, and said to give Kelly a hug for her.

Kelly was standing at the bottom of the stairs with her travel case. "Sally says hi," I said.

"Can you put this in the truck?" she asked. "I want to go check to make sure I haven't forgotten anything."

That reminded me I had to call her school, let them know she was going to be away for a while. She'd already missed the start of class today, and we were likely to be getting a call any moment since I hadn't phoned her in absent. I put in a call to the office, left a message on the machine.

I took Kelly's case, went out the front door and around to the back of the truck. I dropped the tailgate, tossed in the case, and grabbed a three-foot two-by-four scrap that was lying in there. I had a collection of bits and pieces in the garage, and thought this a worthy addition.

I was headed back into the house when a black Chrysler 300 came to a stop across the end of the driveway. I didn't know the car. But when the driver got out, I recognized him, even though we'd never met before.

I stepped into the front hall, leaving the door open a crack.

"Kelly!"

She appeared at the top of the stairs. "Yup?"

"Listen carefully. I'm going outside to talk to a man. Lock this door when I leave. Watch from the window. If something happens, call 911."

"What's going—"

"Have you got that?"

"Yes."

I turned and she scooted down the stairs. Once outside, I listened for the sound of the deadbolt turning into position behind me.

I was still holding the two-by-four.

The driver, a tall dark-haired man in a leather jacket, black pants, and well-shined shoes, came around the front of the Chrysler and leaned against the passenger door. He was wearing sunglasses he didn't bother to take off.

"Can I help you?"

He looked up at the second-floor window that I'd covered over with a sheet of plywood. "Somebody throw a ball through your window, Mr. Garber?"

"Don't leave your car there. I'm backing out."

"I won't be long. I'm just here to pick up something." He folded his arms across his chest. He glanced at the two-by-four in my hand, then disregarded it.

"Pick up what?" I asked. Crossing his arms had brought his sleeves up on his arms, revealing an expensive watch.

"A package your wife was supposed to deliver for her friend. Belinda Morton."

"My wife is dead."

He nodded. "As it turns out, she died the day she was supposed to make this delivery."

"I don't know what you're talking about."

But I was thinking about the envelope, the one Belinda had given to Sheila.

He rubbed his chin with his right hand, like he was mulling over how to deal with me. When he did it, his sleeve pulled back some, revealing a tattoo. An ornate chain design encircled his wrist.

"Looking at my Rolex?" he said.

"A fake?"

He nodded, impressed. "You got a good eye."

"Not really. But that's your specialty, right?"

He eyed me curiously but said nothing.

"You're Sommer," I said. "At least, that's one name you go by. You're in the knockoff business."

That got his attention. I could see his eyes blink behind the shades. "Mr. Twain told you about me." It wasn't a question. I got the sense this was his way of letting me know he'd been watching me, or Twain, or both.

"Why'd my wife call you the day she died?" I asked.

He took his weight off the car, flexed his hands. I tightened my grip on the two-by-four.

"She left a message to say she couldn't make it," he said. "Why do you think that was?"

"I don't know."

"My theory is, she changed her mind. Or had it changed for her. Maybe you had something to do with that."

"You've got that wrong."

Sommer smiled. "Look, Mr. Garber, let's not bullshit each other. I know how it is. You've had money troubles lately. Your wife suddenly has a nice chunk of change in her possession. You think, *Hey, that could take care of a few of our problems.* How'm I doing?"

"Not very well."

Something had caught his eye. "Your neighbor lady always watch everything that goes on out here?"

"Neighborhood Watch," I said.

Sommer's gaze had switched from Joan Mueller's house to mine.

"Seems that everyone's watching us," he said. "That must be your little girl, peeking through the curtain."

Trying to keep my voice as even as possible and gripping the length of wood tightly, I answered, "You threaten her and I'll beat you to death."

He held out his hands, as if bewildered by my tone. "Mr. Garber, you've totally misinterpreted my intentions. Have I threatened you? Have I threatened your daughter? I'm just a businessman, eager to complete a transaction. And here you are, threatening harm to me."

I took a moment to think about how I wanted to handle this. "This money, this package, you say Belinda gave it to my wife to deliver to you."

Sommer's head went up and down a fraction of an inch.

"Why don't you check in with her later today," I suggested. "Maybe she'll have some news for you."

Sommer considered that. "All right then." He pointed to the two-by-four. "But if she doesn't, I'll be seeing you again."

He turned and got back into his car. He sped off so quickly I didn't have a chance to take note of the plate number. Seconds later, the Chrysler turned the corner at the end of the street and was gone.

"I didn't call 911," Kelly reported cheerfully when I came in. "It looked like you guys were just having a nice chat."

THIRTY-ONE

Emily Slocum located her father in the bathroom, shaving.

"Dad, there's someone at the door," she said, her voice flat and emotionless.

"What? It's not even eight o'clock yet. Who is it?"

"Some lady," Emily said.

"What lady?"

"She's got a badge."

Emily went into her parents' bedroom to watch television while Darren Slocum grabbed a towel and wiped the shaving cream off his face. As he was buttoning up his shirt, he looked at her. This was pretty much all Emily had done these last few days. Sat and stared at the TV, not really seeing anything, her eyes glazed over, like she was in some kind of trance.

He did up the last couple of buttons as he walked to the front door. Rona Wedmore was standing on the tiles just inside the door.

"Jeez, Rona, did you tell Emily it was you?" He took her hand and shook it.

Detective Wedmore said, "I did. I guess she forgot."

"I just put some coffee on. You want some?"

Wedmore said yes and followed him into the kitchen. "How are you doing?"

"Not so great," he said, getting down a couple of mugs. "I'm really worried about Emily. She's not crying all the time or anything like that, but it'd almost be better if she did. It's like she's keeping it all bottled up. She just kind of stares."

"You should take her to the doctor. He might suggest she see someone."

"Yeah, maybe. I'm going to let her stay home from school all this week. Ann's sister's been coming over a lot, spelling me off. We've had the visitation—thanks for coming, by the way—and today we're going to have a small, family-only service."

Wedmore said, "I need to ask you a few more questions about Ann's accident, Darren."

"Okay," he said. "Cream, sugar?"

"Black," she said, taking the mug from him. "Have you thought any more about why Ann was down by the harbor so late at night, alone?"

Slocum shrugged. "I don't know. Sometimes, if she can't sleep—if she *couldn't* sleep—she'd take a walk at night, or go for a drive. She might have thought looking out over the Sound, down by the harbor there, would be relaxing."

"But you said she was going out to meet her friend, Belinda Morton."

"That's right. They never hooked up."

"So why did she go down to the harbor first?"

"Like I said, maybe she just needed to clear her head."

Slocum poured cream into his coffee, watching the liquid go from black to light brown.

"You think it's possible," Wedmore asked, "that she was going to meet someone else before she was going to meet Belinda?"

"Like who?"

"I'm asking you."

"What's going on here, Rona? Is there something weird about Ann's accident I should know?"

"Okay, let's start there," she said. "I've been down there, to the harbor, a couple of times. And I've read the investigating officers' reports."

Slocum looked at her curiously. "Yeah?"

"And, I have to tell you, Darren, it's not coming together for me."

He took a sip of coffee. He'd put too much cream in it. He grimaced. "What do you mean?"

"The way it looked, initially, is that Ann noticed she had a flat, she gets out to check, leaving the door open, the motor running, goes around the back, on the passenger side, and takes a look, somehow loses her balance, maybe hits her head on the edge of the pier, and goes into the water." She looked into his face carefully. "Are you okay talking about this?"

"Of course."

"So I've gone down there, and parked in the same spot, and I can't figure how, exactly, she did it. She hadn't been drinking before she left."

"That's right."

"When I was down there, I kind of pretended to stumble, you know?" She did a brief demonstration, like she was tripping over her own feet. "There's plenty of opportunity to catch yourself before you go in."

"But it *was* dark," he reminded her evenly.

"I know. I was down there last night. There's plenty of streetlights." She shook her head. "There's another thing, a big thing."

Slocum waited.

"You know we took Ann's car in, just to give it a going-over. The tech guys didn't notice it at first, but there are these two scratches on the trunk lid."

"Scratches?"

"It's an odd place for them. You get them on the bumper, you get them on the doors, but on the trunk lid? Tech guys said they were very recent."

"I don't know what they would be."

"Ann had rings on both hands," Wedmore said.

"Uh, yes, she did. A wedding ring on her left and another one on her right. Why?"

"If you can picture someone being pushed up against the back of a car, with their hands on the trunk, that's where the scratches are." Wedmore demonstrated, holding her arms out and slightly to the back. "They think the scratch marks could have been made by her rings."

"If she had a flat tire, and went for the spare, she'd have had her hands on the lid." Slocum turned and dumped his coffee in the sink.

"Except there's nothing to suggest she ever attempted to change the tire. She hadn't even turned off the car."

"Why don't you just tell me, Rona, what you think happened."

"I wish I knew. All I know, Darren, is that it doesn't play out the way it looks. It's not playing out the way we're supposed to *think* it looks."

He shook his head. "What are you saying? That it was staged?"

"I'm saying it doesn't feel right. But if that's all there was to it, maybe I'd have to write it off as one of those things. Like you said, maybe she did somehow stumble, then lost her balance and went in. As unlikely as it seems."

Slocum's eyes narrowed. "But you say that's not all there is to it?"

"No. There's this business about why she decided to go out for a drive."

Slocum adopted a puzzled look. "I just told you. Belinda called her. She decided to stop by the harbor first."

"That was the only call she got?"

"Right. Just before she went out."

"She wasn't on the phone earlier that evening?"

"How many times we going to go in circles, Rona?"

"Darren, are you going to keep on playing dumb or you gonna be straight with me here?"

"And why don't *you* just level with *me*? If there's something you want to put out there, just fucking say it."

"What about the call she took in the bedroom? The one the Garber girl heard?"

That stopped him. "Rona, I don't know what people have been telling you, but—"

"Why'd Garber take a punch at you yesterday? What was that all about?"

"Nothing. Just a little misunderstanding."

"The bullet that went through his daughter's bedroom window last night, was that just a little misunderstanding, too?"

"Jesus! You think I had anything to do with that?"

"Whoever shot at that house, they may not have been aiming at the kid, but they were sure sending a message. Did you want to send Glen Garber one after he clocked you?"

"Damn it, Rona, you have got to believe, I did not have *anything* to do with that."

"Convince me. Tell me why he slugged you at the funeral home."

"I'm guessing you already think you know the answer."

She smiled humorlessly. "You were talking to Kelly Garber, without her father's permission. Even though he'd warned you not to. How does that sound?" When he was silent, she continued. "You'd already tried to talk to her before, and her father wouldn't let you, or she wasn't there at the time. How'm I doing?"

"Oh, you're doing just great. I'm fascinated."

"And the reason you've been so desperate to talk to her is, she was hiding in your bedroom closet when Ann was on the phone. She was having a conversation she chose not to tell you about. This is the phone call that prompted her to head out, not the one from Belinda. Kelly Garber was in that closet when your wife was having this conversation, and you really want to know what she overheard." She put out her hands, as though she'd just finished a performance. "How's that?"

Slocum placed his palms on the countertop and pressed down, like he was trying to keep his kitchen from floating away. "I didn't hear that call, and I didn't hear Ann talking to that person. And that's the God's honest truth."

"But you know there was a call. You know Ann was on the phone earlier, and you know the Garber kid was there." Slocum said nothing, so she carried on again. "Here's what I don't get, Darren. First of all, you're a cop, so you're trained to look for things that don't add up. But you don't seem very curious about the circumstances surrounding your own wife's death."

"That's a lie," he said, stabbing an accusing finger at her. "If you know Ann's death wasn't an accident, I want to know what you know."

"The thing is, I'm getting this sense you don't *want* to know," she said. "If it was me, and someone I knew died this way, I'd have a hundred questions. But you don't have any."

"Bullshit," he said.

"And I can only think of two, maybe three reasons why that would be. You had something to do with it, or you know who did and you want to settle the score on your own. Or—and I haven't quite sorted this one out yet—you don't want us nosing around in this because it's going to open up a can of worms you'd rather stayed closed."

"You're really something else," he said. "Going after members of your own department. That give you a little thrill? You know the officers talk, right? About you? About how'd you make detective, anyway? Was it one of those equal opportunity things, trying to make up for the lack of black women detectives in the department?"

Wedmore didn't even blink. "You got anyone who can vouch for where you were all night?"

"What? Are you serious? I was here with Emily."

"So if I asked her now, she could tell me you never left the house? She never went to sleep?"

"I'm not having you bother my daughter at a time like this—"

"So you're saying she wouldn't be able to confirm you were here."

Slocum's face was starting to flush with anger. "We're done."

Wedmore didn't respond.

"You look down on us guys still in uniform. You think, once you make detective, you're hot shit and the rest of us are just a bunch of grunts."

"Another thing," Wedmore said. "I made some calls. You're coming into some money."

"Excuse me?"

"Your wife's life insurance policy. She took it out only a few weeks ago. What's the payout? A couple of hundred grand?"

"Lady, you've got one hell of a nerve—"

"Am I right, Darren?"

"Yeah, okay, so Ann and I both got life insurance. We figured we had enough in the monthly budget to cover the premiums. We wanted to make sure Emily would be okay if something happened to us."

Wedmore's look said she wasn't buying it. "You were married before, weren't you?"

Slocum balled his fists and now his face turned red. "Yeah," he muttered. "I was."

"Did you have a policy on your first wife, too?"

"No," he said. He actually smiled. "Once they'd diagnosed the cancer, it wasn't possible for her to get insurance."

Wedmore blinked. She didn't say anything for a moment, then pushed the mug across the counter in his direction. "Thanks for the coffee. I'll find my way out."

THIRTY-TWO

"I have to make a couple of calls before we leave," I said to Kelly. She rolled her eyes, like we were never going to get out of here, as I went down to my office. My first impulse was to contact the police about Sommer's visit, but as I picked up the receiver I wondered what, exactly, I'd tell them. The guy oozed menace, but he really hadn't threatened me. I was the one who said I'd beat him to death, if he came near Kelly.

So I made the other call. To Belinda's real estate office.

"She's not in right now," the receptionist told me. "If you'd like to leave a message, I'll—"

"What's her cell number?"

She gave it to me. I hung up and dialed the new number. After two rings, an answer. "Glen?" she said.

"Yeah, Belinda."

"Could I call you back? I'm just heading off to show a house."

"No. We need to talk now."

"Glen, if you called to chew me out about the lawyer thing, I told you, I'm sorry about that, I really am. I never—"

"Tell me what was in the envelope," I said, removing the lid from the shoebox under the desk and taking it out.

"Excuse me?"

"The one you gave to Sheila. You answer all my questions about it, and it's yours."

Silence at the other end of the line.

"Belinda?"

"You found it? So it really wasn't in Sheila's car?"

"That depends. You tell me what was in it, and I'll tell you if I've found it."

She started making funny breathing sounds. I wondered whether she was hyperventilating or something.

"Belinda, are you there?"

Her voice small, whispering. "Oh my God, I can't believe it."

"Just tell me."

"Okay, okay, okay, it was an envelope. A brown business envelope. And there was . . . there *was* some money inside."

"So far, so good. How much money?"

"There should be . . . there should be sixty-two thousand in it." She sniffed. She was crying.

I had counted it late last night, and she had it right. "Okay. Next question. What was it for?"

"It was to pay for some merchandise. Some purses. A lot of purses."

"What else?"

"Just . . ."

"Belinda, I'm going to start a little fire in the trash can here. And every time you don't answer my question, I'm going to drop a thousand bucks in."

"Glen, no! Don't do that!"

"What else other than purses?"

"Okay, okay, purses, and also some vitamins and—"

"I'm just getting out my lighter."

"Okay! Not vitamins, exactly. More like pharmaceuticals. Prescription drugs. Discount prescription drugs. Not, like, you know, crack or heroin or anything like that. The kind of drugs that help people. At better prices."

"What else?"

"That's mostly it. A few other things, but mostly purses and prescriptions."

"And where does all this stuff come from?" The receiver felt hot in my hand.

"You know, from purse makers and drug companies."

"I've got a better idea. Instead of setting fire to the money, I'll just hang on to all of it myself."

"Damn it, Glen, what do you want me to tell you?"

"Everything!" I shouted. "I want to know where you get this stuff, what you're doing with it, how Sheila was involved, and why the fuck there's more than sixty fucking grand in an envelope in my house! I want to know why Sheila had this money, why you gave it to her, what she was supposed to do with it. I want to know what the hell happened that last day! I want to know what Sheila did, where she went, who she saw, right up to the moment she drove her car up that ramp. That's what I want you to tell me, Belinda. That's what I want to know."

Once I was done with my tirade, I could hear her weeping. "I don't have all those answers, Glen."

"Tell me the ones you've got. I've got money to burn here."

She sniffed. "The Slocums were the ones who first got into it. Darren, he pulled over some guy driving a van up to Boston one night, for speeding or something. And when he checks out the truck, he finds it full of purses. Knockoffs, you know?"

"I know."

"So instead of giving the guy a ticket, Darren gets asking him about his business, what it's all about. He's thinking this would be a good way for Ann to make some money, because she was losing her job about this time, and the police, they were cutting back on overtime. So the guy, he puts Darren onto his suppliers, people out of New York."

"Okay." I put my free hand to my forehead. I could feel a massive headache coming on.

"Ann said there was a lot of money to be made, and not just in purses. She said there was watches and jewelry and DVDs and building supplies—she had a couple of customers for some of that stuff. But she was finding that running the purse parties kept her busy enough. She didn't want me selling the bags, then we'd be competing with each other, but if I wanted to take on some of the other stuff—and, well, real estate's kind of been slow lately, so I said okay, I'd try the prescriptions."

"Drugs," I said.

"I told you, it's not like that. It's not like I'm running a crystal meth lab. These are legitimate prescription drugs, made overseas. A lot of it comes through Chinatown—you ever been down around Canal Street?"

"How'd Sheila get involved? How'd she end up with all this money? Why was she doing this delivery?"

"She knew how bad things were going for you, Glen. She was taking the course to help you, but then there was the fire, and hardly any jobs on the horizon, and she wanted to do her part. She'd only just gotten into the prescription thing, she'd only made a couple of sales, enough to buy Kelly some new clothes."

Oh, Sheila, I thought. *You didn't have to do this.*

"The money, Belinda."

"Ann and Darren, they had a payment to be made. That was the sixty-two thousand. Sometimes, I'd get it to them. They liked their money delivered in person."

"They?"

"The suppliers. I don't think Ann or Darren had ever really met them, but there was a contact person. I don't know his name for sure, but—"

"Sommer? Tall guy, black hair? Nice shoes? Fake Rolex?"

"That could be him. But the thing was, I'd go into the city, and usually I'd just drop the money off in a mail slot or something, although sometimes, when Ann went in, she'd hand deliver it to the guy. But the day before I was to do the delivery, I had two or three calls from people, wanting to see properties the next day that I had listed, so I asked Sheila, since she was getting interested, and it was already the day she was going to be out for her class, whether she could do the delivery for me."

I squeezed my eyes shut. "And she said yes." Sheila always said yes when a friend asked for help.

"She did. So I gave her the envelope, with a phone number to call if there was a problem."

"Sommer," I said. "Sheila called the number once. To say something had come up. The money never left the house. Why didn't she do the delivery?"

"I don't know, I swear. Glen, they're telling me, if I don't come up with the money soon, they're going to do something! We've managed to pay some of it back. I've maxed out my line of credit and gave seventeen thousand to Darren and Ann, and they put in another eight, for a total of twenty-five. But that still leaves thirty-seven thousand, and if we don't pay soon, there's going to be crazy interest on it. Ann told me, before she died of course, that she'd gotten a life insurance policy, but that could take months to pay out, and these people, they don't want to wait."

"Maybe you should call the police," I said coldly.

"No! No, listen, if I can get the money to them, it'll all be over. I don't want the police involved. George, he doesn't even know I've been doing this. He'd go crazy if he knew I'd gotten involved in all this."

"So what the hell happened?" I said, as much to myself as Belinda. "She didn't make the trip into Manhattan, or if she did, she went without the money. And she didn't make it to her class or—"

"That class," Belinda said. "She was liking it so much at first, but that instructor—she was getting kind of fed up with him."

"You talking about Allan Butterfield? Was he calling her a lot?"

"Yeah. I don't think it was about homework. Sheila would look at her phone, see it was him, and ignore it."

All those missed calls on Sheila's cell. The ones she either didn't hear or chose not to pick up. "Maybe that's why she didn't go to the class," I said. "But where did she go instead?"

"I guess . . . I guess she went somewhere to drink," Belinda said, gently. "I mean, that is kind of what happened. Maybe everything that was going on, she was so stressed out, she just needed to take the edge off, you know? God, I feel like I'm there."

I didn't say anything.

"Glen, I'm so sorry. I'm so sorry about everything that's happened. I'm sorry I involved her in any of this. But we don't know that it has anything to do with what happened later. Maybe . . . maybe she got scared. She had second thoughts about selling the prescriptions and maybe she went to a bar and—"

"Shut up, Belinda. I've heard all I want to hear. You're a hell of a friend. First you get Sheila involved in this, and then you help the Wilkinsons. You're the best."

"Glen," she whimpered. "I answered your questions. I've told you everything I know. I . . . I have to get that money."

"I'll pop it in the mail for you," I said, and ended the call.

THIRTY-THREE

I drove past Belinda's house on the way to the thruway. There was no one home, so I stuffed the envelope through the mail slot in the door and heard it drop on the other side. I'd considered, briefly, slapping some stamps on it and letting Belinda take her chances on the U.S. postal system to get her money back. I was pissed off enough with her to do it, but in the end, common sense prevailed.

Maybe, considering my circumstances, and a pending lawsuit that could wipe me out financially, I should have kept the cash and said nothing. Every little bit helps. But it wasn't mine, and I believed Belinda when she said Sheila had been delivering it for her. The cash was tainted. I didn't want it, and I didn't want any more visits from Sommer.

In one way, the cash had served its purpose. It had leveraged information out of Belinda.

I now knew what Sheila had been up to, what her plan had been to make some extra cash. Whatever Sheila was starting to get mixed up in, she'd been in way over her head. She wouldn't knowingly have gotten involved with someone like Sommer. She'd probably never even met him. She'd had good instincts, and if she'd met this guy, she'd have had nothing further to do with him.

I believed that in my heart.

The more I learned about Sheila's last day, the more convinced I was becoming that she had not gone somewhere to drown her sorrows, then gotten in her car and killed two people and herself, despite how things looked.

There had to be more to it than that. And I was wondering who knew what that was. Sommer? Slocum?

I had more than a few things to talk about with Detective Wedmore next time I saw her.

On the way to Darien, Kelly asked, "How long do I have to go away for?"

"Not long, I hope."

"What about school? Am I going to be in trouble missing school?"

"If you end up being away more than a few days, I'll get some work from your teacher."

She frowned. "What's the point of being away if you have to do work?"

I let that one go. "Look, there's something very serious I have to discuss with you." She studied my face carefully. I felt a pang of guilt. There'd been so many serious things to discuss the last few weeks that she must have wondered how many more there could be. "You need to be really, really careful."

"I'm always careful. Like when I cross the street and stuff?"

"That, sure. But you can't go off doing stuff on your own. You always stay with Grandma or Marcus. No wandering off. No riding your bike or—"

"My bike's at home."

"I'm just saying, you have to stick close to Grandma and Marcus. All the time."

"Fine. This doesn't sound like it's going to be much fun."

As we were coming off the thruway into Darien, there was a woman standing at the bottom of the ramp. She was probably only in her thirties, but looked twice that. By her feet were a ratty-looking backpack and a red plastic basket, the kind the supermarkets have if you're only getting half a dozen items. It had a few water bottles in it and what looked like half a loaf of Wonder Bread and a jar of peanut butter.

She was holding a sign that read, NEED CLOTHES JOB.

"Jeez," I said.

"She was there the other day," Kelly said. "I asked Grandma if we could give her some clothes but she said it's not our responsibility to solve everybody's problems."

That sounded like Fiona. But there was some truth to it. "It's hard to make things right for everyone."

"But if everybody helped just one person, lots of people would get helped. Mom used to say that. Grandma has lots of clothes she doesn't even wear anymore."

"A couple of walk-in closets' worth," I said.

We were stopped at the light and the woman eyed me through the windshield.

"Can I give her something?" Kelly asked.

"Don't put your window down." The woman's eyes seemed dead. She wasn't expecting me to give her anything. Out of every hundred cars that got stopped at this light, how many offered her anything? Two? One? None? What had brought her to this point? Had her life always been this way? Or had she, at one time, had one like ours? A house, a family, a regular job. A husband, maybe. Kids. And if she had known a life like that, was there one event that started the unraveling? Did she lose her job? Did her husband lose his? Did their car die and they had no money to fix it, and couldn't get to work? Did they fall behind on their mortgage and lose their house? And once, having lost it, were they so far behind the eight ball that they could never recover? And it had come to this? Standing at the end of the off-ramp, begging for help?

Couldn't any of us end up this way when one part of our life went horribly wrong, and then the dominoes started to fall?

I fished a five-dollar bill out of my pocket and powered down my window. The woman came around the front of the car, took the bill from my hand without saying a word, and went back to her station.

Kelly said, "You can't get anything for five bucks."

"Tell me what's going on." Fiona stood in her oversized kitchen, with its skylights and marble countertops and Sub-Zero appliances, as Kelly and Marcus talked in the living room.

I told her about the bullet that had gone through Kelly's window. "Between that, and this thing with Darren Slocum pestering Kelly, it made sense to get her out of town. Just take her somewhere fun, that's all I ask."

"My God, Glen, this is all horrible! And why is Ann's husband bugging Kelly?"

My cell rang. I really didn't want to take a call right now, but at the same time, with all that was going on, I needed to know who was trying to reach me.

"Just a sec," I said to Fiona, took out the phone and glanced at the caller ID. It was a number without a name but I was pretty sure I recognized it as the Milford fire department. It was probably Alfie getting back to me. I let it go to message.

"It was this conversation Kelly overheard. The one Ann was having. Slocum thinks if he can get Kelly to remember something about it, it'll help him figure out who she was talking to that night."

"Do you think she can?"

"I don't think so. She didn't hear all that much. The guy's grasping at straws. He's desperate." I paused. "And I kind of get that. It's pretty much how I've been feeling."

I stopped talking as Marcus and Kelly came into the kitchen.

"We're going to get some ice cream," Kelly said happily. "Not to eat there, but to bring home. And we're going to get chocolate sauce and caramel sauce and marshmallow sauce."

"We'll take good care of her," Marcus said.

I gave Kelly a hug before heading out the door, holding on to her so long she finally had to wriggle free.

Once I was back on the road, heading east back to Connecticut, I checked my message.

"Hey, Glen, Alfie here from Milford Fire. Look, your girl Sally called me, and damned if I wasn't going to give you a call today anyway. We sent out those parts from the fire for analysis, and we got the report back yesterday afternoon, a little too late to call, but yeah, what you were calling about, you were right. Those parts, they weren't good enough to keep a pen flashlight going. It was crap. Cheap, knockoff crap. This could put you in a shitload of trouble, my friend."

I dialed his number.

"Sorry about the shitty news," Alfie said.

"Give me the details."

"We sent out the bits and pieces left from that circuit breaker panel for analysis, and it was all rubbish. Wire was so thin, once you applied some current to it, it melted away to nothing. We're seeing more and more of this. I don't mean us, here in Milford, although this stuff is around. But across the country, it's getting bad. Some of the stuff going into new houses, man, I wouldn't use it in my dog's house. Listen, Glen, I have to send this on to the insurance company, you know."

"I know."

"And once they find out that house had equipment in it that didn't meet code, they're not going to pay up. In fact, they might just cancel your entire policy. They're going to figure, if you put that kind of shit in one house, maybe you've put it in any other house you've built."

"I didn't put that crap in, Alfie."

"Not you. Glen, I've known you long enough to know you wouldn't knowingly do this, but somebody working for you did."

"Yeah," I said. "I've got a good idea who. He's not working for me anymore."

"Anybody else that guy *is* working for, they need to know," Alfie said. "He wires up enough houses with that knockoff shit, sooner or later someone's gonna die."

"Thanks for the heads-up, Alfie."

I flipped the phone shut and tossed it onto the seat next to me.

I wanted to find Theo Stamos. I wanted to find Theo Stamos and kill the son of a bitch. But, seeing as how I was now going through Bridgeport, Theo was going to have to wait while I paid a visit to someone else.

THIRTY-FOUR

Belinda Morton couldn't believe it when Glen Garber told her he'd put the money in the mail. An envelope with sixty-two thousand dollars? Surely he wasn't crazy enough to trust all that cash to the mailman. But maybe that was his way of making a point, of showing how angry he was with her.

Not that she could blame him.

She'd just been about to head out for an appointment to show a condo to a couple in their thirties who'd had enough of living and working in Manhattan, had found jobs in New Haven, and were looking for something with a view of the Sound. She phoned and said she'd had a family emergency and had to race home.

And she was almost out the office door when this guy showed up.

Said his name was Arthur Twain, that he worked for some private investigation or security company or something, and he wanted to talk to her about Ann Slocum, and fake purses, and whether she'd been to any purse parties, and did she know that the money that went to buy knock-off products supported organized crime. She could feel herself sweating right through her clothes, even though it was barely sixty degrees out there today.

"I'm sorry," she said, probably ten times. "I don't know anything about this. I really don't."

"But you were a friend of Ann's, weren't you?" Twain persisted.

"I really have to go, I'm sorry."

Ran to her car, squealed out of the lot so fast she nearly ran down a woman on a bicycle.

"Calm down calm down calm down calm down," she kept telling herself. She would have to call Darren, tell him about this Arthur Twain, ask him what she should say if he came to see her again.

She hoped that when Glen said he'd put the money in the mail, he meant the mail slot of her home. She got out of the car so quickly she didn't even bother to close the door. If she hadn't needed her keys to get into the house, she'd have probably left the motor running.

She ran to the door, nearly rolling over on a heel, tried three times to get the key into the slot before she was able to turn it. She swung the door open, looked down onto the floor where the mail always fell.

Nothing.

"Shit, shit, shit," she said. She half stumbled three steps into the house and allowed herself to fall onto the stairs, leaned up against the railing and felt herself starting to shake.

Just because the money wasn't there didn't mean it had been lost, she told herself. Maybe Glen still had it. Maybe he was planning to drop it off later. Maybe he was on his way.

And maybe the son of a bitch really had put it into the mail. That would be just like him. If there was one thing she'd learned from being friends with Sheila all those years, Glen did have a bit of a self-righteous streak in—

She heard a noise in the house.

It sounded as though it had come from the kitchen.

She froze, held her breath.

Someone was running water into the sink. There was the sound of a clinking glass.

Then someone called out, "Honey? That you?"

Belinda felt a weight being lifted off her chest, but only briefly. It was George. What the hell was he doing home?

"Yes," she gasped. "It's me."

He rounded the corner and saw her collapsed on the stairs. He was in the same suit he wore the day before to the funeral. A different shirt, but still with French cuffs, bands of brilliant white between his hands and sleeves.

"You scared me half to death," she scolded him. "What are you doing here? Your car's not in the driveway."

"When I got to work, I wasn't feeling all that well," he said. "I think it might be that fish you made last night. So I decided to come home, work from here today. I'm not going back to the office, so I put the car in the garage." George ran his management consulting business out of New Haven, but it was just as easy for him to work from home. "And what about you? I thought you had a showing?"

"I . . . it was canceled."

"What are you doing on the stairs? You look like you've been crying."

"I'm . . . I'm fine."

"Are you sure?" George asked, reaching into his suit jacket and pulling out a brown envelope. "Is it possible it has something to do with not finding this?"

Belinda was on her feet. She recognized the envelope immediately. By its thickness, and her own handwriting on the outside. "Give me that."

She went to grab for it but he pulled it away, slipping it back into his jacket.

"I said give it to me," she said.

George shook his head sadly, as though Belinda were a child who'd just come home with an F. "So you *were* expecting this," he said.

"Yes."

"There's sixty-two thousand dollars here. I counted it. It was dropped through the mail slot. You knew this was coming?"

"It's business. It's a down payment on a property down on East Broadway."

"What's this phone number on it? And who makes a down payment with cash, and doesn't even get a proper receipt? And is it just a coincidence I saw Glen Garber's truck driving away from the house when I turned down the street? Is Glen the one putting a down payment on a property? Would you mind if I asked him about it?"

"Don't meddle in my affairs, George. You've done enough already, making me talk to those lawyers about Sheila. Do you know how much that hurt Glen? Do you have any idea what that may do? It could wipe him out. It could bankrupt him."

George was unruffled. "People need to be accountable, Belinda. They need to be held to a certain standard. And if Glen wasn't cognizant of problems Sheila was having, when he should have been, then there's a price to pay for that. And envelopes stuffed with cash, dropped through a mail slot, do not meet those standards. Don't you realize the sort of risks that exposes us to, to have that kind of cash around the house?"

Cognizant. She wanted to kill him. All the years she'd put up with this. Thirteen years of his sanctimonious bullshit. The fool had no idea what he was talking about. No idea how deep she was in. And no sense that this money, this envelope stuffed with cash, was her ticket to digging herself out.

"What I'm going to do," George continued, "is I'm going to put this money away someplace safe for you, and when you can show me what exactly it relates to, and assure me it's going to be handled in a responsible manner, then I'll be happy to hand it over."

"George, no. You can't do this!"

But he was already walking away, heading to his ground-floor study. By the time she caught up, he was already across the room, swinging out the hinged portrait of his equally sanctimonious, judgmental, ramrod-stiff, son-of-a-bitch father—dead, thank God—to reveal a wall safe.

"I need that money," Belinda pleaded.

"Well, then you better explain where it came from and what it's for." George turned the dial on the safe and opened it in seconds. He tossed the envelope in, closed the door, and gave the combination a spin. "I hope this doesn't have anything to do with those illegitimate women's accessories Ann used to sell. Those dreadful parties."

She glared at him.

"You know how I feel about the sanctity of trademarks and copyright. Selling bags that are not what they purport to be, that are not authentic, that's just not right. The fact is, I don't even know why a woman would want a bag that said it was a Fendi or whatever when in fact it was not. You know why? Because you'd always *know.* What pleasure is there in carrying around something you know to be fake?"

She looked at his comb-over attempt.

"For example," he continued, "if I could get a car that looked like a Ferrari for a fraction of the price, but underneath it was a Ford—well, that's not a car I would want."

George in a Ferrari, Belinda thought. She could no more picture a donkey piloting an airplane.

"What's happening to you?" she asked. "You've always been a self-righteous, pretentious asshole, but these last few days there's something else going on. You're sleeping on the couch, saying you're sick but you don't have the flu or anything, and you freaked out when I tried to join you in the shower, you—"

"You're not the only one who has stresses."

"And now you're adding to them. You have to give me that money."

"It's up to you. Tell me what's going on."

"You have no idea what you're doing," Belinda said to him.

"Oh, I know," he said. "I'm doing the responsible thing."

She wondered if he'd still be saying that after a visit from Sommer.

THIRTY-FIVE

I found my way to the Bridgeport Business College and parked in a visitor's spot. It didn't look all that much like a college. It was a long, flat, industrial-looking building without an ounce of academic charm. But it reportedly had good courses, and that was what had led Sheila to come here for her night classes.

I didn't know whether Allan Butterfield was part of the regular faculty, or merely taught an evening course here on the side. I went through the entrance doors and approached a man sitting at the information desk in the drab foyer.

"I'm looking for a teacher, his name's Butterfield."

He didn't need to consult anything. He pointed. "Take that hall to the end, go right, office is on the left. Just look for the signs."

I was standing outside Allan Butterfield's door a minute later, and rapped on it.

"Hello?" said a muffled voice from inside.

I turned the knob and opened the door on a small, cluttered office space. There was just enough room for a desk and a couple of chairs. Papers and books were stacked helter-skelter.

Butterfield wasn't alone. A redheaded woman in her early twenties sat on the other side of the desk from Butterfield. An open laptop was balanced on her knees.

"Excuse me," I said.

"Oh, hi," Butterfield said. "Glen, Glen Garber." He remembered me from our meeting after Sheila's death, when I'd been attempting to trace Sheila's final hours.

"I need to talk to you," I said.

"I'm just finishing up here with—"

"Now."

The woman closed her laptop and said, "That's okay, I can come back later, Mr. Butterfield."

"Sorry, Jenny," he told her. "Why don't you pop in tomorrow?"

She nodded, grabbed a jacket she had draped over the back of her chair, and squeezed past me to get out the door. I took her chair without being invited.

"So, Glen," he said. First time I met him, I put him in his early forties. Five-five, pudgy. Mostly bald, a pair of reading glasses perched on the end of his nose. "Last time we spoke, you were trying to track down Sheila's movements the day of the . . . well, I know you were extremely concerned. Have you gotten some answers to your questions? Achieved some sort of closure?"

"Closure," I repeated. The word tasted like sour milk in my mouth. "No, no closure."

"I'm so sorry to hear that."

No sense beating around the bush. "Why are there so many calls from you to my wife's cell phone before she died?"

He opened his mouth but nothing came out. Not for a good second or two. I could see he was trying to think of something, but the best he could come up with on short notice was "I'm sorry—I—what?"

"There's a slew of calls from you to my wife. Missed calls. It looks to me like she was receiving them, but didn't want to take them."

"I'm sorry, but I don't know what you're talking about. I mean, I'm sure, occasionally, I may have had reason to call your wife about the course she was taking, she had questions related to the assignments, but—"

"I think that's bullshit, Allan."

"Honestly, Glen, I—"

"You need to know that I'm having a very, very bad day, which happens to be part of a very, very bad month. So when I tell you I'm not in the mood for bullshit, you need to believe me. Why all the calls?"

Butterfield appeared to be assessing his chances at escape. The office was so crowded, he'd never get out from behind that desk and through the door without stumbling over something before I could block his path.

"It was totally my fault," he said. There was a slight tremor in his voice.

"What was your fault?"

"I behaved, I behaved inappropriately. Sheila—Ms. Garber—she was a very nice person. Just a naturally nice person."

"Yes," I said. "I know."

"She was just . . . she was very special. Considerate. She was someone . . . someone I could talk to."

I didn't say anything.

"I don't really have anyone in my life, you see. I've never been married. I was engaged once, in my twenties, but it didn't work out." He nodded sadly. "I don't think I was . . . she said I tried a little too hard. Anyway, I rent a room upstairs in a nice old house on Park. I have this job, and I like it, and the people here, they're good to work with, but I don't have a lot of friends."

"Allan, just tell me—"

"Please. The thing is, I'm not accustomed to kindnesses. Your wife was very nice to me."

"Nice how?"

"One night, I happened to mention in class that I wasn't quite my usual self, that my aunt had just died. My mother died when I was only ten years old, and my aunt and uncle took me in, so she was very close to me. I said I had to leave class a little early, because I was going to stay with my uncle for a few days. He was never very good at looking after himself at the best of times, and now, well, I needed to make sure he was taking care of himself. We have a break halfway through class, and evidently Sheila went to the ShopRite, then she quietly took me aside and handed me this bag with a coffee cake and some bananas and some tea and said, 'Here, that should get you through tomorrow morning with you and your uncle.' And you know what she did? She *apologized* for the coffee cake. Because it was store-bought. Said if she'd known, before class, she'd have made something herself. I was so touched, by her thoughtfulness. Did she ever tell you about that?"

"No," I said. But it did sound like Sheila.

"This is very hard for me to say to you," Butterfield said. "I mean, it'll just seem, I don't know, maybe it'll seem strange to you, but I was very much affected when she passed away."

"Why all the calls, Allan?"

He frowned and looked down at his messy desk. "I made a fool of myself."

I decided to let him tell it at his own speed.

"I told you, before, that Sheila and I had gone out for a drink one night. That was all it was. Honestly. It was nice, just having someone to talk to. I told her, when I was younger, that I wanted to be a travel writer. That I had this dream of going all around the world and writing about it. And she said to me, she said, if that's what you want to do, you should do it. I said, I'm forty-four. I have this teaching job. I can't do that. She said, take a vacation, go someplace interesting, and write about it. See if I could sell the story to a magazine or newspaper. She said, don't quit. Try to do it on the side, see where it goes." He nodded happily, but looked as though he might cry. "So, next week, I go to Spain. I'm going to do it."

"That's great," I said, still waiting.

"So after I booked the trip, I wanted to thank her. I asked her out to dinner. I suggested she come early on a class night, and I would take her out. To show my gratitude."

"And she said?"

"She said, 'Oh, Allan, I couldn't do that.' I realized that what I had asked her for was a date. A married woman, and I had asked her for a date. I don't know what I was thinking. I was so sorry, so embarrassed by my actions. I just . . . liked talking to her. She was so encouraging. She made me believe in myself, and then I did something so stupid."

I still didn't know what the calls were about, but figured he was just about to get to that part of the story.

"I guess I never felt a single apology was sufficient. I phoned a couple of times, said I was sorry. And then I was worried maybe she would drop the course, so I phoned her again, but she stopped taking my calls." He looked crushed. "I thought, if she would answer just one last time, I'd make a final apology, but she didn't. Someone reached out to me, and I ended up pushing them away." He sighed. "It's kind of what I do."

"Do you think she intended to come to class that night?" I asked. "She never said anything to me about not going."

"It's kind of what I've wondered, too," Butterfield said. "And she was really liking the course, and looking forward to helping you. The week before, she told me about her plans for a business of her own."

"What did she say about that?"

"She wanted to run a business from her home, maybe set up a website where people could order things."

"What kind of things?"

"Common prescription items. I—I told her I wasn't sure that was such a good idea. That the quality of the goods, it might be difficult to verify, and that if they didn't do what they were supposed to do, she might open herself up to certain liabilities. She said she hadn't thought about that, and she would look into it. She said she'd hardly sold anything so far, and if she had reason to believe the drugs were dangerous, she wouldn't sell them."

I got up and extended a hand. "Find lots to write about in Spain."

I was almost to the Milford exit when I called the office.

"Garber Contracting," said Sally Diehl. "How may I help you?"

"It's me. You don't look at call display anymore?"

"I just had a glazed donut," she replied cheerfully, "and was too busy licking my fingers to notice it was you."

I wondered if there was a way to find out from her where I might find Theo without letting her know I wanted to murder him.

"You hear back from Alfie?" she asked.

"Not yet," I lied. "I was hoping to ask Theo a couple of things first. You know where he is?"

"Why do you want to see him?" Sounding defensive.

"I just need to ask him a couple of things," I said. "No big deal."

She hesitated. "He's rewiring a house down on Ward, right near the harbor, around the corner from your place. It's a huge reno."

"Got an address?"

She didn't have the number, but said I wouldn't be able to miss the place. If the house was being totally remodeled, there'd be a Dumpster out front, and of course, it wasn't hard to spot Theo's truck, what with his name being on the side and that set of plastic testicles dangling from the back bumper.

"That it?" Sally asked.

"Yeah, for now."

"Thing is, I was going to give you a call. Doug went home."

"What, is he sick?"

"I don't think it was like that. He didn't even call the office to tell me. I got a call from KF. He said Doug got a call, he thinks from his wife, and flew out of there like a bat out of hell."

"No idea what happened?"

"I tried him on his cell and he talked to me for like three seconds. He said, 'They're taking my house. And that was it.' "

"Shit," I said. "Okay, look, I'm going to take a ride by there and see what's going on."

"Let me know, okay?"

"Sure."

I kept on 95, going past the Connecticut Post Mall on my left, and got off at Woodmont Road. Five minutes after that, I was pulling up in front of Doug and Betsy Pinder's place.

The front yard was in total disarray.

It looked as though the Pinders had decided to move, had gathered all their possessions in front of the house in a matter of minutes, and then canceled the moving van.

There was a dresser with drawers hanging out, half-open suitcases with clothes spilling everywhere, pots and pans scattered on the grass, a Rubbermaid cutlery holder sitting on the sidewalk. Three kitchen chairs, a television, DVD player, a scattering of DVD cases. An end table, lamps on their sides. It was as though someone knew they had ten minutes to empty the house before it blew up, and this was what they'd managed to save.

But the house had not blown up. It was still standing. But there was a new lock affixed to the door, and some official-looking notice stapled to it.

Wandering about, in the midst of this wreckage, like people scavenging for mementos in a house that's just been ravaged by a tornado, were Doug and Betsy Pinder. She was doing more crying than looking, and Doug was just standing there, slumped and pale, appearing to be somewhere between dumbfounded and in shock.

I got out of the truck and walked up the drive, past Doug's old truck and Betsy's Infiniti. Whatever authorities had come and brought things to a head this way were long gone.

"Hey," I said. Betsy, standing by one of the metal and vinyl chairs from their kitchen set, looked at me through teary eyes, then turned away.

Doug glanced up and said, "Oh, Glenny. Sorry, I had to leave the site."

"What's happened here, Doug?"

"They locked us out," he said, his voice breaking. "The sons of bitches locked us out of our own home."

"And you let them," Betsy snapped. "You didn't do a goddamn thing to stop them."

"What the hell was I supposed to do?" he shouted at her. "Did you want me to shoot them? Was that what you wanted me to do?"

I put my hand on Doug's arm. "Tell me what happened."

Now he turned on me. "And no thanks to you," he said. "I came to you for help and you didn't give a shit."

"Whatever kind of trouble you're in," I said, keeping my voice low and calm, "I don't think a week or two of advance pay was going to solve it. You know that and I know that. So what happened?"

"They foreclosed," he said. "They came in and kicked us out."

"That kind of thing doesn't happen overnight," I said. "You have to be at least, what, three months behind on your mortgage? And they send a letter, and put a note on your door and—"

"You think I didn't see it coming? Why the hell do you think I was asking you for help?" He shook his head. "I should have made that call about you."

"All that unopened mail, all those bills," I said, ignoring his last comment. "Maybe a few of the warnings were in there."

"What the hell am I going to do?" he said, waving his arms at his belongings. "What the hell are *we* going to do?"

"Oh great, *now* you're thinking about a plan," Betsy sniped. "Too bad you hadn't been thinking about something a little sooner, Einstein."

Doug glared at her. "Yeah, you're totally blameless. You didn't have a goddamn thing to do with this. How could you? You were never home. You were at the *mall*."

Betsy's eyes filled with rage. She pointed her finger at her husband and jabbed into the air repeatedly. "Maybe you should have manned up, taken control of the situation. Who's supposed to have a handle on things? Huh? Who's supposed to be some kind of a goddamn provider? *You?* Don't make me laugh. When have *you* ever stepped up to the plate?"

"You know what you do?" he spat. "You don't just suck the money out of me. You suck the *life* out of me, that's what you do. I got nothing left. *Nothing*. You've got it all, babe. You've got all I ever had to give."

"Really? Is that why now I've got nothing but *shit*? Because that's all you've ever given me since—"

Doug moved on her. He had his hands out in front of him. He was going for her neck. Rather than run, Betsy stood, frozen in place, wide-eyed, as Doug bolted forward. He had about ten feet to close between them, which gave me enough time to get my arms around him from behind before he could latch onto Betsy.

"Doug!" I shouted into his ear. *"Doug!"*

He tried to wrestle away from me. He was a strong, wiry guy, like most people who work in construction. But I was just as fit, and I'd locked my fingers together on his chest, pinning his arms in place. He squirmed around for a second or two, then went docile.

Once Betsy saw that he was under control, she resumed her taunting, that finger jabbing into the air again. "You think *this* is what I wanted? You think I like standing out on my own goddamn lawn, can't get into my home? You think—"

"Betsy!" I shouted. "Shut up!"

"And who the hell do you think you—"

"Both of you! Just shut up for a second."

Betsy lowered the finger as I released my grip on Doug. "Look," I said, "I get it. You're upset and want to kill each other. If that's what you want to do, maybe I should just let you. God knows I got enough other things to deal with. But it's not going to solve your problem. You need to deal with the situation."

"Easy for you to say," Doug said.

I'd had enough. "Listen to me, you dumb son of a bitch. You've known this day was coming. You can blame Betsy, or me, or Sally for not bailing you out, but the fact is you and Betsy own this mess." I turned on Betsy. "Same goes for you. You can either deal with this mess now and try to get your life back together, or you can stand out here screaming at each other. Which is it?"

Betsy had tears in her eyes. "He wouldn't even open the bills. He just stuffed them in a drawer."

Doug countered, "What was the point of opening them? It's not like we could pay them." To me, he said, "They ripped us off. The banks. They sold us a bill of goods. Said we could get this place for, like, nothing down, then when it came time to renew, they're all like, Hey, we told you this was going to happen. But they didn't, Glenny, the bastards didn't tell us anything like that. Those fucking bankers, they take government bailouts and give themselves fat fucking bonuses and people like us get screwed!"

"Doug," I said, too tired to say anything else.

He picked up the stack of DVDs and threw them across the yard, flinging them like Frisbees. Then he grabbed a kitchen chair and smashed it several times into the dresser. Betsy and I stood back and let him do it. When he was done, he put the chair down, sat himself on it, and hung his head.

To Betsy, I said, "Where can you stay?"

"My mom's, I guess. In Derby."

"She's got room for both of you?" I asked.

"Yeah. But she's gonna rub our noses in it."

"If she'll give you a place to live, suck it up and take it," I told her.

"I guess."

"Doug," I said. He didn't look up. "Doug." Slowly, he lifted his head. "I'll give you a hand, putting this stuff in your truck. You can store it at the shed." That was the building where we kept equipment, out back of the Garber Contracting office off Cherry Street. "Probably going to take a couple of loads."

He got up slowly, picked up a single DVD—a *Predator* movie—and walked it over to his truck like a condemned man. He opened the tailgate and tossed it in.

Loading up was going to take a long time at this rate.

I stuffed some clothes that were spilling out of a suitcase and managed to zip it shut. "This'll probably go to your mom's, right?" Betsy nodded. "So you might as well put it in your car."

Moving equally slowly, she took the case and threw it into the back seat of her Infiniti. Neither of them said a word for the next half hour as the three of us picked up their belongings from the front yard and put them either in the car or truck. The dresser and the end tables wouldn't fit anywhere, so Doug said he'd come back for those later.

"You heading over to the office?" he asked me.

"No," I said. "I've got another stop to make."

THIRTY-SIX

Finding the right house on Ward was a piece of cake. There are a lot of older, quaint, seaside-type homes down in that part of Milford, places that shared the kinds of architectural details you'd expect to find on houses on Martha's Vineyard or somewhere up on the Cape. Sheila and I used to talk about shifting over a few blocks into this neighborhood, but whether you moved down the street or across the country, you still had to pack the same amount of stuff.

But those discussions had been a long time ago.

It was a two-story, green, wood-shingled house with gingerbread trim, and as I'd guessed, there was a Dumpster in the driveway. Parked in front and to the side of it were three pickups, one advertising a plumber on one door, another the name of a contracting company, and the third with *Theo's Electric* on the side. A few feet away from the back of the truck, a worker had set up a couple of sawhorses for a makeshift table and was cutting two-by-fours into shorter lengths with a circular saw.

"Hey," I said. "How's it going?"

He nodded, then took in my name on the door of my truck. "Can I help you?"

"Glen Garber," I said. "You in charge here?"

"Naw, I'm Pete. You'd be looking for Hank. Hank Simmons. He's inside."

I knew Hank. Over time, you got to know the other people in town who were doing the same kind of work.

"How about Theo? He around?"

"His truck's right there, so he can't be far."

"Thanks." I took a step toward him, admiring the circular saw. "Nice. A Makita?"

"Yeah."

"Mind if I have a look?"

He got a good grip on the saw and handed it to me. I took it from him, felt the heft of it in my hand, squeezed the trigger for a millisecond to make it whine. "Very nice," I said. I gave a couple of tugs on the extension cord so I could move around to the back of Theo's truck with it.

"What are you doing?"

I crouched down where the decorative, flesh-colored sack was suspended from the bumper. I got myself into a secure stance. When you performed a delicate operation like this, you didn't want any accidents.

"Jesus, what are you doing there?"

I pulled back the housing that shielded the circular blade, held it there with one hand, then hit the trigger with my index finger. The saw buzzed to life. Carefully, resting my elbow on the top of my knee for support, I sliced through the top of Theo's bumper decoration. I eased off the trigger as the truck nuts dropped to the driveway.

I let the shield drop back into place, and when the saw had stopped whining, handed it back to Pete.

"Nice piece of equipment," I said. "Thanks."

"Are you out of your mind?" he yelled. "Are you crazy?"

Bending from the waist as though I were picking up a golf ball, I picked up the nuts and tossed them a couple of times in my hand. "You say Theo's inside?"

Pete, dumbstruck, nodded.

"Good, I'll give these to him," I said, and left Pete standing there, no doubt wondering whether to keep working or follow me inside to see what happened.

He decided to stay outside, but he didn't turn the saw back on.

I walked through the open front door and could hear the sounds of workmen echoing through the house. A hammer tapping, the pneumatic sound of a nail gun, men kibitzing back and forth, the noises echoing because the house was without furniture.

A man in his sixties standing in the front hallway looked me up and down. "Hey, Glen Garber, you old son of a bitch! How you doin'?"

"Not bad, Hank," I said. "Still building houses that fall down if you slam the door too hard?"

"Pretty much," he said. He spotted the truck nuts in my hand. "I like to keep mine in my pants but to each his own."

"I'm looking for Theo."

"Upstairs. Anything I can help you with?"

"No, but I might be able to help you with something. I'll catch you on the way out."

I went up the stairs, which were lined with clear plastic to protect the carpeting underneath. When I got to the second floor, I called out Theo's name.

"In here!" he shouted.

I found him in an emptied master bedroom, down on his knees, stripping wires for new outlets. I stood in the doorway.

"Hey, Glen," he said. "What brings you here?"

I tossed the detached truck nuts onto the floor in front of him. "I believe those are yours," I said.

He looked down at them and his face flushed red with anger. "What the fuck?"

"It was you, you son of a bitch," I said.

"What?" he said, getting up onto his feet. "What was me?"

"I heard back from the fire department."

"Yeah, so?" He glanced down again at the rubber testicles, like they were a dog that had been run over in the road.

"So, you burned my house down. Those parts you put into the circuit breaker panel were shit."

"I don't know what you're talking about," he said.

"I figure this is how it works," I said. "You cost out a job based on what true-blue, American parts cost, then you buy this knockoff crap from China or wherever it comes from for a fraction of what the real stuff costs, and you make yourself a tidy little profit. Only problem is, the stuff doesn't meet code, Theo. The stuff can't handle the load. And the breakers don't trip. And then you've got a house on fucking fire."

Hank Simmons was standing in the hall behind me. "What's going on here?"

"Have a listen," I said over my shoulder. "You're going to want to know about this."

"You can't go around saying stuff like that," Theo said. Taking one last glance at his castrated bumper adornment, he added, "And you don't fuck around with a man's truck."

"I just felt a guy who doesn't have any's got a lot of nerve hanging a pair from his bumper," I said.

I was ready for him.

When he took a swing at me, I ducked under it and put my right fist hard into his gut. As fights go, it lacked excitement. My punch took the wind out of him and he dropped to the floor.

"Shit!" he howled, clutching his stomach.

Hank grabbed my arm but I shook him off. "Jesus, Glen, what the hell are you doing, coming in here and—"

I pointed to the man on the floor. "Hank, if I were you, I'd take a good long took at anything he's installed in this house. This guy burned one of my places down."

"It's not . . . my fault!" Theo gasped.

"That house on Shelter Cove?" Hank asked.

"He put bogus electrical parts in it," I said.

"Goddamn."

"Yeah, no kidding. And insurance companies don't much like to pay off when you build a house with that kind of stuff."

"He's done a couple of my other jobs," Hank said worriedly. Looking down at Theo, he said, "This true? I swear to God, if you've—"

"He's lying!" Theo wheezed, getting onto his knees. "I'm gonna have you charged! I'm gonna have you charged with assault!"

I turned to Hank. "Did you see him take a swing at me first?"

Hank said, "I believe I did."

"See you later, Theo," I said.

I turned and started down the stairs. By the time I was out the front door, I could hear Theo coming up behind me. I spun around, figuring he was going to try to jump me, but he wasn't making any aggressive moves.

"You got me all wrong, man," he said. "It's not my fault." There was the sound of pleading in his voice.

"Sure," I said. I stood my ground. "You're finished. You're done. I'm going to tell everyone the kind of work you do. There's not going to be a contractor in Connecticut who'll hire you."

"Don't do this, man. I only tried to do my best. You've always done right by me."

"You're lucky you didn't actually end up killing anybody," I said. "You nearly killed me."

I got in my truck, feeling exhilarated. It was almost a kind of high, working out my anger and frustrations on Theo. He had it coming.

But it didn't take long for the elation to fade away into regret. I'd just punched Theo Stamos, the man Sally Diehl was intending to marry, to spend the rest of her life with. I'd just promised to make it impossible for him to ever work in this state again.

Sally was going to be pissed.

THIRTY-SEVEN

When I got to the office, Sally'd been crying.

"I need to talk to you," I said.

"I already heard." She wouldn't look at me.

"Sally, come into my office."

"Go to hell," she said.

"Damn it, get in here." I took her gently by the arm and led her into my office and put her in a chair. Rather than get behind the desk, I pulled over another chair and sat up close to her.

"He says you cut off the thing," she said. "From his truck."

"*That's* what he's upset about?" I asked.

"And he says you hit him. How could you do that? How could you hit him?"

"Look, Sally, he took a swing at me. I was defending myself." I didn't tell her how much I'd provoked him. I pulled a couple of tissues from a box and handed them to her. "Pull yourself together."

She dabbed at her eyes and blew her nose. "You already heard from Alfie, didn't you?"

I nodded.

"What did he say?"

"He said the circuit breaker panel didn't meet code. It was garbage. Cheap knockoff parts."

"And right away you blame Theo?"

"Sally, he did the work."

She crumpled the tissue in her hands. "That doesn't necessarily mean it's his fault. Like, what if someone gave him the wrong parts and he couldn't tell the difference?"

"Look, Sally, I'm really sorry about this. I'm sorry about how this affects you, because you're special to me. You know that Sheila, when she was still around, and I have always thought the world of you. Kelly loves you. I'd bend over backwards to give Theo the benefit of the doubt, because I know he means a lot to you, but—"

"I don't know."

"You don't know what?"

"I don't know exactly how much he means to me. But he's all I've got at the moment."

"Well, look, that's something you have to work out. And what I have to do, Sally, is I have to protect myself, and this company, and the people like you who work for me, and if someone does work for me that's unacceptable, that leaves us exposed to possible lawsuits, that could end up getting someone killed, for crying out loud, then I have to do what I have to do." I put my hand on her shoulder. "But I'm sorry I've hurt you."

She nodded, dabbed at her eyes again. "I know."

"And I know that this has been a tough time for you. Losing your father. No other family here to help you out."

"He was just . . . one minute he was okay and the next he was gone."

"I know," I said. "It's hard. Look at my dad. One second he's hauling plywood off a truck, the next he's dead."

She nodded. "You were there," she said.

"Yeah, I was there when he died."

"No, I mean, my dad's funeral. I couldn't believe it when you came to the funeral."

"Sally, I wasn't going to not be there for you."

"Yeah, but you had a funeral to get ready for, too. I always felt bad."

"You always felt bad about what?"

"That I didn't come to Sheila's."

"Don't worry about that."

"No, I feel real bad. I mean, if you could come to my dad's, why couldn't I go to your wife's funeral the day after?"

"It was hard for you," I said. "You're just a kid, really. No offense. You get older, you can handle these things." I tried to make a joke. "You learn to multi-grieve."

"I thought I was the office multitasker." Her eyes filled with tears again. "'Give it to Sally, she can handle a hundred things at once.' I guess not always." After a couple of more dabs at her eyes, she asked, "Is Theo finished? Is he ever going to get work around here again?"

"I don't know."

"He said you're going to ruin him."

I let out a long sigh. "He's ruined himself."

That, evidently, rubbed her the wrong way. Abruptly, she pushed back her chair and stood up. "You're a hard guy to love, Glen. Sometimes, you can be such a hard ass. Now we're going to have to move away, and I'm going to have to get a job someplace else." She stormed out of the room with one last shot. "I hope you're happy."

I wasn't, particularly.

Sally went home after that. It was, after all, quitting time. The last thing she'd told me, in short, clipped sentences, was that Doug had left his truck, full of stuff, around the back of the shed, then taken off with Betsy in her Infiniti to go see the bank before it closed about the mess they were in. Sally said Doug had asked, if I had a chance, would I mind unloading his truck.

I put my head in my hands for a few moments. Then I opened my bottom desk drawer and took out a half-full bottle of Dewar's and a shot glass, and poured myself a drink. I put the stopper back in the bottle and tucked it into the drawer.

I downed the drink, then went to the shed. I didn't know that I could do much for Doug in his current predicament, but letting him and Betsy store their stuff here was at least something. There was a lot of room in the shed, and if their things were stacked efficiently they wouldn't take up that much space. Unloading Doug's truck would mean one less thing he had to deal with when—and if—he showed up for work tomorrow morning.

I felt sick about Doug. It was a strained relationship we had at times, particularly lately. We'd worked side by side for several years while my father was alive, more or less equals on the job. We not only worked together. We played. Everything from golf to video games. Our wives commiserated while their two grown men would kill an afternoon immersed in a Super Mario Bros. time-waster. And to prove we weren't just children, we would get drunk at the same time. Doug had always been a carefree guy, someone who didn't see much point in worrying about tomorrow when it was a whole night's sleep away, and the unfortunate thing was he'd married someone who worried even less. Not, as today's events proved, an ideal match.

His lackadaisical approach to life hadn't been a problem when we worked together, but after my father died and I took over the company, and Doug became an employee instead of a coworker, things changed. First of all, we no longer hung out as a foursome. When I became the boss, Betsy didn't like the way the scales had tipped between her and Sheila. Betsy imagined Sheila somehow lording it over her, like I'd somehow morphed into Donald Trump and Sheila was Ivana, or whomever Trump was married to these days.

The qualities that had once endeared Doug to me now occasionally drove me to distraction. His work was always good, but there was the odd day he phoned in sick when I knew he was hungover. He wasn't as attentive as he could be to customers' concerns. "People watch too many of those home reno shows," he often said. "They expect things to be perfect, but it's not like that in the real world. Those shows, they've got big budgets."

Clients didn't like to hear those kinds of excuses.

If we hadn't at one time been buddies, Doug probably wouldn't have felt he could hit me up for advances on his salary. If we hadn't at one time been buddies, I would have said no the first time he asked, and not set a precedent.

I wanted to help him out, but I couldn't rescue Doug. He and Betsy were going to have to hit rock bottom before they were able to pull themselves up again. I understood what he said about the banks, about those mortgages that were all too good to be true. He wasn't the only one that got sucked in.

A lot of people were learning their lessons. I just hoped Doug and Betsy were able to learn theirs before they killed each other.

I opened the tailgate of Doug's truck and the window of the cargo cap above it. Because the Pinders had not had time to organize their things, everything had been tossed in loose. I opened the door to the shed and cleared a spot in one corner for the stuff, and brought out a couple of chairs, a DVD player, some linens. They probably should have taken that to Betsy's mom's place, but they could sort that out later.

I had the truck nearly emptied when I noticed a couple of cardboard boxes, about the size a dozen bottles of wine would come in, tucked up close to the cab. I crouched down and walk-squatted the length of the truck bed. You spend enough time in construction, you can walk in the back of a pickup like that without getting a groin injury or pulling a hamstring.

Once I reached the boxes, I got down on my knees. I wasn't sure whether this was stuff from Doug's house or something he'd already had in the truck that belonged to the business. So I folded back the cardboard flaps and had a peek inside. There was a lot of crumpled newspaper, which had been used as packing material. I took out bits of paper to see what it was protecting. The box was filled with electrical parts. Coils of wire, outlets, junction boxes, light switches, parts for circuit breaker panels.

It might have been interesting to read some of the stories on the newspaper scraps, but they were all written in Chinese.

THIRTY-EIGHT

It wasn't immediately obvious these parts were all junk. As knockoff electrical bits went, they looked pretty authentic. But sitting in the back of Doug's truck, studying them, I was able to spot things that didn't pass muster. The circuit breaker parts, for one, had no certification marks on them. Anything legit would have had them. The color of the plastic used for the light switches was off, not consistent throughout. You handle parts like these long enough, you just know.

I had a terrible, sinking feeling. There was something Sally had said. *"What if someone gave him the wrong parts and he couldn't tell the difference?"* Maybe Theo hadn't been in the business long enough to spot this kind of thing, to have an instinctive feel for it.

Shit.

What the hell was junk like this doing in the back of Doug's truck? Was he the one who'd substituted parts like this on the Wilson job? Had he done it on any others?

I slid the two boxes along the truck bed until they were positioned on the tailgate, then carried them, stacked one atop the other, to my own vehicle. I tossed them into the back, put up the tailgate, then locked the shed, the office, and the gate that led into the property.

I called Doug on his cell phone, hoping his service hadn't been cut off for nonpayment. Surely the bill had been one of those tucked, unopened, in his kitchen drawer.

I got lucky.

"Yeah, Glen?" He sounded weary.

"Hey," I said. "You get settled in with Betsy's mom?"

"Yeah, but man, this is no way to live. She's got five fucking cats."

"Have any luck at the bank?"

"They were closing when we got there, so we're going to go first thing in the morning, try to talk some sense into them. This is totally unfair, man, really."

"Yeah. Listen, I need to see you."

"What's up?"

"We need to talk, in person. I know you've got a lot on your plate at the moment, but it's important."

"Yeah, well, I guess."

"I can drive up to Derby, but I don't know where your mother-in-law's place is." Doug gave me an address. I was pretty sure I knew the street. "Okay, I'm heading up there now."

"Can you stay for a beer?" he asked. "Because, listen. That thing I said the other day, kinda threatening you, that was out of line, you know? I feel bad about that. Elsie—that's Betsy's mom—she's got some beer in the fridge and she says I can take three a day out of there. I'll save you one."

"That's okay," I said. "See you in a bit."

It wasn't that far to Derby, but it felt like a long drive. I'd really wanted to lay all this on Theo. I'd never liked the guy, and I'd never been that crazy about his work. If the fire had to be blamed on him, well, that suited me fine. Even considering that Sally was supposedly going to marry the guy.

I would never have wanted Doug to be the bad guy. I wondered what my father's reaction would have been to finding out that one of his supposedly most loyal employees had done something that could destroy the company.

He'd have fired his ass, that's what he would have done.

I found the street, turned down it, and about halfway up, in a driveway on the left, I spotted Betsy's Infiniti. I wondered how much longer she'd have that. I could see a ten-year-old Neon in her future.

I parked in front of her mother's house, a brick two-story. A Siamese cat was watching the street through the front window. I went up the drive and was about to knock when the door opened.

"You made good time," Doug said, a cigarette dangling between his lips. "Usually you run into some rush-hour traffic this time of the day."

"The roads were pretty clear."

"Which way did you come? When I come, I usually take—"

"Doug, cut it."

"Yeah, sure, okay. But you want that beer?"

"No."

He took a long drag on the cigarette, then threw it to the ground. Smoke continued to waft up from it.

"Listen, I really appreciate your help this afternoon, and for kind of, you know, defusing a tense situation. If you hadn't been there, I swear, I don't know what I might have done to Betsy."

"Emotions were kind of running high," I said.

"Now, here at her mom's, I got two of them going at me. Elsie takes Betsy's side in everything. She doesn't know how to see the big picture. And the place smells like cat piss."

"Walk with me," I said, leading him down the driveway to the truck.

"What's on your mind, Glenny?"

"Just wait a minute. There's something I need to show you."

"Sure. I don't suppose it's a bag full of cash?" Doug forced a laugh. I didn't respond.

I unlocked the tailgate and opened the window.

"I unloaded your truck for you," I said.

"Oh, that's good of you, man. 'Preciate it. Hope it doesn't take up too much room in the shed."

"I found these two boxes up by the cab." I paused, waiting for a reaction. Getting none, I said, "You recognize these?"

He shrugged. "They're boxes."

"You know what's inside them?"

"Beats me."

"No idea?"

"Can we open 'em up?"

I pulled back the cardboard flaps on the first one, tossed aside some Chinese newspaper clumps, and lifted out a circuit breaker switch. Doug, uncrumpling a balled-up piece of newsprint, said, "How does anyone read this shit? Have you ever wondered how the Chinese do typewriters when there's, like, a million letters? Their computers must have keypads the size of driveways. How do they do that?"

"I don't know," I said.

"This stuff was in my truck?" Doug said, tossing the paper aside.

"Yeah. The other box is full of the same. Switches, outlets, all that kind of thing."

"Huh," he said.

"You saying you don't recognize this?"

"They're switches and shit. Sure, I recognize that kind of thing. But I don't know what it's doing in my truck. Just supplies, I guess. You know everything that's in the back of your truck?"

"This stuff, none of it's up to code," I said. "It's made overseas, made to look like legitimate parts made here."

"You think?"

"I know. This is what caused the fire at the Wilson house, Doug."

"This stuff here? It doesn't looked burnt or nothing."

"Stuff just *like* it. I got the news from Alfie today, over at the fire department."

He took the part from my hand. "Looks okay."

"It's got no certification stamp. Although some, I gather, do, but the stamps are fake."

He turned it around in his hand. "Damned if it don't look like the real McCoy."

I took the part from him and tossed it into the box. "I just accused Theo Stamos of installing this in the Wilson place. It got a bit ugly. He swore up and down it wasn't his fault. I didn't believe him. Thing is, I still don't. I think he installed it. But what I'm wondering now is, did he knowingly do it?"

"Knowingly?"

"I wonder if the parts got switched on him."

"Why would someone do that?" Was Doug really this thick, or was it an act?

"You substitute knockoff parts for the real thing, you can return the real stuff to the store and make a tidy little profit."

"Yeah, I suppose—*You*? You mean *me*?"

"That's what I want to know, Doug. I want to know if that's what you did."

"Jesus, are you kidding me? You think I'd do something like that?"

"I never would have, but now, I don't know anymore. You went behind my back with Sally, tried to get an advance on your salary. That was wrong. You threatened to call the IRS on me. You're in the middle of a financial meltdown, and your wife spends money like she's printing it off the computer."

"Come on, man. That's a serious accusation."

"I know. And I want you to explain to me why this stuff is in your truck."

Doug swallowed, glanced up and down the street. "I swear to you, I don't know anything about this, Glen."

"No idea," I said.

"Nope." A lightbulb seemed to go off. "You know what I think?"

"Tell me."

"I think I'm being set up or something."

"You're being framed?"

"Yup."

"Who's framing you, Doug?"

"If I knew that, don't you think I'd tell you? Maybe it's KF."

"Ken Wang," I said.

"He's Chinese," he said. "Maybe those are his newspapers in the box there."

"He's grown up in America," I said. "I don't even know if he knows Chinese."

"I've heard him speak it. Remember that time we went into that Chinese place for lunch, Ken was talking to the owner?"

"I don't remember that," I said.

"Well, I do. He was all 'egg foo this and moo shu that.' You should talk to him, that's what you should be doing."

"The stuff is in *your* truck, Doug."

Betsy popped her head out the front door and shouted, "What's going on?"

"Go inside!" Doug shouted at her, and she did.

"You know what I think?" I asked him.

"What?"

"I think you've let me down. Big-time."

"No way, man. We go way back."

"That's why this hurts so much. I know you're in deep shit, Doug. I know the wolves are at your door. But you ask for help. You don't betray a friend. You don't put everything he has at risk."

"Seriously, I don't know nothin' about those boxes."

"Don't come in tomorrow, Doug. Except to pick up your truck."

"What about the day after that? What are you saying?" Something occurred to him. "Can I still leave our stuff in the shed?"

I slammed the tailgate shut and walked around to the driver's door, Doug trailing me.

"Come on, man! This is the worst day of my life, and now you're, what—firing me? Is that what you're doing? What the fuck?"

I got in the truck, slammed the door and locked it. Through the closed window I could still hear Doug shouting at me.

"You're supposed to be my friend, you son of a bitch! Why are you doing this to me? Huh? Your old man would never treat me like this!" A pause to catch his breath, then, "I should have let you burn!"

I hit the gas and was on New Haven Avenue when I had to pull off into a service station parking lot. I threw the truck into park, rested my elbows on the steering wheel, and pressed the heels of my hands into my forehead, taking deep breaths all the while.

"Damn it, Doug," I said under my breath. I'd never felt more let down, more betrayed.

You think you know people.

"I don't know anybody anymore," I said to myself.

When I got home, it was dusk.

I didn't like coming back to an empty place. I knew sending Kelly away was the best thing to do, but right now, I wished she was here. I needed someone. And while I wouldn't have poured my heart out to Kelly the way I would have to Sheila—I was hardly going to burden her with my disappointment in Doug—I would have hugged her, and felt her arms around me in return, and maybe that would have been enough.

With all the spring in my step of a dead man walking, I went to the front door, and as I was about to slip the key into it, I noticed it was slightly ajar.

I knew that when I'd left I'd closed and locked this door.

I pushed, ever so gently, against it, just far enough to slip inside. I thought I heard some kind of jostling in the kitchen.

It looked as though I was going to get my wish after all. There was someone in the house.

THIRTY-NINE

Slocum was coming out of the Connecticut Post Mall, where he'd gone to buy a few things for Emily to try to cheer her up—some markers, a pad, a stuffed dog, and a couple of books by someone named Beverly Cleary that he had no idea whether Emily would like but the lady in the store said they were good for an eight-year-old—when the man called out to him, saying, "Officer Slocum? Do you have a minute?"

He stopped just as he was about to head out into the parking lot and whirled around.

"My name's Arthur Twain," he said. "I wonder if you have a moment."

"No, I don't."

"First of all, I'm very sorry to hear about your wife, Mr. Slocum. I need to ask you some questions about her business, the parties she held, where she sold handbags. The company I work for has been engaged to investigate trademark infringement. I suspect you know what I'm talking about."

Slocum shook his head. "I got nothing to say to you." He scanned the lot, looking for his pickup. He spotted it and started walking.

Twain followed. "What I'd like to know, Officer, is where you were getting the merchandise. I believe you know a man who goes by the name Sommer?"

Slocum kept on walking.

"Did you know, sir, that Sommer is a suspect in a triple homicide in Manhattan? Are you aware that you and your wife have been doing business with a man with significant criminal connections?"

Slocum hit the button on his remote and opened his door.

"I think it might be in your interest to help me," Twain said, speaking more quickly now. "You let yourself get in too deep, there'll be no coming back. If you'd like to talk to me, I'm staying at the Just Inn Time for the next—"

Slocum settled in behind the wheel, closed the door, and keyed the ignition. Twain stood there and watched as he drove away.

Detective Rona Wedmore waited until it was dark before she returned to the harbor for the third time. The temperature had dropped sharply since the sun had gone down. Had to be in the high forties, she figured. Should have worn a scarf and some gloves. As she got out of her unmarked car she pulled her jacket together in front, zipped it up to her neck, stuffed her hands into the pockets.

Not as many boats in the harbor now as there were even a week ago. Many owners had taken them out of the water and put them into storage. It seemed so dead down here this time of year. The place was so full of activity in the summer; now these boats seemed mournful in their abandonment.

The car Ann Slocum had been driving was no longer here, of course. It remained, on Wedmore's orders, in a police garage.

Those scratches on the trunk lid bothered her a lot. And she'd just learned something else. The flat tire was caused by someone sticking a knife blade into the sidewall, right at the rim's edge. Ann hadn't driven over a nail, and it didn't appear that the tire had been driven on flat. The air had gone out of it after the car had been stopped.

This so-called accident was looking less like one with each new development.

She'd caught Slocum in a lie. He'd denied knowing that Ann had been on the phone prior to the call from Belinda Morton. Wedmore knew, after her talk with Glen Garber, that Slocum was covering up something.

His story about how his wife liked to take a drive in the evening to clear her head was pure fiction. Wedmore wanted to know why a cop, who should be smart enough to spot inconsistencies at a crime scene, was willing to accept his wife died in an accident when so many clues pointed to suspicious circumstances.

Of course, Darren Slocum's attitude made perfect sense if he was the one who'd killed her.

Wedmore knew the stories about Officer Darren Slocum. The allegations that he'd helped himself to some drug money. Stories of extreme force during arrests. The guy was a loose cannon. Everyone knew his wife ran an off-the-books business, and that he helped her with it.

He could have done it. He had no solid alibi. He could have slipped out of the house while his daughter slept. But suspecting it and proving it were two entirely different things. There were the life insurance policies the two had taken out on each other. That provided a decent motive, especially when they were having financial problems, but it wasn't enough to nail the guy.

As for Slocum's first wife, Wedmore had confirmed that she really had died of cancer. Rona kicked herself for that one. She should have known the facts before raising the issue. Felt like a bit of a shit, too.

She stood there in the cold night air, looking out over the Sound, as though the answers to her questions might magically wash ashore. She sighed and was walking back toward her car when she noticed the light.

It was coming from a moored cabin cruiser. She could see shadows moving back and forth behind the windows.

Wedmore strode out onto the dock, the heels of her boots echoing off the wood planks. As she came up alongside the boat she could hear muffled talking inside. She leaned out over the water, rapped on the hull, and called out, "Hello? Hello?"

The talking stopped, and then the door to the cabin opened. A thin man in his late sixties or early seventies, with a neatly trimmed gray beard and reading glasses, emerged.

"Yeah?"

"Hi!" Wedmore called out. She identified herself as a detective with the Milford department. She thought, *What's the phrase?* "Permission to come aboard?"

He waved her on, extended a hand to help her but she managed on her own. He invited her into the cabin, where a white-haired woman was seated at a table, sipping on a cup of hot chocolate. The smell of cocoa filled the cabin.

"This is a police detective," the man said, and the woman brightened, as though this was the most interesting thing that had happened in quite some time.

They introduced themselves as Elliot and Gwyn Teale. When they retired, they sold their house in Stratford and decided to live on their boat full-time.

"Even in the winter?" Wedmore asked.

"Sure," Elliot said. "We've got a heater, we've got water, it's not so hard."

"I love it," Gwyn said. "I hated the upkeep with a house. This is so much easier."

"When we need groceries or to do the laundry, we get a taxi and run our errands," Elliot said. "It's close quarters, I'll give you that, but we have everything we need. And it means when our kids want to come visit, they have to take a hotel. There's a lot to be said for that."

Wedmore was impressed. She had no idea anyone could live here year-round, and doubted any officers who'd been down here investigating Ann Slocum's death would have thought to look for anyone.

"I wanted to ask you about the woman who died here the other night."

"What woman was that?" Elliot asked.

"Just over there? Friday night? A woman fell off the pier. Struck her head, drowned. Her body was found there later that night when an officer noticed her car sitting there, the door open, the motor running."

"That's a new one on us," Gwyn said. "But we don't have a TV, or listen to the radio much, and we don't get a paper. And we sure don't have a computer here, so we're not on the Internet. Christ Himself could rent a boat here and we wouldn't know about it."

"That's the truth," Elliot agreed.

"So you didn't see the police early Saturday?"

"I did notice a couple of police cars," Elliot said. "But it didn't seem to be any of our business, so we stayed on the boat."

Wedmore sighed. If they hadn't been curious enough to check out a swarm of police cars, it wasn't likely they'd noticed much of anything going on around here.

"I don't suppose you saw anything out of the ordinary late Friday night, early Saturday morning, then?"

The two looked at each other. "Just those cars that drove down, wouldn't you say, hon?" Gwyn asked Elliot.

"Just that," he said.

"Cars?" Wedmore asked. "When was this?"

"You see, when anyone drives down that ramp there toward the pier," Gwyn explained, "their lights flash right into our bedroom." She smiled, then pointed to the forward hatch, where Wedmore could make out a bed that tapered toward the bow. "It's not much of a bedroom, but there are some very small windows in there. And I guess it was around ten or eleven, something like that."

"Did you notice anything else?"

"I got up on my knees and took a peek outside," Elliot said. "But it must not have been the same thing you're talking about."

"Why do you say that?"

"Well, there were two cars. Not just one car came down. Some woman was getting out of her car just as another one was pulling in right behind her."

"The first car, it was a BMW?"

Elliot frowned. "Could have been. I don't pay much attention to makes of cars."

"And the car that pulled in behind it, can you remember what it looked like?"

"Not really."

"Would you at least be able to remember whether it was a pickup truck? A red one?"

He shook his head. "Nope, wasn't a pickup truck. I think I would have noticed that. It would have sat up more, been shaped different. I think it was just a regular kind of car, but that's about all I could tell ya."

"Did you see who was in it?"

Another shake. "Couldn't tell ya. That's when I dropped back down and went to sleep. I have to tell you, I've never slept better than since I started hearing the sound of waves lapping up against the hull at night." He smiled. "It's like a lullaby."

FORTY

Standing just inside the door, hearing an intruder moving around in my kitchen, my heart pounded as I tried to figure out how to handle this.

I could charge in there and surprise whomever it was. But there were problems with that. First, they might not be surprised. They might be waiting for me. And if the person waiting for me was Sommer, I knew he carried a weapon. I did not. So, not such a great plan.

I could try something really radical, like calling out, "Who is it?" But that had all the drawbacks of the previous strategy. Someone waiting for me could come out of the kitchen and shoot me just as easily as waiting for me to walk in there.

A third option made the most sense. Back quietly out of the house and call the police. I reached noiselessly into my jacket for my phone. Worried that the beeping would alert whoever was in the house to my presence, I opted to wait until I was outside before punching in 911.

I was turning to slip back out when the woman shrieked.

"Oh *God*! You gave me a *heart attack*!"

She was standing in the kitchen doorway, a beer bottle in one hand, a plate of crackers and cheese in the other.

My own heart did a flip, too, but I managed not to scream. "Jesus, Joan, what are you doing here?"

All the color had drained from her face. "Were you walking on your tiptoes or something? I didn't hear you come in at all."

"Joan—"

"Okay, okay, first of all, why don't you take this beer?" She smiled and took a couple of steps toward me. She was wearing tight jeans, and that top again that showed a hint of bra. "You look like you could use it. I'd planned to nurse this one till you got here, but you take it and I'll crack open another one. I figured it was okay to put some snacks out now."

"How did you get in here?"

"What, Sheila never told you?"

"Told me what?"

"That I had a key? We had keys to each other's place, in case there ever was a problem. You know, like if Kelly came to my place after school, but there was something she needed at home, or who knows? Kelly *is* away, right? I mean, I saw you putting her little suitcase in the truck, so I just figured maybe she was going to stay with Fiona for a day or two after the house getting shot up and all. Is that what you decided to do? It makes sense, it surely does."

I stood there, stunned. "Go home, Joan."

Her face fell. "I'm sorry. I know what you've been going through and I just thought, When's the last time anyone's done anything nice for you? It's been a while, am I right? Sheila told me her mother's never cottoned to you, so I know the last thing she's been to you these last few weeks is a comfort."

"Carl Bain doesn't have a wife," I said. "At least not one that he lives with. She ran off when Carlson was only a baby."

Joan stood there, frozen. The plate of crackers and cheese suddenly looked very heavy.

"Why did you tell me that story?" I asked. "Because it was all a story, right? The boy, he never said anything about his father hurting his mother. And you never told Sheila you were wondering what to do. Because it was all bullshit, right? You made those lies up."

Joan's eyes started to mist.

"Just tell me why," I said, although I thought I'd already figured it out.

I saw panic in her eyes. "Tell me you didn't talk to him."

"It doesn't matter how I know. I just do. You can't do something like that." I shook my head. "You can't." I took the beer and the plate from her hands and walked them into the kitchen. When I turned around, she was standing there, looking very small.

"I keep thinking maybe he'll just walk in the door one day," she said.

"That the rig went down, but somehow Ely clung onto some part of it, and maybe he got picked up by some ship somewhere, without any ID, and maybe he lost his memory, like in that Matt Damon movie, you know the one? But then Ely gets his memory back, and he comes home." She dug a tissue from her jeans pocket, dabbed her eyes and blew her nose. "But I know it's not going to happen. I know that. But I miss him."

"I know," I said. "I'm sorry."

"Ely, he was always there for me. He protected me. He watched out for me. No one does that for me now. I just, I just wanted to be protected from something, to have someone doing the protecting..."

"So you made up that story, so I..."

Joan tried to look at me but she couldn't. "It felt so nice, you know?" Her face crumpled and more tears trickled. "Knowing you were there? That I could call on you?"

"You can call on me," I said. "For something real."

"And the other thing is, I wanted to look after someone. Ely, he looked out for me, but I looked out for him, too. And now, after what you've gone through, you need that. You need someone to look after you. I thought... I thought I could do that for you. And the other thing I said, about the money that's coming, that's true, I swear to God. I've got a big settlement coming."

I was about to take a couple of steps closer to her, but held my distance. This had the feeling of something that could go very wrong very quickly if I allowed it to.

"Joan," I said gently, "you're a good person. A kind person."

"I noticed you didn't say 'woman.'"

"You're that, no question," I said. "But... I don't want this. It's not just with you, but with anyone. I'm not ready. I'm a long, long way from ready. I don't have any idea when that will be. The only thing I care about now, the only thing I'm looking after now, is my girl."

"Sure," Joan said. "I get that."

We both stood there another moment. Finally, Joan said, "I'm going to go, okay?"

"Sure."

She started for the door.

"Joan," I said.

She stopped, and there was this ever-so-slightly hopeful look on her face, that maybe I'd reconsidered, that I wanted to deal with my loneliness and loss and grief the same way she did, that I would hold her in my arms, take her upstairs, and in the morning, she would make me breakfast just the way she did for Ely.

"The key," I said.

She blinked. "Oh yeah, okay." She fished it out of her pocket, placed it on the kitchen table, and left.

How many other times, I wondered, had Joan let herself into the house when I wasn't here, and what might she have been up to?

I also wondered, for a moment, if she'd be interested in a business teacher I knew.

FORTY-ONE

As I ate the cheese and crackers and drank the beer, I tried to get my head around the other events of this day.

Sommer's visit. The sixty-two thousand dollars Belinda had wanted Sheila to deliver to him. The crappy electrical parts that had caused the fire in the house I'd been building. The showdown with Theo Stamos. Finding the knockoff parts in the back of Doug Pinder's truck.

My head was spinning. There was so much information—and at the same time, so little—that I didn't know how to process it. My fatigue level didn't help. There had been too many sleepless nights.

I finished my beer and picked up the phone. Before I crashed, I needed to be sure Kelly was okay.

I speed-dialed her cell number. It rang twice before she answered.

"Hi, Daddy. I was just about to go to bed and was hoping it was you."

"How's it going, sweetheart?"

"Okay. Kind of boring. Grandma's wondering if we should drive to Boston for something to do. At first I wanted to go but I really just want to come home. I thought maybe if I came here I wouldn't be so sad but Grandma is sad so it's kind of hard not to be. But she says there's a big aquarium there. It's like the Googleheim. You know, the museum where you start up at the top floor and you keep going around and around until you get to the first floor? The aquarium is like that. It's this big tank and you start at the top and keep going until you get to the bottom."

"Sounds like fun. Is she there? Your grandmother?"

"Hang on."

Some fumbling. "Yes, Glen."

"Hi. Everything okay?"

"Everything is fine. Is there something you wanted?"

"I just wanted to be sure Kelly was okay."

"She is. I guess she told you we're talking about whether to take a trip."

"Boston."

"But I don't know if I'm up to it."

"Just let me know what you decide," I said. Fiona passed the phone back to Kelly so I could say good night.

A second later, the phone rang. I picked up without glancing at the caller ID. "Hello?"

"Glen?" A man.

"Who's this?"

"Glen, it's George Morton. I wonder if you might be able to meet me for a drink."

He was waiting for me in a booth at a place over in Devon. It was a bit down-market for George, but maybe he wanted a place he thought would suit me.

A couple of tables away from the booth were four young guys. If they'd been carded, I had to guess their IDs were borrowed from older friends. But this seemed to be the kind of place where they didn't worry much about that kind of thing.

George made no move to stand as I arrived. He let me slip in opposite him. My jeans got caught on sticky spots as I shifted in. George was dressed casually this time, a button-down shirt and a denim jacket. There was a bottle of Heineken in front of him.

"Thanks for coming," he said.

"You didn't want to say what this was about when you called," I said.

"It's not the sort of thing to discuss over the phone, Glen. Can I get you a beer first?"

"Sure."

George caught the waitress's eye and I asked for a Sam Adams. George sat with his hands on the table, folded together, his arms forming a defensive V around his beer.

"This is your meeting, George," I reminded him.

"Tell me about that envelope full of cash you delivered to my house."

"If you know about it, but you don't know what it's for, that tells me Belinda hasn't told you. But she told you it was from me?"

"I saw you put it through the mail slot," he said.

I glanced over at the table with the boys. They were starting to whoop it up. They had three pitchers of beer on the table and their glasses had been filled.

"Well, there you go. Anything else you want to know, ask Belinda."

"She's not very forthcoming. All she'll say is the money is a down payment on a property. Are you buying another property, Glen? Tearing down a house and putting up a new one on the site? Reason I ask is, I had the sense things were a bit tight for you right now."

The waitress delivered my beer and I took a sip. "Look, George, I don't know where you get the idea I owe you a favor or an explanation for anything. I understand you're the one who persuaded Belinda to open up to the Wilkinson lawyers, to tell them Sheila had the odd drink and once smoked pot with your wife and—"

"If you read the transcript of my wife's statement closely, you'll see that it says Sheila smoked marijuana in my wife's presence, but it does not state that Belinda was also smoking it."

"Oh, I see. So you don't mind tearing my wife down, but you're careful to protect yours at the same time. Did the Wilkinson woman promise you a cut if she gets everything I own? Is that how it went down?"

"I was doing what I thought was right." He unclasped his hands, extended an arm and tapped the table dramatically with his index finger. "Here's a woman who's lost her husband and a child, and you want my wife to lie and deny them justice?"

"If my wife had a history as a pothead and a record for driving around stoned, you might be on to something, George. But she had no history, and she didn't drive around stoned. So blow your self-righteous crap out your ass."

He blinked furiously. "I believe in doing things right. I believe people need to live up to a certain standard. And envelopes stuffed with cash, without any explanation, that's just not the way one does business."

Three of the boys were chanting *"Chug! Chug! Chug!"* as the fourth downed a glass of draft in a matter of seconds. They refilled his glass and started chanting again.

I looked back at George, down at his tapping finger, then suddenly dropped a hand down on his extended arm, pinning it to the table. George's eyes opened wide. He tried to pull his hand away but he couldn't do it.

"Let's talk about standards," I told him. "What sort of standards would a man have to have to let a woman other than his wife slap some handcuffs on him?"

When he'd stuck out his arm, I'd gotten a good look at his wrist. It was red and angry, all the way around. In a couple of spots, the skin was just beginning to heal, as though it had been scraped recently.

It was, I knew, a stab in the dark. But George Morton was within Ann Slocum's circle. And Ann, in that snippet of video I'd seen, wasn't exactly talking to a total stranger.

"Stop it!" he whispered, still trying to wriggle free. "I don't know what you're talking about."

"Tell me how you got those marks. You've got two seconds."

"I—I—"

"Too long."

"You just, you caught me off guard. I did that—I did that working in the garden."

"Both wrists, same marks? What kind of gardening injury was this?"

George was stammering, none of the words making any sense.

I let go of his hand and wrapped mine back around my beer. "Ann Slocum did that to you, didn't she?"

"I don't know what you're—I don't know what you're talking about," he blustered.

"Since you're all about being honest and forthright, why don't I ask Belinda to join us, save you having to tell this story twice." I started reaching for my phone.

He reached out and held my arm, giving me an even better look at the marks. "Please."

I pushed his hand away but didn't go for the phone. "Tell me."

"Oh my God," he whimpered. "Oh my God."

I waited.

"I can't believe Ann would have told Sheila this," he moaned. "And that Sheila would tell you. That's how you found out, right?"

I smiled knowingly. Why tell him I'd learned about this from my daughter's cell phone, and from what she'd taken from Ann Slocum's purse? Try explaining *that,* I thought. And the truth was, for all I knew, Ann *had* told Sheila about this, although I seriously doubted it.

"So you know," he said. "I can't believe Ann told her. That she would admit to what she was doing. Oh my God, if Ann told Sheila, she could have told..."

He had his face in his hands. He looked like he was going to have an instant nervous breakdown. "You don't know how long I've been living with this, worried that someone... anyone might find out that..."

"Tell me," I said, sitting there, looking as smug as a goddamn Buddha.

It came out in a torrent. "Ann needed money. They were always running short, her and Darren, even with selling purses on the side. I'd always found her... compelling. Attractive. Very... forceful. She could tell, she could tell I was interested. I wasn't the one who suggested it. I never could have done that. But she asked to meet me for coffee one time, and she... made a proposal."

"A business proposal," I said.

"That's right. We met, a couple of times at a motel here in Milford, but that seemed a little too risky, being right in town, so we started going to a Days Inn in New Haven."

"So you paid her to handcuff you, and...?"

He looked away from me. "We kind of worked up to that. At first, it was just, you know, regular sex."

"Things not good at home, George?"

He shook his head, unwilling to get into it. "I just... I just wanted something different."

"What'd you pay her?"

"Three hundred, each time."

"I guess none of this came up when you were at the lawyer's office offering up judgments on my wife's character," I said. "Although I don't know why it would. Totally different things, really."

"Glen, look, I'm asking for your complete discretion here, you get that, right?"

"Oh, sure." *You stupid son of a bitch.*

"The thing is, she wanted more."

"She upped her rates?"

"Not exactly," he said. I took a sip of my cold beer and gave him a minute. "Ann said it'd be a terrible thing if Belinda ever found out. First time she said it, I thought, Yeah, I totally agree. Second time she said it, I realized what she was getting at. She wanted more money to keep quiet. I thought she'd never tell. That'd be crazy. She and Belinda were friends, had been a long time, and if she told, it would all come out, Darren would find out—"

"Darren didn't know?" That did make sense, given Ann's orders to Kelly to keep quiet about what she'd heard.

"He didn't know anything about it. I really didn't think she'd ever tell, but I didn't want to take the chance. The thing was," and his voice got very quiet, "she took a picture, once, with her camera phone, when I was, you know, hooked up to the bed. Just me in the shot. She said, wouldn't it be funny, if somehow that got emailed to Belinda. I'm not even sure she actually took the picture. She might have been faking, but I just didn't know. So I started giving her an extra hundred each time, and that seemed to satisfy her, until, well . . ."

"Until she was dead."

"Yeah."

The boy who'd been chugging beer had stopped. "I can't do any more," he protested, laughing. "I can't."

"Wanna bet?" one of his friends said. One grabbed him from behind, a second held his head, and the third put the pitcher right to his lips. He started tipping and beer slipped down the boy's chin and all over his shirt. But a lot of it seemed to be going down his throat, judging by the way his Adam's apple was bobbing.

The boy was going to be very drunk, very soon. I just hoped these clowns weren't planning to drive—

"When she had that accident," George said, "I was stunned, you know? I felt sick, and I couldn't believe it. But part of me, I hate to say this, a part of me was relieved."

"Relieved."

"She didn't have any hold on me anymore."

"Unless that picture's really out there somewhere. On her phone."

"I keep praying it's at the bottom of the harbor. Every day that goes by, and the police don't get in touch . . ."

I said, "You might get lucky on that score."

"Yeah, I hope."

I poked the inside of my cheek with my tongue. "I've got a favor to ask of you, George."

"What?"

"I'd like you to get Belinda to rethink what she told those lawyers. That the whole pot thing, she got it wrong. It was just some Turkish cigarettes or something. She might also say that any time she ever saw Sheila drink, she was very responsible about it, which as far as I'm concerned, is the truth."

I looked long and hard at George to see that he was getting the message.

"You're going to blackmail me, too," he said. "If I don't do this, you'll tell Belinda."

I shook my head. "I would never do that. I was thinking I'd tell Darren."

He swallowed. "I'll see what I can do."

"Don't think I don't appreciate it."

"But that money. That sixty-two grand. What the hell is that about?"

"Like I said, you'll have to ask Belinda."

If they weren't calling Ann's death an accident, I might have been less inclined to make him that deal. Because if Ann had been murdered, George would be a prime suspect.

So would Darren and Belinda, for that matter. If they knew what had been going on.

I was so bone-tired I didn't have the energy to think about these new revelations. I went home, and to bed.

Sleep came pretty quickly this time. That might have been a blessing, if it hadn't been for the nightmare.

Sheila was in a chair, a kind of dentist's chair, with gleaming chrome and red padding and straps and belts that secured her into it. And forced into her mouth was a funnel, jammed in so far it had to be pushing up against the back of her throat. Tipping into the funnel, supported from brackets bolted to the ceiling, a bottle the size of a refrigerator. A vodka bottle. Vodka was spilling out, overflowing the funnel, splashing onto the floor. It was like some alcoholic form of waterboarding. Sheila was struggling, trying to turn her head, and somehow I was in the room with her, screaming, telling them to stop, whoever it was that was doing this, screaming at the top of my lungs.

I woke up, tangled in the sheets, soaked through with perspiration.

I was pretty sure what had triggered the nightmare. It was those kids at the other table. Chugging beers. My mind kept coming back to the moment when three of the guys pinned their friend's arms and started forcing him to drink even more alcohol.

They poured the beer down his throat.

The kid was going to get drunk on his own, anyway, that was pretty clear. But what if that hadn't been his intention? What if he hadn't wanted to get drunk? There wouldn't have been a damn thing he could do about it.

You could make someone drink too much. You could force them to get drunk. It wasn't all that complicated.

And then I thought, *What if they'd put that kid in a car? What if they'd put him behind the wheel?*

Jesus.

I sat up in bed.

Was it possible? Could it have happened that way?

What if Sheila had been compelled to drink too much? So much that she lost all sense of judgment and got into her car. Or what if someone put her in the car, after making her consume a large quantity of alcohol?

Was that so crazy? In a word, probably yes.

But the more I thought about it, the more convinced I became that it was at least possible. I thought, again, of the Sherlock Holmes line Edwin had quoted me. As far-fetched as this scenario was, it made more sense to me than the one I'd been led to believe, that Sheila had willfully gotten drunk and driven her car.

The trouble was, if I started to buy into a theory as wild as this, it raised a couple of very huge questions.

Who would force her to drink so much?

And why?

When the phone rang, I jumped. The digital clock read 2:03 a.m., for Christ's sake. I had a feeling that it would be Joan. I wasn't up for any more of her problems.

"Hello?" I said.

"Glen, it's Sally." She sounded frantic. "I'm so sorry to call you so late, but I don't know what to do, I didn't know who else to call or—"

"Sally, Sally, just hold on," I said. I picked at my shirtfront, feeling how wet it was. "Just slow down and tell me what's happened. Are you okay? What's wrong?"

"It's Theo." She was crying. "I'm at his place and he isn't here. I think something may have happened to him."

FORTY-TWO

Sally gave me directions. My hand shook slightly as I wrote them down.

Theo lived in a trailer on an empty lot out in the countryside west of Trumbull. I took the Milford Parkway up to the Merritt and headed west. Once I was past Trumbull, I got off and went north on Sport Hill Road, then hung a left onto Delaware, at which point I phoned Sally's cell. She'd warned me that the driveway into the property wasn't easy to spot, especially at night, so if I called her then she'd be sure to be down by the side of the road so I'd see her.

It took me the better part of an hour to get up there. When I pulled over to the shoulder, it was coming up on 3:30 a.m. Sally was leaning against the back of her Chevy Tahoe, and when she saw headlights moving over off the road, she took a few steps, checking that it was me. I hit the inside light a second and waved so she didn't have to worry that I was a stranger.

This really was the middle of nowhere. I didn't see any other houses along this stretch of road.

She ran up to the truck and I gave her a reassuring hug as she fell into my arms. "There's no one inside, but Theo's truck is here," she said.

Theo had left it at the bottom of the driveway, which explained why Sheila hadn't pulled her Tahoe off the road. As I walked past I noticed Theo had not yet replaced the decoration I'd removed from below the rear bumper.

We walked up the two ruts that constituted Theo Stamos's driveway.

It was about a hundred feet up to the trailer, a fifty- or sixty-foot rust-streaked mobile home that had probably been manufactured in the seventies. It was set on an angle, the side with the two doors—one forward and one aft—facing northwest. There were lights on inside, providing enough illumination so we could see where we were walking.

"How long's he lived here?" I asked.

"Long as I've known him," Sally said. "That's a couple of years. I don't get where he would be. I talked to him on the phone a couple of hours ago."

"At one in the morning?"

"Around then."

"Kind of late for a phone call?"

"Okay, so, we kind of had a fight, you know?" She sighed. "Because of you."

I didn't say anything.

"I mean, Theo was pretty pissed at you, and he was going on about it to me, like it's my fault or something because I work for you."

"I'm sorry, Sally," I said. I meant it.

"And then I find out that something has happened since then, with Doug." Even in the darkness, I could make out her accusing look. "Something that might get Theo off the hook."

I hadn't gotten around to telling her about finding the bogus electrical parts in Doug's truck. "I was going to fill you in on that," I said.

"Doug had those fake parts? Boxes of them?"

"That's right," I said.

"Did it occur to you then that maybe it wasn't Theo's fault? I mean, if Doug had those parts now, couldn't he have had them when the Wilson house burned down?"

"I don't know," I said. "But regardless, Theo installed them, and he should have been able to spot the difference."

"You're impossible."

"How did you hear about Doug?" I asked.

"He called me. He was so upset. Especially after you've been friends for so long, how he saved your life and everything."

I winced mentally.

"And I told Theo," Sally continued. "And he was super mad, he kept calling me about it, the last time around one, I guess. So I thought, I better come over here and try to calm him down."

"And he wasn't home?"

We'd arrived at the steps that led up to the trailer door.

"No," Sally said. "But if he's not here, why's his truck here?"

"You've been inside?"

She nodded.

"You've got a key?"

Another nod. "But it was open when I got here."

"He's not in there passed out or anything?" She shook her head. "Let's have a look just the same."

I swung open the metal door and stepped inside the trailer. It was pretty spacious, as trailers go. I stepped into a living room, about ten by twelve. There was a couch and a couple of cushy chairs, a big-screen TV sitting atop a stereo unit, a scattering of DVDs and video games. There were half a dozen empty beer bottles around the room, but it wasn't quite a frat house in here.

The kitchen, to the left of the partition as you walked in, was another story. The sink was overflowing with dirty dishes. There were several empty takeout containers littering the countertop, a couple of empty pizza boxes. Theo's truck keys were on the kitchen table, next to a stack of invoices and other work-related papers. While the place was a mess, nothing looked particularly out of order. It wasn't like there were upturned chairs and blood on the walls.

I picked up the keys and jangled them. "Wouldn't think he'd go far without these," I said, as though they were some sort of clue.

On the far side of the kitchen was a narrow hallway that led down the left side of the trailer. There were four doors off it—two small bedrooms, a bathroom, and a larger bedroom at the tail end. The smaller bedrooms had been turned into storage rooms. Empty stereo boxes, clothes, tools, stacks of *Penthouse* and *Playboy* magazines, and others raunchier than those, filled each of them.

I didn't, at a glance, see any boxes of counterfeit electrical equipment.

The bathroom was about what you'd expect of a single guy. Just one step above an interstate highway gas station restroom. And the large bedroom was an explosion of work clothes and boots and tossed covers.

"You ever stay here?" I asked Sally. It wasn't a question about her sex life. I just couldn't picture her tolerating this mess.

She shuddered. "No, God. Theo'd sleep over at my place."

"When you guys get married, you moving in to your house?" I almost called it her father's place.

"Yeah," she said.

"Anything look funny here to you?" I asked.

"Just the usual horror show," she said. "Where would he go?"

"Would he have gone out with a friend? Maybe someone came over and they went out for a drink or something."

Sally pondered a moment. "Then why didn't he take his keys and lock up when he left? He's not going to want someone to steal his truck."

"Did you try his cell?" I asked.

She nodded. "Before I came over. And his phone here. Both went to message."

I thought. "We should give it another try." I walked back up the narrow hallway and picked up the phone on the kitchen counter. "Hang on," I said. "Let's check the history. If somebody called him on his landline, invited him out, we'll see who it is."

I found Sally's number on there, but nothing else in the last several hours. "Just you," I said.

"Maybe he called somebody," Sally suggested.

"There's an idea," I said, and hit the outgoing call list. It showed not only the last number called, but the last ten.

There were three calls out in the last eight hours. One was to Sally's cell, another to her home phone, and the third, the most recent, to a number I knew well.

"He called Doug's cell," I told Sally. "Looks like maybe an hour after the last time he talked to you."

"He called Doug?" Sally said.

"That's right." I suddenly had a bad feeling. If Theo really hadn't known those parts he'd installed were bad, and believed Doug Pinder was responsible, he might have been inclined to have a face-to-face meeting.

But then again, Theo's truck was still here. Could someone else have picked him up and taken him to see Doug? But then we were back to why he hadn't taken his keys with him. You want to lock up, and you don't want to leave your keys so someone can steal your truck.

"I wonder if I should call him," I said.

"Who?" Sally asked. "Doug or Theo?"

I'd been thinking Doug, but if Sally hadn't tried Theo in some time, it made sense to try him again.

I moved through the kitchen to the door, looked outside, hoping maybe we'd see Theo coming up the driveway.

"Try him," I said to Sally.

Sally got out her cell and hit a button. She put the phone to her ear. After a few seconds, she said, "Nothing."

I wasn't sure, but I thought I'd heard something. "Try it again," I said.

I went out onto the step and stood very still, holding my breath. Nothing but the sounds of night. And then, off in the woods, I was pretty sure I heard a phone.

Sally came outside. "I tried it again, but still no answer."

"See if there's a flashlight around," I said. I had one in the truck, but didn't want to have to run all the way down to the road.

Sally went back in, returned a moment later with a heavy-duty Maglite.

"Stay here," I told her, getting a grip on the flashlight. "Keep trying the number."

"Where are you going?"

"Just do it."

I went down the steps, walked across what passed for a yard out front of the trailer, and approached the edge of the woods.

"Did you dial it?" I shouted back to the trailer.

"I'm doing it now!"

Ahead of me, to the right, a phone rang. After five rings, it went off. Theo must have set it to go to voicemail at that point.

I walked through some tall grass, casting the flashlight beam back and forth.

"Again!" I shouted.

A few seconds later, the phone began ringing again. I was getting closer.

There was a cluster of trees to the right. The ringing seemed to be coming from the other side of them.

The phone stopped ringing.

I moved through the grass, continued to wave the light in front of me.

"What do you see?" Sally called to me.

"I think he must have dropped his phone out here," I called back. "Do it again."

This time when the phone rang, it made me jump, it was so close. Behind me, and to my right. I whirled around, and the flashlight beam landed on where the noise was coming from.

The phone was probably still in one of Theo's front pockets. The ring tone must have been set pretty loud, which made sense, considering that Theo worked noisy construction sites. Otherwise we never would have heard it, because Theo was lying on his stomach.

His arms reached out beyond his head, and his legs were splayed awkwardly. In the flashlight beam, the puddles of blood on the back of his shirt gleamed like oil.

FORTY-THREE

I didn't realize Sally had come up next to me, and when she started to scream I nearly jumped out of my skin. I put my arms around her and turned her back to Theo's body so Sally couldn't see it. And now, with the Maglite pointing up into the trees, she wouldn't get a very good look at him even if she could peer around me.

"Oh my God," she moaned. "Is it him?"

"I think so," I said. "I didn't get real close, but it sure looks like him."

She clung to me, shaking. "Oh my God, oh my God, Glen, oh my God."

"I know, I know. We need to get back to the trailer."

It occurred to me, suddenly, that whoever had done this to Theo might still be close by. We could be in danger in this isolated spot. We needed to get away from here and call the police. I wasn't convinced that being back in the trailer was the safest place to do that from.

"Come on," I said.

"Where are we going?"

"My truck. Come on. Quickly."

I hurried her along, out of the woods, across the yard and down the rutted lane to my truck. I got her into the passenger side, giving her a boost up to the seat, then ran around to the driver's door. The whole time I was scanning the surroundings, as pointless as that was a couple of hours before the sun came up, wondering if whoever murdered Theo now had us in his sights.

I didn't know for sure Theo had been shot, but it was my best guess. Out here, in the country, you could fire off a shot or two and it was unlikely anyone would hear it, and even if they did, they probably wouldn't do anything about it.

We were sitting ducks right now, even in the truck. Sally was still muttering "Oh my God" repeatedly as I keyed the engine and dropped it into drive.

"Why are we leaving?" she asked. "Why are we running away? We can't just leave him there . . ." She started to cry again.

"We'll be back," I said. "After we call the police."

I tromped my foot onto the accelerator, kicking up gravel as I pulled away from the shoulder. The back tires squealed as they hit pavement.

Maybe a quarter mile on, doing sixty, something caught my eye in the rearview mirror.

Headlights.

"Hello," I said.

"What?" Sally said.

"We got someone coming up behind us."

"What do you mean? *Following* us?"

I couldn't make out whether it was a car or a truck, but I could tell this much: The headlights in my mirror were getting bigger.

I took the truck up to seventy. Then seventy-five.

Sally had twisted around in her seat. "Is he falling back?"

"I don't think so." I was looking in my mirror every couple of seconds. I could feel my heart pounding in my chest. "Okay, let's see what he does if I slow down."

I took my foot off the gas and let the truck coast down back to something approaching the speed limit. The headlights started to loom large, and extremely bright, in my mirror. I could see now that they sat up high, so it was a truck or SUV of some kind.

And the son of a bitch was riding with his high beams on. I reached up and hit the mirror with my fist to shift the glare out of my eyes.

The vehicle was almost on my bumper now.

"Hang on," I told Sally.

I hit the brakes, not hard enough that the driver behind would hit me, but enough to slow my truck so that when I turned in to the gas station I wouldn't end up sending us ass over teakettle.

A horn started blaring the moment my brake lights flared. And the horn kept going as I swerved into the gas station lot. The truck steered briefly into the oncoming lane, but instead of slowing down, sped up even more. As I slammed harder on the brakes I glanced to my left.

It was a black Hummer, its horn blaring as it drove off into the night.

Sally and I were both panting as we sat there by the dimmed gas pumps.

"False alarm," I said.

I got out my cell, punched in the three digits, and waited to talk to the emergency dispatcher.

Dawn was breaking when we got back to the scene. A police car had met us at the gas station. I had turned around and led the cop back to the end of Theo's driveway. With the sun coming up, it was easier to lead the officer into the woods and find the body. When we got to within ten feet of it, I pointed and stood back with Sally.

It wasn't long before another half a dozen state police cars had arrived and that stretch of road was closed off. A black cop by the name of Dillon did a preliminary interview with Sally and me, trying to get the sequence of events right. He said a detective would be wanting to talk to us all over again, which turned out to be right, but we had to wait an hour for that round of questioning.

We'd been told not to leave, so we spent a lot of our time sitting in my truck, listening to the radio. Sally seemed numb. For long stretches she just sat there, staring at the dashboard.

"You okay?" I asked every few minutes, and usually she'd just nod once.

I reached over one time to give her a comforting pat on the arm, and she pulled away.

"What?" I asked.

She turned and studied me. "You set all this into motion."

"Excuse me?"

"Going around accusing Theo and Doug of things."

"We don't know what happened here, Sally."

She looked back through the windshield, avoiding eye contact. "I'm just saying, you go see Theo, and then you go see Doug, and in the night they were talking to each other, and something happened."

I wanted to defend myself, to tell Sally I acted on the information I had, and on the things I had discovered. That I never intended for anything like this to happen. But instead I said nothing.

I decided it was best to wait for the facts to come in. Maybe, when they did, it would turn out that everything Sally was saying was right.

And I'd have to deal with it then.

I told the lead detective, whose name was Julie Stryker, that we had found Doug Pinder's number on Theo's outgoing call list. I had to tell her where the police could find him, up at his mother-in-law's place.

"But he's a good guy," I said. "He wouldn't do anything like that."

"No kind of bad blood between them?" Stryker asked.

I hesitated. "Not . . . really. But they might have had a few things to say to each other. There'd been some developments yesterday."

Detective Stryker wanted to know what those were. I filled her in on the report I'd had from Alfie at the fire department and how that related to Theo. Then I explained about the stuff I'd found in Doug's truck and how that tied in as well.

"So, these two, they might be wanting to blame each other for what happened at your job site," Stryker reasoned.

"It's possible," I agreed. "I can call Doug, see if—"

"No, Mr. Garber. Do not make that call. We'll have a word with Mr. Pinder ourselves."

Ken Wang phoned me.

"Hey, boss, Stew and I are ready to get to it, but there's nobody here," he said in his Southern drawl. "Where's Sally? She usually opens things up."

"Sally's with me."

"What?"

I could picture the eyebrows going up. "She had some trouble in the night. And I don't think Doug will be coming in, either. Listen, Ken, I'd rather have this conversation in person, but I'm going to have to ask you this now."

"Sure. What's on y'all's mind?"

"I need you to step up. I need you to be Doug. My second in command."

"Shee-it. What's up with Doug?"

"Can you do it?"

"Sure. I get a raise?"

"When I see you, we'll talk. It's your show today. Figure out what needs to get done and do it." Before he could say anything, I ended the call.

When Stryker returned, she wasn't interested in answering our questions, but we did manage to learn that Theo had been shot. Three times, in the back.

Sally tried to hold it together, but wasn't having much luck.

"Who shoots someone in the back?" she asked me.

I didn't answer that question. Instead, I asked, "Has Theo got family around here?"

Sally managed to tell me he had a married brother in Boston, a sister in Utica who'd recently been divorced, and his father still lived in Greece. Theo's mother had died three years ago. Sally figured, where notifying next of kin was concerned, police should start with Theo's brother. He was someone who could get things done, who'd make the funeral arrangements, empty out the trailer, that kind of thing.

"Do you want me to call him for you?" I offered.

"Won't the police do that?"

"I think so."

"I can't do it," Sally said. "I can't."

"Listen," I said, "if there's anything else you need, tell me."

She looked at me with wet eyes. "I'm sorry I freaked out on you."

"It's okay."

"I know you did what you had to do. It's just, I thought he was my one shot. I mean, he wasn't Mr. Perfect, but I think he loved me."

We didn't talk for a few minutes. There was something on my mind. It had been there since before I'd fallen asleep, and even in the midst of the horrible events of the last few hours, it had never been far from the surface.

"I need to ask you something," I said to her.

"Yes?"

"This is going to sound totally crazy, but I need to bounce it off you."

"This is about Theo?"

"No, it's about Sheila."

"Yeah, sure, whatever, go ahead, Glen."

"You know Sheila's death, it's never made sense to me."

"I know," she said quietly.

"Even though I've never been able to get my head around the fact that

Sheila would get behind the wheel drunk, I've never been able to come up with any kind of rational explanation for what happened. But I have one now."

She tilted her head, curious. "What is it?"

"It's so simple, really. What if someone *forced* her to drink?"

"What?"

"Maybe the tests the forensic people did are right. Sheila was drunk. But what if someone made her drink a lot, against her will?"

"Glen, that's crazy," Sally protested. "Who would do such a horrible thing to Sheila?"

I squeezed the wheel. "Yeah, well, I don't know exactly, but there's been so much strange shit going on lately. It would take forever to tell you all of it but—"

"Like your house getting shot at?"

"Yeah, that, and a lot of other shit, too. There's this guy, Sheila was going to deliver something to him the day she died. It was all part of the purse party stuff Ann did. Belinda was into it, too. And not just purses."

"I don't get where you're going, Glen."

"It doesn't matter. The thing is, Sheila never met up with him, never made the delivery."

"Okay, I'm on information overload here," Sally said. "First Theo, then this theory of yours about Sheila. But, Glen, Jesus, what you're saying—that someone forced Sheila to drink because they *wanted* her to have a car accident? I mean, how could you even know that would work? She might fall asleep just turning the key, or drive into the first ditch she passed. You couldn't count on her driving up some ramp and doing what she did."

I let out a long breath of exasperation.

"Sorry," she said.

"I know what you're saying," I said. "I do. But for the first time, I've got a theory. A real, honest-to-God theory about how Sheila might have died. Maybe . . . maybe she was already dead before her car got put on the ramp. Someone got her drunk, knocked her out, put her in the car and left it there."

I looked over at Sally. She had such a look of pity on her face, I felt embarrassed.

"What?" I said.

"I just, I just feel so bad for you," she said. "I know how much you loved her. I mean, if I was you, I think I'd be doing the same thing. I'd be trying to figure out how something like this could happen, but, Glen, I mean . . ."

I reached out and took her hand. "It's okay. I'm sorry. You've got enough on your plate right now without my dumping crazy theories on you."

When the police were done with us, and it took nearly until noon, I walked Sally to her Tahoe and made sure she was belted in behind the wheel. "You're sure you're okay to drive?"

She nodded and took off down the road.

I got in my own truck, and set out to find Doug Pinder, if the police hadn't found him already.

I tried his cell first but there was no answer. I didn't have a number for Betsy, or her mother's place, so I decided to just drive there first. When I pulled up out front of the house around one, there was a police car parked across the street. The only car in the driveway was an old Chevy Impala, which I guessed belonged to Betsy's mother.

As I got out of the truck an officer got out of the police car and said to me, "Excuse me, sir!"

I stopped.

"May I have your name please?"

"Glen Garber," I said.

"I need to see some ID." He was closing the distance between us. I dug out my wallet and slid my driver's license out of it for him to examine. "What's your business here, sir?"

"I'm looking for Doug Pinder," I said. "That who you're waiting for, too?"

"Do you have any idea where Mr. Pinder may be?"

"I'm guessing he's not here, then."

The officer said, "If you have any idea, you need to tell us. It's important we speak with him."

"I know," I said. "I just came from the Stamos place. I know what this is about. I made the 911 call. Is Betsy in?"

He nodded. He didn't seem to want me for anything else, so I walked up to the door and knocked. A woman in her mid-sixties answered. Several cats gathered about her feet as she opened the door, and three of them scooted outside. "Yeah?" she said.

"I'm Glen," I said. "You must be Betsy's mother." When she didn't deny it, I said, "Is she here?"

"Bets!" the woman screamed back into the house. "I swear," she said to me, "it's like a goddamn three-ring circus around here."

Betsy came through the living room and the look on her face said she wasn't very pleased to see me. "Yeah, Glen, what is it?"

"I'm looking for Doug," I said, stepping inside, being careful not to squish a cat in the door as I closed it.

"You and fucking T. J. Hooker out there," she said. "What the hell's going on?"

"I don't know," I said bluntly. "I need to find Doug and talk to him."

"You talked to him enough yesterday. Accusing him like you did. I thought you were his friend."

"I am his friend," I said, although I knew I didn't have much business saying so. "When did he leave here?"

"Beats me," she said. "Middle of the night he disappeared, took off in my car." So far as I knew, Doug's truck was still at the office, so that made sense. "I got no way to get around. Where the hell is he? What do the cops want with him? They think we don't have enough problems already? Is this what they do to people who lose their houses? Start treating them like criminals? We're supposed to go to the bank today to try to get our house back. How the hell are we supposed to do that if he's out wandering around somewhere?"

I was going to ask her to tell him to call me if he came home, but I figured, what with the cops waiting for him out front, he wasn't going to have a chance to do that.

"What the hell do they think he did?" Betsy demanded.

"Did Doug say he was going to see Theo?"

"He didn't say anything to me. You talking about that Greek electrician?"

"Yeah."

"What about him?"

"He's dead," I told her.

"Dead?"

"Someone shot Theo last night. The police need to talk to Doug. If he went out there to see Theo, he might have seen something, heard something, that would help the police catch who killed Theo."

"So it's not like the cops think Doug had anything to do with it," she said. "He's, like, a witness?"

"They just need to find him, Betsy. That's all."

"Well, I hope he's got my car with him when they do, because I've got to go to the bank and try to get our goddamn house back."

I decided to try the office next. The chain-link gate that seals off Garber Contracting from the street was in place. With no one to watch the office, Ken had locked the place up before heading off to whichever job site he felt had priority. There was no sign of Betsy's Infiniti, but there was another police car sitting across the street, and I had to go through the same routine again, explaining that I was not Doug Pinder.

I wondered if Doug might have found a way to slip in anyway, and once the cop was done with me I unlocked the place and walked through the office and shed, checking to see whether Doug might be sitting in his truck around back. It was still there, but there was no sign of him.

Once I had the place locked up again, I set off for the house Doug and Betsy had lost the day before. Even though they no longer lived there, I wondered whether Doug might try to break in, grab a few extra things he and Betsy hadn't been able to drag out onto the lawn with the little time they'd been given yesterday.

As I came around the corner, I saw the Infiniti sitting in the driveway. Doug sat slumped on the front step, his arms resting on his knees, a bottle of beer in his right hand, a cigarette in the other.

"Hey, pardner," he said, a smile crossing his face. "Can I get you a cold one?" It sounded as though he'd had a few.

I walked toward him. "No, I'm good."

The lock on the door appeared intact. If Doug had gotten into the house, he'd found some other way to do it.

"What are you doing here?" I asked.

"This is my house," he said. "Why the hell shouldn't I be here?"

"It's the bank's now, Doug," I said.

"Oh yeah, thanks for reminding me," he said glumly, taking a swig from the bottle. "But I always liked sitting out here havin' a beer. I can still do that." He patted the concrete slab next to him. "Pull up a chair."

I sat down on the concrete step.

"Where've you been?" I asked.

"Oh, here and there," he said, drawing on the cigarette, blowing the smoke out through his nose. "You sure you don't wanna wet your whistle?" He pointed to the six-pack at his feet. It had one bottle left in it.

"I'm sure. You go out to see Theo last night?"

"Huh?" he said. "How you know about that?"

"He called you."

"Damn right. Cell going off didn't wake anybody up but me, though, because I'm sleeping down in the basement on my own." He blew out more smoke, took another drink.

"What?"

"Yeah, get this. Betsy's old lady won't allow me and her sleeping together under her roof. Says it makes her uncomfortable, the idea of people having relations in her house, so I'm in the basement and Betsy's upstairs. She treats us like we're a couple of unmarried teenagers or something. Can you believe that? Just between us, I don't think Betsy's mom thinks much of me, but I'll tell you this, she doesn't have to worry about me and her daughter getting it on. Hasn't been much of that in a long time. Betsy goes along with these rules, I think, because it means her and her mom can talk about me into the night without me being there."

"What did Theo want?"

"Said he needed to talk to me, is all. I said, what the fuck is so important you need to talk to me in the middle of the night? And he said, 'Get your ass up to my place and I'll tell ya.' Or something like that."

"So you went."

"Is there some sort of problem here, Glenny?" he said.

"Just tell me what you did."

"I took a drive up. He gave me some directions and I went up there. You know what I think?"

"Tell me."

"I think he was playing some sort of joke on me."

"What do you mean?"

"I went all the way up there and the Greek son of a bitch wasn't even there."

"He wasn't?"

"Nope." He shook his head.

"You looked around?"

"His truck was there, but I couldn't find him around anyplace. I looked in his trailer—he lives in a trailer, did you know that?"

"Yeah."

"I went inside, looked around, stupid bastard wasn't no place to be found."

"What did you do then?"

"Drove around." He finished off the beer and tossed the bottle onto the grass. "You sure you don't want that last one?"

"Positive. Maybe it would be better if—"

"Don't worry about me," he said, grabbed the beer and twisted off the cap. "This one's a bit warm. But what the hell."

"So you just drove around."

"Well, I was already up, and I didn't much want to go back to Betsy and her mom. No fun up there. And the Infiniti, it's nice to drive, and God knows how much longer we'll have it before it's repoed. Parked down by the beach for a while, must have had a little nap, because before I knew it, it was after ten."

"Then what?"

"Picked myself up some beer and decided to sit here for a while and contemplate my future." He grinned. "It's a tad grim."

"You never saw Theo at all?"

"Not to the best of my recollection," he said, and chuckled. He finished his cigarette and tossed it in the direction of the bottle.

"What do you think he wanted to talk to you about?"

"I don't know, but I sure knew what I wanted to talk to him about."

"What was that?"

"Why'd he put those boxes of shit parts in my truck?"

"Did he tell you he did it?"

"Fuck, no."

"But you think it was him? Last time we talked, you were talking like it was KF."

He offered up an elaborate shrug. "I think I might have been guilty of what they call racist profiling, Glenny. Shame on me." He theatrically slapped the back of his hand that was holding the beer. "But fuck, Theo? The heat's already been on him for this. I mean, if he's the one put that stuff into that house, makes sense he was the one put it into my truck. If

I can figure that out, I don't know why you can't. I was interested to ask him why he's trying to screw me over. And I still will, next time I see the bastard."

"Theo's dead," I told him, looking for a reaction.

He blinked tiredly. "Come again?"

"He's dead, Doug."

"Well, shit, that's going to make it difficult to talk to him, isn't it?" He took a long swig from his last beer. "He electrocute himself? Be fitting."

"No. He was shot."

"Shot? You say *shot*?"

"That's right. Doug, tell me you didn't shoot Theo."

"Jesus, you're really something else, you know that? First you accuse me of burning our own houses down, now you think I'm going around shooting people?"

"So the answer is no," I said.

"You gonna believe me if I say so? Because lately, you're not exactly what I would call a great guy to have in my corner."

"I'm sorry, Doug. Maybe I, I don't know, maybe there's some explanation—"

"Hello, what's this?" he said, looking down the street.

It was a police car. No siren, no flashing light, just coming up the street. The car stopped at the end of the drive and a female officer got out.

"Douglas Pinder?" she said.

He waved. "That'd be me, sweetheart."

She said something into the radio clipped to her shoulder, then started walking our way.

"Mr. Pinder, I've been asked to bring you in for questioning."

"You got something to ask, ask."

"No, sir, you'll need to come in."

"Okay if I finish my beer?"

I said, "Doug, do what she says." To her, I said, "He's had a little to drink, but he's harmless."

"Who are you, sir?"

"I'm Glen Garber. Doug works for me."

He swung his head around. "I got my job back? That's good news. We've lost a lot of the day but there's still probably some work we can get done. Just don't expect me to hammer a nail in straight. And I probably shouldn't operate heavy machinery."

Two more police cars were coming up the street.

"What's this, a convention?" Doug said. "Glenny, do a donut run."

"I need you to come with me, sir," the cop said. "Peacefully."

"Well, fine then," he said, and put down his beer. "But first I have to get my wife's car back to her." He grinned at me. "Bet the bitch wants to go to the mall."

"Sir, the Infiniti there, that's yours?"

The other cop cars had stopped and an officer was coming out of each one.

"It's Betsy's," he said. "You know, to be honest, I probably shouldn't drive it back right now, anyway. Last thing I need at the moment is a DUI, know what I'm saying?"

The woman gave a nod to the closest approaching officer, and he opened the door on the Infiniti. He leaned in for a look.

"If you want to take it for a spin," Doug said, "I got the keys in my pocket here somewhere."

"Sir," the officer said, more sternly this time than before.

Doug stood, wobbled, and said, "Okay, so what's the deal-ee-o? What you want to talk to me for?" He looked at me. "This about Theo?"

"Don't say anything," I warned.

"Why's that?" He asked the officer, "Is this about Theo Stamos? My boss here says somebody shot him. That's pretty weird because I went out to see the son of a bitch last night."

"Doug," I said. "For Christ's sake."

"Come this way, please," the officer said, leading him toward her car. He went without objection.

The officer looking into the Infiniti came back out, reached into his pocket, and drew out a latex glove. He pulled it over his hand, snapped it, and leaned back into the car again.

"It's not *that* dirty in there," Doug said as he walked past the Infiniti.

This time, when the officer came out of the car, he had something dangling from his baby finger on the trigger guard. A gun.

"Whoa," Doug said, just before he was put into the back seat of the police car. "Hey, Glen, check it out! Betsy's keeping a goddamn gun in the car! I'm definitely gonna have to start being a little nicer to her."

FORTY-FOUR

I watched them take Doug Pinder away in one car while the other cop staked himself out by the Infiniti, seemingly guarding it. I had a feeling Betsy wasn't going to get her car back anytime soon. It was headed for the lab, along with the gun that had been found inside.

What a mess.

I wondered whether to give Betsy a heads-up, but figured she'd be up to speed in very short order. That cop posted at her mother's house was about to get word that Pinder had been found, Betsy's car impounded. *Which would upset her more?* I wondered. That her husband was being questioned in a murder investigation, or that she'd lost her expensive wheels?

Their entire world had fallen apart in the last twenty-four hours, on every goddamn level. I felt sick about it for a host of reasons, not least of which because I didn't believe Doug had it in him to kill someone. I'd allowed myself to believe he'd try to make a buck by using shitty electrical parts, but it was another thing altogether to believe he was a murderer.

But the problem there was, Doug had been up to see Theo. He had reason to be angry with him. And there was a gun in the car. Maybe he had done it, and gotten so drunk after that he didn't remember. Or was even drunk when he pulled the trigger.

Three times.

You had to be pretty sober to nail someone in the dark—in the woods—three times.

I didn't know what to think. So I got in my truck and drove back to Garber Contracting. I opened the gate that led onto the property, then unlocked the office. It felt like a weekend. No one around, the place quiet.

The light on the phone was flashing. I picked up and logged into the voicemail. Seventeen messages. I grabbed a pen and a pad of paper and started taking them down, one by one.

"We're here with the drywall, Glen. Where the hell are you guys? Nobody working today? Was there a holiday no one told me about?"

"I called last week? You put a Florida room on the back of our house last summer? And we're getting bees in the room, we think they're getting in someplace and wonder if you could come out and have a look?"

"My name's Ryan and I wondered if I could drop off a résumé? My mom says if I don't get a job she's going to kick me out."

They went on from there. I noticed, just as Sally had the other day, that none of them were prospects for future jobs. Everything really was turning to shit.

Once I'd made a note of all seventeen, I started calling people back. I was there until nearly five, dealing with subcontractors, suppliers, past customers. It didn't make me forget my litany of problems, but it at least distracted me from them for a period of time and let me focus on something I was good at.

When I'd dealt with as many calls as I could, I sat back in the chair and let out a long, exhausted sigh.

I looked at the picture of Sheila on my desk and said, "What the hell am I doing?"

My mind went back to the day I was supposed to clean out my father's garage after he'd passed away. I suddenly found a number of projects that had to be done around my own house. I'd nailed down some loose shingles, fixed a broken screen, replaced a porch step that was starting to rot.

Sheila'd stood there, watching me cut the board to size. When the saw stopped its buzzing, she said, "If you run out of projects here to keep you from dealing with your dad's stuff, you could try the neighbors. The Jacksons' chimney's kind of crumbling."

She always knew when I was avoiding something. And that's what I was doing now. I was doing more than avoiding an unpleasant task.

I was avoiding the truth.

The time I'd spent here, catching up on work, writing down phone messages—there was a much bigger problem I wasn't addressing. I was sweeping leaves off the driveway when the funnel cloud was only a block away.

I'd had no trouble harping at anyone who'd listen that Sheila wasn't the type to drink and drive. But once I'd gotten the notion that Sheila'd been forced to do what she did, all these horrific images starting coming into my head. Images as bad as those in my nightmare. Flashing before my eyes during every waking moment.

I believed someone had done something horrible to Sheila.

Someone was behind her death. Set it up somehow.

"Someone murdered her," I said.

Out loud.

"Someone killed Sheila."

I had nothing concrete. I had no evidence. What I had was a gut feeling born out of the swirling vortex that involved Ann Slocum, her husband, this thug Sommer, Belinda and that sixty-two thousand dollars she wanted Sheila to deliver for her.

It all added up to something.

I believed it added up to murder. Someone put my wife into that car, drunk, and let her die.

And killed two other people at the same time.

I was as sure of it as I'd ever been of anything.

I picked up the phone, called the Milford police, and asked for Detective Rona Wedmore.

"Your wife's accident didn't happen in my jurisdiction," Wedmore reminded me over coffee. She'd agreed to meet me at the McDonald's out on Bridgeport Avenue an hour after I put the call in to her. She thought I'd called wanting to know whether the police had learned who'd shot at my house. I'd said if she knew, I'd like to know, but if she didn't, I wanted to talk about something else.

"You don't strike me as the kind of person who'd use that as an excuse not to look into something," I said.

"It's not an excuse," she said. "It's a reality. I start sniffing around in another department's case, they don't take kindly to that."

"What if it's related to a case that's local?"

"Like?"

"Ann Slocum."

"Go on."

"I don't think my wife's death was an accident. Which has got me wondering if maybe Ann's death isn't exactly what it seems. They were friends, our daughters played together, they were both involved in the same sideline, although to varying degrees. There are just a hell of a lot of coincidences here. And you know Darren's been on edge about that call Kelly heard. I'm no cop, okay, but it's kind of like houses. You walk into a place, it might look okay to most people, but I go in, I see things other people don't see. Maybe the plaster's wavy in one place, like it's been patched over in a hurry to cover up where water's getting in, or you feel the way the boards move beneath your work boots, and you know there's no subflooring. You just know something's not right. That's how I feel about my wife's accident. And Ann's, too."

"Do you have any evidence, Mr. Garber, that Ann Slocum's death was not an accident?" she asked.

"Like what?"

"Something you've seen, or heard? Anything definitive that supports what you have to say?"

"Definitive?" I repeated. "I'm telling you what I *believe*. I'm telling you what I believe to be the *truth*."

"I need more than that," Wedmore insisted.

"You don't ever go on hunches?" I asked her.

"When they're *mine,*" she said, and half smiled.

"Come on, are you telling me you don't believe it, too? Ann Slocum goes out in the middle of the night after that crazy phone call and ends up falling into the harbor? And her husband accepts the whole thing without question?"

"He's a Milford police officer," Wedmore said. Was she really standing up for him, or playing devil's advocate?

"Please," I said. "I've heard about the allegations against him. And you must know he and his wife, they were running this knockoff purse business on the side. You don't buy that stuff wholesale from Walmart, and you don't get your start-up money from Citibank. You have to deal with some very shady people. The Slocums had other people involved in selling knockoff stuff, and not just purses. Prescription drugs, for one thing. And stuff for construction."

It occurred to me then, for the first time, that the Slocums could easily have been the suppliers of the breaker panel parts that burned down that house of mine. I vaguely recalled Sally saying Theo had done some work for the Slocums once. And if the parts had actually come through Doug, there was a connection there, too. Betsy had met Ann at the purse party she'd thrown at our house. And it was likely they'd known each other before that.

"The day Sheila died," I said, "she was doing a favor for Belinda. She was delivering cash for her to a man named Sommer. The money was to pay for all these goods. But it never got delivered. Sheila had her accident. And this Sommer guy, he's a menacing son of a bitch. He came to see me the other day, and Arthur Twain says he's a suspect in a triple homicide in New York."

"What?" Wedmore had taken her notepad out and was scribbling away, but had looked up when I got to Twain and the triple homicide. "Who the hell is Arthur Twain and what triple homicide?"

I told her about my visit from the detective and what he'd told me.

"And then Sommer came to see you? Did he threaten you?"

"He thought I might have the money. That maybe it didn't burn up in the accident."

"Did it burn up in the accident?"

"No. I found it. In the house. Sheila'd never taken it with her."

"Christ," she breathed. "How much money are we talking here?" I told her. Her eyes widened. "And you *gave* it to him?"

"Belinda had already called me, hinting around, asking if there was a package with some cash in it, because I think Sommer had been leaning on her pretty hard to make good on the payment. So when I found the money, I gave it to Belinda to pay the guy off. I didn't want any part of that money."

Wedmore put down her pen. "Maybe that's what the call was about."

"The one Kelly heard?"

"No, the one Darren admitted to. Just before Ms. Slocum went out, Belinda Morton called her. But she never said that was what it was about."

"You've talked to her?"

Wedmore nodded. "I was out to her house."

I debated with myself whether to tell her the messy truth about George Morton's relationship with Ann Slocum, and how she'd been blackmailing him. At the moment, withholding that information was my leverage with Morton to get Belinda to back off her story about Sheila. I weighed being totally open with Wedmore against the financial future of my daughter and myself, and decided, at least for now, to look out for my own. But if and when I found out Morton's handcuff games had anything to do with Sheila's situation—I didn't see how they could, unless Sheila really did know about them and that knowledge had gotten her into trouble—then I'd tell Wedmore everything I knew.

"Were you about to say something?" she prodded.

"No. That's it for the moment."

Wedmore made a couple more notes, then looked up.

"Mr. Garber," she said, adopting the same tone my doctor used when telling me not to worry while I awaited test results, "I think the best thing for you to do is go home. Let me look into this. I'll make some calls."

"Find this Sommer guy," I said. "Bring in Darren Slocum and ask him some tough questions."

"I'm asking you to be patient and let me do my job," she said.

"What are you going to do now? When you leave here?"

"I'm going to go home and make some dinner for myself and my husband," Wedmore said. She glanced over at the McDonald's counter. "Or maybe just take something with me. And then, tomorrow, I'm going to give your concerns all the attention they deserve."

"You think I'm nuts," I said.

"No," she said, looking me right in the eye. "I do not."

Even though I believed she was taking me seriously, her comment that she'd wait until tomorrow to look into this wasn't good enough.

So I'd have to start doing something tonight.

She said she'd be in touch, got up, and joined the line to place an order. I watched her a moment, and then did something of a double take.

There were two teenage boys ahead of her, jostling each other playfully, both looking down at an iPhone or some other kind of device one of them was holding. One of the boys I recognized. He'd been with Bonnie Wilkinson when I bumped into her at the grocery store. He'd stood there when she told me that I was going to get what was coming to me. And not long after that came news of the lawsuit.

Corey Wilkinson. The boy whose brother and father were dead because Sheila's car was blocking that off-ramp.

I didn't want to be sitting here when they walked past with their food. I couldn't even look at him.

I was sitting in my truck, about to turn the key, when the two of them came out of the McDonald's, each holding a brown paper bag and a drink. They walked briskly across the lot, then got into a small silver car. Corey got in on the passenger side while the other kid slid in behind the wheel.

The car was a Volkswagen Golf, a model from the late nineties. Stuck onto the top of the stubby antenna, which angled up from the back of the roof, was a decorative yellow ball, slightly smaller than a tennis ball. As the car drove past, I could see a Happy Face painted on it.

FORTY-FIVE

Arthur Twain was propped up on the bed in his room at the Just Inn Time, his laptop resting on the tops of his thighs, his cell phone next to him on the bedspread. He had definitely stayed in better places than this, but everything else in town was booked.

He wasn't making much progress. Belinda Morton didn't want to talk to him. Darren Slocum didn't want to talk to him. The only one who'd talked to him at all was Glen Garber. But he had other names, other women who'd attended purse parties Ann Slocum had given. Sally Diehl. Pamela Forster. Laura Cantrell. Susanne Janigan. Betsy Pinder. He'd give Milford another day or two, see if he could talk to some of them, get a better idea how many different places the purses that were being sold out here were coming from.

One thing Twain was certain of: Slocum and his dead wife were like the hub of a wheel out here. They'd brought all sorts of merchandise into this part of Connecticut. Ann sold the purses, they had a couple of people taking pharmaceuticals off their hands and reselling them, and they even dabbled in some home construction supplies, at least the goods that were easy to move, like electrical components. No toxic drywall.

It wasn't that Twain didn't care about all that other stuff, but it was the fashion companies that were paying his tab. If following a drug trail led him to the bogus purses, terrific, but otherwise he wasn't being paid to worry about all those other things. One time, tracking down some fake Fendis, he'd stumbled upon a DVD counterfeiting lab in the basement of a house in Boston. They were stamping out about five thousand copies of movies, some that were still in theaters, every single day. Twain made a call to the authorities who cared about that sort of thing, and the place was raided within the week.

He was composing an email back to the office about how his investigation was unfolding when there was a rapping at the door.

"Second!" he shouted. He set aside the laptop and swung his stocking feet onto the floor. He was over to the door in six steps and peered through the security peephole. There was nothing but black. Twain had never looked through the peephole before. Maybe it was broken, or someone had stuck gum to it on the outside. It was the kind of place where someone might do that, and where the cleaning staff would never notice.

Or maybe someone was holding a finger over it.

"Who is it?" he asked.

"Glen Garber."

"Mr. Garber?"

He hadn't remembered telling Garber the name of his hotel. He hadn't even booked in here yet when he went to visit him. He'd given Garber a card, he was sure of that. So why didn't the man phone him, instead of tracking him down here?

Unless there was something he wanted to tell Twain that he didn't feel safe discussing over the phone.

If it was Garber.

"Can you stand a bit back from the door?" Twain asked, putting his eye to the peephole again. "I can't quite see you."

"Oh, sure," the man on the other side said. "How's that?"

The peephole was still black. Which meant it wasn't working, or the man was still holding his finger over it.

"Can you give me a minute?" Twain asked. "I just got out of the shower."

"Yeah, no prob," the voice said.

Twain's briefcase was on the desk. He opened it, reached into the pouch on the underside of the lid, took out a short-barreled handgun, felt its reassuring heft in his right hand. He looked at his shoes, on the floor next to the bed, and considered slipping them on, but decided not to take the time. He returned to the door, checked the peephole again.

Still black.

He slid back the chain with his left hand, then gently turned the handle.

It all happened in seconds.

The door slammed into him with tremendous force. If all it had done was hit his body, that would have been bad enough. But the bottom of the door mashed the toes of Twain's shoeless left foot. He screamed in anguish as he went sprawling across the carpet.

A figure came into the room. Low, and fast. Twain had never seen him in person before, but he knew instantly who he was. And he could see that Sommer's hands were gloved, and that one of them was holding a gun.

Somehow, despite the pain, Twain had managed to hold on to his. His back pressed to the industrial carpet that looked like crushed caterpillars, his legs splayed awkwardly, Twain arced his arm swiftly, desperate to get a bead on Sommer.

Pfft.

Twain felt something hot under his right arm and dropped the gun. He wanted to reach for it, but this new pain, this was something very different than the pain in his foot. It was sapping him, instantly, of all strength.

Sommer moved toward him, stomped a foot on his wrist to make sure he couldn't get to his weapon. Twain looked up into the barrel of Sommer's weapon, noticed the silencer attached to the end.

Pfft.

The second shot went directly into Twain's forehead. A couple of twitches, and then nothing.

Sommer's cell phone rang. He tucked his gun away and took out the phone.

"Yes?"

"What are you doing?" Darren Slocum asked.

"Taking care of that thing you told me about."

Slocum hesitated, like he was going to ask, then thought better of it. "You said you were going to Belinda's to get the money, that Garber said to check with her by the end of the day."

"Yes. I called her. She said she had the money but there was a problem. Something to do with her husband."

Sommer looked down and took a step away from the body. The blood was moving, and he didn't want any to get on his shoes.

"That'd be George. He can be a bit of a tight-ass."

"It won't be a problem."

"I'm coming with you. If she has that money, eight grand of it's owed to me. I've got a funeral to pay for."

FORTY-SIX

I threw the truck into drive and fell into traffic behind the silver Golf.

The night of the shooting at my house, the cop had told Wedmore that my neighbor—Joan Mueller—had seen a small silver car with something round and yellow on the antenna drive past.

This car being driven by Corey Wilkinson's friend matched that description very nicely.

I moved over a lane and got in behind them. I made a note, on the pad I kept mounted on the dashboard, of the car's license plate. I suppose I could have stopped following right then and called the plate number into the cops, but that wasn't the way I wanted to handle it.

I followed them all the way to the Post Mall, where the kid behind the wheel dropped Corey off at the doors near the Macy's. Corey took all the McDonald's trash as he got out, waved as his buddy drove off, and shoved the stuff into a nearby garbage bin. He was starting up the steps to the mall when I pulled over, powered down the window, and called out to him.

"Hey, Corey!"

The kid stopped and turned. He looked at me for a good three seconds before he realized who it was. Then he made a "What the fuck?" face and turned to continue on into the mall.

"Hey!" I shouted. "It's about my window."

He stopped again, turned more slowly this time. I tried to coax him over with a wave, but he didn't move. So I said, "We can either have a chat, or I can just call the cops. I got your friend's license number. Which do you think he'd like you to do?"

He walked over, stood about a foot away from the door. "Get in," I said.

"What's your problem?"

"I said get in. You can get in, Corey, or I can call the cops."

Corey gave it another three seconds, then opened the door. I hit the gas and headed for Route 1.

"Who's your buddy?" I asked.

"What buddy?" he said, looking straight ahead.

"Corey, I can find out who he is. So why don't you just stop playing dumb and tell me?"

"Rick."

"Rick who?"

"Rick Stahl."

"How'd it work the other night? Did Rick drive? And you took the shot?"

"I don't know what you're talking about."

"Okay, hang on, I gotta do a U-turn up here."

"Why, what?"

"I'm just going to drive you straight to police headquarters. I'll introduce you to Detective Wedmore. You'll like her."

"Okay, okay! What's your deal?"

I shot him a look. "My deal? Is that what you said? You want to know what my *deal* is? You clowns shot at my house. You blew the window out in my daughter's bedroom." I jabbed a finger at him. "In my daughter's fucking bedroom! You got that? And she was in the room! That's what my fucking deal is."

"Hey, man—"

"I'm as sorry as I can be about what happened to your dad and your brother, and I understand who you believe is responsible, but I don't care if you think my wife wiped out your entire fucking family tree, you do not shoot into my daughter's bedroom." I reached over, took his arm in a vise grip and shook it. "Do you hear what I'm saying to you?"

"Ouch! Yeah," he mumbled.

"I didn't hear that."

"Yeah!"

I held on to him. "Who fired the shot?"

"We didn't know anyone was in the room," he said. "We didn't even know whose room it *was*." I squeezed harder. "It was me. I did it. Rick drove—I don't have my license yet—and I was in the back seat with the window down and I took the shot as we drove by and I swear to God I just thought I'd hit the house or your car or something like that. I didn't think I'd actually hit a window. Or that anyone would be inside."

I gave his arm a painful twist, then let go. We drove the next few miles in silence. Finally, I asked, "Just tell me."

"Huh?"

"What was the thinking behind this?"

"Thinking?"

I almost laughed. "Okay, I get that there wasn't very much thinking going on, but what the hell was going on in your head?"

"I just wanted to do something." He said it quietly. "I mean, my mom, she's suing you, but I wanted to be able to do something, too." He glanced over and I could see the tears welling up in his eyes. "It wasn't just her that lost people. I did, too. My dad and my brother."

"You wanted to put a scare into us."

"I guess."

"Well, you did that. You scared me. You know who else you scared?"

He waited for me to tell him.

"You scared my daughter. She's eight. Eight. Years. Old. The bullet came in about six feet away from her, through her window. She was screaming her head off. There was glass all over her bed. Do you hear what I'm saying to you?"

"I hear."

"Do you feel better now? Do you feel better about what happened to your brother and your dad now that you terrified a little girl who'd never done anything to you? Is that the justice you're looking for?"

Corey didn't say anything.

"Whose gun was it?"

"It was Rick's. Like, it was Rick's dad's. He's got all kinds of them."

"I'm going to give you half an hour," I said.

"I don't—"

"If I don't see you in half an hour, I call the cops and I'll tell them just what you did. You get on the phone to your friend Rick. You two are going to be at my house, in half an hour, with that gun, and you're going to hand it over."

"His dad's not going to let him—"

"Half an hour," I repeated. "And there's one more thing."

He glanced at me anxiously.

"Bring your mother."

"What?"

"You heard me." I pulled the truck over to the side of the road and stopped. "Get out."

"Here? This is, like, nowhere."

"That's right."

He climbed out of the truck. I saw him in my rearview mirror, talking on his cell phone, as I drove off.

They were at my door in thirty-seven minutes. I was actually prepared to give them forty-five before making the call to Wedmore. The two boys, looking very nervous, were accompanied by Corey's mother. Bonnie Wilkinson was pale and haggard. She eyed me with a mixture of contempt and apprehension.

Rick had a paper bag in his hand.

I opened the door and motioned for them all to come in. No one said anything. Rick handed me the bag. I unrolled the top and looked inside.

The gun.

I said to Bonnie Wilkinson, "They filled you in?"

She nodded.

"If it were just him," I said, nodding to Rick, "I'd call the cops. But I can't turn him in without turning in your boy." The kid had just lost both his father and his brother. I couldn't be part of dumping any more grief on the Wilkinson family, regardless of the crippling suit the mother had filed against me.

"But if either of them ever tries anything like this again, if they so much as look at my daughter the wrong way, I will press charges."

"I understand," Mrs. Wilkinson said.

Rick said, "What am I going to tell my dad when he notices his gun's missing?"

"I have no idea."

"I'll talk to him," Mrs. Wilkinson told Rick. No one spoke for a moment. Finally, she said, "I didn't know Corey was going to do something stupid like this. I'd never have allowed it."

I was going to tell her I knew that. I was going to tell her that I appreciated that her strategy was to kill us in court, not on the street. But all I did was nod.

It seemed we were done here. As they started to turn for the door I said, "Rick. One last thing."

The kid looked at me, scared.

"Lose that ball off your antenna before the cops spot it."

FORTY-SEVEN

Shortly after they left, the phone rang.

"Mr. Garber, Detective Julie Stryker here." The woman investigating Theo Stamos's murder. "I have a question for you. Why might Theo Stamos have been writing a letter to you?"

"A letter?"

"That's right."

"Was it threatening? I'd told him he couldn't work for me anymore. You found a letter like that?"

"It was shoved under some papers on the kitchen table. Looks like he was making notes about what to say to you in a letter, or maybe on the phone. Getting his thoughts in order."

"What did the notes say?"

"He appears to have been trying to draft some sort of apology, maybe even a confession. Can you think of anything he might want to confess to you?"

"I told you about that house he wired for me that burned down."

"There was an incident between the two of you the other day. I spoke to a Hank Simmons. Mr. Stamos was doing some work for him."

"Yes." I had a feeling she might find out about that sooner or later. "I confronted him with some news. I'd just heard from the fire department that electrical parts he'd installed were no good. It was what caused the fire."

"You didn't mention this earlier." Stryker didn't sound pleased.

"I told you about the electrical parts."

"According to Mr. Simmons, you cut some . . . rubber testicles off Mr. Stamos's truck?"

"Yes," I said.

A pause, then, "I can't say I blame you there."

Talking to her, I realized, was probably unwise. *Hang up and call Edwin,* I thought. I really might need a lawyer. Was my confrontation with Theo about to make me into a murder suspect? After all, I'd been up there, too, to his trailer. I'd found the body. Was Stryker thinking I had something to do with his murder?

But if she considered me a suspect, would she be interviewing me over the phone? Wouldn't there have been a police car parked out front, waiting for my return?

And of course, they did have Doug in custody.

"So is that what the apology's about?" I asked. "The fire?"

"Hard to say. At the top of the page is your name, and under that some words. Let me read you what he wrote. Keep in mind, it doesn't make a lot of sense. Just phrases jotted down in very messy handwriting. And he wasn't much of a speller, either. Let's see here . . . Okay. 'Mr. Garber, you judged me, not fair' and 'sorry about Wilson.' Who's Wilson?"

"It was the Wilson house that burned down."

"Okay. Then, 'just trying to make a living' and 'thought parts up to' and it looks like *c, o,* maybe a *b,* and—"

"Probably 'code.' The parts were up to code, he thought."

"And 'can't cover it up anymore.' Does that make sense?"

"No," I said.

"And then the last thing scribbled down is 'sorry about your wife.' Why would Theo Stamos be sorry about your wife, Mr. Garber?"

I felt chilled. "Is there anything else?"

"That's it. What's he got to be sorry for where your wife is concerned? Is she there? Would you be able to put her on?"

"My wife's dead." I heard the bleakness in my voice.

"Oh," said Stryker. "When did she pass away?"

"Three weeks ago."

"That recently."

"Yes."

"Had she been ill?"

"No. Her car got hit in a traffic accident. She was killed."

I could sense her interest growing. "Was Mr. Stamos at fault in that accident? Would that be why he was sorry?"

"I don't know why he would say that. He wasn't driving the other car."

"So he wasn't involved in the accident?"

"No . . . no," I said.

"You seemed to hesitate there."

"No," I repeated. What the hell did it mean? Why had Theo written that? Of course, plenty of people had said something along those lines to me in the past weeks. *Sorry about Sheila.* But it was out of context here. It didn't make sense.

"I don't get it," I said. "Now I have a question for you."

"Shoot."

"Are you sure about Doug? Do you really think he killed Theo?"

"We charged him, Mr. Garber. There's your answer."

"What about the gun you found in the car? I'll bet, even if it's the gun that killed Theo, that Doug's fingerprints aren't on it."

A pause. "What makes you say that?"

"I haven't been there for Doug lately. But I am now. I don't think he did it. He hasn't got it in him to kill somebody."

"Then who did?" she asked. When I couldn't think of an answer, she sighed. Then she said, "Well, if you come to some conclusion, give me a call."

There was a banging on the front door.

"Betsy," I said, in surprise, as I opened it.

She stood there on the porch, a hand on one hip, looking like she wanted to punch my lights out. There was a car idling at the curb, her mother behind the wheel.

"I came for Doug's truck," she said.

"Excuse me?"

"The police got my car, they took it to some crime lab or something, and I need wheels. I want Doug's truck."

"Come by tomorrow," I told her. "When I'm at the office."

"I got a set of keys for his truck, but I don't have a key for the gate. Give me that and I can go get it."

"Betsy, I'm not giving you the keys to anything. Your mother can drive you around until tomorrow."

"If you don't trust me and think I'm going to run off with all your precious little power tools, then come on down and unlock the place so I can get the truck. Won't take five minutes."

"Tomorrow," I repeated. "It's been a long day and I have things I have to do."

"Oh, really," she jeered, hands on both hips now. "It's been a bad day for *you*. First I lose my home, and the day after that my husband gets arrested for murder. But *you've* had a bad day."

I sighed. "You want to come in?"

She weighed the offer, then, without saying anything, stepped into the house.

"Tell me how Doug is," I said.

"How he is? How the fuck do you think he would be? He's in *jail*."

"Betsy, I'm really asking here. How is he?"

"I don't know. I haven't seen him."

"They won't let you see him?"

She didn't like the question, looked off to the side. "I haven't exactly had a chance. But they've probably got him locked up where I couldn't see him anyway." She looked, briefly, at her hands, which appeared to be trembling ever so slightly. "God, I'm a nervous wreck." She shoved her hands into the front pockets of her skintight jeans.

"Have you got him a lawyer?"

She laughed. "A lawyer? Are you kidding me? How the hell am I supposed to afford a lawyer?"

"Can't you get a court-appointed one?"

"Yeah, right. And how good would one of those be?"

I thought about the money between the studs in my study. I could hire a lawyer for Doug with that.

"Besides," Betsy added, "I've had stuff to do."

"Getting the truck? That's your number one priority?"

"I need wheels. My mom needs her car back."

"Have you written him off, Betsy? Is that it? You don't care what happens to Doug?"

"Of course I care. But they've got him. They wouldn't have charged him if they didn't have the goods on him, that's what my mom says. I mean, I guess they know he was there, up at Theo's trailer. There's the gun in the car, and they say it was the one that shot him. What more do they need? I have to tell you, I didn't even know he had a gun." She gave her head a shake. "You think you know someone."

"I didn't know you were this cold, Betsy."

"I just want a decent life," she spat. "I deserve better than this. That makes me some kind of criminal?"

"Doug said to me one time, like he was making a joke, that he wondered if you had some money tucked away someplace. Why would he say that?"

"If I had some secret stash, would I be living with my mom and begging you to let me get at my husband's piece-of-shit pickup truck?"

"That's not an answer, Betsy. Is Doug right? Do you have some money stashed away? I noticed those stacks of bills in your kitchen didn't stop you from going out shopping. You still had some money somewhere even as your cards were probably getting canceled."

"I can't believe you. I really can't. You think I'm turning tricks or something?"

"No," I said, although I thought it was an interesting thing to say, given what I'd found out about Ann Slocum.

She shook her head angrily. "Okay, so sometimes, my mom helps me out. She gives me a little something here and there."

"Betsy, level with me here."

"Okay, look, she may not look like she's living the high life, but there was some money, she had this uncle a couple of years back, there was about eighty thou after his house was sold. She was the only relative left, so she got it all."

"And Doug didn't know about this?"

"Hell, no. I'm not crazy. Mom snuck me some once in a while, when we were short, or if we couldn't pay the minimums on the Visas." She laughed. "If all those different banks wanted to keep sending us credit cards, it seemed wrong not to use them. I'm not one to be ungrateful."

"This has lost you a house, Betsy."

The hands came out of the pockets and went back on the hips. "When did you start thinking you were so much better than everybody else? Is it something you're born with, or do you develop the attitude over time?"

"What were you doing when Doug went out to Theo's place?"

"Huh?" she said. "What are you talking about?"

"I'm just asking, Betsy. What were you doing while Doug was out?"

"I didn't even know he'd gone until I got up in the morning and my car was gone. What do you mean, what was I doing? I was sleeping."

"You ever been up to Theo's place?"

"What? No. Why would I have been there?"

"How did you know he lived in a trailer?"

"What?"

"Just a minute ago, you mentioned Theo's place was a trailer. How did you know that?"

"What the hell are you getting at? I guess the cops must have told me, I don't know. What's wrong with you? And are you going to let me get that truck or not?"

"Drop by tomorrow," I said. "If I'm not there, Sally might be. Or KF. Someone will help you out. But right now, we're closed."

I showed her out the door and closed it behind her.

Something was bothering me. I kept thinking about what Doug had said, how he and Betsy didn't even sleep together when they were at her mother's house. When Doug left the house to go see Theo, for all he knew, Betsy wasn't even home at the time.

She could have been anywhere.

I wasn't sure where I was going with this, why I was suspecting Betsy of... something. It must have had to do with her apparent lack of concern for what had happened to Doug. She hadn't even been to see him since his arrest. She seemed content to accept the police version of events.

Like Darren Slocum, Betsy Pinder wasn't interested in challenging the facts. She was okay with things just the way they were.

FORTY-EIGHT

Sommer brought the Chrysler to a stop half a block down from Belinda Morton's house, turned off the headlights and killed the engine.

Slocum, in the passenger seat, said, "I gotta ask you something."

Sommer looked at him.

"Tell me you weren't trying to kill Garber's kid? When you shot out her window?"

Sommer shook his head tiredly. "It was kids doing a drive-by. They went past when I was parked there. After that, it wasn't safe to hang around, so I went to see Garber the next morning."

"Jesus, you couldn't have just told me that? Here I'd been thinking you'd nearly killed my daughter's best friend."

"And yet here you are, still doing business with me," Sommer said.

"What about Twain? Did you—"

Sommer held up a hand. "Enough. Are you coming in with me?"

"No," Slocum said. "So long as you give me my share, I don't need to."

Sommer got out of the car, leaving the keys in the ignition. The warning bell chimed briefly as the overhead light came on. Slocum watched as Sommer walked purposefully toward the Morton house. Silhouetted by the streetlights, Sommer looked like Death, Slocum mused.

George Morton was sitting in the family room, watching *Judge Judy* on the forty-two-inch plasma. "Honey, come in here and watch this," he said. "Judy's really going to town on this woman."

Tonight, it was some mother who was making a million excuses for her dumbass son, who'd taken the family car without permission to a party where lots of underage kids were drinking. One of the son's drunk friends had taken the car for a spin and totaled it, and now this mother wanted the parents of the other kid to pay for the damages, ignoring the fact that if her own son hadn't taken the car and let a drunk friend drive off with it, none of this would have happened.

"Are you coming in here or not? You're not still mad, are you? Listen, honey, I want to talk to you about something."

Belinda was in the kitchen, standing at the counter, looking over various real estate documents, unable to concentrate at all. Mad? He thought she was *mad*? More like homicidal. Sommer was expecting his money and that asshole husband of hers was still stubbornly holding on to it, keeping it locked up in his study safe, refusing to hand it over until Belinda told him what it was for. Totally improper, George kept saying, these large cash transactions. After all, he said, you're not in business with criminals.

When he was in the bathroom, she'd tried to open the safe using numbers from his Social Security card, his license plate, his birthday, even his mother's birthday, which he never failed to remember, even in years when he forgot Belinda's. But she hadn't stumbled upon the right sequence yet.

So now she was back in the kitchen, working on a new strategy. Something more dramatic. She would go down to the basement, get a hammer from her husband's toolbox, then invite him into his study. There he'd find her standing next to that model galleon he'd spent about two hundred hours building several years ago, threatening to smash it into a million pieces if he didn't open that goddamn safe right this second and give her the envelope stuffed with cash. There was no way he'd allow her to destroy that model. And she'd do it, there was no doubt in her mind. She'd smash it until it was nothing more than a pile of toothpicks.

George called out, "Did you hear me, hon? I want to talk to you about something."

She came into the room. George picked up the remote, extended his arm and muted the judge. *This must be something really important,* she thought. She also wondered, *What did George do to his wrist?* It was the first she'd noticed it. He'd been so modest the last few days, not letting her see him naked, wearing long-sleeved shirts.

"I've been thinking about this lawsuit that Wilkinson woman has launched against Glen," he said.

Belinda waited. It was her experience that George was never that interested in what she had to say, so she might as well see where this was going.

"It's a terrible thing," he said. "It could wipe Glen out. And there he is, trying to raise a child alone. He'll never be able to send her to college. It'll set him back for years and years if the Wilkinson woman wins."

"You're the one who was all high and mighty about doing what was right."

"I'm a little less sure now what, exactly, is right. I mean, just because Sheila might have experimented with marijuana, it doesn't mean she was smoking it the night of her accident. And from what I hear, it wasn't drugs they found in her bloodstream but alcohol."

"What's going on, George? You never change your mind about anything."

"All I'm saying is, next time you meet with the lawyers, you should say that maybe you were wrong about these things. That since you first spoke, you remember these events more clearly, that Sheila really didn't do anything that wrong."

"Where's this coming from?"

"I just want to do what's right."

"You want to do what's right? Open that goddamn safe."

"Well now, Belinda, that's really a separate matter. I still want *you* to explain to *me* what that's all about, and I want you to know I'm willing to be flexible about this. I'm wondering if maybe, just this once, I overstepped my bounds where—"

"What the hell happened to your wrist?"

"What? Nothing."

But she had grabbed hold of his arm and tugged the sleeve back. "What did you do to yourself? This didn't just happen. It looks like it's already healing. When'd this happen? You've been covering this up for days. Is this why you've been so weird lately? Not letting me see you naked, not sleeping with me, not—it's *both* wrists?"

"It's a rash," he said. "Don't touch it or you'll catch it. It's very contagious."

"What, is it poison ivy?"

"Something like that. I was just trying to protect—"

The doorbell rang. That stopped both of them.

"Well, there's someone here," George said. "You want to go see?"

Belinda glowered at George as he hit the button to restore Judge Judy's lecturing. She headed for the front door, swung it open without even thinking, because she wasn't expecting Sommer. She'd told him to call and they'd arrange a meeting tomorrow, by which time she was counting on finding a way to persuade George to unlock the safe.

It looked as though there had been a change in plan.

"Oh God," she said. "I thought we said tomorrow. I need another—"

"No more time," Sommer said, stepping in and closing the door behind him.

"Who is it?" George called out.

"My husband's home," Belinda whispered.

Sommer gave her a "So what?" look. "You *do* have the money."

She tipped her head in the direction of her husband's voice. "He found the cash, thought there was something fishy about it, and he won't take it out of his safe until I tell him what it's for."

"So tell him."

"I told him it was a down payment for a property. But he doesn't believe me. George is a stickler for proper paperwork and receipts and documentation."

Sommer sighed, looked off toward the family room. "I'll show him some documentation," he said.

And Belinda thought, *What the hell, I've tried everything else.*

Slocum got out his cell phone, hit a button, put the phone to his ear.

"Hi, Daddy," Emily Slocum said.

"Hi, sweetheart."

"Did you want to talk to Aunt Janice?"

"No, I just wanted to talk to you."

Darren Slocum kept his eyes on the house up the street, hoping Sommer would return shortly. These situations made him very uncomfortable. He had no illusions about what kind of person Sommer was. He knew full well what he was capable of. Ann had told him what had happened on Canal Street, what she'd seen him do. Sitting out here in the car, wondering just how far Sommer might take things, it worried him.

But if Sommer got his money, if this went without incident, this could be the end. You're all paid up, he'd tell him. Go find someone else to sell your stuff out here. With Ann dead, Slocum wanted out. No more purse parties, no more bringing in prescription drugs for Belinda to sell. No more home construction stuff for Theo Stamos.

Slocum wanted out. Out of this business. And out of Milford.

He figured his days as a cop were numbered. His bosses were still looking into that stolen drug money, the cash he'd used as start-up money for their business. Even if his bosses couldn't nail him for it, the stench around him was only going to get worse. Maybe he'd hand in his badge. If he walked away, odds were they'd deep-six the investigation. Getting him off the force would satisfy them. He'd move. Maybe upstate New York. Pittsburgh. Get a job in security or something.

In those moments when Slocum felt shame about the path he'd decided to take, the choices he'd made, the people with whom he'd aligned himself, he phoned his daughter. A man who loves his daughter, he told himself, can't be all bad.

I am a good man. My little girl means more than anything to me.

So, waiting for Sommer to show, he placed the call.

"Where are you, Daddy?" Emily asked.

"I'm sitting in a car waiting for someone," he said. "What are you doing?"

"Nothing."

"You must be doing something," he said.

"Aunt Janice and I were on the computer. I was showing her how many friends I've got and what their favorite things are. I wish you'd come home." Her voice was so sad.

"I will, soon. Once I wrap up a few things."

"I miss Mom."

"I know. I do, too."

"Aunt Janice said we should go on a vacation. Me and you."

"That's a good idea. Where would you like to go?"

"Boston?"

"Why Boston?"

"That's where Kelly says she might go."

"Kelly Garber's in Boston?"

"Not right now. She's at her grandma's."

"Well, I think it'd be good for me and you to go someplace, and if you want it to be Boston, that's okay with me."

"They have an aquarium."

"That'd be fun," Slocum said, watching a set of headlights coming up the street. "See all kinds of fish and sharks and dolphins."

"When do I have to go back to school?"

"Next week, I guess," Slocum said.

The car was stopping across from the Morton house, pulling over. The headlights went off.

"Sweetheart," Slocum said, "Daddy has to go. I'll call you again later."

Belinda led Sommer into the family room. George shifted in his leather recliner when he sensed her approach. He grabbed the remote, hit the mute button again.

"Hey," he said, seeing only Belinda first.

"Someone here to see you," she said.

George peered up and saw Sommer standing there. "Well, hello. I don't believe we've—"

Sommer grabbed hold of George by the back of the neck, hauled him out of the chair, and propelled his head directly into Judge Judy. The plasma TV shattered.

No one got out of the car right away after the headlights went out. But Slocum thought he could make out the driver looking at the Morton house. Thinking about what to do, maybe.

Slocum thought, *Who the hell is this?*

The flat-screen TV shattered. George screamed. Belinda screamed.

Sommer dragged George away from the TV. The top of his head was bloodied and he was flailing his arms about wildly, trying to strike out at Sommer, getting in the occasional slap that might have worked with a mosquito but wasn't going to have much effect here.

"Where is it?" Sommer asked.

"What?" George whimpered. "What do you want?"

"The money."

"My study," he said. "It's in my study."

"Lead the way," Sommer said, but held on to George by twisting a fistful of shirt at the back of the neck.

"You didn't have to do that!" Belinda shouted at Sommer. "He's bleeding!"

With his free hand, putting his palm directly on her right breast, Sommer shoved her out of the way. Belinda stumbled back against the doorjamb.

"It's in a safe, is that right?" Sommer asked.

"Yes, yes, it's in the safe," George said, steering them into his study and around his desk. "It's in the wall, behind that picture over there."

"Open it," Sommer said, shoving George across the room until his face was forced into the portrait of his father.

Sommer let up on the pressure slightly so George could swing the picture out of the way to reveal the safe with the combination lock.

"So this is the kind of people you're doing business with," George spluttered at Belinda.

"You stupid bastard!" she screamed at him. "You brought this on yourself!"

George put his fingers on the dial, but they were shaking. "I . . . I don't know if I can do it."

Sommer sighed. He switched his grip on George from his right to his left hand, then pulled him out of the way so he could twist the dial himself. His hand was rock steady.

"Tell me," he said.

"Okay, okay, okay, spin it a couple of times around to the right, then left to twenty-four, right to eleven—"

I'll be damned, Belinda thought. *He used my birthday.*

Just as George was about to call out the third number, which Belinda was now able to predict, there was a ringing in the room.

A cell phone.

Belinda kept hers on when she was home, but it wasn't her ring tone. George always turned his off when he wasn't out somewhere. So it had to be Sommer's. But with one hand on George and the other still spinning the dial, he didn't have much choice but to ignore it.

The driver's door opened. Slocum squinted, trying to get a look at who it was.

The person started crossing the street.

"Get under the light, get under the light," Slocum whispered through gritted teeth.

It was as though Slocum's pleadings could be heard. The person stood, just for a moment, under the streetlamp. Still looking at the house. Slocum could now make out who it was.

"Shit, no," he said, and reached into his pocket for his cell phone. He flipped it open, called up Sommer's number, hit the button.

"Pick up, pick up, pick up."

Sommer spun the dial to the last number, heard the tumbler fall into place, and swung open the safe door. By the time he'd done that, his cell had stopped ringing. He let go of George's shirt and reached in for the cash-stuffed envelope.

"At last," he said.

George, sensing an opportunity, started to bolt. But he wasn't fast enough for Sommer, who dropped the envelope, turned, grabbed George by the arm and threw him into the leather office chair. It pitched over as George fell into it.

Sommer reached into his jacket and pulled out his gun. He aimed it straight at George and said, "Don't be an idiot."

But Belinda screamed when she saw the weapon, so George barely heard Sommer's warning.

And none of them heard the doorbell.

FORTY-NINE

Once Betsy and her mother had driven off, I went upstairs to the bathroom and splashed some water on my face. I looked in the mirror, at the bags under my eyes. If I'd ever been this run-down before, I couldn't remember when.

I came out of the bathroom and sat on the edge of the bed I'd shared with Sheila. I ran my hand across the spread, over to where she used to sleep. This was where we'd come to rest every night, where we'd shared our hopes and dreams, where we'd laughed and cried, where we'd made love, where Kelly had begun.

I put my elbows on my knees and my head in my hands and stayed that way for a few moments. I could feel tears welling up, but I refused to let them out. This wasn't the time.

I took a few deep breaths, tamped down the hurt and the pain and the sorrow.

"Pull it together, dipshit," I said. "You got places to go, people to see."

I wasn't entirely sure what all those places, or who those people, might be. I couldn't sit still. I wasn't going to sit around while Rona Wedmore ate her Big Mac and fries and then went to bed and waited until tomorrow to follow up on the things I'd told her. I wanted to find things out now. I had to keep moving, keep asking questions.

I had to know what had happened to Sheila.

I knew what she would say to me right now if she could: *"Make one of your lists."*

I kept a notepad and a pen on the bedside table for the times I woke in the middle of the night, thinking something like *This is the day the countertops are going into the Bernsteins' place, I gotta make sure the cabinet guys are ready.* I'd make a note so I wouldn't forget.

When I put pen to paper, I found I wasn't so much making a list of things to do, but a list of questions that remained unanswered.

What had Sheila done in her final hours? How did she get so drunk? Was she, as I was strongly inclined to believe now, murdered? And if Sheila's death was murder, did it follow that Ann's was, too?

Could Ann have been murdered by her husband Darren? Or George Morton, whom Ann was blackmailing? Or even Belinda, who might have found out what was going on? And what about Sommer, who was already a murder suspect, according to Arthur Twain? The Slocums were tight with him.

It could have been any of them. Did it make sense that, whomever it turned out to be, that same person also killed Sheila?

My gut said yes. But my gut didn't have a lot to go on.

And what about Belinda? By her own admission, she was the one who gave Sheila the money to deliver to Sommer. I couldn't help but wonder whether Belinda knew more than she'd told me so far. I wanted to talk to her again, preferably without George hovering over us.

Finally, there was Theo. How did his murder figure into all of this? Was it related at all? Or was it as simple as it looked? He and Doug had gotten into a fight and Doug had shot him?

I just didn't know, but I kept scribbling.

The very last question I underlined four times: *Why did Theo write me a letter saying he was sorry about Sheila?*

I looked at everything I'd written down and wondered if, and how, all these puzzles might be connected. If I could get the answer to just one of these questions, would I have the answer to them all?

I knew who I wanted to see first.

On the way out the door, I grabbed the paper bag with the gun in it. It was going to end up in Long Island Sound, or maybe Milford Harbor, or Gulf Pond. Some body of water deep enough to swallow up this gun forever.

I locked up the house and got into my truck, tucking the bag under my seat. I hit the headlights as I backed out of the drive. I didn't have all that far to go. Just from one Milford neighborhood to another.

When I got to the house, I rolled the truck to a stop. I was parked across the street from it, looked at the house for a moment, thought about what I wanted to say. Some of these questions were going to be tough to ask. One of them I would leave right to the end.

Finally, I opened the truck door, slammed it shut behind me, and crossed the road, the streetlamps illuminating my way. There was no one out on the road, just one car parked at the curb a few houses down.

I went up to the door and leaned on the bell. Waited. I rang it again. I was about to ring it a third time when I could hear someone approaching.

The door opened.

"Hey," I said. "We need to talk."

"Sure," Sally said, looking a little surprised to see me. "Come on in."

FIFTY

Sally gave me a hug as I stepped into the front hall. She took me into the living room.

"How are you doing?"

"Not so great," she said.

"I know. You're probably still in shock."

"I think, maybe, yeah. It doesn't seem possible that he's dead."

"I know."

"Theo's brother from Providence called me. He's coming down to make all the arrangements once they, you know, once the body's been released by the police. The father's coming over from Greece tomorrow or the next day. They're going to ship the body home."

"To Greece?"

"I think so." She offered up a short, sad laugh. "We were going to go there one day."

I didn't know what to say.

"I just feel so mixed up. I mean, I loved the guy, but I know he was no prize. I'm not even sure I wanted to spend the rest of my life with him. But sometimes, a girl's gotta do what she's gotta do if she doesn't want to be alone forever."

"Sally."

"It's okay, I'm not fishing for compliments or anything. Not that I'd object if you wanted to throw any my way." Another laugh, accompanied by a tear. "And he'd *almost* finished my bathroom. Can you believe it?

Floor heats up nice, but he still had to fix a few of the tiles, caulk the tub. I was thinking the two of us would have had a bubble bath in it by next weekend."

I must have looked away.

"Am I embarrassing you?" Sally asked.

"No, not at all. I just . . . feel bad."

"You and me, we're quite a pair, yeah?" Sally said. "I lose my dad three weeks ago, you lose Sheila, now this."

That actually brought a smile to my lips. "Yeah, we're a couple of good luck charms, we are."

Something that had never occurred to me until this moment prompted me to ask, "Sally, when your dad was still alive, and you were having to buy all those drugs for him, you never bought any from Sheila, did you? Or Belinda? Or get them from any place but a drugstore?"

I had this horrible thought that maybe Sally had been sold ineffective, knockoff prescriptions that could have contributed to her father's death.

Sally was perplexed. "What? Why would I buy drugs from Sheila or anyone else?"

I let out a sigh of relief. "Before she died, she was thinking about starting up a little business, selling common prescriptions for way less than what they cost at regular drugstores."

Sally's eyebrows went up. "Wow. I could have used those."

"No, you wouldn't have wanted them. They could have been totally useless." We sat down opposite each other.

Sally said, "What's the latest on Doug?"

"All I really know is they've charged him."

"I can't believe it," Sally said.

"Me neither."

"I mean, we've worked with him for years. I never would have thought."

Sally's definition of "I can't believe it" was evidently different from mine. She was shocked, but accepting. I really, truly did not believe it.

"I think I know what happened," Sally said. "I mean, it's only a theory. But I think once Theo realized Doug had substituted those bad parts, they got into a fight, and maybe Doug was afraid Theo would tell you what he'd done."

"Maybe," I said, with little enthusiasm. "But it's not like him. I don't see Doug shooting someone in the back."

"A lot of people have done things lately we didn't think made much sense," she said, and I knew she was talking about Sheila.

"Let me get to what I came to ask you about," I said. Sally looked at me expectantly. "I got a call from Detective Stryker. She said Theo was writing some kind of a note, maybe not long before he got killed."

"What kind of note? Where did she find it?"

"On the kitchen table in the trailer, I think, under some other papers. Stryker said it looked like he was writing something to me. Making notes, trying to figure out what he was going to say."

"He did that," Sally said. "Writing wasn't something he was all that good at. He'd jot down ideas and bits and pieces of what he wanted to say before he'd write a letter. What were the notes?"

"They were kind of disjointed, didn't make all that much sense, but there was one thing that stood out. He said something along the lines of 'Sorry about your wife.'"

"Sorry about *Sheila*?"

I nodded. "What do you make of that?"

"I don't know," she said. "I mean, it probably means just what it says. He was sorry Sheila passed away."

I shook my head. "I don't get that. Theo and I were hardly friends. Especially after that blowup we'd had. And it's been a few weeks now since Sheila died. Why tell me now?"

Sally shook her head. "It is kind of screwy, isn't it?"

"It's why I asked you how well you really knew him. Do you think it's possible Theo had anything to do with Sheila's death?"

Sally stood up. "Oh God, Glen, really. I can't believe you."

"I'm just asking," I said.

"I know you didn't like him, that you thought he did shit work, that those truck nuts hanging off his bumper offended your fine sensibilities, but Jesus, are you kidding me? Thinking Theo killed your wife? Glen, *no one* killed Sheila. The only one who can be blamed for Sheila's death is Sheila. Look, I know how much it hurts you for me to say that, but it's the truth, and the sooner you accept that, the sooner you can move on with your life and stop torturing the rest of us."

"But Theo sounds like he was feeling guilty about something."

She shook her head. She was furious, her cheeks flushed.

"This is, like, this is the most unbelievable thing you've ever said to me," she said.

I stood up. I knew we were done here. "I'm sorry, Sally," I said. "I don't mean this as an attack on you."

She was moving toward the front door. "I think you should go, Glen."

"Okay," I said.

"And I think I'd like to give my notice."

"What?"

"I don't think I can work for you anymore."

"Sally, please."

"I'm sorry, but I think I need to move on. With my personal life, with work. Maybe I just need to start all over again. I bet I could get a good price for this house. I could go live someplace else."

"Sally, I'm really sorry. I think the world of you. We need to let things settle down. We're all on edge. There's been so much happening the last month. For me, for you. Take a couple of weeks off. Maybe talk to somebody. Honestly, I've been thinking about doing that. Some days, I think I'm going to go out of my head. Just take—"

She had the door open. "Go, Glen. Just go."

I went.

FIFTY-ONE

Rona Wedmore had gone home with two Big Macs and a large order of fries. No Cokes, no milk shakes. There were drinks in the fridge at home. No sense paying takeout restaurant prices for something you already had at home. And besides, McDonald's didn't have beer.

She pulled in to the driveway of her Stratford house and let herself in.

"I'm home," she called out. "And I've got Mickey D's."

There was no reply. But Detective Wedmore showed no concern about that. She could hear a TV going. Sounded like an episode of *Seinfeld*.

Lamont loved to watch *Seinfeld*. Rona hoped one day he might even laugh during an episode.

She took her gun from her belt and locked it in a desk drawer in a spare bedroom she used as an office. Even if she was only going to be home for a short while, she always took off her weapon and put it in a secured location.

That done, she came into the kitchen and walked through it to a small room at the back of the house, the one they'd fixed up before Lamont went over. Not big, but big enough for a loveseat and a coffee table and a TV. They spent a lot of time in here together. Lamont spent almost all of his time in here.

"Hey, babe," she said, walking in with the brown takeout bag. She leaned over and kissed her husband on the forehead. He kept staring straight ahead at the adventures of Jerry, Elaine, George, and Kramer. "You want a beer with dinner?" Lamont said nothing. "A beer it is."

She set up two TV trays in front of the loveseat, then went into the kitchen. She put the Big Macs on plates and split the large order of fries between them. She squeezed some ketchup out onto Lamont's plate. She'd never really cared for ketchup on her fries. She just liked them salty.

She put the plates on the trays, then went back into the kitchen. She filled a glass with water from the tap for herself and reached into the fridge for a beer. She returned to the TV room. Lamont had not started his burger or eaten a fry. He always waited for her. He wasn't much on the "please" and "thank you" thing these days, but he never began a meal until she'd sat down with him.

Rona Wedmore took a bite of the Big Mac. Lamont did the same.

"Every once in a while," she said, "these just hit the spot. Don't you think?"

The doctor had said that just because he didn't have anything to say didn't mean he didn't want her to talk to him. She'd gotten used to carrying on these one-sided conversations for several months now. She wished Lamont would get so sick of listening to her blather on about work and the weather and could Barack pull it together for a second term that he'd finally turn and say to her something like "For the love of God, would you please just shut the fuck up?"

How she'd love that.

Lamont dipped a french fry in ketchup and put it into his mouth whole. He watched Kramer whip open the door, slide into Jerry's apartment.

"I never get tired of that," Rona said. "It kills me every time."

When the commercials came on, she told him about her day. "This is the first time I ever had to investigate a cop," she said. "I've got to walk on eggshells on this one. But this guy, there's something seriously bent about him. Isn't the slightest bit curious about how his wife died. What the hell do you make of that?"

Lamont ate another fry.

The doctor said he might snap out of it tomorrow, maybe next week, maybe in a year.

Maybe never.

But at least he could be home. He functioned, more or less. Could take a shower, dress himself, slap a sandwich together. She could even phone and he'd check the caller ID and if it was her he'd pick up and she could give him a message. Just so long as she didn't need him to answer back, she was okay.

Sometimes she just called to say she loved him.

And there'd be silence on the other end of the line.

"I hear ya, babe," she'd say. "I hear ya."

As a police detective, she'd seen things. Working in Milford, maybe she didn't see, with any regularity, the kinds of things cops in L.A. or Miami or New York saw, but she'd seen some things.

But she couldn't imagine what Lamont had witnessed over there in Iraq. She'd been told by others what it was—about the Iraqi schoolchildren, how they'd blundered into that IED—but she still couldn't get her head around it.

Guess Lamont couldn't, either.

When he was finished with his burger and fries, Wedmore took the dishes into the kitchen and put away the TV trays. She returned and sat next to him on the couch.

"I'm gonna have to go out for a bit," she said. "I don't think I'll be long. But I talked to this man today, his wife died in a car accident a few weeks ago, and this guy, and his daughter, you wouldn't believe the shit they've been going through. He thinks there's something fishy about how his wife got killed. I think there is, too."

Lamont picked up the remote and started surfing through channels.

"Even though I told him I wasn't going to do anything with this until tomorrow, I'm going to try to talk to someone tonight. You okay if I head out for a bit?"

Lamont landed on an episode of *Star Trek*. The original one, with Kirk and Spock.

Wedmore gave him another kiss on the forehead. She put her gun back on her belt, slipped on her jacket, and went out the door.

She drove back over the bridge into Milford, past Riverside Honda, which was still in the process of being rebuilt after that fire, then found her way into Belinda Morton's neighborhood and parked across the street from the house. She looked at it a moment, then got out. She did a quick scan of the street, something she always did out of practice. Saw a dark Chrysler parked a few houses down.

It was quiet.

She went up to the door and rang the bell.

It was almost comical, in a way. The moment she hit the button, there came a scream from inside the house, like maybe she'd caused it to happen.

Rona did three things in very quick succession. She got out her phone, hit a button, and said, "Officer needs assistance." And she rattled off the address. The phone went back into her pocket, the gun came off her belt.

This time, instead of using the doorbell, she banged on the door with her fist.

"Police!" she shouted.

But the woman was still screaming.

Wedmore didn't have the luxury of waiting for backup. She tried the door, found it unlocked, and swung it open, stepping back out of the doorway at the same moment. Carefully, she peeked her head around, both hands on her weapon, arms locked. There was no one in the front hall.

The screaming had stopped, but now a woman, presumably the one who'd been making all the noise, was pleading, "Please don't kill him! Please. Just take the money and go."

A man's voice: "Give me the envelope."

Wedmore followed the voices. She went through the dining room, then past a room where a large television hung crookedly from the wall, the screen smashed.

Now, a second man's voice, whimpering, "I'm sorry! I'm sorry. Just take it!"

Wedmore considered her options. Hold her position in the hall until help arrived? Shout out from where she was that the police were in the house? Or just—

The woman screamed again. "Don't shoot him! No!"

Wedmore appeared to be out of options. She came through the door. In a nanosecond, she took in the scene.

The room was a study. On the far side of the room, a broad oak desk. Heavily stacked bookshelves lined walls. To the right, a window that looked out onto the backyard.

On the wall behind the desk, a framed picture on hinges was swung back to reveal an open wall safe.

A woman Rona Wedmore recognized as Belinda Morton was standing off to one side, her face raw with horror. A middle-aged balding man Wedmore believed was George Morton, his head smeared with blood, was on his knees, looking up into the barrel of a gun. Training the weapon on him was a lean, well-dressed man with gleaming black hair. Wedmore did not recognize him.

With her arms set rigidly before her, and both hands on her gun, she shouted with a voice she barely recognized as her own: "Police! Drop it!"

The man was quicker than she had anticipated. One moment he was facing Belinda Morton's husband, and now his entire upper body had shifted and he was looking right at Wedmore.

The gun had moved, too. The barrel was now little more than a black dot in Wedmore's eye.

She pushed herself to the right at the same time as she shouted, again, "Drop—"

She barely heard the *pfft*.

Sure felt it, though.

She got off one shot in return. Didn't have a chance to see whether she'd hit her target.

Wedmore was going down.

FIFTY-TWO

Darren Slocum, sitting out on the street in the Chrysler, heard the shot.

"Oh shit," he said aloud.

He reached over for the keys, which were still in the ignition, got out of the car, and stood with the passenger door open, wondering what he should do. Much depended on who'd been shot. If anyone had been at all. It could have been some kind of warning shot. A gun might have gone off by accident. Someone might have fired at someone else and missed.

What Slocum did know was who'd gone into that house. He'd watched Rona Wedmore get out of her car, cross the street, and bang on the door. From his position, he thought he'd heard some commotion in the house, but wasn't sure. He'd seen Wedmore get out her phone and make the briefest of calls before unholstering her weapon and entering the premises.

Not good.

If Wedmore had shot Sommer, the smartest thing he could do was disappear. And not in Sommer's car. Best to toss the keys back in, leave the Chrysler on the street, let everyone believe Sommer came to the Morton house alone. If Slocum left in the car, and police couldn't find one outside the house, they'd know Sommer had an accomplice.

Darren didn't want anyone looking for an accomplice.

Of course, it was also possible Belinda or George had been shot in whatever mayhem had taken place inside that house. And the absolute worst-case scenario, Slocum concluded, would be if Milford police detective Rona Wedmore had been shot.

By Sommer.

Which would mean Slocum was waiting out here for a cop killer.

Again, not good.

Slocum thought, *Let it be Sommer.* It'd be for the best, really. If Sommer was dead, he wouldn't be doing much talking. He wouldn't be able to tell about his involvement with Darren and his wife. Sommer was, even to Darren, who'd dealt with some pretty scummy people in his time as a cop, scarier than hell. Darren knew he'd sleep better at night knowing the guy was dead.

He stood there by the car, thinking all these things, debating with himself. Stay with the car? Go up to the house? Just take off? He could make it from Cloverdale Avenue to his place on Harborside Drive in ten minutes on foot.

And then? What if his fellow cops put it all together? When they showed up at his door, would they slap the cuffs on him, even if Sommer was dead and hadn't said a word?

When he got home, should he pack up Emily and make a run for it? And how far could he expect to get, realistically? He wasn't prepared for anything like this. He didn't have another identity set up. The only credit cards he had were in his own name. How long would it take the authorities to track him down? A man on the run with a little girl in tow?

A day? If that?

He couldn't decide what to do. He needed to know what had happened in that house before—

Someone came out the front door.

It was Sommer. Holding a gun.

The man ran down the walk toward the car. Slocum started running toward him. "What the hell happened in there?" he shouted.

"Get in the car," Sommer said, not quite shouting, but firm. "I got the money."

Slocum stood his ground. "What was that shot? What happened?"

Sommer was nose to nose with him now. "Get in the damn car."

"I saw Rona Wedmore go in there. A cop! And you coming out, alone. What went down in there?" Slocum grabbed hold of the lapels of Sommer's jacket. "Goddamn it, what did you do?"

"I shot her. Get in the car."

In the distance, the sound of approaching sirens.

Slocum gently released his grip on Sommer's jacket, let his arms settle by his sides. He stood there, shook his head a couple of times, as though some kind of peace had come over him.

"Now," Sommer said.

But Slocum didn't move. "It's over. All of this. It's over." He looked to the house. "Is she dead?"

"Who cares?"

Slocum surprised himself when he said, "I do. She's a fellow cop. A lot more cop than I am. There's an officer down, and I have to help."

Sommer pointed his gun at Slocum. "No," he said, "you're not." And pulled the trigger.

Slocum clutched his left side, just above his belt, and looked down. Blood appeared between his fingers. He dropped to his knees first, then fell onto his side, still holding himself.

Sommer went over to the car, closed the passenger door, then went around and got in behind the wheel. He went to turn on the engine.

"What the—"

The keys he'd left in the ignition were no longer there. He opened the door to activate the overhead light to see if they had fallen down onto the floor mats.

More sirens.

"Goddamn!" he said. He got back out of the car and strode over to Slocum, who was still clutching his stomach, as if he could somehow hold himself together.

"The keys. Give me the keys."

"Fuck you," Slocum said.

Sommer knelt down, started feeling around in Slocum's pockets. His hands became smeared with blood. "Where are they, damn it? Where are they?"

He happened to glance up at that point, at the Morton house.

Staggering out the front door, one hand holding a gun, the other pressed up against her shoulder, was Rona Wedmore. She glanced back into the house and shouted, "Stay in there!"

Sommer was thinking things couldn't get any worse.

Then a pickup truck turned the corner and started driving up the street.

FIFTY-THREE

I'd already made up my mind, even before I'd left home, that I'd drop in on Belinda after I'd been to see Sally.

I felt bad as I stepped out her door. It looked as though I was going to lose her as an employee, and a friend. But I'd had to ask her what Theo could have meant when he wrote that he was sorry about Sheila.

It was not some token note of condolence. There was more to it.

I pondered at the connections as I walked back to my truck. It stood to reason that Theo might have gotten his electrical supplies through Darren and Ann Slocum—assuming Doug wasn't the one who'd procured them. And Darren and Ann's troubles were very much intertwined with Sheila's and mine.

But how it all stitched together, I couldn't begin to guess.

I figured I would go see Belinda, and then I'd pay a visit to Slocum. I didn't know, exactly, the questions I was going to ask, or the approach I was going to take, with either of them. Particularly Slocum. The last time I'd seen him had been at the funeral home when I'd slugged him.

As I turned onto Cloverdale Avenue and approached the Morton house, I could tell right away something was not right.

A black woman had just come out the front door. Stumbled almost. She had her left hand pressed to her right shoulder and in her other hand was a gun.

I recognized her as Milford police detective Rona Wedmore. That was probably her car parked just ahead, on my side of the street.

About three houses beyond the Morton place, I saw a black Chrysler 300 at the curb, facing my way. It was the same kind of car Sommer had been driving when he came to the house yesterday morning, looking for the money. The driver's door was open, but I couldn't see anyone at the wheel.

Then I spotted a man kneeling on the grass, between the edge of the street and the sidewalk, only a short distance ahead of the Chrysler. As I nosed the truck into the curb, my lights splashed across him, and I could see he was crouched over something. It was another person, on the ground, apparently injured.

The kneeling man was Sommer. I couldn't tell who the injured man was, but Sommer was searching through his pockets for something.

I threw the transmission into park and opened the door.

Rona Wedmore was looking my way and the moment my feet touched the pavement she shouted, "No! Get back!"

"What's happened?" I said, still shielded by the truck door.

I had a better look now at Wedmore, standing under the porch light of the Morton house, and could see red oozing between the fingers of the hand she was pressing to her shoulder. She leaned up against a post, briefly, then started coming down the steps, taking her hand from her wound to use the railing.

I could hear a chorus of sirens.

Wedmore, now at the bottom of the steps, waved her weapon in the direction of Sommer and shouted at me. "Get out of here! He's got a gun!"

At that moment, Sommer raised his and pointed it at Wedmore. I barely heard the shot, but the wooden railing she'd been holding a second earlier splintered.

Sommer went back to searching the man, grabbed something, and ran to the open door of the Chrysler.

I glanced back into my truck. There, just sticking out from under the seat, was the paper bag. I hadn't yet gotten rid of the gun the boys had given me.

The smart thing to do at that moment would have been to throw myself into the truck and lie low until Sommer had driven off. But like that time I'd tried to put out the fire in the basement of the Wilson house and became lost in the smoke, I didn't always do the smart thing.

I grabbed the bag, ripped it open, and grabbed the weapon.

I didn't know a lot about this gun. I had no idea what make it was. I couldn't have hazarded a guess when or where it was made.

And I certainly had no idea whether it was loaded.

Would Corey Wilkinson and his friend Rick have been dumb enough to bring a loaded gun to my house? They'd been dumb enough to take a shot at it, so I thought there was a chance the answer was yes.

I firmed my grip on the handle as Sommer got into the car. I heard the engine turn over. The headlights came on like fiery eyes. Rona Wedmore was running, somewhat haltingly, across the Mortons' lawn, heading for the street. Her footing was off, like maybe she was going to lose her balance. She was raising her gun hand, pointing it down the street at Sommer's car.

The Chrysler's tires squealed as it started barreling up the street.

As Wedmore came off the curb and her right foot hit the pavement, it gave out under her. She stumbled and went down on her side into the street. Sommer steered the car toward her.

I came around my pickup's open door and started running to where Wedmore had fallen. The black car was still approaching. I stopped, steadied myself, put both hands on the gun and raised it to shoulder level.

Rona Wedmore shouted something, but I couldn't hear what it was.

I squeezed the trigger.

Click.

Nothing happened.

The car continued toward us.

I squeezed the trigger a second time.

The recoil forced my arms up into the air and I felt myself stumble back half a step. The windshield on the Chrysler spiderwebbed out from the passenger side. Sommer turned the wheel hard left, missing me by no more than ten feet as he screeched past. I threw myself out of the way, hitting the pavement and rolling to within a few inches of Wedmore.

There was a loud thunk, the screech of scraping metal, and then a crash.

By the time I'd turned around to see what had happened, the Chrysler had already bounced over the curb, driven into the middle of a yard, and slammed into a tree.

"Stay down!" Wedmore screamed at me.

But I was already on my feet, gun still in hand. My heart was pumping so hard, the adrenaline rushing through me with such speed, that I was immune to reason or common sense.

I ran over to the Chrysler, coming around it cautiously from behind, the way I'd seen cops do it on TV. I noticed a length of angled gray metal sticking out from under the car, and surmised that before Sommer hit the tree, he'd mowed down a street sign. Steam billowed out from beneath the buckled hood as the engine continued to run, but instead of the usual growl, it sounded more like nails in a blender.

As I got closer, I spotted a deployed airbag, and coming up alongside, I saw Sommer.

There wasn't much need to train the gun on him.

The edge of a white metal sign reading SPEED LIMIT 25 had caught Sommer on the forehead and just about taken the top of his head clean off.

FIFTY-FOUR

Two ambulances were dispatched to the scene. Darren Slocum, whose condition was deemed more serious than Rona Wedmore's, was taken away first to Milford Hospital. The bullet had gone right through him, on his far left side, and while no one was able to say anything with certainty at the scene, it looked as though it had missed any vital organs. Wedmore's shoulder had been grazed, and while she'd lost some blood, she was standing on her own before the paramedics forced her to lie down on the stretcher.

The Mortons were more or less unharmed, although George's head had been cut open when it was slammed into the television. For sure, they were both traumatized. Belinda told me what had happened inside the house. Wedmore had burst into the study, then dived for cover as Sommer took a shot. Sommer had grabbed the money-stuffed envelope and fled. He must have figured the detective had already called for backup and he didn't have much time to get away.

For the longest time, I could not stop shaking. I wasn't actually hurt, but the paramedics wrapped me in blankets and sat me down to make sure I was okay.

The police had plenty of questions for me. Fortunately, before she was taken away, Wedmore put in a good word for me.

"That stupid bastard just got a guy who tried to kill two cops," she told them as they loaded her into the ambulance.

They wanted to know about my gun.

"Is it yours?" they asked.

"More or less," I told them.

"Is it registered?"

"Not to my knowledge," I said.

I had a feeling I was going to get some sort of slap on the wrist for this, but nothing more. I didn't think the police would like the optics—hassling someone who'd saved one of their own from getting run down in the middle of the street.

But even though they took a conciliatory tone with me, the questioning at police headquarters went on until dawn. Around seven they drove me back to my truck, and I found my way home.

And went to bed.

I woke up around three. The phone was ringing.

"Mr. Garber?"

"Hmm?"

"Mr. Garber, Rona Wedmore here."

I blinked a couple of times, glanced at the clock, totally discombobulated. "Hey," I said. "How are you?"

"I'm okay. Still at the hospital. They're going to let me go home in a few minutes. I just called to tell you that what you did was one of the stupidest, dumbest, most moronic things I've ever seen anyone do. Thanks."

"You're welcome. What have you heard about Darren Slocum?"

"He's in the ICU, but it looks like he's going to pull through okay." She paused. "He might be sorry he made it after the department's through with him."

"He's in a lot of trouble," I said.

"He came with Sommer to the Mortons'. He may face accessory charges and God knows what else."

"What else do you know? Anything about my wife? Or Darren's wife?"

"There's still a lot we don't know, Mr. Garber. Sommer's dead, so we're not going to learn anything from him. But we're talking about one very nasty son of a bitch here. We can't assume anything, but it wouldn't surprise me to learn he somehow arranged the deaths of both your wife and Mrs. Slocum. And early indications are he killed a private investigator named Arthur Twain, as well, at the Just Inn Time hotel."

I sat up in the bed and threw off the covers. "Arthur Twain?"

"That's right."

I felt numbed by the news.

"I don't know how, exactly, Sommer might have done it," I said, "but given the kind of person he was, it's possible he killed Sheila. Somehow got her drunk, set her up in that car, knowing someone would run into it sooner or later."

Wedmore was quiet.

"Detective?"

"I'm here."

"You don't buy that?"

"Sommer shot people," Wedmore said. "That's what he did with anyone who got in his way. He'd never have gone to the kind of trouble you're talking about to kill someone." She paused. "Maybe, Mr. Garber, and I mean no disrespect when I say this to you, you're going to have to accept that, in your wife's case, things are exactly as they appear. I know that can't be easy, but sometimes the truth is a very difficult thing to accept."

Now it was my turn to be quiet.

I stared out the window, at the large elm tree in our front yard. Only a handful of leaves still clung to it. In another few weeks there'd be snow out there.

"Anyway, I just wanted to say thank you," Rona Wedmore said, and ended the call.

I sat there on the edge of the bed, my head in my hands. Maybe this was how it ended. People died, and their secrets died with them. I'd get the answers to some of my questions, but not all.

Maybe this was as far as I could go. Maybe it was over.

FIFTY-FIVE

I phoned Kelly.

"I'm going to come get you today."

"When? When are you coming?"

"This evening. I've got a few things to get out of the way first."

"So it's all safe to come home?"

I paused. Sommer was dead. Slocum was in the hospital. And I knew who was responsible for the shot window. If there was anyone else out there to be worried about, I couldn't think who it was.

"Yeah, sweetheart. It's safe to come home. But there's something I have to tell you about."

"What?"

I could hear the worry in her voice. So much had already happened to her, she must have been getting to the point where she was expecting bad things to happen.

"It's about Emily's dad. He got hurt."

"What happened?"

"A very bad man shot him. I think he's going to be okay, but he's going to be in the hospital for a while."

"Did somebody get the bad man who shot him?"

Kelly would probably hear the whole story at some point, if not from me, then someone else. But I didn't see the need to get into the details now. So I said, "Yes."

"Did he die?"

"Yes."

"A lot of people are dying lately," Kelly said.

"I think things are going to calm down now," I said.

"I know why Emily's dad didn't die."

That caught me off guard. "Why's that, sweetheart?"

"Because God wouldn't let a girl lose her mom *and* her dad. Because then there wouldn't be anybody to look after her."

"I never thought of it that way."

"Nothing will happen to you, right? That couldn't happen, could it?"

"Nothing's going to happen to me," I said. "It can't, because you're my number one priority."

"Promise?"

"I promise."

I stumbled around the house for a little while. Made some coffee, poured some cereal into a bowl. Brought in the newspaper that had been on the stoop for hours. There was nothing in it about what had happened last night. It was probably too late to get into a morning newspaper. The story was probably online, but I didn't have the energy to check it.

I made a couple of calls. One to Ken Wang, to tell him he was still in charge. Another to Sally, but she wasn't answering her cell or home phone. I left a message. "Sally, we should talk. Please."

When the phone rang shortly after, I thought it might be her, but it was Wedmore again. "A quick heads-up," she said. "They're putting out a detailed press release on what happened. Your name's in it. You're a hero."

"Super," I said.

"I'm just saying, there's a good chance the media's about to descend on you like a plague of locusts. If you're okay with that, enjoy."

"Thanks for the warning."

It made sense to get out of the house as soon as possible. I went upstairs and had a shower. As I was stepping out of the stall, the phone rang. I tiptoed across the tiled floor, careful not to slip with wet feet, and into the bedroom. The ID was blocked. Not a good sign.

"Hello?"

"Is this Glen Garber?" A woman.

"Can I take a message?"

"It's Cecilia Harmer, at the *Register*. Do you know when he'll be in, or where I might be able to reach him?"

"He's not here and I'm afraid I don't have any way to reach him."

I dried off and put on some fresh clothes. The phone rang again and this time I didn't even bother. I thought of something I should have told Ken, but didn't have the energy to talk to him. If I sent him an email, he'd get it right away on his BlackBerry.

I went down to my basement office, checked to see that the piece of paneling hiding my money was still in place. It was. I turned on the computer and, when it was ready to go, opened up my mail program.

There wasn't all that much there, aside from a few spam messages. One thing caught my eye, however.

It was from Kelly.

I'd forgotten that I'd asked her to email me the video she'd shot from her phone when she was hiding in the closet in the Slocums' bedroom. I'd never gotten around to taking a closer look at it, and while there didn't seem to be much point now, I was curious.

After all, it was that sleepover that had kick-started the nightmare of these last few days. Of course, the real nightmare had begun the night Sheila died, but just when I'd hoped we might be able to get our lives back to normal, there'd been that incident with Ann Slocum.

I clicked on the message and opened the video.

I put the cursor over the "play" icon and clicked.

"Hey. Can you talk? Yeah, I'm alone... okay, so I hope your wrists are okay... yeah, wear long sleeves until the marks go away... you were wondering about next time... can do Wednesday, maybe, if that works for you? But I have to tell you, I've got to get more for... expenses and—hang on, I've got another call, okay, later—Hello?"

I clicked the "stop" icon. I was pretty sure I knew now what this was all about. Ann was talking to George about the handcuffs. I dragged the "play" indicator back to the beginning and started the video again, but this time I let it go past *"Hello?"*

Ann Slocum said, *"Why are you calling this... my cell's off... not a good time... kid's got someone sleeping... Yeah, he is... but look, you know the arrangement. You pay and... something in return... mark us... down for a new deal if you've got something else to offer."*

And then, abruptly, the image blurred and went dark. It was at this point that Kelly evidently had put away her phone.

I went back to the beginning to play it again, thinking, *I should send this on to Detective Wedmore, for what it's worth,* and that didn't seem to be much. Maybe, if Kelly had recorded the entire call, where Ann talked about putting a bullet in someone's brain, it might have provided some useful information.

But I was still intrigued by what little there was, particularly when Ann took the other call. Was this the person who'd asked Ann for a meeting? Was this why she had gone out that night?

I listened.

"Why are you calling this . . . my cell's off . . . not a good time."

Ann was saying things in the gaps that weren't audible. I turned up the volume on the computer, then blew up the image full-screen, thinking maybe I could read Ann's lips.

"Why are you calling this . . . my cell's off—"

Stopped, went back. I was pretty sure, in that first gap, Ann said "phone" and another word or two.

Played it again. Listened, watched Ann's mouth. It was there. "Phone." And I thought I could make out the other words. She was saying, *"Why are you calling this phone, oh yeah my cell's off."*

I grabbed a pen and a sheet of paper and wrote down what I believed the conversation to be.

Listening over and over again to small snippets, I started filling in the gaps.

"Why are you calling this phone? Oh yeah, my cell's off. This is not a good time. My kid's got someone sleeping . . ."

I couldn't get the next word, but assumed it was "over." Went back, started again.

"Why are you calling this phone? Oh yeah, my cell's off. This is not a good time. My kid's got someone sleeping over." And then there was a six- or seven-second gap here where Ann said nothing, was listening to her caller. Then, *"Yeah, he is, in the kitchen. No, but look, you know the arrangement. You pay and get something in return."*

It must have taken me the better part of twenty minutes to piece that much together. I continued on.

". . . mark us . . . down for a new deal if you have something else to offer."

There was something very short in that gap.

I played it again, watched Ann's mouth. Lips open, then closing. Looked like an "m" sound.

Played it again.

And again.

I was pretty sure I had it. Ann had said, *"I'm."*

Which means she'd said, *". . . mark us I'm down for a new deal if you have something else to offer."*

That didn't make any sense at all. I read it aloud to myself.

"Mark us I'm down for a new deal if you have—"

Holy shit.

Not "mark us."

Marcus.

Ann had said, *"Marcus, I'm down for a new deal if you have something else to offer."*

I had to get Kelly.

FIFTY-SIX

"Are you sure you're okay if I go out?" Fiona asked her granddaughter. She'd been sitting on the couch in front of the coffee table, doing her best to comfort the child, sipping some white wine.

"Yup," Kelly said.

"Because I know you've had some very upsetting news. That's a terrible thing about Emily's father."

"I'm okay."

"It's just that we're really low on everything, and since your father says he's not coming to get you until this evening, we need something for dinner because we are absolutely not ordering in pizza or anything like that."

Then, with something of a flourish, she set her wineglass on the table and got up.

"We'll have a great time," Marcus said, and rubbed his hand on top of the girl's head. "Won't we, sweetheart?"

Kelly glanced up at him and smiled. "Sure. What do you want to do?"

"We could watch a movie or something," he said.

"I don't really feel like a movie."

"I'm sure you two will think of something," Fiona said.

"Why don't we go for a walk?" Marcus said.

"I guess," Kelly said without enthusiasm.

Fiona grabbed her purse and dug out her car keys. "I shouldn't be too long," she said. "An hour or so."

"Sure," Marcus said.

The moment she was out the door, Kelly noticed Fiona had forgotten her cell phone. It was sitting on the table in the hall, hooked up to the charger.

"Don't worry about it," Marcus said. "She's not going to be gone that long." He invited Kelly to come sit with him on the back deck. It looked out on the well-manicured backyard, and beyond that, Long Island Sound.

"So, going home today," he said.

"I guess," Kelly said, sitting on one of the wicker chairs and swinging her legs back and forth.

"I think this is the first time just the two of us have had a chance to talk since you got here."

"I guess."

"Your grandmother told me the news. Sounds like things have settled down at home. Everything your father was worried about is taken care of. That's a good thing, isn't it?"

Kelly nodded. She wished her father could pick her up right now. She'd rather have dinner with her dad. Being with Grandma and Marcus once in a while was okay, but living with them was pretty boring. Fiona was always reading books or fancy magazines about homes where famous people lived, and Marcus watched television. That would have been okay if he watched anything interesting, but he always had it on the news. Kelly knew for sure she wouldn't want to live and go to school here and be away from her dad all week. Grandma and Marcus were, well, they were *old*. Her dad was old, too, but not this old. Fiona would do things with her some of the time, but then she'd tell her to go find something to do, something *quiet*. And she really hated the way Marcus smiled all the time. It was one of those old people smiles where they really don't mean it.

Kind of like the way he was smiling now.

"This has been a crazy time for you," Marcus said. "Starting with that sleepover at your friend's house."

"Yeah," Kelly said.

"Fiona—Grandma—when she was asking you all those questions about what happened, when you were hiding in the mother's closet, I could tell that made you pretty uncomfortable."

Kelly nodded. "It did kinda."

"Of course it would."

"I really wasn't supposed to talk about it. I mean, Emily's mom said that, and Dad didn't want me talking about it, either. Especially to Emily's dad, who was all upset about it and wanted to know what I'd heard."

"But you didn't tell him," Marcus said.

Kelly shook her head side to side.

"But now, the bad guy's dead," Marcus said. "I guess none of it matters anymore. It's one of those things you can put behind you."

"Maybe now," Kelly said, "I can erase the video from my phone."

Marcus blinked. "Video? What video is that, Kelly?"

"The one I took when I was hiding in the closet."

Marcus coughed. "You took a video when you were hiding in the closet? Of Ann Slocum? When she was talking on the phone?"

Kelly nodded. Marcus's smile struck her as particularly forced right now.

"Do you have your phone on you?" he asked. When Kelly nodded, he said, "Show it to me."

Kelly reached into her front pocket for it, tapped a couple of buttons, and then went over and sat next to Marcus so she could hold it as he looked on.

"Okay, so I just press this, and here it is."

"Hey. Can you talk?"

"What's this?" Marcus asked. "When was this?"

"This was just when she came in. She was phoning somebody who hurt their wrist."

". . . if that works for you? But I have to tell you, I've got—"

"Who's she talking to here?" Marcus asked.

Kelly shrugged. "I don't know. I don't know who either of her callers were."

"There were two callers?"

"Okay, you just missed it because you were talking so much," she scolded him. "She gets another call, so she says goodbye to the first person. I'll move it back so you can hear it."

"Why are you calling this . . . my cell's off . . ."

"See, this is the other person," Kelly said.

"Shh!"

He said it so harshly Kelly felt it like a slap. Marcus wasn't smiling anymore.

". . . something in return . . . mark us . . . down for—"

"Turn it off," Marcus said.

"But there's a little bit more," Kelly said.

"Stop it. Stop it right now."

Kelly thought it was funny that all of a sudden he didn't want to see any more. He'd been so interested just seconds earlier.

Kelly shifted away from him on the wicker couch. Marcus stood up. He was brooding. She thought it was weird how fast grown-ups could go from a good mood to a bad one.

"Go find something to do," he snapped.

"Fine," she said. "I hope my dad comes soon."

She went to the spare room she used when she stayed here and started taking what few clothes she had brought out of the drawer. She was especially glad to be getting out of here if Marcus was going to start acting all weird.

She had her bag packed in a couple of minutes, then took out her phone to delete the video. She was just about to do it when she decided to watch it again, since Marcus had kept her from watching it to the end.

Kelly got the earbuds she brought along for when she used the phone for music and plugged them in. And then she played the video.

She played it again.

And again.

She had no idea what had made Marcus angry, but she'd discovered something interesting that she had never noticed before.

She unplugged the earbuds and decided to go looking for him, even if he was being all cranky. Kelly found him pacing back and forth in the kitchen.

"You want to know something really weird?" she said.

"What?" he said. He still sounded grumpy.

Holding up the phone, Kelly said, "You know, in the video? It sounds like Emily's mom is saying your name."

FIFTY-SEVEN

First, I phoned Fiona's house. After five rings, it went to message. "Fiona, call me," I said. Then I tried her cell, which went to eight rings before the voicemail kicked in. "Fiona, it's Glen. I tried the house and there was no answer. Call me as soon as you get this. My cell. Call my cell."

And then I tried Kelly's cell phone. She'd set hers to go to message after five rings. Which was exactly what it did.

"Hi! It's Kelly! Leave a massage!" Her little joke.

"Kelly, it's Daddy. Call my cell the second you get this, okay?"

I grabbed my truck keys. I swung open the front door.

"Mr. Garber! Mr. Garber!"

On the walkway leading up to the porch, a smartly dressed blonde woman brandishing a microphone, and alongside her, a cameraman. There was a news van parked across the end of the driveway.

"Mr. Garber, we'd like to talk to you!" the woman shouted. "Police are saying you brought down the man who shot and wounded two Milford police officers and we wondered if we could get—"

"Move that fucking van out of my way," I said, moving past her and shoving the cameraman to one side.

"Hey, watch it, pal."

"Please, Mr. Garber, if we could just—"

I got in my truck. Neither the reporter nor the cameraman was making a move toward the van, and I didn't have time to wait. I turned on the engine and backed partway down the drive, then cut across the lawn, narrowly missing the tree and dropping over the curb with a thud.

Just before I put the truck into drive and sped off down the street, tires squealing, I noticed Joan Mueller standing in her living room window, watching all the commotion.

As the engine roared, I told myself it all made some kind of sense. Marcus had met Ann Slocum at the purse party at our house. And I knew Ann had caught his eye. If he'd started seeing her—

What if Ann had pulled the same stunt with Marcus that she had with George? Suppose she'd started seeing him and then threatened to let it slip to Fiona that he was being unfaithful to her? Told him she'd be happy to keep quiet if he paid her off?

What was it she'd said on the video? He paid and got something in return. Her silence. Marcus was evidently trying to cut some kind of new deal with her. A way to reduce the blackmail payments, maybe?

That was why he wanted to see her.

Ann had left the house that night to meet with Marcus.

I sped in the direction of the turnpike, running yellow lights, totally ignoring stop signs. I floored it when I hit the ramp onto the westbound 95. Darien was about a half-hour trip. I was hoping to trim about ten minutes off that if the traffic allowed it. The truck wasn't exactly built for speed, but it could still do eighty or more if I pushed it.

I wondered why no one was answering their phones.

So Ann goes out to meet Marcus. They have some kind of argument down by the harbor. Ann ends up dead.

I felt it in my bones. Marcus Kingston had murdered Ann Slocum.

But did that also mean he'd had something to do with Sheila's death? I'd come, over time, to believe the two were related.

Was it possible Marcus had somehow staged the accident that claimed Sheila's life? Gotten her drunk? Put her car on that ramp and waited for someone to hit it?

If he did, why? Did Sheila know he'd been having some kind of affair with Ann? Had Sheila threatened to tell her mother? And Marcus killed her to keep her quiet?

I had no fucking idea.

All I knew for sure was, my daughter was staying in the same house with Marcus. A man I now believed was capable of something very terrible.

I tried Fiona's house again. Still no answer. Same for her cell phone and Kelly's. When did that ever happen? That no one would be answering their phones?

There were other people I needed to call, but I didn't know their numbers, and I was driving so fast I couldn't safely spend time on the phone trying to get them.

I hit one of my presets randomly. And, after several rings, got Sally's message.

"You've reached Sally Diehl. I can't take your call right now but please leave a message."

"Sally, damn it, it's Glen and if you're there pick up! Kelly's in trouble and—"

A click, and then, "Glen?"

"Sally, I need help."

"Tell me."

"I can't explain it all now, but I think Marcus may have killed Ann Slocum. Maybe even Sheila."

"Jesus, Glen, what are you talking—"

"Just listen! Take down this address. Fifty-two—"

"Wait, wait, I have to get a pencil. Okay, shoot."

I rhymed off Fiona's address in Darien. "Kelly's there, unless she's out someplace with Fiona or Marcus. You have to call Detective Rona Wedmore."

"Hang on. Rona . . . Wedmore."

"She was in Milford Hospital today, but she should be out now. Call the main police line, tell them you *have* to talk to her. And if you can't get her, talk to somebody, tell them to get in touch with the police in Darien and get someone to that address."

I glanced down at the speedometer. I was almost at ninety. The truck was shaking and rattling and felt as though it was starting to float.

"Have you got it?" I asked.

"Yeah, but Glen, this sounds—"

"Do it!"

I ended the call, just in time to avoid rear-ending a tractor-trailer. I swerved around it, felt the back end of the pickup fishtail slightly, and kept my foot pressed to the floor.

FIFTY-EIGHT

"Let's have a look at that," Marcus said, taking the phone from Kelly.

He played the video from beginning to end.

"Did you hear it?" Kelly asked. "She says, like, 'Marcus I'd down with it' or whatever. Did you catch that?"

"Yes," he said. "I think I did."

The house phone rang. When Marcus made no move to answer it, Kelly said, "Do you want me to get that?"

"No, just let it ring. They'll leave a message if it's important."

Seconds later, Fiona's cell on the front hall table began to make a racket.

"What about that?" Kelly asked.

"Don't worry about it," Marcus said, still holding on to Kelly's phone. When it went off in his hand, Kelly became alarmed.

"That's mine!" she said. "I have to answer it."

Marcus raised the phone up next to his head. "Not right now you don't. We're talking."

"Can I see who it is?"

Marcus shook his head. "You can check it later."

"That's not fair," Kelly protested. "That's *my* phone."

Once it had stopped ringing, Marcus slid the phone into the front pocket of his pants. Kelly watched in amazement that he would do such a thing.

"Kelly," Marcus said, "is that the very first time you've noticed that on the video?"

"Huh?" She still couldn't get over the fact that her grandmother's husband had stolen her phone from her. "Yeah, I guess so."

"Has anyone else ever noticed that?"

"I don't think so. The only other person who's ever even seen it is my dad. I emailed it to him."

"So," Marcus said. "Just the two of you."

"Why were you talking to Emily's mom that night?"

"Stop talking, please."

"Give me my phone back."

"In a minute, child. I need to think."

"What do you have to think about?" she asked. "Please can you give it to me? I didn't do anything wrong around here. I put away my things and I always do what you and Grandma tell me to do."

"You know how we talked about taking a walk earlier? That might be fun to do now."

Kelly didn't like the look on Marcus's face. He wasn't even managing one of his fake smiles now. She wanted to go home. She wanted to go home right now. "Give me my phone so I can call my dad."

"I'll give you your phone when I'm ready to give you your phone," he told her.

Abruptly, Kelly turned and walked out of the room, heading for the closest home phone. She picked up the receiver and started entering the numbers of her father's cell.

Marcus snatched the receiver from her hand and slammed it down hard.

"No calls, you little bitch," he said.

Kelly's lip quivered. Fiona's husband had never spoken to her this way before. Marcus grabbed her by the wrist and squeezed. "Shut up, just shut up."

"You're hurting me," Kelly said. "Let go! *Let go!*"

"Sit down here," he said, forcing Kelly onto the couch by the coffee table. He stood right next to her, crowding her so that she could not get up. The girl whimpered.

"That's getting on my nerves," he told her. "If you don't stop it, I'll snap your neck."

Kelly tried to stifle her cries, making funny noises in her throat. She ran her index finger under her nose, tried to wipe her tears from her cheeks.

For several minutes Marcus just stood there, muttering to himself. "Have to do something," he said. Suddenly, he reached down and grabbed the girl by the wrist. "A walk. We're going to go for a walk."

"I don't want to," Kelly protested.

"It'll be fun. It's good to get outside."

"No!" Kelly shouted. "I don't want to!"

At that moment, the front door opened and Fiona stepped in. "I can't believe I left here without my—"

It was quite a sight that greeted her. Marcus, red and shaking, holding on to Kelly. The child crying, her eyes wide with fear.

"Grandma!" she shouted, straining to get free, but Marcus would not let go.

"What's going on?" Fiona demanded. "Marcus, let go of that child."

But he did not. Kelly continued to cry.

"Marcus!" she shouted. "I told you to—"

"Shut up, Fiona," he said. "Shut the fuck up."

"Have you lost your mind? What are you doing?"

He bellowed at her. "What did I just say? Did you hear what I said? I told you to shut up. And if you don't, I'll snap her neck. I swear to God I will."

Fiona took a few tentative steps into the room. "Marcus, just tell me—"

"Where are your keys?"

"What?"

"Your car keys. Where are they?"

"Marcus, whatever you're thinking of doing, this is crazy."

Marcus put his arm around Kelly's neck.

"They're in the car. I left them in the ignition."

"Get out of my way. Kelly and I are leaving."

"Please, Marcus, just tell me what this is all about."

"It's about Emily's mom," Kelly blurted.

"What?"

"Don't listen to her," Marcus said. "She's just a stupid—"

Outside, the sound of a truck door slamming.

FIFTY-NINE

The first thing I saw when I ran into Fiona's living room was Marcus with his hand around Kelly's neck. Then Fiona, her face white with fear.

"Stop right there," he said, and I did.

"It's okay, honey," I said. "It's going to be okay. Daddy's here."

"Did you block Fiona's car?" Marcus asked. "Because we're getting out of here."

"It's too late, Marcus. I know. The police know."

"They don't know anything," he said.

"Know what?" Fiona asked. "What is it?"

"Ann went out to meet you that night, didn't she?" I said. "Because she was blackmailing you. You lured her out that night to kill her."

Marcus's eyes blazed with anger. "That's not true." He looked at Fiona. "It's not true."

Fiona looked at me and back to Marcus, disbelieving. I said, "Oh, it was you. Ann says your name. On the video."

"I only wanted to talk to her," he said. "She fell. It wasn't my fault. It was an accident. You ask the police. The tire was flat. She got out to check it."

I wondered how Marcus could possibly know that, unless he'd set things up to look that way.

Fiona, standing next to the coffee table, said, "Marcus, this can't be true."

"It's over, Marcus," I said. "I've emailed that video, where Ann says your name, to everyone on my mailing list. Everyone's going to know, Marcus. Let Kelly go."

But he hung on to her.

"Please," I said. "She's just a little girl."

"I want a head start," he said. "I take her with me, you give me half an hour, I'll drop her off somewhere."

"No," I said. "But I'll give you a head start if you let Kelly go. And if you answer one question for me."

"What?"

"Sheila," I said.

"What about her?"

"Why Sheila?"

Marcus screwed up his face. "I don't know what you're talking about."

"I don't know how you did it, exactly, but I need to know why. Did she know? Did she know you were having an affair with Ann? Did she threaten to tell her mother? Is that why you did it?"

Fiona's mouth opened. She was too stunned to speak at first, but finally, in a whisper, she said, "No."

His eyes met hers. "Fiona, it's all bullshit. Glen's lying, that's—"

"You killed Sheila? You killed my daughter?"

Marcus tightened his arm around Kelly's neck. She coughed, put her hands on Marcus's arm and tried to free herself, but she was no match for the strength in a grown man's arm.

"Stand aside and let me leave," he said.

"You can't run," I said. "The police will find you. Hurt Kelly and it's only going to be worse for you. You're not leaving here with her. It's not happening."

Kelly struggled some more, kept pulling on Marcus's arm. I glanced again at Fiona. She was a lit firecracker with an inch of fuse left.

Marcus nodded. "Yes, yes I am. If you take even a step toward me, I'll twist her head right off. I swear—*Jesus!*"

Kelly had brought up her right leg, then driven her heel down into the top of Marcus's foot with everything she had. When he screamed, his grip on Kelly slackened.

In that same moment, Fiona grabbed the wineglass on the coffee table and swung it against the table's edge. She held on to the base of the glass, which was now a mass of glistening, jagged edges.

Kelly squirmed free and ran toward me.

Fiona lunged, thrusting the glass forward, a primal scream escaping from her throat. Even before she reached Marcus, there was blood spilling from her fingers where the broken glass had cut her. But she was oblivious to any pain of her own. She had only one thing on her mind, and that was to kill her husband.

I would have moved to intervene, but Kelly had thrown herself around me.

Marcus raised his arms to deflect Fiona, but she was possessed of a strength that was not her own. She kept coming at him, thrusting the shards of glass toward his neck.

Caught him, too. Blood began to spurt from his throat in several places. He made anguished gagging noises and clutched his hands to his throat. Blood dribbled through his fingers.

I screamed, "Fiona!" and pulled Kelly off me. I grabbed Fiona from behind as she continued to wave the broken glass in the air.

Marcus dropped to the carpet.

I looked at Kelly and said, firmly and without panic, "Hit the police button on the security system."

She ran.

As Marcus continued to clutch his neck, trying to stanch the flow of blood, I said to Fiona, "It's okay, it's okay. You did it. You did it. You got him."

Fiona began to weep, to wail, as I held her. She dropped the glass to the floor, turned, and wrapped her bloody arms around me.

"What have I done?" she wept. "What have I done?"

I knew she wasn't talking about what she'd just done to Marcus. She was talking about having brought this man into her life and unleashing him on her family.

SIXTY

Seconds after Kelly hit the emergency button on the security system, their monitoring people phoned. I took the call and told them to send an ambulance as well as the police.

I'd barely hung up and the police were there. But they'd been dispatched as a result of Sally's call to the police in Milford, who in turn got in touch with their counterparts in Darien.

The paramedics went to work quickly on Marcus and, to my amazement, managed to stabilize him. I figured he was a goner. The ambulance wailed as it tore out of the driveway.

Even while Marcus was still gurgling and writhing on the floor, I got Kelly out of the house. I didn't want her to see any more of this than she already had. I picked her up and she wrapped her arms around my neck as I took her out the front door. I kept patting her back softly, moving slightly from side to side to soothe her. "It's over," I said to her.

Her mouth pressed close to my ear, she said, "He killed Emily's mom."

"That's right," I said.

"And Mom?"

"I don't know, sweetheart, but it kind of looks like it."

"Was he going to kill me?"

I wrapped my arms around her more tightly. "I would never have let him hurt you," I said. Not mentioning that if I'd gotten there five minutes later, things might have worked out very differently.

In the minutes before the paramedics arrived, Fiona stayed in the house with Marcus. I caught a glimpse of her at one point, perched on the edge of the coffee table, just looking down at him, waiting, presumably, for him to die. I was worried she might do something rash—not to Marcus, but to herself. She was in a highly agitated state for a while there, screaming about what she had done, what she had allowed to happen, and it would have been good if I could have stayed with her. But I had only one priority, and that was to get Kelly out of the house.

When the police cars started showing up, I told them the woman in there was probably traumatized—hell, I think we all were—and within a minute or two they had brought Fiona out front, too.

She seemed almost catatonic.

She took a seat on a small bench she'd installed by the front gardens and sat there, saying nothing.

"Fiona," I said gently. She seemed not to hear me. "Fiona."

Slowly, she turned her head. She was looking in my direction, but I wasn't sure she was seeing me. Finally, she said, "How are you doing, sweetheart?"

Kelly twisted her head around on my shoulder to look at her. "I'm okay, Grandma," she said.

"That's good," Fiona said. "I'm sorry you haven't had a very nice visit this time."

In talking to the police, I tried to cast Fiona in the best possible light.

Marcus was holding on to her grandchild, threatening to break her neck. He had pretty much admitted killing Ann Slocum. His intention was to use Kelly as a hostage as he made his getaway. When Kelly stomped on his foot, it was Fiona's one chance to stop him before he did anything else.

On top of all that, she attacked him believing that he had killed her daughter.

My wife.

Marcus hadn't admitted any responsibility for Sheila's death. I didn't think that would hurt Fiona where her actions were concerned, but it was troubling to me.

Not overly. But troubling.

Why would he acknowledge a role in Ann's death but not Sheila's? It was possible, of course, that even having confessed to all his other crimes, he couldn't admit, in front of Fiona, that he'd murdered her daughter. Maybe it was one crime too many to cop to.

I didn't really know what to think. Maybe Marcus had murdered Sheila, and maybe he hadn't. Maybe someone else had.

And there was always the other possibility. The one Rona Wedmore had alluded to.

No one had killed Sheila. She had done it to herself. She'd gotten drunk, gotten in her car, and caused the accident. I'd been fighting that version of events for so long. With all the things that had been swirling around Sheila—thousands of dollars in cash that were to be delivered to a hit man, counterfeit goods, blackmailing wives—it seemed inevitable her death was connected. Could there be this much mayhem going on in Milford and then, on top of all of it, Sheila has an accident that's totally unrelated?

At first, I was furious with Sheila, that she would do something so stupid. Then, as I began to believe she was blameless, I felt guilt over the way I'd felt, the things I'd shouted to her in my head.

Now, I had no idea what to feel.

After all I'd been through these last few days, I had my suspicions, but I didn't really know any more now than I had before.

Maybe there are some things we're better off never knowing.

SIXTY-ONE

It would be wrong to say that things got back to normal. I had my doubts that our lives would ever really return to that. But over the next couple of days, some routine started to return.

But not the first night.

Kelly, after witnessing the horrors that had happened in Fiona's home, did not sleep well. She tossed and turned and, at one point, began to scream. I ran into her room, sat her up in bed, and she looked right at me, eyes open, but there was a vacant glaze to them I'd never seen before. As she shouted "No! No!" I realized she was still asleep. I said her name over and over again until she blinked and came out of it.

I found a sleeping bag in the basement, rolled it out on the floor next to her bed, and slept there the rest of the night. I rested my hand on her mattress and she held on to it till morning.

I made eggs for breakfast. We talked about school, and movies, and Kelly had some interesting things to say about how singer Miley Cyrus had turned from a girl she would have liked to hang out with into some kind of skank.

"You don't have to go to school today," I said. "You can go back when you want to."

"Maybe when I'm twelve," she said.

"Dream on, pardner."

And she smiled.

I took her to work with me that day. She accompanied me to a couple of job sites and played on my computer when we got back to the office. It was nothing short of a shambles. Dozens of unreturned voicemails. Invoices that had not been paid.

Ken Wang said he'd done his best to hold things together, but without Doug and Sally around, he was barely treading water.

"What's happening with Doug?" he wanted to know. "We need him."

"I don't know," I said. "He's still in custody."

"You want my opinion? If he did kill Theo, it was totally justifiable. I thought about doing it myself a couple of times. And where the hell is Sally?"

"She doesn't work here anymore."

"Don't say that."

"That's what she told me."

"Let me give y'all a bit of friendly advice. If you have to get down on your knees and beg, you get that woman back in here. You might think you run this outfit, and if it makes you happy to live with that delusion, that's fine with me, but she's the one makes this place work."

I sighed. "She's not coming back."

"I hope you don't mind my saying, you being the boss and all, but you must have fucked up big—oops, sorry, Kelly."

"It's okay," she said, swinging around in my chair. "I've seen and heard worse lately."

Kelly had been talking online, and on the phone, with Emily. Her aunt Janice continued to care for her while Darren Slocum's stay in the hospital continued. He was likely to be there another week or so, and even after he returned home he was going to need some help.

"Emily says her dad isn't going to be a policeman anymore," Kelly said.

"That so."

"She says he's going to do something different. And they might move. I don't want her to move."

I touched the top of her head. "I know. She's a good friend, and you guys need each other."

"She wants me to come over tomorrow night. Maybe for pizza. But *not* a sleepover. I'm never going on another sleepover for the rest of my life."

"Good plan," I said. "I guess you could go over for a visit. We'll talk about it tomorrow."

"What job sites are we hitting tomorrow?"

Rona Wedmore dropped by the office to see me. She had her arm in a sling.

"I thought it was your shoulder," I said.

"They say it'll heal better if I don't keep moving my arm around. I saw you on the news, yelling at that news lady as you came out of your house. That was smooth."

I smiled.

"My department's going to give you some kind of award," she said. "I tried to talk them out of it, told them you were some kind of nut, but they're insisting."

"I really don't want anything," I said. "I'd like to forget about all of it. I just want to move on."

"And what about your wife? Are you able to move on there?"

I leaned up against a filing cabinet and folded my arms across my chest. "I don't know that I have much choice. All I can figure is, she got into something so deep, she went off the deep end that night. She acted in a way she never had before because she was in a mess like she'd never been in before. But she should have talked to me about it. We could have worked things out."

Wedmore nodded sympathetically.

"Do you believe things happen for a reason?" she asked.

"Sheila did. I've never really subscribed to that."

"Yeah, I'm like you. At least, I used to be. Now, I'm not so sure. I think I got shot for a reason."

I unfolded my arms, slid my hands down into my pockets. "I can't think of any good reason to get shot, unless it's going to get you off work for the next six months at full pay."

"Yeah, well." She looked away from me for a second. Then she said, "When I got admitted to the hospital, they went and got my husband, brought him down. You know what he did when he saw me?"

I shook my head.

"He said, 'You okay?'"

It didn't seem like much of a story to me, but it seemed like the most important thing in the world to her.

"I think I should take a cake," Kelly said. "If Emily's buying the pizza, I should bring dessert."

"Okay."

It was the next day, and I had talked to Janice on the phone to see whether it was really okay for Kelly to come over. Janice said Emily had done nothing all day but talk about her best friend coming for a visit.

I offered to stop at a traditional bakery on our way over, but Kelly insisted we go to the grocery store and get a frozen Sara Lee chocolate cake. "It's Emily's favorite. Why are you rubbing your head, Daddy?"

"I've been having a lot of headaches the last couple of days. I think it's just stress, you know?"

"I get that."

Emily had been watching for us and ran out of the house as we pulled in to the driveway. Janice followed her out. The girls threw their arms around each other and ran into the house.

Janice stayed outside to speak with me. "I want to thank you, for what you did, stopping that man who shot Darren."

"I was kind of looking out for my own neck, too."

"Still," she said, touching my arm briefly.

"What's going to happen to him?"

"He's resigned from the force, and he's got a good lawyer. He's offered to tell everything he knows, about what Sommer did, about what he knows about the people he worked for. I'm hoping, if he still gets jail time, that it'll only be a few months. After that, he can look after Emily. He loves her more than anything in the world."

"Sure. Well. I hope it works out, for Emily's sake. I'll come back for Kelly in a couple of hours. That be okay?"

"That'd be fine."

I got back in the truck, but I didn't head home. There was one other stop I needed to make.

About five minutes later I was parked out front of a different house. I walked up to the door and rang the bell.

Sally Diehl opened the door a few seconds later. She was wearing rubber kitchen gloves, and was carrying a caulking gun.

"We need to talk," I said.

SIXTY-TWO

"You have to come back," I said. "I need you."

"I told you, I quit," Sally said.

"When I was in a jam, when I needed help the other day when I was going for Kelly, you were the one I called. You're the one who always knows how to get things done. You've always been the go-to girl, Sally. I don't want to lose you. Garber Contracting is falling apart and I need you to keep it together."

She stood there, brushed back some hair that had fallen across her eyes.

I said, "What's with the caulking gun?"

"I'm trying to finish up around the tub. Theo did this new bathroom but he never quite finished it."

"Let me come in."

Sally looked at me for another second, then opened the door wide. "Where's Kelly?"

"She's at Emily's. They're having some pizza."

"That's the kid whose dad got shot?"

"That's the one."

Sally asked what had actually happened at Fiona's house and I filled her in, even though it wasn't something I liked to talk about.

"Jesus," she said. She'd gotten rid of the caulking gun, peeled off the gloves, and taken a seat at the kitchen table. I was leaning up against the counter.

"Yeah, no kidding," I said. I rubbed my temples with my fingers. "God, I'm getting such a headache."

"So Marcus killed Ann?" Sally asked.

"Yeah."

"And Sheila, too?"

"I don't know. Maybe, when he recovers enough that he can talk again, he'll be willing to tell us everything, although I'm not counting on it. I'm starting to come around to the fact that, you know, maybe Sheila did it."

Something seemed to soften in Sally's face.

"I tried to tell you," she said. "But you haven't been in the right place."

"I know." I shook my head. It was still throbbing. "What about Theo?"

"Funeral was yesterday. It was horrible, Glen, honestly. Everybody crying. I thought his brother was going to throw himself on top of the casket when they lowered it into the ground."

"I should have been there."

"No," she said firmly. "You shouldn't have."

"I regret the things I said, Sally. Maybe Theo meant exactly what he was saying when he was writing that note to me, that he was sorry. I turned it into something else." I rubbed my head. "You got any Tylenols or anything? My head feels like it's about ready to explode."

"In the drawer right behind your butt," she said.

I swiveled around, pulled out the drawer, and found a veritable pharmacy in there. Different pain remedies, bandages, syringes. "You got an entire Rite Aid in here," I said.

"It's a lot of stuff for my dad. I haven't gotten around to clearing it out yet," Sally said. "I'm going to have to do that."

I found the Tylenols, closed the drawer, and got the cap off.

"Tell me you'll at least think about coming back to work," I said. "KF's about to have a nervous breakdown."

I shook two pills out onto the counter. When I'd get headaches on the road with Sheila, and didn't have water to wash down the pills I kept in the glove box, she'd insist we stop somewhere so I could get a drink.

"You can't take them dry," Sheila'd say. "They'll get stuck in your throat."

So I said, "Glass?"

"In the drying rack," Sally said.

I looked at the rack next to the sink. There were a couple of glasses there, a single plate, some cutlery. As I reached for the glass, I saw something I wasn't expecting to see.

A baking dish.

The lasagna pan I hadn't seen in over three weeks. Browny-orange in color.

What Sheila always called "persimmon."

SIXTY-THREE

I carefully lifted the pan out of the rack and set it on the counter.

Sally laughed. "You gonna drink out of that?"

"What's this doing here?" I asked slowly.

"What?"

"This lasagna pan. I recognize this. It's Sheila's. What's it doing here?"

"Are you sure?" she said. "I'm pretty sure that's mine."

Sheila and I had a routine over the years. She cooked dinner, I cleaned up. You spend year after year cleaning the same dishes and bowls and glasses and baking dishes, you get to know them like the back of your hand. If this dish had come from our house, it would have a smudge on the bottom near one corner, where the residue from a price tag had never worn away.

I turned the dish over. The smudge was there, right where I expected it.

"No," I said. "It's ours. This is the dish Sheila always made lasagna in."

Sally had gotten out of the chair and walked over to have a look. "Hand it over." She examined it. She looked inside it, flipped it over, and checked the bottom. "I don't know, Glen. If you say so, then I guess it is."

"How'd it get here?" I asked.

"Jeez, I don't know. I know it didn't fly in through a window. I guess Sheila must have brought lasagna over sometime and I forgot to return it. So shoot me."

"Sheila made up a lasagna the day of her accident. She left two plates of it for Kelly and me. But there wasn't any more of it. I decided to try making lasagna the other day and I couldn't find the pan." I held it up. "Because it was here."

"Glen, please. Is there a point to this?"

"Your father died the same day Sheila did. I remember telling Sheila on the phone, just before she was going out, that your dad had passed away. She said we'd have to think of something to do for you. But the minute she hung up, she must have decided to take you the rest of the lasagna. That's what she did. When people died, she'd always take food to the family. Even people she didn't know all that well. Like her business teacher."

"Honestly, Glen, you're starting to scare me here."

"She came here, didn't she?" I said. "She came here to see you, to comfort you, and that's why she didn't go into the city. That's why she didn't have the money with her, why she hid it in the house."

"What money? What are you talking about?"

"She didn't want to be carrying it around. She came here to bring you a lasagna, to help you deal with losing your father. That afternoon. She thought it was more important to look after a grieving friend than run an errand for Belinda. If she came by here that day, why didn't you tell me?"

"Glen, Jesus," Sally said, and with the pan still in one hand, pointed with the other to the Tylenols on the counter. "Take those. I think there's something wrong with your head."

It was pounding more than ever as I tried to figure out why the baking dish was here. I looked away from Sally, just for a second, at the pills, then thought of something else I wanted to say to her.

I turned back and said, "I was going crazy, trying—"

All I saw was the baking dish, coming at me. And then everything went black.

I was at the doctor's, getting my flu shot.

"This isn't going to hurt a bit," he said as he put the needle into my arm. But the moment it pricked my skin and he found the vein, I shouted out in pain.

"Don't be such a baby," he said. He injected the serum and withdrew the needle.

"Now," he said, producing another syringe, "this isn't going to hurt a bit."

"You already gave me my shot," I said. "What are you doing?"

"Don't be such a baby," he said. He injected the serum and withdrew the needle.

"Now," he said, producing another syringe, "this isn't going to hurt a bit."

"Wait, no! Stop! What are you doing? Stop it! Get that motherfucking needle away from me you son of a—"

My eyes opened.

"Oh good, you really are alive," Sally said, close enough to me that I could smell her perfume. I had to blink a couple of times to bring her, and the rest of the world, into focus.

That world was sideways, and above me. I was lying on Sally Diehl's kitchen floor. A few feet away from me, scattered across the linoleum, was Sheila's lasagna pan, or what used to be Sheila's lasagna pan. It had shattered into countless pieces.

"You got one hard head," Sally remarked as she knelt over me. "I was afraid I hit you too hard, killed you. But now, I can make this work."

She moved back from me and I could see that she was holding a syringe in her hand. "I think that'll be the last one," she said. "You're full up now. You put it straight into the bloodstream, I don't think you need as much as if you were drinking it."

I attempted to roll over so I could look behind me, but there was an obstacle at my back. I realized after another second that it was my hands. They were bound behind me. I could feel something stuck to the hairs on my wrist. Duct tape. Lots of it.

Sally had crossed the room, grabbed a chair, and dragged it back across the floor toward me. She sat on it backwards, her legs straddling it. She rested her arms on the chair back. In one hand she held a gun.

"I'm sorry about this, Glen. Between you and Sheila, fuck, you guys. She was too nice, and you, you're a dog with a goddamn bone."

My head was pounding and I could taste blood in my mouth. I sensed I had a pretty good wound in my forehead and the blood had run down my face.

In addition to the headache, there was something else. A different kind of feeling. Woozy. The room seemed to be circling around me. At first, I figured that was the head injury. But now I wasn't so sure.

I was feeling . . . I was feeling a little drunk.

"It's hitting ya, right?" Sally asked. "Starting to feel a little three sheets to the wind and that kind of thing? Got pretty used to giving my dad his insulin. But that's not what I shot you up with. You're full of vodka."

"Sheila," I said. "This is what you did to Sheila."

Sally didn't say anything. She just kept looking at me, then at her watch.

"Why, Sally? Why did you do it?"

"Please, Glen, just let it kick in. You'll be feeling pretty good very soon. Nothing'll seem very important then."

She was right. I was already feeling woozy in a way that had nothing to do with getting hit in the head with the lasagna pan.

"Just tell me," I pleaded. "I have to know."

Sally's lips pressed tightly together. She looked away, then back at me.

"He wasn't dead yet," she said.

The words didn't make any sense.

"I don't . . . What?"

"My dad," she said. "It hadn't worked yet."

"I . . . I don't get you."

"When I talked to you that morning, told you he was dead, he *almost* was. I'd given him a double dose of heparin, was waiting for it to make him bleed to death internally. But then, the son of a bitch, he rallied a bit. And that was when Sheila came over with the fucking lasagna. She comes right in, doesn't even knock, she's all 'Oh, Sally, I'm so sorry for you, here's something you can put in your fridge for later.' And then she sees my dad, still barely breathing, and she's like, what the hell? 'He's alive?' she says. And then she starts going on about how we had to call an ambulance."

I blinked. Sally was going in and out of focus. "You killed your father?"

"I couldn't take it anymore, Glen. I gave up my own place—I couldn't afford the rent spending all my money on his medicines—and I moved in here, but the cost of the drugs, Jesus, and pretty soon I was going to have to put him into care someplace, and do you have any idea what that costs? I'd have to put this place up on the market, too, and with the economy the way it is, what do you think I could even get for this dump? I figured, the day after I ended up on the street, he'd just die anyway. I needed to move things along."

She sighed. "I couldn't have Sheila telling the cops I killed my dad. I hit her in the head, shot her up with booze."

"Sally, you're making this up . . ."

"How you feeling, Glen? It must be working, right? Feeling no pain and all that?"

"The . . . accident." I was trying not to slur my words.

"Just let it go," she said. "It'll be better that way."

"How . . . did you do that?"

Another sigh. "Theo helped. Came over, couldn't believe what I'd done, but I knew he'd bought those bogus parts from the Slocums, put them in the Wilson house, so he couldn't say no to me. I drove her car up the ramp, got her behind the wheel, and Theo gave me a lift back. But I'm gonna have to do this one on my own tonight."

"Sally, Sally," I said, trying to keep my head clear despite what was coursing through my veins, "you . . . you were like family . . ."

She nodded. "I know. I feel bad, I do. But I gotta say, Glen, lately? You've been a bit holier-than-thou, you know, acting like I wasn't making the best choices. I've made my choices, Glen. I've chosen to look out for myself. No one else will."

"Theo's note," I said. "Saying he was sorry . . ."

"I know he was an asshole to you, but the guy had a conscience. It was eating him up. The fire. Sheila. He wanted to confess."

"Doug," I whispered. "You set him up . . . right? Put those boxes in his truck, take the heat off Theo."

"I don't want to talk about this, Glen. It's all very painful."

"How . . . wait a . . . fuck no . . . you killed Theo. That was you."

For the first time, I thought she actually looked sorrowful. She rubbed her eyes. "I only did what I had to, okay? Like right now. I'm doing what I have to do."

"Your . . . fiancé . . ."

"He phoned me from his trailer, saying he couldn't stay quiet any longer. Said he had to tell Doug it wasn't his fault. I said, Theo, don't do anything till I get there, and when I did, I said okay, call Doug, invite him over, tell him in person, that was the honorable way to do it. And as soon as Theo got off the phone, I walked him into the woods. I'd brought one of my dad's guns."

A tear ran down her cheek.

"I hid my car, then parked Theo's truck down by the road so Doug would have to walk in. When he was looking around the trailer, I slipped the gun into his car. Betsy's car."

I was just able to understand it, but my brain was getting cloudy.

"The thing is, Glen, I'd rather be single, and on the outside, than married and sitting in a jail cell the rest of my life. You have to get up."

"What?"

She got off the chair and knelt down beside me. She held on to the gun with one hand and grabbed my elbow with the other. Yanking on me, she said, "Let's go. Up. Up!"

"Sally," I said, on my knees now and weaving, "you puttin' me on an off-ramp, too?"

"No. It has to be different."

"What . . . how?"

"Come on, please, Glen. You can't change how this is going to go. Don't make it hard for both of us."

She pulled hard and got me off my knees. She'd always been in good shape, and had the edge on me in size. Plus she had the added advantage of being sober. I tried to get my wrists apart but Sally had done a good job taping them. With enough time, I might have been able to free them. "Where are we going?"

"To the bathroom," Sally said.

"What? I don't have to go to the bathroom." I thought a moment. "Maybe."

I swayed. I was definitely drunk.

"This way, Glen. Just take it a step at a time." She walked me patiently out of the kitchen, through the dining room, where I bumped into a chair, and into the hall that led to the bedrooms and the bathroom.

I didn't know what, exactly, Sally had planned, but I had to do something. Try to make a break for it.

Suddenly, I threw my weight into her, ramming her into the wall with my shoulder. She knocked a commemorative Wedgwood plate, adorned with a profile of Richard Nixon, off its hook and to the floor, where it shattered.

I turned to run, but my feet caught on the carpet runner and I went down. Without hands to break my fall, I landed on my cheekbone. Pain rocketed through my jaw.

"Damn it, Glen, stop being such an asshole!" Sally shouted. I turned enough to see her standing over me, the gun pointed at my head. "Get the fuck up, and this time I'm not helping you."

Very, very slowly, I got to my feet. With the gun, she pointed to the door to the bathroom. "In there," she said.

I stood in the doorway of Sally's refinished bathroom. Theo's handiwork was everywhere. The toilet, sink, and tub were gleaming white porcelain. Uneven black-and-white checkerboard tiling covered the floor. Some of the grouting was chipped, and there was a glimmer of the heating cable beneath the tile. It hadn't been properly covered.

The new tub had fresh caulking about halfway around. The tub, I was guessing, had never been used.

But it was full of water.

"Down on your knees," Sally said.

Even in my drunken stupor, it was starting to become clear. Like Sheila, I was going to be found dead in my truck, with a very high blood-alcohol count. But they weren't going to find me on an off-ramp.

They were going to find me in the water.

If I was doing this to someone, I'd run them off the road at Gulf Pond. Put my victim behind the wheel, roll the truck into the water, and let it sink. Hoof it home from there. When they hauled out the body, the lungs would be full of water.

"It . . . it won't work, Sally," I said. "They'll put it together eventually."

"On your knees," she said again, sounding only a little impatient. "Face the tub."

"I'm not doing it. I'm—"

She kicked me, hard, in the back of my right knee, and I dropped like a stone.

The tiles were hard beneath my knees. Even through my pants, I could feel warmth radiating through them. My left knee straddled two uneven tiles. One made a crunching noise beneath my weight, an indication that the tiling job was a joke.

If the tiles were cracked, if water could seep through, then—

It all happened very quickly. Sally tossed the gun onto the counter next to the sink, then pounced on the upper half of my body. She threw all her weight onto my shoulders, forcing my head over the edge of the tub.

All I managed to say was "Jesus, no—" before my head went into the water.

I guess I was expecting it to be warm, like bathwater, but it was ice cold. My mouth and nose filled instantly. Panic at not being able to breathe overwhelmed me.

I knocked her off me for half a second, raised my head above the water and gasped. But then Sally was on me again, one hand grabbing hold of my hair to keep my head down, the other grabbing hold of my belt at the back of my jeans, trying to tip me forward. Even though I didn't have my arms free, water was being splashed everywhere.

Let it splash.

My mind was racing. With what little mental faculties and oxygen I had left, I was desperately trying to figure a way to get out from under Sally. The edge of the tub was acting as a lever for her, helping her keep my head under the water. She was expecting me to fight her, to try to push back, and she was well positioned to keep it from happening. I wondered if I could throw her off if I suddenly stopped resisting and allowed the rest of my body to fall into the tub.

I gave it a try.

Suddenly, I let my head go forward even deeper into the tub. My forehead banged the bottom. I felt Sally's hand slip free of my belt, and then I twisted around and rose up, bringing my head above water. Now I was sitting with my butt on the bottom, my back against the wall.

I gasped again, trying to get as much air into my lungs as quickly as I could.

Water swelled and coursed over the edge of the tub, spreading across the floor and dribbling down into the heat vent and the numerous cracks between the tiles. I threw my body around, forcing more water out of the tub. Not only would that make it harder for Sally to submerge my head, it was getting the water out where I wanted it.

Fingers crossed that Theo's work was consistent.

I pulled my legs back, then shot them forward, catching Sally hard in the chest. The motion knocked her back onto the floor and tipped me sideways into the tub. One of my legs was still dangling over the edge of the tub.

Sally had thrown her hands back to break her fall. Her palms landed flat on the tile surface, water nearly up to the top of her knuckles.

Something happened.

There was the sound of sparking. Suddenly, Sally seemed to freeze. Her eyes opened wide.

Then the lights in the bathroom shorted, then went out. But there was faint illumination from a hall light. Enough to see Sally's body fall onto the floor with a soft splash.

She lay there, staring at the ceiling, not moving a muscle.

The heated floor. The water had shorted it out and electrocuted her.

That sort of thing wasn't supposed to happen if it was wired in correctly, if the proper parts were used. If the tiling was any good.

Theo. Master electrician. God bless him.

Staggering, I managed to get myself into a standing position in the tub. My shoes, and all my clothes, were soaked. When the lights went out, I knew the breaker had popped, and that it was safe to step out.

I weaved my way down to the kitchen, backed up to a drawer and managed to get out a knife. If I'd been sober, I might have been able to cut through the tape in a minute or two, but it took me nearly ten. I kept dropping the knife.

Once I was free, I went to Sally's phone and made two calls. The second was to 911. The first was to Kelly's cell.

"Hey, sweetheart," I said. "Everything's okay, but there's been a little accident at Sally's, and I'm going to be a while."

THREE WEEKS LATER

EPILOGUE

I pulled the tape gun across the top of the large cardboard box, then said to Kelly, "Run your hand along there and make sure it's stuck good to the flaps."

She pressed both hands down on the strip of tape, rubbed it all over several times. "That's really on there," she said.

"You're sure you're okay with this?" I said.

She looked up at me and nodded. There was sadness in her eyes, but certainty, too. "I think Mom would want us to do this," she said. "She liked to help people."

"Yeah," I said. "She was all about that." I looked inside the nearly bare closet. "I guess this is the last one. We better get it to the front door. They said the pickup would be between ten and noon."

I carried the box downstairs and set it down with four others of similar size just inside the front door. I supposed I could have put everything into garbage bags, but that seemed wrong. I wanted everything properly folded. I didn't want everything all mashed together when it got to its destination.

"Do you think that homeless lady in Darien will get any of these?" she asked.

"I don't know," I said. "Maybe not. But there might be someone here in Milford who will, and if we hadn't seen that lady the other day, and felt bad for her, then someone in our own town would never get these."

"Then what about the other lady?"

"Maybe someone from Darien will have seen a person needing help in Milford, or New Haven, or Bridgeport. So when she donates some clothes, it'll go to that woman."

I could see that Kelly was not convinced.

Together, we got the five boxes onto the front step. Kelly wiped her brow dramatically when we were done. "Can I ride my bike?" she asked. I'd been pretty protective lately, keeping her close.

"Just along the street here," I said. "Where I can see you."

She nodded. She went over to the garage, which was open, and wheeled out her bike.

"Emily's dad is out of the hospital," she said.

"I heard that," I said.

"They really are moving. Emily's dad has relatives in Ohio, so they're going to go there. Is Ohio far?"

"Kind of."

She didn't look happy about that. "Is Grandma still coming today?"

"She said so. I thought we'd all go out to dinner."

Fiona was moving, too, but not to Ohio. She was getting a condo in Milford so she could be close to us. Close to Kelly, anyway. She hadn't gone back into her house since the incident. She'd been staying in a hotel. She had the place on the market and was hiring movers to sort everything out so she wouldn't have to set foot in it. She'd also started divorce proceedings against Marcus, who, once he was released from the hospital, was going to move in to a nice cell while prosecutors built a case against him in the death of Ann Slocum. So far, no one had rushed to post bond for him.

No charges had been filed against Fiona for attacking Marcus, and weren't likely to be. Turns out, had there been, she'd have had plenty of money to hire the best lawyer. Marcus had been lying when he said she'd lost money in that huge Ponzi scheme. He just didn't want Kelly coming to live with them, and figured if I thought Fiona really couldn't afford to send Kelly to a private school, I'd make sure it didn't happen.

Kelly put on her helmet, snapped it into place, and rode down to the end of the drive. She hung a left and pedaled madly.

She really was her mother's daughter. It had been her idea to donate Sheila's things to one of the agencies in town that provided clothes to the disadvantaged. There were a few things we both wanted to keep. Sheila's jewelry, such as it was. She wasn't much for diamonds, although perhaps if I'd bought them for her more often, she might have been. She'd had a red cashmere sweater Kelly said always felt nice against her cheek when she snuggled in with her mother on the couch when they watched TV. Kelly wanted that.

She didn't want any of the purses.

Kelly was back at school, where things were much better. The papers and newscasts had a lot to do with that. Once the truth, in particular the fact that Sheila was not responsible in the Wilkinson deaths, came out, the other kids started leaving her alone. And Bonnie Wilkinson had dropped her $15 million lawsuit. Not much of a case anymore. I had Kelly seeing a counselor, to help her with all the tragedy that had happened around her, and so far, it seemed to be helping. Although I was still sleeping on her floor every other night.

Charges were dropped against Doug Pinder, who was back working for me. Betsy stayed in her mother's house, and Doug found a one-bedroom apartment on Golden Hill. They were heading for divorce, but no nasty fights over property were expected.

I didn't know whether I'd ever be able to make it right with him. I'd accused him of things he hadn't done. I hadn't believed him when he'd professed his innocence. I tried to apologize, in some small part, by paying, from that stash of money in the wall, Edwin Campbell to expedite the process of his release.

What made me feel most guilty was Doug's forgiving attitude. When I attempted to tell him how bad I felt, he waved his hand and said, "Don't worry about it, Glenny. Next time you're in a burning basement, I'll grab a beer first."

There were still things to be worked out. I was still battling it out with my insurer over the Wilson house. I was arguing that far from being negligent, I was the victim of a crime. Edwin was hopeful.

Business appeared to be picking up. I'd been out this week giving estimates on three jobs, and I was interviewing for someone to work in the office and keep us organized.

Kelly had been up to the corner and was pedaling back. "Watch!" she said. "No hands!" But she was only able to release her hold on the grips for a second. "Wait, I'm going to do it again."

A cube van was working its way down the street, slowly, the driver checking addresses. I stood and walked down the steps from the porch, waved and caught his attention.

He stopped out front and slid open the back door before coming across the lawn toward me.

"Nice day," he said. "But who knows, in a couple of weeks we could have snow."

"Yeah," I said.

"All these boxes?" he said.

"That's right," I said.

"Good to get rid of stuff, isn't it?" he said cheerfully. "You clear out the closet, wife's got room for new stuff, am I right?"

We managed all the boxes in one trip. Setting the last one into his truck, shoving it down next to the other bags and boxes of donations, he said, "This one's kind of heavy."

"That's the one with all the purses," I said.

He slid the door down, said "Thanks" and "So long," and got back into his truck. It started up and began to pull away from the curb.

And then I heard her. It wasn't like the other times, where I could imagine what she might say. This time, I could hear her voice.

"You're going to be okay."

"I should have known from the beginning," I said. "But I blamed you. Doubted you."

"None of that matters. Just take care of our girl."

"I miss you," I said.

"Shhh. Look."

Kelly flew past on the sidewalk, arms outstretched. "No hands!" she squealed. "For real!"

And then she grabbed the handlebars and brought the bike to an abrupt, skidding halt. She put both feet on the sidewalk and stood there, straddling the bike, her back to me, her head all helmet, and watched the truck go to the end of the street and turn the corner. She kept watching for a good ten seconds after it disappeared, hoping, maybe, like her father, that it would come back, that we could change our minds.

ACKNOWLEDGMENTS

I'm glad all I had to do was write this book. So many others helped bring it to fruition. In particular, I'd like to thank Juliet Ewers, Helen Heller, Kate Miciak, Mark Streatfeild, Bill Massey, Susan Lamb, Paige Barclay, Libby McGuire, Milan Springle, and The Marsh Agency.

I also want to thank my son, Spencer Barclay, and his Loading Doc Productions crew—Alex Kingsmill, Jeff Winch, Nick Storring, Eva Kolcze—for the book trailers they've been cranking out for me.

Last, but definitely not least, the booksellers and readers. They make it happen.

ABOUT THE AUTHOR

LINWOOD BARCLAY is a former columnist for the *Toronto Star,* and the author of nine novels, including *Never Look Away, Fear the Worst, Too Close to Home,* and *No Time for Goodbye.* He is currently at work on his next thriller, to be published by Bantam Books.